T0354785

Red, White and Black

An American Story

ROBERT HUMPHREYS

authorHOUSE®

AuthorHouse™
1663 Liberty Drive
Bloomington, IN 47403
www.authorhouse.com
Phone: 1 (800) 839–8640

Published by AuthorHouse   08/09/2016

ISBN: 978-1-5246-1040-1 (sc)
ISBN: 978-1-5246-1039-5 (e)

Library of Congress Control Number: 2016908246

Print information available on the last page.

Any people depicted in stock imagery provided by Thinkstock are models, and such images are being used for illustrative purposes only. Certain stock imagery © Thinkstock.

This book is printed on acid-free paper.

Acknowledgements

Our Friend Jeff White, my brother in law Billy Vanlandingham, my son Robert D. Humphreys, and my wife Kay Humphreys, for their guidance and direction with this book.

Dedication

——

The mothers of my grandchildren, Stephanie Cherry and Erica Humphreys. I love you, and I am proud of you both.

Chapter 1

The summer of 1965

Peter pulled the red Datsun pickup off the gravel road and parked in a patch of low weeds at the edge of the tree line. He was a tightly wound bundle of frayed nerves.

As he sat in the darkness mustering his courage, a set of headlights flashed in his rearview mirror. He ducked down quickly, lying across the bench seat of the compact truck. The stick shift stabbed him in his side. Despite the discomfort he remained motionless, frozen by fear. If questioned, he had no plausible reason for his whereabouts. The passing car slowed as it came alongside the pickup. Peter held his breath and struggled to control his anxiety. The panic stung for several minutes after the car moved on. Lying across the seat in the silence he imagined black men plotting to steal or strip parts from what they might think was an abandoned vehicle. On the other hand, he thought they saw him and were waiting to assault him when he exited the sanctuary of his truck. Cautiously sitting up, he rubbed his side where the gear shift had stabbed him. He scanned the area for imagined assailants. He uttered a racial slur and profanity. He knew blacks occupied the passing car because no good

1

white person, not even white trash, would live in this part of rural Shelby County on the outskirts of Memphis.

After fumbling in the glove compartment he pulled out a package of C-4 explosives and placed it on the seat beside him. He took his Zippo lighter from his pocket to make sure it was operational. When he clicked the shiny chrome device open, a whiff of lighter fluid filled the cab. He used his thumb to turn the course steel wheel against the flint, and instantly a flame appeared. He quickly extinguished the fire with a whispered curse, realizing its light could be plainly seen in the stark darkness of the rustic landscape. From his other pocket he withdrew a .38 caliber over/under derringer. He opened the firearm to reconfirm it was loaded.

Opening the door, he bemoaned his stupidity when the dome light in the pickup came on. Leaving the safety of his truck he locked the door and crept into the tree line. He felt like an elephant lumbering through the lightless woods. He could barely see and was stumbling into holes, tripping over undergrowth and entangling himself in vines hanging from the trees. His energy rapidly diminished and his misery grew with each step. Insects swarmed around his sweat-soaked body as thorns and thistles pulled on his clothing. When he finally reached the clearing, he swore once more because the white framed church was still more than a hundred yards away.

Although he was covered in black clothing, he was afraid to expose himself by crossing the clearing toward the church, so he continued to fight through the thicket at the edge of the tree line. When he reached the rear of the church, exhausted from his harrowing tromp through the woods, he leaned against the building.

After taking a quick breather, he stuck the white clay-like substance to the wooden siding of the structure. Then, taking the lighter from his pocket he ignited the C-4. In a flash, the clay substance burst into a brilliant hot blaze that illuminated the outside wall of the church. When he was convinced the building would burn to the ground, he dropped a piece of self-composed Klan literature so it would be easily discovered during an investigation. He was confident the white supremacists would gladly take responsibility for his act of terrorism.

Turning to leave, he heard voices rapidly approaching. Alarmed, he darted into the woods. Footsteps thundered behind him. As he ran through the forest, low hanging branches slashed his face. Undergrowth and saplings wrapped around his legs. He tripped and fell several times, but he bounced up and continued scrambling through the woods. His pursuer apparently fared no better in the darkness and didn't seem to be gaining ground.

Arriving at the road where he left his truck, he found himself approximately fifty yards from his vehicle. He sprinted towards the pickup in a shallow rain ditch that paralleled the gravel road. With the sound of footsteps now gaining on him, he tripped on a fallen tree branch lying hidden in the darkness. Clambering to get up, he was hit from behind with a ferocious jolt and a great weight drove him back to the ground, squeezing the breath out of him like a collapsing accordion. Stunned and breathless, Peter was pinned to the ground by a man sitting on top of him. Giant hands gripped tightly around Peter's throat, choking the life out of him. Peter and the black man were on the ditches incline. Instinctively, Peter used the downward slope to unseat his assailant. While Peter battled to his feet, the black man grabbed Peter's leg with such force he nearly pulled his pants down, making it impossible for Peter to escape.

Holding on to the waistband of his trousers, Peter kicked and scrambled, but he couldn't free himself from the man's grip. While both men strained for breath, Peter reached into his pocket and withdrew his derringer.

"Let go or I'll shoot" Peter cried. He aimed the shaking derringer at the man clutching his leg.

Unconcerned by the threat, the man pulled harder on Peter's pant leg. When Peter began to teeter, the black man grabbed at the derringer. Peter pulled the trigger. The blast from the gun rang in Peter's ears, and the man's grip released. Peter bolted for the truck. He cursed himself again for locking the truck's door as he groped through his pockets to find his keys. Jerking the keys from his pants, they slipped through his fingers and fell to the ground. With the derringer still in his right hand, he dropped to his knees and searched blindly in the darkness with his left hand. He sighed loudly with relief when he found them among the weeds. He braced himself against the side of the truck and rose to his feet. He unlocked the door and started to climb into the truck when he was startled by a noise behind him. It was the black man again on his feet, ready to pounce.

Peter raised the derringer to eye level and shot the man point blank in the face. The man fell back with a loud blood-curdling shriek as he crashed to the ground like a felled tree. Peter got into the truck and sped away. With his adrenaline subsiding, he drooped against the steering wheel. His lungs burned, his chest hurt, and his pulse thumped. Still assuming his mission was accomplished, he smiled to himself, happy that he had made a clean getaway.

Chapter 2

Fifteen years earlier, October 1950, City of Memphis Hospital, Negro Wing.

Mary reclined on a thinly padded examining table. Initially, the cool surface provided some relief for her aching back. However, before long the discomfort returned. She was embarrassed to wear such a revealing hospital gown; its cheap, green cloth left little to the imagination, as did the thin lace loosely tying the back of the gown together. With her feet propped in the metal stirrups of the exam table, her genitalia was exposed to any curious stranger who happened to enter the room. She was nauseated by the antiseptic smell and ill at ease with the white doctors and nurses rushing through the halls carrying clipboards, pushing carts, and wearing serious expressions on their pallid faces.

She was temporarily living with her mother, in the small dilapidated shack where she grew up. Her only transportation was limited to either walking or riding the bus so her mother, using a neighbor's phone, summoned a city ambulance to take her daughter to the municipal hospital. Mary's mother was suffering from numerous infirmities that were common among the poor blacks. The stress of her daughter having a baby caused her pressure and sugar to rise, and because her mother was feeling so poorly, Mary went unaccompanied to birth her first baby.

The chart said she was twenty-two years old. He would have guessed the girl with the skinny arms and legs was less than eighteen. As he had recently told his nurses, he invariably had difficulty estimating the age of colored people. Like most of his patients at the charity hospital, she lacked prenatal care, so complications were a constant possibility. Not that he was particularly interested in his patient's well-being. He was more concerned at how much time a complicated delivery would require.

The only sound the doctor made when he entered the room was the door being closed, followed by his footsteps crossing the tile floor to his examining stool. He took his seat and perused Mary's medical chart without any introductions. His silence added to her emotional anxiety.

"I don't know what I'm going to name this child," Mary winced in a huff between contractions, craving to make connection with another soul. She had been lying in the tiny exam room alone and scared for some time.

"Name your baby whatever you want," the doctor finally replied. He spoke slightly louder than a mumble, looking up from the medical chart, hoping she would be the last indigent patient and end his fifteen-hour day.

When he stopped analyzing her chart he glanced between her legs and was met with wafts of pungent body odors. After his examination, he knew the baby would be born soon, and he hoped to be on his way home prior to the delivery.

"I've got to have a name before the baby is born," Mary said, almost pleading for help.

"If it's a boy, you can name him after his father." There was no inflection in the doctor's voice as he held her wrist and checked her pulse. "If it's a girl, name her after you or your mother."

The doctor, who was named after his father, hoped the lack of interest displayed in his voice would end the conversation.

"I don't know who that is."

"You don't know who... who is?" he asked, eager to leave.

"The baby's daddy," she replied, gritting her teeth and exposing a nugget of gold in her mouth that gleamed in the harsh light of the hospital room.

"What do you mean you don't know who the baby's daddy is?"

The doctor was no longer shocked at the immorality among the people he was assigned to treat during his medical training in Memphis. Coming from a well-to-do and socially prominent family in Nashville, it took him a while to become accustomed to his clientele from the cotton fields of Mississippi and the rice patties of Arkansas.

Her body stiffened from a contraction, and beads of sweat glistened on her forehead.

"You people are unbelievable," he said, glaring at her with a deep frown. He checked her balloon belly with his stethoscope. "Are you trying to determine a last name or a first name for your baby?" he asked, his frown turning to an arrogant smirk, feeling some superiority as he verbally assaulted the woman.

"I know the last name. It is Johnson, just like me and my mama's," Mary answered, slightly aggravated at being referred to as you people. "I need a first name."

"Wait until you see if it's a boy or a girl." The doctor realized he was spending an excessive amount of time with this woman who couldn't afford to pay for his attention and care.

"I may not be up to naming a baby after it comes. I want to name it now to be sure it gets a proper name. I don't want a white woman naming my baby." When a single black mother didn't have a name for her newborn, a nurse at the charity hospital occasionally made up a name for the birth certificate to expedite the paperwork for the legal portion of the birth. These babies were sometimes given documented names such as Pajama, Rectal, Infectious and Ether, which the nurse pronounced slightly different than the spelling. Many of those names were laughed at and talked about during breaks and over meals by the white hospital staff.

"Name it after someone you know, someone you admire," the doctor suggested. It had crossed his mind to suggest naming the baby for a Bible figure, like he had observed many of his patients do over the past few months. However, due to her promiscuous circumstance and him being Baptist, he thought a Biblical name would be blasphemous.

"I don't admire anybody except my mama and what if it's a boy?" She cringed with another contraction but was happy to be in a conversation with another person, even if it was a pompous white man. "I need a fitting name for a boy or a girl," she said after the contraction eased.

"I don't name babies. I only deliver them," the doctor said, wondering how this woman was possibly going to raise a child to be a productive citizen when she appeared to take no responsibility for her own life.

"You're a doctor, ain't you? Ain't you supposed to help me?"

The doctor cleared his throat, apparently annoyed by Mary's outburst. "Where are your mother and father? They ought to be here to help you."

"My daddy's dead, and Momma is ailing. So she ain't coming. You're the only person here who can help me," she retorted, trying hard not to cry.

"Maybe I'll name my baby after you," she mumbled, barely loud enough for him to hear.

This idea irked him. He didn't want to be the black baby's namesake; so he asked, "What interests do you have?"

"What do you mean?"

"What do you like to do? Maybe you can name your baby after something related to what you like to do."

"I like to go to the dog track." She tells him, though because of her young age she had only been a couple of times. Older men, regulars to the track, had snuck her in and showed her a good time.

"Good! Then name the baby after the dog track in West Memphis. Call him Southland," the doctor said, smiling.

"That ain't a fitting name for a child," she breathed heavily from the contractions while becoming increasingly scared by the more frequent pains.

"What's the name of your favorite dog?" he asked. He wanted to finish the examination and leave before he got stuck delivering the baby. Nevertheless, he thought it would be hilarious if this woman named her baby after a dog.

She shut her eyes and flinched in pain from another contraction. When she opened her eyes, she said, "I don't know."

"What are the names of some of the dogs who have won money for you?" He really wanted to get out of there now.

"I won the trifecta not long ago." Actually, the man she was with won the trifecta. She had never won anything of value in her life.

"What's a trifecta?" the doctor asked, knowing little about wagering and nothing about dog racing.

"That's where you pick the first three dogs in a race in the order they finish."

Tickled that he would be able to tell other members of the hospital staff that he had convinced this woman to name her newborn after a form of gambling, he insisted she name her baby Trifecta. Mary took to the name immediately, claiming this baby would bring her three times the luck.

With the issue settled, the doctor thought he would take one last look between her legs before he made his exit and went home. However, with that glimpse, he realized it was too late. He would have to deliver the baby, Trifecta.

Chapter 3

The beginning of the school year, 1965, and two years prior to the desegregation of Central High School in Memphis, Tennessee. Almost 16 years following the birth of Trifecta Johnson.

He blended into the crowd of boys and girls lingering in the school hallway. He stood motionless gawking in bewilderment at Marcie McDougal. She was talking with a group of students, who, by their appearance and poise were obviously the cool kids on campus. Seeing her among the popular students caused a feeling of hollowness to grip his soul. Because of her apparent social status he thought she was unapproachable. Even though he wanted to belong, he had learned in junior high school that he was not part of the in-crowd. Plus since puberty he had grown painfully self-conscious around girls.

They had been neighbors as young children, but her family moved and he hadn't seen her for three years. He remembered her as being snot nosed, sweaty and flatulent. She brandished skinned knees, dirty fingernails, crooked teeth and unruly hair. However, she had morphed into a

10

voluptuous young woman. In comparison, he felt he was lacking the essential sophistication to have a successful social life in high school.

He watched her until she turned and looked directly at him. For an instant, their gazes locked like magnets. Recognizing her childhood playmate, Marcie's face began to glow, like a full moon, with a sincere smile. Embarrassed because he was caught spying on her he lowered his head, quickly turned, and walked away.

He threaded his way through the clamor in the hallway, trying to distance himself from her. He hadn't gone far before he was startled by the school year's first bell, giving him three minutes to be at his desk. Looking at the room numbers above each door, he realized he was not only going in the wrong direction; he was also on the wrong floor. His heart sank, and his self-esteem plummeted further when he realized he was going to be late for class on his first day of high school.

Marcie's smile disappeared as soon as Henry turned tail and melded into the gaggle of students. She was heart sickened by the snub of her former playmate. While Marcie was a shoo-in to be one of the school's most popular co-eds, her feelings were crushed like a grape in a wine press by Henry's unexplained behavior.

*

As fate would have it, Henry passed her in the hall every day between second and third periods. She was constantly surrounded by her elite friends, including several boys who were vying for her attention. People were attracted by her luscious looks, effervescent smile and buoyant sense of humor. From the first day of high school, Marcie enjoyed consummate popularity while Henry was invisible to most of the other students. Even though she haunted his imagination, due to her popularity, he became self-conscience and faint-hearted anytime he was near her. Rather than approaching her and risk being rejected, he would turn his head and pretend he didn't see her, causing her to think of him as a snob.

As the school year progressed, so did Henry's envy. Every time he saw her, she was laughing, talking, and flirting with other boys. He often wondered what all her wooers would think if they knew he had kissed her hundreds of times, and had seen her naked on several occasions.

Henry and Marcie were born months apart in 1950. They grew up best friends and inseparable companions. They lived two doors from each other. Being the only children their age in close proximity of their homes, Henry played tea party and house with Marcie. She reciprocated by playing cowboys and sports with him. It was while they played "house" that Marcie and Henry innocently kissed, mimicking the actions of their parents.

As young children Marcie and Henry were in the same class in elementary school and played together every afternoon. They were together so often they could have been considered siblings and felt as comfortable in each other's homes as they did their own. Being at liberty to roam Marcie's house, there were occasions when Henry innocently walked into Marcie's bedroom while she was dressing and got a glimpse of her shapeless, hairless body.

Their neighborhood was located just east of East Parkway and consisted of small brick homes built as part of the post-war construction boom. Marcie shared their three bedrooms and one-and-a-half bath home with her parents and older brother. Henry's home had two bedrooms and one bath; he shared a bedroom with his older brother.

Marcie's father was an attorney whose family was from New England. Her mother was a blue blood Memphian. They chose to live in the same neighborhood as Henry's family until Marcie's father became a full partner in his law firm. They couldn't afford both country club dues and a larger house, so they opted for the country club. Because of Marcie's mother's pedigree, her family belonged to the Memphis Country Club, the oldest and most exclusive private club in the city.

Marcie's mother was constantly at the club, which was evidenced by her deep tan, which she developed playing golf, tennis and lounging around the swimming pool. Henry's mom was a housewife. His dad was the manager of a dry cleaner. Neither of his parents were blue bloods or members of a country club.

Marcie's family was athletic. Her father had played football and baseball in college. Her brother played several sports in park commission leagues, and played golf and tennis competitively at the country club. Despite being a girl, Marcie never had a problem rivaling Henry in athletics.

Marcie's and Henry's brothers played little league baseball and basketball together. The baseball team they played on was coached by Beau Campbell who was a sports writer for the evening paper. Beau's team was predominately society kids. Henry's brother was invited to play for the team because of his association with Marcie's family. The years their brothers played baseball for Beau, Marcie and Henry attended every game. When Henry was old enough to be a player he was invited to join Beau's team. Even though Marcie's skills at baseball were equal to Henry's and most of the other boys on the team, girls didn't play organized baseball during the late fifties. However, she did practice with the team and because of her proficiency at fielding and hitting she was considered part of the team even though she wasn't allowed to play in the games. Beau usually picked up Henry and Marcie along with a couple of the other kids for their weekly practices.

It was Beau who first tweaked Henry's interest in becoming a newspaper reporter. While riding to baseball practice, in the backseat of Beau's car, Henry looked at pictures Beau had taken of athletes from various high schools, local colleges and minor league baseball players in the Southern Association.

Henry was so intrigued with Beau's pictures that he wanted to know everything he could about being a sports writer. Henry asked so many questions that Beau finally invited him and Marcie to join him in the press box at a Memphis Chick's baseball game.

While the children agreed to be on their best behavior in the press box, Marcie's dad stayed at the game to make sure the kids didn't become a nuisance. It's a good thing he did because Marcie was soon bored of sitting quietly among old men who smoked, grumbled, and pounded on typewriters. By the bottom of the second inning, Marcie joined her father in the bleachers where she enjoyed eating peanuts and hotdogs. Henry remained next to Beau; motionless and hypnotized by the chaos and excitement of the press box. Beau was so impressed with Henry's interest he asked Marcie's dad if it was alright for Henry to go to the newspaper with him to file the story. Marcie's dad called Henry's parents and got the okay.

At the newspaper, Henry followed Beau to a huge room filled with desks, typewriters, and telephones. At that hour of night the place was lifeless. Because most of the lights were turned off, the room was dim and full of shadows. Henry sat on a wooden chair beside Beau's desk. He watched Beau's fingers whisk over his typewriter keys with precision and dexterity. When out of the shadows, Henry glimpsed the figure of a man approaching them.

"Was it a good night, Beau?" the man asked, unconcerned that he might be interrupting Beau's work.

"Oh, hi Scoop," Beau said, glancing up. "It was a good game, lots to write about."

Scoop was the nickname for the retired city reporter who became a fixture at the newspaper since his wife passed away several years prior.

Not wanting to waste time with the retiree, Beau said, "Scoop, this is Henry. Henry is a future reporter. Do you mind sitting here with him while I turn in my story?"

"Glad to," Scoop said, pulling up a chair as Beau left the room. He was exhilarated to have a virgin audience to listen to his litany of tales about being a news hound.

Thirty minutes later, when Beau returned to his desk, Scoop had barely taken a breath in his embellished but exciting recapitulation of his forty-five years at the newspaper. That was all the time Henry needed to be convinced that he wanted to be a reporter.

*

In the spring of 1958, when Marcie and Henry were in the third grade, Marcie's mom became pregnant. Just after Thanksgiving, when Marcie was in the fourth grade, her mother gave birth to a baby girl. Marcie and her new sister shared a bedroom.

By the spring of 1961, when Marcie was in the sixth grade and looking forward to attending junior high school, her parents decided that with three growing children, their family needed a larger house. The residence they found was in Hein Park, an old money neighborhood approximately two miles away from Henry's neighborhood and in a different junior high school district.

At the beginning of the school year in 1961, Marcie blossomed into a princess, and Henry discovered what it was like not only to be alone, but to be lonely.

Chapter 4

A history of Peter Golovach, and the summer of 1965

In 1947, when Peter was five years old, his family of three immigrated to the United States from Russia. Peter's father, Ivan, had been a high-ranking officer in the Soviet army during World War Two. Having worked closely with the American military during the war, Ivan was acutely aware that the Soviets were no match for their western allies in armed warfare. It was obvious to him that a showdown between the two superpowers was imminent.

Unlike many post-war immigrants to the United States, the Golovaches' purpose for migration was not social, economic, or religious. Their goal, along with other faithful communists, was to infiltrate and destroy the United States government from within its own borders. Patriotically, he packed up his wife and young son, left the motherland, and relocated to the United States. His new assignment was to serve with the GRU, or the Glavnoye Razvedyvatel'noye Upravleniye, which was the CCCP's foreign military intelligence agency. Once stateside he settled among other Russians in Brighton Beach, New York, also referred to as "Little Odessa," after a city on the Black Sea. From

Brighton Beach he waged his own cold war against capitalist democracy. He thought it ironic that he intended to use the liberties and personal rights the U.S. gave him to do all he could to take away those same privileges and freedoms from American citizens.

Ivan's front was operating an import-export business. This cover allowed him to travel internationally as well as in the United States without causing any suspicion from the authorities. His covert mission was to create anarchy in American society by intensifying social problems regardless of whether the domestic disorder was caused by labor, civil rights, student unrest, or politics. He was aided by a number of subordinates as well as financed with money generated by the sale of illegal drugs in the U.S. Having both sufficient people and funds he was able to support both sides of any social conflict to ensure that no issue could be solved amicably. Personally, he postured as an ultra- conservative, while many who were under his command posed as radicals or revolutionary liberals.

Growing up in the United States Peter enjoyed the advantages and freedoms of America, while escaping the economic shortages, tyrannical government, and lack of opportunity in the Soviet Union. Still he was constantly inundated with the merits of communism by his parents and their associates. Because his father and the Kremlin intended for Peter to follow in his parent's footsteps, he spent many of his adolescent summers in Moscow, Peking, Havana, and Budapest, being indoctrinated with communism, and taught revolutionary tactics.

After Peter was commissioned by the Soviet Secret Service in 1964, he was assigned to exploit the American civil rights movement. His Stalinist and Marxist mentors trained him to promote fear, hate, and unrest, among the poor and uneducated. The civil rights movement seemed like a perfect venue to sow discord, due to the history of prejudice and distrust that existed between the white and black communities in the United States.

In the spring of 1965 Peter relocated to Memphis, Tennessee. The communist party thought with the rampant racism and the poor living conditions of many blacks residing there, the city was primed to be a hot bed of civil unrest.

Even so, Memphis was one of the few cities in the south where blacks had been encouraged to vote. So the strife normally associated with voter's registration in Tennessee and Mississippi was averted in the Bluff City. E. H. "Boss" Crump, who previously served as the mayor of Memphis, used blacks as an important part of his political machine. He went so far as to assist many of them in registering to vote. Some of his opponents claimed Crump bought the black vote.

Peter's initial assignment in Memphis was to burn Sanctified House of Prayer Apostolic Church with the intention of inciting the black community. There had been no church burnings in the immediate area prior to Peter's attempted arson. While Peter was not successful in terms of burning down the church, he was effective in causing fear along with cries for justice and revenge within the black community by murdering Hercules Jones.

The morning following the attempted arson and slaying, Peter discovered the newspaper had reported that a Caucasian man loosely fitting his description and driving a red pickup truck had murdered Hercules Jones. A reward was offered for any information about the owner of the vehicle that led to a conviction.

The local Ku Klux Klan publicly denied any knowledge of the crime and claimed never to have seen or used the literature found at the church. Even if the Klan was telling the truth, law enforcement agencies were aware that these terrorist frequently employed out-of-town Kluxers to carry out missions. Their strategy was to complicate criminal investigations by the lack of local participation. So the KKK remained a prime suspect in the investigation.

During their investigation the police found out that Hercules and his friends had received a telephone call from a neighbor who reported seeing Peter's truck parked on the side of the gravel road. The woman, who called them, saw a white man in the same truck snooping around the previous day.

Hercules and three other men went to the church, suspecting the man was up to no good. When they arrived at the church they saw the building was on fire, and they spotted Peter escaping into the woods. Hercules raced after him. His companions stayed to extinguish the fire.

It was a slow news day across the country so the event drew national attention, both from the media and civil rights organizations. With the possibility of an interstate conspiracy, the FBI joined the investigation. Special Agent Bill Ball from the Memphis field office partnered with Detective John Gillespie of the Memphis Police Department in the investigation. Cooperation between the agencies was rare. However, Agent Ball served on the Memphis Police Department for several years prior to joining the Bureau; ergo many of the city's policemen knew and respected him.

While Agent Ball and Detective Gillespie were conducting a field investigation, Special Agent in Charge (SAC) Sam Reid contacted the Cointelpro's (An acronym for the undercover, **Co**unter **Intel**ligence **Pro**gram within the FBI). The Cointelpro had operatives working in all major white supremacy groups including the Ku Klux Klan, The White Citizens Counsel, and the American Nazi Party. Even though there were no black agents in the FBI, the Cointelpro placed paid informants in every national civil rights organization, as well as in most local civil rights groups. Although they provided SAC Reid with an extensive list of suspects involved with Aryan groups in West Tennessee, Eastern Arkansas and North Mississippi, none of their sources provided a lead on who killed Hercules Jones, or what motivated the attempt to burn The Sanctified House of Prayer Apostolic Church.

SAC Reid sent the piece of the alleged Klan literature found at the church to the office of the FBI's headquarters, hoping they would be able to identify the chapter of the Klan where the literature originated. They also obtained warrants to bring several local Klan leaders in for questioning.

Ball and Gillespie re-interviewed the men who went to the church with Hercules. The men were cooperative but not much help. They gave minor details such as approximate height and weight of the perpetrator.

After that they interviewed Eula Livingston, the lady who drove past Peter's truck on the night of the murder, and called Hercules and his friends. Other than a vague description of the suspect and his vehicle, she was of no help.

She said all white men looked the same to her.

Ball showed her several mug shots of the most notorious Klan members in the area. She didn't recognize any of the men in the pictures.

After reporting to SAC Reid about his interview with Eula Livingston, Reid contacted several surrounding law enforcement agencies with a list of known white supremacists and asked them to find out if any of the men on the list owned a red pickup. In the meantime Agent Ball and Detective Gillespie met with Apostle Roscoe Simpson, pastor of the Sanctified House of Prayer Apostolic Church. The Apostle was extremely hostile, accusing law enforcement and the government of being racist and unconcerned about black citizens. Simpson provided no information that helped in the murder investigation.

The next morning there was a predawn roundup of leading white supremacists in Memphis, north Mississippi, and eastern Arkansas. While interrogation experts from the FBI grilled the ringleaders from the Klan, White Citizens Counsel and other extremist groups, Agent Ball worked the phone to find out if anyone found any information on the red pick-up.

With enrollment in the Klan and other white militant organizations growing, along with escalating civil rights activity, Ball spent the afternoon and evening in the field with a list of the newest suspected Klan members in an attempt to coerce some information from them. He reasoned a rookie Klansman could be intimidated easier than a veteran who had experience in dealing with law enforcement.

Some of the Klan's new recruits were rabble-rousing punks, but a portion of the fledging Klansmen were older men, who, other than their Klan association, appeared to be good citizens. Many of these men felt threatened by civil rights, feminists, the counter culture, rock and roll, and communism.

While Ball gained some personal satisfaction from harassing the punks, he experienced empathy with a number of the good citizens who had become faint hearted and discouraged over the state of the nation and turned to the Klan in desperation. Still, for all his efforts, he didn't discover any information that would help him solve Hercules Jones's murder.

When he returned to his office that evening he received a telephone call from Detective Gillespie.

"Good news, Bill," Gillespie said. "I just got a lead."

Chapter 5

History of Mary Johnson 1936-1955

Trifecta's earliest recollection from his childhood was when he and Mary stayed with his grandmother, Caledonia Johnson. They lived in a decrepit clap board shack located in Memphis' poorest ghetto. The run down accommodations barely kept them from freezing in the winter and the building was insufferably hot in the summer.

Caledonia's lights and water were disconnected as often as the utilities were operational. The white people at the Memphis Light, Gas and Water department had neither mercy nor grace for the poor blacks of the city. "Not paying their light, gas and water bills is just another example of Negroes' irresponsibility," was a common remark made by the white women who worked as cashiers at the city's utility. Of course, none of them ever had to choose between rent, buying food, or paying the utility bill. Despite the hardships, life in Memphis was more pleasant than share cropping in Mississippi.

When Trifecta was five-years old, Mary announced to his grandmother, "Mama, we're moving out."

"Where are you going?" Caledonia asked.

"We are moving in with Maurice."

"Who?"

"Maurice."

"The man who mows people's yards for a living?"

"Yes, ma'am."

"That's where you've been all these evenings when you should have been home with Trifecta and me?"

"I visit him some evenings."

"He's a drunk."

"Just because he drinks doesn't make him a drunk. Anyway, he said if I move in with him he'll stop drinking."

"Don't you believe him," she snapped. "A man is on his best behavior when he is courting. After you move in with him, you'll really find out what he is like. I didn't bring you from Mississippi to live with a worthless man."

"He isn't worthless; he works every day."

"He ain't going to make enough money to support you and Trifecta."

"I still get my welfare check."

"Not if you're married."

"I didn't say anything about getting married."

"You're making a mistake, but you're grown and you ain't got to listen to me, but I'm warning you: the man ain't no good, particularly if he isn't willing to marry you."

Staying with Maurice proved to be a challenge. The trio moved often, leaving most residences hours before the sheriff arrived with an eviction notice. Without a place to live, they sometimes moved in with Maurice's friends or relatives until he found a new place to live.

Mississippi

Mary was the younger of two daughters born to Mississippi share croppers. Her daddy died when she was six years old, leaving her with sparse and cloudy memories of him and life in Mississippi.

The journey to Memphis for Mary's family began shortly before dusk; Caledonia was sitting in a crudely constructed homemade chair on the weathered gray porch of her cabin. She was watching the other blacks returning from the fields, weary from the heat and labor among the rows of cotton. All who went by Caledonia's small sway back shack spoke, most of them either near or distant relatives. Ruby, a field hand and one of Caledonia's eight living siblings, stopped by Caledonia's squalid tenant house for a chat.

"Mr. Myers come by today," Caledonia said.

"What did the white scoundrel want?" Ruby asked leaning against the hoe she had used to chop cotton.

"He said it is time for me to leave."

"Do what?"

"He said that without a man we can't do enough work to stay in this shack."

"Jonah ain't been passed but a month," Ruby said, referring to Caledonia's recently deceased husband.

"It's been almost two months. He said if I can't get a man to move in with me who is willing to work, I've got to leave. And there ain't any men around here fit to take Jonah's place, so I reckon I've got to go."

"That white trash got the heart of the devil. So where are you going?"

"Memphis, I reckon."

"Do you know anyone in Memphis?"

"Jonah has some people there."

"Do they know you're coming?"

"I mailed them a letter this morning. Mr. Myers gave me a week to move out, so I figure by the time we get to Memphis they'll be expecting us."

"Do you have any money?"

"Counting my change, I have five dollars and thirty-two cent," which comprised all of Caledonia's and Jonah's life savings.

"It'll take all that to get the three of you to Memphis on the bus."

"I know. I've got to get someone to carry us there."

"What're you going to do for work once you get there?"

"I don't know, but surely I can come up with something better than share cropping without a husband."

Within days, Caledonia found a small-time truck farmer who was always looking for an excuse to go to Memphis and sew some wild oats. The farmer agreed to take Caledonia and the girls to Memphis for free, anticipating the pleasure of female companionship for the thirty-mile journey. Several of Caledonia's relatives cautioned her that the man she would be traveling with was a womanizing drunk, and she best be careful; not only for herself, but for her little girls.

The Saturday Caledonia was scheduled to leave, her neighbors and relatives held a farewell party for her. They presented her with some hand-me-down clothes for the children to take to the city and ten dollars in cash. Ten dollars was an amazing sum for the black sharecroppers to contribute, particularly before the cotton was picked and sold.

When the farmer arrived to take Caledonia to Memphis, Mary and Josephine whined about leaving the only home they ever knew, but Caledonia ordered her girls into the bed of the truck and climbed in after them.

"Don't you want to ride in the front with me, Miss Caledonia?" the farmer asked.

"I'll be fine back here with my children," Caledonia replied.

At first the farmer was disgruntled when Caledonia refused his invitation, but he soon reasoned that he would rather spend the evening with a sweet-smelling city-woman than be tied down to a dusty corn pone like Caledonia.

Memphis

Caledonia quickly discovered that providing the bare necessities for her daughters in Memphis required two jobs. Even with the two jobs, which kept Caledonia working night and day, the paltry wages paid to black women kept the small family in abysmal poverty. During the day Caledonia cleaned rooms at the Claridge Hotel located on Main Street. At night she cleaned restrooms in the Sterick building. Her schedule left little time for her to spend with or supervise her children. When Caledonia was home she was so exhausted she couldn't do much more than sit in a chair and prop up her sore feet. Still, she felt blessed to have the work because it was 1936 and the country was still recovering from the Great Depression. Jobs were scarce to come by even for well-educated white men, let alone a black woman who was practically illiterate.

With no options for child care, Caledonia put Josephine in charge of the household while she worked. Josephine despised taking care of her younger sister, preferring to be on the street with girls her own age. When Caledonia came home Mary frequently met her at the front door frowning, if not in tears, complaining that Josephine had been mean, or hit her, or tormented her in some other way.

As teens, neither girl was good academically or athletically, but both were very attractive. As they grew the friction between them escalated. In a fight Mary was no match for Josephine physically. Josephine also had a quicker wit, leaving Mary to concede most verbal arguments in frustration. However, Josephine was inordinately shy around boys, while Mary was confident and flirtatious. Any time Mary overheard Josephine mention a boy to one of her friends, Mary would direct her attention toward him, and within days he would be walking Mary home from school.

The more provoked Josephine became with Mary's dallying, the more salacious Mary grew. She used her looks to get the boy's attention and her suggestive playfulness to keep several suitors on a short leash. The more boys she had chasing her, the more envious Josephine seemed to be, which encouraged Mary to do whatever it took to attract more boys.

Mary never indulged in more than kissing and inappropriate touching with her boyfriends, until one summer night she went for a drive with a twenty-two-year-old man. He was six years older than she; with straightened hair shining with pomade. He had a job, a car and the ability to buy cheap, fruity wine. The night Mary lost her virginity she stayed up vomiting the sweet wine that had allowed her date to take advantage of her in his 1938 Rambler sedan with reclining seats. She never saw the man again, but their brief affair set Mary on a new course of taking her relationships further with more boys.

"You're going to get your black butt pregnant," Josephine warned.

"You're just jealous because you ain't got a fella chasing after you," Mary sassed.

"I ain't jealous of you girl, but I'm not going to listen to your mouth, and I'm not going to take care of you and your love child neither."

"I ain't asking you for nothing, and I'm not pregnant," Mary responded.

"You're going to be if you don't stop acting like a dog in heat, spreading your legs for any man that comes sniffing around you."

"It ain't none of your business what I do, and you're not an angel yourself."

"It's not going to be any of my business when you wind up like mama, with kids to feed and no man around. You'll be working night and day just to keep them fed and in diapers. And when that happens, don't come begging me for help."

"Shut up!" Mary screamed, stomping her foot.

"You shut up yourself," Josephine replied turning and walking away, leaving Mary grumbling to herself.

Except for an early miscarriage that no one knew about, Mary didn't get pregnant during three years of promiscuity. When she had her baby she was mortified that Josephine's repeated prediction was true and she would find herself with a baby and no man. As soon as her belly began to swell the men who seemed to be constantly under foot vanished, and when she was on the street toting Trifecta on her hip, most men steered cleared of the once popular girl. Several men suspecting the child might be his.

When Trifecta was five, Mary met Maurice. Maurice seemed to be a wonderful man who cared about her as well as Trifecta. His only apparent faults were that he sometimes drank too much, and he didn't have a steady job. However, when he suggested that Mary move in with him, she jumped at the chance, thinking she could influence him to quit drinking, and find stable employment.

Things didn't work out the way Mary dreamed. Within weeks of her moving in, Maurice was drinking more, working less and began physically abusing her.

Maurice blamed Mary for everything that was wrong with his life. He wanted her to account for every minute of her time, and would get angry if she socialized with anyone when he wasn't with her. He went from being generous when they were dating to stingy once they began living together. He barely gave her enough money to keep sufficient food in the house to feed Trifecta. Even though he always squandered her welfare check on carousing and raising Cain, he insisted that she get a job, and pay her share of the expenses. Being black with no skills and lacking a high school education, the only thing she could do was day work. Domestic employment was difficult for her to find because she had no experience with housework, and she had to take Trifecta with her to the houses where she applied for a job. It was a hard pill to swallow, but it was evident that Caledonia had been right about Maurice.

Chapter 6

Fall 1962

By the seventh-grade, Marcie matured into a charming young woman with a sunny personality and a captivating smile. Her mother, anticipating the anxiety Marcie would experience attending a new school, had been observing the fashions of junior and senior high school girls at the country club. With a significant amount of money and the assistance of some young sales clerks at Levi's and Goldsmith's department stores, Mrs. McDougal made sure that Marcie would begin the seventh grade outfitted in the most popular teenage styles, making her transition into an acceptable social circle at Snowden Junior High School almost effortless.

Henry, on the other hand, struggled to find his niche at Fairview Junior High. He was inexperienced and unprepared for the social burdens of the seventh grade. For the first time in his life, he was separated from Marcie, and overwhelmed when he realized he was without a best friend.

At the beginning of the school year he ate lunch with some casual acquaintances from elementary school. After lunch he hung out in the hall, feeling secluded and detached.

He had no place to go, nothing to do and no one to talk to. On the third day of school, after eating lunch he wandered into the boy's restroom. The titled room was crowded with boys holding cigarettes cupped in their hands, standing quietly in a cloud of smoke and looking anxiously at him. When they realized Henry was not a teacher, they resumed their smoking and talking. Unsure what he should do, Henry went to the urinal but was unable to pee. When he turned to leave one of the boys asked, "Want a drag?" He extended a cigarette to Henry that he had been sharing with a classmate.

Wanting to appear cool, Henry said, "Sure."

The cigarette was hot boxed from being smoked too quickly. When Henry put the cigarette to his mouth, the filter was wet with the other boy's saliva, and he could feel the heat from the long hot ash on his lips.

Henry sucked the smoke into his mouth and immediately blew it out.

"You've got to inhale," coached the boy who handed him the cigarette.

Henry looked perplexed. Neither of Henry's parents smoked, and he had never spent much time with a smoker, so he wasn't sure what he was being instructed to do.

"You got to breathe the smoke all the way into your lungs."

Henry put the cigarette to his mouth again and tried to breathe the smoke in, but the smoke refused to go down. He tried to swallow the smoke, but to his dismay the smoke lodged in his throat. It felt like a boulder in his wind pipe. He gagged and then coughed the smoke out. He felt very uncool.

"You almost got it. Try again," encouraged the boy.

Reluctantly, Henry raised the cigarette to his lips, but just as he was beginning to take a puff the bell rang. The boy reached for the cigarette, which Henry willingly surrendered, took one quick drag, and then flicked the cigarette into the toilet, leaving Henry alone in a haze of smoke.

By the end of fifth period Henry needed to pee, so he stopped by the restroom on the way to his next class. To his surprise, the restroom on the second floor was filled with smoke just like the restroom on the first floor. Henry walked toward the urinal, and when he had finished his business, he was met by the boy from lunch.

"Try it again," the boy said, offering a lit cigarette to Henry.

Henry took the cigarette and puffed on it. He sucked in a large volume of air through his mouth, making an audible sucking sound, trying to force the smoke into his lungs. This time the lump of smoke passed through his throat and landed hard in his lungs. Henry coughed uncontrollably; he thought he was going to vomit. The smoke rubbed his throat raw as he coughed it up; tears came to his eyes and he handed the cigarette back to the boy. The bell rang and the restroom cleared. Henry rushed to class, his head spinning.

The next morning when Henry arrived at school he went to the restroom around the same time as the previous day. Several boys were smoking but he didn't see the boy from the preceding day. Not knowing what else to do he stepped up to the urinal. He couldn't go, so he pretended to pee. Suddenly, the door flew open banging against the tile wall. Coach Walker, a math teacher and football coach, stepped into the room. Instantly fear and guilt appeared on each boy's face and cigarettes were thrown into toilets, or onto the floor. Several boys tried to slip past Coach Walker but he blocked the door.

"I saw you, you and you smoking," Coach Walker said, pointing to three different boys. One of them still had a cigarette cupped in his hand, attempting to hide it by holding it close to his leg. "Let's go to the office, and the rest of you get to class. And I'd better never see any of you smoking."

Henry stood at the urinal as the other boys filed out of the restroom. When everyone else was gone, Henry zipped up his fly and walked towards the door. He blushed as he walked by Coach Walker, who gave Henry a cold and threatening stare. The tardy bell rang as he stepped into the hall. He was late for his class.

The next morning before homeroom Henry went into the first floor restroom and the boy who had previously invited Henry to share his smoke was lighting up. As Henry approached him, the boy handed him the cigarette. Henry took a drag. With a deep breath the smoke went into his lungs. He handed the cigarette back to the boy.

"You about got it," the boy said.

Henry felt a little light-headed but was pleased with his accomplishment. The boy took a puff and handed the cigarette back to Henry. Henry took a drag. He didn't have to struggle quite as much to inhale the smoke. When he returned the cigarette to the boy, he immediately began to feel flush, and his head began to swim. The boy took a puff and handed the cigarette back to Henry. This time, Henry inhaled the nicotine a little easier, but his head reeled more, and he became nauseated. He leaned against the wall, afraid he might pass out. The smoke from the cigarette was becoming increasingly bitter, as a long ash glowed like a hot ember on the end of the cigarette. Henry took another draw and his nausea and dizziness intensified. He felt like he might be running a fever. The bell rang. The boy took one last drag and flipped the cigarette into the toilet. "See you at lunch," the boy said as he walked away. Henry was so lightheaded he didn't feel he could walk straight, so he continued to lean against the wall. A cloud of smoke lingered as the room emptied, leaving Henry alone. The silence of the deserted restroom rang in his ears as his head and stomach continued to twirl.

Fearing he would be counted absent he decided to try to make it to class. The empty halls echoed with his footsteps.

He felt like he was staggering as he made his way to home room. When he entered the classroom the teacher asked him where he had been.

"The restroom," Henry said weakly.

"Do you feel alright?" his homeroom teacher asked, noticing Henry's ashen features.

"No ma'am," Henry replied, embarrassed, thinking he might throw-up.

"Why don't you go to the school nurse?"

When Henry arrived at the sick room the first question the nurse asked was, "Have you been smoking?"

"No ma'am," Henry answered in a faint voice.

"You smell like you've been smoking," the nurse said, not believing Henry.

"There were boys smoking in the restroom."

"Do you know who they are?"

"No ma'am," Henry answered. "I'm new here."

The nurse checked his temperature; Henry didn't have a fever, so she made him lie down until he felt better. By the time he was situated on the cot, the effects of the cigarette were gone, but he continued to lie still, scared that if he recovered too quickly the nurse would become more suspicious about his smoking.

When he got up and told the nurse he felt better. She reminded him about the rules against smoking on campus and sent him to his first period class with a written excuse for his tardiness.

At lunch Henry returned to the boy's room. His companion was just lighting up.

"Hey," Henry said as he approached the boy.

"Hey."

"Can I have a smoke?" Henry asked.

"Sure," the boy said, bending over and pulling a cigarette out of the elastic rim of his sock, where he hid his cigarettes during school.

"My name is Henry."

"I'm Alan," the boy responded. Alan flipped the top of his cigarette lighter, and offered Henry a light.

When Henry inhaled the first puff of smoke, he became slightly dizzy but nowhere near as woozy as that morning. Afraid a teacher might come in at any moment he stood inside one of the stalls, while remaining near enough to Alan to talk. When he noticed Alan's attention was somewhere else he puffed on the cigarette, but he didn't inhale. He wanted to avoid being sick while still acting cool.

Chapter 7

Summer 1965

Isabel Carter appeared to be in her late sixties or early seventies. She called the police department in response to an article she read in the previous morning's newspaper. The article was about a black man who was murdered on the outskirts of the city. The newspaper gave a vague description of the suspect, along with a description of his pickup truck.

Mrs. Carter lived on Vinton Avenue, a street lined with mature oak trees and arrayed with stately old brick homes built in the early years of the twentieth century. She was a widow and to supplement her income, she rented a furnished garage apartment, which in more genteel times had been the servants' quarters. She preferred to rent to students attending one of the local colleges.

Her most recent tenant, Pete Burns (AKA Peter Golovach), drove a red Datsun pickup. She thought it was unusual not to have seen him or his vehicle for several days. When she went into his apartment to check on him, she found that all of his possessions were gone. That's when it occurred to her that her renter and the person described in the newspaper could possibly be one in the same. She immediately notified the police department.

Detective Gillespie telephoned Agent Ball, and the two arranged to ride to Mrs. Carter's residence together.

"He seemed like such a nice young man," Mrs. Carter said. "Quiet, well dressed, clean-cut, and he was very punctual paying his rent."

"Did he pay with cash or check?" Ball asked.

"He always paid with cash."

"How long did he live here?"

"He moved in just prior to the spring semester."

"Was he a student?"

"Yes, he went to Memphis State. He wants to be a high school teacher."

"Do you know where he was from?"

"He told me he was from Alabama, but I thought it was strange he didn't talk like he was from the south."

"What do you mean?" Ball pressed.

"He had a strange accent, sort of northern, but I never questioned him about it."

"Did you get any references on him?"

"No, but I did get an address and telephone number for his parents, as well as the license plate number of his truck. Even though I require the first and last month's rent in advance there have been times I have had to call a student's parents to collect my money. However, I never had any trouble collecting from him."

"May we have his parents address and phone number?"

"Certainly, let me get it for you."

She went to her desk and returned with a piece of paper containing all the information she had for Peter.

The only description Mrs. Carter could give was that Pete Burns was a nice-looking young man, of medium height, medium weight, with brown hair and clean shaven.

Agent Ball arranged for a technical team to follow up at the scene to get fingerprints and anything else in the apartment that might help them locate Pete Burns.

Mrs. Carter had provided them with a home address in Decatur, Alabama, a home telephone number for his parents and his license plate number, which indicated that the vehicle was registered in Shelby County, Tennessee where Memphis is located.

After leaving Mrs. Carter's home, the two law men drove to Memphis State University. There was no Pete Burns registered in any classes. They cruised around the campus looking for a red Datsun pickup with Pete's license plate number. After completing their unsuccessful search at Memphis State, they decided to check out Christian Brothers College and Southwestern College. No Pete Burns was registered at either institution, and they didn't find the suspected vehicle on either campus.

After dropping off Gillespie at the police precinct and returning to his office, Agent Ball called the telephone number Mrs. Carter gave him. Mr. Leonard Mitchell answered the phone; the man had never heard of Pete Burns, nor did he have a son attending college in Memphis. Plus he was only thirty-three years old. Not only did he not live at the address Mrs. Carter gave Agent Ball; he didn't even live in Decatur. Ball called the Decatur police department and asked them to send a patrol car to the address Mrs. Carter gave them. There was no such address within the city.

Locally, the FBI did not have a file on Pete Burns. However, the FBI headquarters had two files with that name. One lived in Kansas City, the other in Milwaukee. Both men were much older than Agent Ball's suspect, but he thought there was a possibility they were related. The telephone number for Peter Burns in Kansas City was disconnected. There was no answer at the number in Milwaukee.

In the meantime, Detective Gillespie called saying he had tracked down the license plate number they had obtained from Mrs. Carter.

"The plates were issued to a Dr. and Mrs. William Davenport, on Eastlawn Drive. The plates belong to a blue Chrysler Imperial," Gillespie told Ball on the phone. Ball drove to the police station and picked up Gillespie. The Davenports lived at the top of Eastlawn Cove, just a few houses from Henry Murphy.

The Davenports lived in a ranch-style house. Their home was much larger than any other house in the middle-income neighborhood. The yard was covered in thick Bermuda grass that was fertilized so green it appeared to be blue. Immaculately trimmed bushes surrounded a fashionable home that was shaded by huge oak trees.

The door was answered by a black maid in a pale green uniform with a white scalloped apron.

"Dr. Davenport is not in, but Mrs. Davenport is here. May I ask whose calling?"

"I'm Agent Ball of the FBI, and this is Inspector Gillespie of the Memphis Police Department."

Excusing herself, the black woman shut the door leaving the officers standing on the front porch. Moments later a distinguished woman wearing a purple suit with a pearl necklace came to the door.

"I'm Helen Davenport, how may I help you?" she asked with an air of southern sophistication.

The two detectives explained the situation with the license plates, and Mrs. Davenport seemed mildly alarmed. She escorted them to the garage where her blue Chrysler Imperial was parked. The sleek and shiny land yacht had current Tennessee tags. Mrs. Davenport had no idea if they were the proper tags. After examining the vehicle registration, the tag that belonged to the Davenports' automobile was the tag Mrs. Carter said was on the red Datsun pickup. Inspector Gillespie called the DMV to trace the license plate on the Davenport car, and discovered it belonged to Ophelia Wilcox.

Mrs. Wilcox was an elderly woman who lived in a small but neat white asbestos-sided house in the Berclair subdivision. She told Ball and Gillespie that she had been a widow for several years, and she had no idea how her license plates could have been on the Davenports' car. When the three went to the carport, behind Mrs. Wilcox's house, they discovered there was no license plate on her 1960 Ford Falcon. Mrs. Wilcox was visibly shaken, afraid she was somehow liable for a mix-up in car tags.

Detective Gillespie completed a police report on the stolen tags, so Mrs. Wilcox could replace her car's license plates.

*

Within an hour of murdering Hercules Jones, Peter called his father in Brighton Beach. Ivan advised his son to leave his garage apartment and get rid of the truck. After that he was to go to a specific used car lot on Lamar Avenue where they would sell him a vehicle for cash with no paper trail. Then he was to find a new place to live.

Additionally, Ivan gave Peter instructions to be carried out over the next several days and contacts to assist him.

*

Ross's relationship with Peter Golovach and the communist party had nothing to do with politics. As far as he was concerned one form of government was as oppressive to blacks as another. So being a co-conspirator with the Russians had nothing to do with ideology and everything to do with personal gain. To keep Peter out of harm's way, Ross's first assignment was to recruit two nonentities, to do the grunt work and be exposed to the greatest risk in carrying out Peter's subversive mission.

Reverend Lucas Moneypenny found a hand-addressed letter in his mailbox. In the envelope was fifteen dollars along with a message telling him to be at Red's Pool Hall at ten o'clock the following morning. Reverend Moneypenny was a minister without a church, without any theological training, without a Bible, and most importantly, without a call from God.

The same day, Leroy Sims received an identical letter as Lucas Moneypenny. Leroy survived without any productive labor. Instead he defrauded the welfare system, constantly flimflammed lonely women, and swindled local charities.

Chapter 8

1958-July 1961

When Trifecta was six years old, Mary started doing day work for Mrs. Churchill. The Churchills owned a grand home in Chickasaw Gardens, an exclusive area of Memphis.

Even though Mary lacked experience and was only moderately literate, Mrs. Churchill hired her because she looked and smelled clean, and was reasonably attractive. She had grown tired of Negro mammies who swiped at furniture with a dust rag, then turned sully or sassy when told how to clean properly. Despite Mary's gold tooth, Mrs. Churchill thought she could dress up this somewhat appealing girl, teach her to serve and do housework, and she would become the envy of all her socialite friends—many of whom complained of their domestics being lazy and impudent.

Mary worked five days a week and was paid four dollars per day plus bus fare, meals and crisp laundered uniform dresses. Before Trifecta was old enough to attend school, Mary was allowed to bring him to work with her and feed him breakfast and lunch. On days when it was raining, Mrs. Churchill met Mary and Trifecta at the bus stop and drove them to her home. When it was raining after work, Mrs. Churchill took them home even though she disliked going into the ghetto where Mary lived.

Trifecta was always remembered by the Churchills on his birthday and at Christmas. On each occasion, he would receive three gifts, one from each of the Churchill boys, and a gift from Mr. and Mrs. Churchill.

In 1960, Memphis was governed by "Jim Crow laws," meaning the Memphis City Zoo, the Public Library, the Pink Palace Museum, and other public facilities were segregated. The only time blacks were allowed visit these attractions was on "Black Thursdays". Schools remained segregated despite the Supreme Court ruling on Brown versus The Board of Education in 1954. Blacks remained confined to sitting in the back of city buses, drinking at separate water fountains, and using designated restrooms. Blacks were prevented from eating in white restaurants, and could only stay at hotels specified for blacks.

For a long time, neither Trifecta nor Mary gave much thought to the Jim Crow laws; they just accepted the restrictions as being the way of life. However, throughout the 1950s and 60s, the attitude of the rank and file blacks was changing. Many black people were ready to break from bigoted traditions; unfortunately, tradition is a hard thing to break, particularly in the south.

On March 19, 1960, eight black college students participated in the first civil rights protest in Memphis. A sit-in was staged at the main branch of the Memphis library. This protest started a chain reaction of nonviolent protests across the city. As the number of protests escalated, Mrs. Churchill warned Mary not to get involved in the trouble-making activities that were stirring within the colored community because it was only going to disrupt the racial harmony that Memphis had enjoyed for years. Even though

Mary respected Mrs. Churchill, she didn't think there was any racial harmony in Memphis.

*

Maurice was a handy man. He made money cutting yards and doing odd jobs for various white people. When the Churchills were looking for a yard boy in the fall of 1961, Mary recommended Maurice, never letting on she cohabitated with him. Based on her recommendation Maurice was hired and worked two days a week for the Churchills. He started during the winter, performing repairs and general maintenance around the house. When spring came he got really busy, receiving an endless list of orders as well as constant scrutiny by Mrs. Churchill. He planted, pruned, cut, weeded, fertilized, trimmed, cultivated, watered and aerated. From eight in the morning until late into the afternoon, he groomed and pampered the Churchill's lawn, bushes, and flower gardens. He felt he worked like a slave under the watchful eye of Mrs. Churchill. Like Mary, he was provided lunch. However, he wasn't allowed to eat in the house. He could eat on the back porch or in the garage. He often complained to Mary that Mrs. Churchill treated the family dog better than she treated him because the dog was free to eat in the kitchen. Mary was always quick to defend Mrs. Churchill and pointed out the Churchills didn't pay their dog, nor did the dog sweat as much as Maurice.

Throughout July, 1961, Mrs. Churchill observed that Maurice was becoming increasingly uncooperative. In addition, she routinely noticed the smell of alcohol emanating from him. She had always forbidden domestics from drinking on her premises.

One day after Maurice cut the yard things came to a climax. "It looks like Maurice edged the yard with a dull axe," she said as she walked out the back door to confront her yard boy. When she found him in the garage, he wreaked so acutely of alcohol she concluded he had just taken a drink. An argument ensued, and Maurice's language became abusive. Having listened to all she could tolerate, Mrs. Churchill said, "I have never been addressed by a white man with such language, and I'm certainly not going to listen to words like that from one of my Negroes. I'll get your wages for the day, and you may leave." Mrs. Churchill was on her way out of the garage before the tittering Maurice could respond. Fortunately Maurice's drunken reflexes were slow, because being called one of her Negroes enraged Maurice to the point he could physically strike her.

By the time Mrs. Churchill returned with a five-dollar bill in hand, Maurice was on the back porch complaining to Mary. Mary stood just outside the door with her face cupped in her hands, sobbing.

Thrusting the money toward Maurice, Mrs. Churchill said, "I'm paying you for the entire day even though you don't deserve it. Now please leave and don't come back."

Maurice started to respond but Mary screamed, "Don't say another word; just leave."

Maurice's eyes were inflamed as he swayed drunkenly before the two women. He turned, spit on the ground, and staggered down the driveway, money in hand, with a bottle of whiskey peeking out of the back pocket of his dungarees.

As Mary cried harder, Mrs. Churchill embraced her. With Mary's face buried in her shoulder, Mrs. Churchill whispered in her ear. "It's alright, honey; settle down, I'm sorry you had to be a part of such a horrible thing."

"But you don't understand. Maurice is my husband." Mary whimpered, embarrassed by Maurice's actions and humiliated because she was living in sin with him.

Being surprised but still under control, Mrs. Churchill said, "Let's go inside and talk about it."

"I'm so ashamed." Mary said, still sobbing as she followed Mrs. Churchill into the house.

Mary and Mrs. Churchill talked for an hour. Mrs. Churchill contributed a few tears of her own. When there was nothing left to say, Mrs. Churchill offered to take Mary and Trifecta home. Mary protested because she had not started preparing the Churchill's supper. Mrs. Churchill assured her that Mr. Churchill would be happy to take her out to dinner that night.

Trying to avoid another altercation, Mary insisted Mrs. Churchill drop them a block from her house because she was frightened Maurice would be home.

Maurice didn't show up at the house until the next morning when Mary was getting ready for work.

Chapter 9

July 1965

Lucas Moneypenny arrived at Red's pool hall just before ten o'clock. He was leery but curious about the fifteen dollars he found in his mailbox. He hoped he would be able to collect the additional funds promised in the note that was enclosed with the cash. A closed sign hung on the front door of the pool room. There was a man sitting in a wooden chair in front of the building. Lucas pulled the note from his shirt pocket to confirm the address.

"Are You Sims?" the man in the chair asked.

"No."

"You must be Moneypenny."

"Who wants to know?" Moneypenny asked.

"The door is unlocked. Go in and have a seat. We'll be with you in a minute."

"Who are you, man?"

"I'm the cat that's going to make you some money. Now go inside and when Sims gets here we'll talk."

Moneypenny went into the dimly lit pool room. A table and chairs were set up just inside the door. As Lucas took a seat on the vinyl covered chair, he noticed a light-skinned black man with reddish hair sweeping the floor around three pool tables. Moneypenny assumed the man's name was Red, as in Red's Pool Hall. The room stunk of spilt beer and yesterday's nicotine. A sense of foreboding crept over him as the only sound inside the room came from the rhythmic swishing of the broom across the rough wooden floor and the whirl of a fan oscillating in the corner.

Moneypenny considered himself to be a street hustler who lived by his wits. However, he was nothing more than a mooch living off simple minded women, temporary friends and an occasional relative. If someone asked about his occupation, he claimed to be a preacher. Asserting to be a man of the cloth gave him an opportunity to panhandle in the name of the Lord.

In a few minutes, the man who had been sitting outside entered the pool room accompanied by a man whom Moneypenny guessed was Sims. When the two men entered, the bright skinned man sweeping the floor disappeared through a door at the rear of the room.

When all three men were at the table, the man from outside put ten dollars in front of Moneypenny and Sims. Neither man moved.

"Go ahead and pick it up."

Moneypenny quickly stashed the cash in his shirt pocket but Sims remained motionless.

"What is the bread for?" Sims asked, wearing a poker face, trying to ignore the mounting tension.

The man explained they were being paid to burn crosses in front of an FBI agent's home, and at a black church.

"You're crazy," Sims said. "Why would two black men burn a cross at a black church and at an FBI agent's house?"

"Because you've been paid, and if you don't there will be some unpleasant circumstances."

"This doesn't make any sense," piped up Moneypenny, afraid the man was capable of making good on his threat.

"It makes perfect sense," the man said. "You've been paid, and you're going to do the job. If you don't, you'll wish you had."

"Why did you choose us?" Moneypenny asked with fear tightening his stomach.

"You've been chosen because you like to make easy money," the man said, looking at Moneypenny. "And if you turn up missing, nobody will care. So no one will be looking for you or calling the pigs if you don't do what you've been paid for.".

"Who are you?" Moneypenny asked.

"My name is Ross."

"That's your first name or last name?"

"It's just Ross."

Even though it wasn't apparent, Sims was as scared as Moneypenny. He reluctantly picked up the money.

Leaving the poolroom through the back door they passed Red sitting against the building drinking whiskey straight from a pint bottle. Red did nothing to acknowledge them as they passed within a few feet of him.

The truck they would use was hidden in a ramshackle garage. They could sense the harsh smell of kerosene as they approached the tottering building.

"If the law stops us, they're going to be curious about that stink," Moneypenny said.

"Then don't get stopped," Ross said. "I'll meet you both here at midnight tonight. Don't be late and don't even think about disappointing me."

*

At twelve-thirty in the morning, Ross called the Lamp Lighter Lounge from a payphone. The bartender asked the man sitting at the bar nursing a beer if his name was Peter. Peter took the phone. "They are on their way," Ross reported. Peter took a sip from his Pabst Blue Ribbon and left.

Chapter 10

Fall 1962 three years earlier

Henry had fantasized so long about being a reporter that he was convinced all he lacked was a press-pass to be a certified ink slinger. So it was inconceivable to him when his homeroom teacher announced that Hilda was going to be the class correspondent for the school newspaper, instead of him.

When homeroom was dismissed Henry approached Miss Farber.

"I'm a good newspaper reporter." Henry said.

"I'm sure you are," Miss Farber replied.

"Then why can't I be the class reporter? Henry asked.

"In my class there are standards for students who are given a leadership position. Hilda's reputation is without flaw. Additionally, she is a positive influence on the other students."

"I'm a good influence."

"Henry, it is common knowledge among the teachers that you are a smoker. Not only do you smoke off campus, but I suspect that you disregard the school policy and smoke with your cohorts in the boys' rest room. I don't feel it's appropriate to allow someone with such disrespect for the school to have a leadership position in my class. I have to consider the message that will send to the other children."

"I do not smoke," Henry lied.

"Come now Henry, you smell like a smoke stack every morning. You smell like an ash tray right now. Teachers observe things Henry, and we talk to one another about our students. Frankly, you have been associating with the wrong group of boys."

Realizing his dream of being a reporter was slipping away he said, "I'm new at this school, I don't know who to be friends with."

"Henry, the decision has been made."

"It's not fair, I'm a good reporter," Henry blubbered, close to tears.

"It is more than fair. If you can't control yourself, I will be forced to send you to the principal's office."

"Give me a chance, I'll change," Henry plead. "I'll do anything to be on the newspaper staff."

"You'll quit smoking?"

"Yes ma'am."

An influx of students filtered into the classroom as the bell rang. Mrs. Farber was beginning to think Henry was sincere when he promised to quit smoking. However, Hilda was a good student and such a pretty girl. Miss Farber couldn't bring herself reverse her decision for class reporter. She decided she would look for an alternative solution that would allow Henry to work on the newspaper.

"Henry, let me see what I can do. Report to me immediately after school I'm sure I can find some compromise. I'm doing this because I believe you want to be a good example for the other students and you promised to stop smoking. Now let me write a note explaining why you are late to your next class."

"Yes, ma'am," Henry said humbly.

Confident that he had successfully manipulated Miss Faber, and with a tardy note in hand, Henry went to the restroom and lit a cigarette.

That afternoon Miss Farber told him he could be a freelance sports reporter.

Daydreaming of being a great sports writer, Henry rode a bus to the Scripts Howard publishing company to see his baseball coach Beau Campbell.

The newspaper office was a flurry of activity. Beau was at his typewriter when Henry approached his desk.

"Hi Henry, Beau said, extending his hand.

Henry shook Beau's hand and said, "I need some help. I've joined the school newspaper staff, and I've been assigned to cover sports. I thought you might be able to give me some pointers."

"I'd be glad to. But why aren't you playing ball rather than writing about it?"

"You know I'm probably not good enough to make the team, and I really want to be a writer like you."

"Well, how can I help you?"

"I need to know how to write a story."

"Every article must have five elements: who, what, when, where and why. If you cover all those points, you'll have a good story. However, you might want to talk to Scoop. I'm sure he would love to help you write some stories," Beau said, having neither the time nor desire to help Henry develop a childhood writing career.

"I didn't know Scoop covered sports," Henry said, hoping Beau would help him.

"He probably hasn't in a long time, but Scoop is a professional reporter. He can write about anything, and if you want to be a newspaper man you need to be able to write on a variety of subjects. You can learn a lot from a veteran like Scoop."

"Is there any other advice you can give me?" Henry asked, apprehensive about contacting Scoop. He figured

Scoop wouldn't remember him, and wouldn't be willing to help him.

"My best advice is to get Scoop to help you. He can answer your questions and steer you in the right direction. Let me give you his telephone number." Beau thumbed through a rolodex on his desk and wrote down Scoop's home telephone number.

"Do you think Scoop will remember me?"

"I'm sure he will, but if you want, I'll give him a call and tell him you'll be in touch."

"That would be great."

Henry called Scoop later that evening. He was disappointed to find out that Beau had forgotten to call the old reporter.

"Sure, I'll be glad to help you," Scoop said. "Tell you what we can do; let me meet you after school, at the practice field, and we'll take a look at the team."

"Okay," Henry said, remembering the surly look coach Walker gave him the day he caught three boys smoking in the rest room.

"What's wrong?" Scoop asked, sensing the hesitation in Henry's voice.

"I don't know if Coach Walker will allow us to watch practice. He's pretty strict."

"The first thing you have to learn if you're going to be a reporter is you can't let anybody or anything prevent you from writing a story. The second thing you have to learn is you never give up until you have the story right. The only way to get the story right is to experience your story first hand."

*

The next day after school, Henry stood by the driveway that ran between the school building and the practice field waiting for Scoop. He watched the football players begin their calisthenics under the direction of Coach Lincoln, the assistant coach.

The longer Henry waited the more concerned he became that Scoop was not going to show up. Just as Henry contemplated leaving, he noticed Scoop and Coach Walker walking together towards the practice field. Henry could see that Scoop was carrying a long narrow pad in his hand. As Scoop and the coach approached the field, Scoop looked at Henry quizzically not sure he was the boy he agreed to meet. Henry waved weakly, and Scoop smiled, acknowledging him.

When practice started, Scoop joined Henry.

"What are you writing?" Henry asked meekly.

"Making some notes for our story," Scoop responded. "Do you know the quarterback's name?"

"No," Henry replied.

"It's Jeff White. He became the starting quarterback last year when a kid named Billy Vanlandingham broke his leg. Billy is the back-up quarterback at Messick High School this year."

"How do you know all that?"

"I interviewed the coach. That's what reporters do."

*

The next morning Henry went into the boy's restroom. Alan was there, smoking.

"Can I have a cigarette?" Henry asked Alan.

"Now that I have taught you how to smoke, you need to learn how to buy," Alan said, passing Henry the cigarette he was smoking.

As Henry took his first drag on the cigarette the door burst open and Coach Walker entered the room. Instantly, Henry threw the cigarette into the commode. Lowering his head, and with a huge knot in his belly, he walked towards the door holding his breath, trying not to exhale the smoke.

Several boys were walking past the coach and through the door in front of him. When the coach recognized Henry as the boy who had been with Scoop, he grabbed Henry's arm.

"Have you been smoking?" The coach's voice was gruff and angry.

Henry couldn't help looking into the coach's fiery eyes. "No, sir," Henry squeaked, still trying to hold his breath, but his attempt was useless. He had to breathe, and his weak answer was followed by a puff of smoke escaping his mouth.

Pulling Henry by the arm, the coach took Henry to his private office in the gym. Henry was afraid his career as the school's sports reporter was over before it began because the coach had caught him smoking and he was sure Mrs. Farber would find out.

"I'm going to give you three licks for smoking," the coach said, waving a paddle in front of Henry that looked to be two feet long. "Then I'm going to give you three licks for lying. Normally I would have you suspended for lying but because Scoop is trying to help you: I'm just going to paddle you. But don't you ever lie to me again, do you understand?"

Henry wanted to answer but was afraid he would cry, so he nodded his head.

"Answer me boy, do you understand?" Coach Walker bellowed with the tone of a Marine Drill Sergeant.

"Yes, sir," Henry said, his voice cracking and tears starting to run down his cheeks.

"Grab your ankles son," the coach said in a softer tone, "and quit your sniveling."

Henry bent over taking a firm grip on his ankles. The coach swatted Henry's butt six times.

Nothing was said by either Coach Walker or Miss Faber, about Henry forfeiting his position on the newspaper staff.

The first game of the season, Fairview played their arch-rival, Bellevue Junior High School. Scoop met Henry after school and he was able to get Henry into the press box where the lone official operated the score board. Scoop told Henry what to write in his notes.

Fairview won the game six to nothing on a twelve play drive that culminated with an end run by the Jeff White. They failed to make a two point conversion. Scoop and Henry went to the offices of the Press Scimitar where they sat at Beau's desk and composed an article. Scoop was careful to let Henry write the story, while making sure he got the article right.

*

"They changed the story," Henry told Scoop over the phone.

"What do you mean they changed the story?"

"They left out parts and changed some of the words."

"That's part of the business. It's called editing," Scoop said, trying not to display his contempt towards a junior high school teacher who had the nerve to edit what he helped Henry write.

Despite the editing, Henry's article received rave reviews from the athletes, students, and teachers. A few teachers were cautious with their praise of Henry's work because of his reputation as a smoker.

Chapter 11

1959 three years earlier

George Washington Smith, who everyone called G.W. had been married to his wife Yolanda for over fifteen years. They still lived and share cropped in the same county where slave traders had sold their ancestors to local plantation owners one hundred and fifty years before.

In 1959, approximately seventy percent of the population of that rural county was black, yet fewer than fifty blacks had ever been registered to vote and less than a dozen actually cast a ballot.

During that summer, G.W. and several hundred black citizens were persuaded to register to vote during a mass meeting at one of the local churches. Wednesday was the only day the voters-registration office was open. There was one person in the courthouse authorized to enroll new voters, and when new black voters began registering, he intentionally moved at a snail's pace. While waiting to register, the sheriff required blacks to stand in line outside the courthouse. He didn't allow them to sit or move into the shade. They were to remain on the walkway leading to the courthouse under the ardent July sun.

The first day blacks were registering to vote, Sylvester Jenkins and G.W. were in line talking when G.W.'s eyes began to sting. Within seconds, Sylvester's exposed skin began smarting. Soon a cloud of red pepper enveloped the line of potential voters. The pungent condiment was drifting from the roof of the courthouse. The once orderly line scattered as the budding voters tried to escape the acrid substance covering them. Law enforcement standing outside the billow of red pepper screamed at the blacks to get back in line while white spectators laughed at the rabble.

When the air cleared, G.W. and the others reformed the line and continued to wait in the stifling heat. By noon several people were overcome by the oven like weather and had to be taken home. Others persevered and waited their turn to enter the courthouse. Due to a slow-moving line, only a smattering of people, were registered each day. Every Wednesday, when blacks lined up for an insufferable wait, they were assaulted with some substance from the roof of the courthouse. The sheriff ignored these acts of aggression, but threatened to disperse the blacks if they failed to remain orderly.

"G.W., have you been working the cotton this year like you're supposed to?" Bubba Simmons asked G.W. one Wednesday, while he stood in line outside the courthouse. Bubba owned the land G.W. share cropped.

"Yes, sir," G.W answered.

"It appears to me that you have been spending a lot of time in town instead of in the field where you belong."

"I'm working the cotton and if the man in the courthouse would do his job I would be in the field right now."

"Boy, let me make sure you understand, if we don't have a good crop, I'm holding you responsible, and you don't want to face the consequences of a poor crop. You hear me?"

"We're going to have a good crop," G.W. replied, as silent rage boiled within him.

534

"I don't need your uppity sass boy. You understand me?" Bubba spewed. "Plumb foolish; you coloreds don't know anything about voting."

For the Smiths, like all share croppers, the summers were sweltering. With back-breaking work and a paltry pay off in the fall. Yolanda was sure Bubba cheated them out of the money that was due to them each harvest, but G.W. was afraid to say anything. "Being cheated out of something is better than having nothing," G.W. often said. G.W. and Yolanda both knew that if they complained they risked being evicted from the land, and no other land owner would take them on.

On election-day for the Democratic primary, G.W. got up early and went to town so he could vote as soon as possible and get back to the fields. Several blacks had the same idea. As the blacks huddled in a small group waiting for the poll to open, racial slurs and obscenities could be heard from passels of whites scattered over the courthouse lawn.

When the poll opened, a line formed. The group of black voters stood together amid an ever-increasing number of crude and vile remarks. Somehow a reluctant G.W. was the first black in line. When G.W entered the courthouse, the polling official looked up from his registrant book.

"What do you want, boy?" the white man asked, looking up from a ledger containing a list of registered voters.

"I'm here to vote, sir," G.W. said, removing his hat respectfully.

"You got it all wrong, boy," the polling official said. "This is the white democratic primary. Ain't any darkies supposed to be voting today."

G.W. was confused and unsure what to do when a deputy sheriff appeared next to the polling official.

"You coloreds heard what he said; the only folks supposed to be voting today are whites. You all need to go on home before there's trouble." The deputy was joined by several other ruthless-looking white men.

The group of blacks started to leave the courthouse with their heads hung, feeling embarrassed and intimidated. When G.W was walking across the courthouse lawn, Bubba Simmons and three other men blocked his path.

"I told you boy. You coloreds don't know anything about voting. Now get back in the field where you belong."

G.W. had been verbally abused by Bubba Simmons most of his adult life, however his blatant disrespect in front of other blacks caused an anger to fill G.W.'s heart he could barely control. He stared Bubba squarely in the eye with a scowl upon his face. Bubba experienced a moment of fear, and a fight might have ensued, but one of the other black men took G.W. by the arm, pulling him away as he said, "Let's go home, man. We got things to do." When G.W. and the other blacks left, Bubba's fear turned to laughter.

Chapter 12

July 1961, two years later

Mary was almost dressed for work, when the screen door on the front of the meager house slammed with such intensity it sounded like a gun shot.

"Where are you going?" Maurice growled, looking at Mary through blood shot eyes. He reeked of alcohol and sweat as he walked into the bedroom.

"Work."

"You're going to quit that job."

"How are we going to eat? How are we going to pay the rent? Because you ain't working anymore," Mary said with a little sass in her voice.

"We're leaving," Maurice said in a domineering tone, almost daring Mary to oppose him.

"Where are we going?" Mary asked, accepting his challenge and becoming more belligerent.

"Chicago."

"What are we going to do in Chicago?"

"My brother can get me a job." Maurice's hands were balled into fists.

"How are we going to get there?"

"Bus."

"Where are you going to get the money and what about our stuff?"

"I'm selling it," he said.

"What?"

"I'm selling it today."

"Who are you going to sell it to?

"The furniture man; he should be here anytime."

Tears clustered in Trifecta's eyes. He was afraid the argument might become physical. He silently prayed to God that Maurice wouldn't hit his mama as he had seen him do on many occasions.

"What about my baby?" Mary looked defiantly into Maurice's face.

"He'll have to go to your mama's," Maurice said, now staring down at Mary. His eyes locked onto hers, unblinking. He hadn't tolerated the white woman's mouth the day before, and he wasn't going to listen to this black girl's lip today.

"What?" she said defiantly, swelling up like a bull frog, stretching and standing on her tip toes to put her face closer to his as a threatening gesture. Violence didn't scare Mary. She had been abused by tougher men than Maurice, and probably would be again.

"Just until we get settled, then we'll come get him," Maurice said more gently, stepping back from the angry woman. He was too tired and hung over to get in a physical confrontation with this hellcat.

"Why do we have to go?"

"Because I'm tired of this city; it ain't nothing but a big plantation. I'm tired of being treated like a field slave. I'm sick of white people like Ms. Churchill. Her husband sits up all night on his lily-white butt drinking liquor. Then she looks down her pointy white nose at me for having a little taste of whiskey while I'm working in the heat." Maurice's voice shook as he stared down at Mary.

"So if you want to come you best pack your things; if not, I'm selling out and leaving you and your child here."

Mary emotions raged, she sat on the edge of the bed shaking, and began to cry. Maurice turned and walked out the front door, slightly less contentious than when he had entered. Still distraught, Mary got up and reluctantly started packing their clothes in a cardboard suitcase. She bundled Trifecta's clothes in a paper grocery sack. Most of Trifecta's clothes were high-quality hand-me-downs, donated by Mrs. Churchill.

With tears cascading down Trifecta's cheeks, he put his arms around his mother's waist. Mary hugged Trifecta, unsure what the future held for them.

"Mama, do we have to go?" Trifecta asked.

"Don't cry, baby "she said, trying to soothe him. "It will be alright. Mama has to leave for a little while, but you know I love you."

"I love you," Trifecta said, snuggling into his mother's breast.

Composing himself, Trifecta began assembling his most treasured possessions in a grocery sack. A transistor radio that Mr. and Mrs. Churchill had given him the previous Christmas, along with a basketball and a model airplane the Churchill boys gave him.

"Mama, do you remember the day we built this plane?"

"I sure do; we had a fine time, just you and me having fun talking, and building your plane."

"Will we ever be able to do that again?"

"We sure will, honey, just as soon as me and Maurice has some money. I'll come back and get you, and we'll go to Chicago and have us a good time every day."

"Mama, I'm sorry."

"What do you have to be sorry for?"

"I've been bad. If you stay, I'll be good."

"Oh baby, you ain't been bad. You are a good boy. My leaving ain't got nothing to do with you. We just got to go where the work is."

"I wish you'd stay here and work for Mrs. Churchill, even if we haven't got any money."

"I know baby, but you know I have to go where Maurice goes."

Trifecta's felt the physical pain of a broken heart, thinking his mother preferred the company of that low-down man over him.

Mary had just carried the suitcase and grocery sacks onto the front porch, when a white man and his black helper got out of a truck that was parked in front of their house. Maurice and the white man talked a minute, and then Maurice led both men into the house.

Mary and Trifecta could faintly hear the men speaking. Suddenly, Maurice was almost shouting as he spewed profanity. Moments later he was out on the front porch, holding a twenty-dollar bill.

"He said it's old and full of roaches. This is all he gave me," Maurice grumbled, showing Mary the twenty dollars clutched in his hand. "We done paid one hundred and fifty dollars two years ago for that furniture and all we get now is twenty dollars. White people got us again."

Trifecta's heart filled with hope, thinking twenty dollars might not be enough money to take his mama to Chicago.

Chapter 13

July 1965: Sims and Moneypenny get Agent Ball's attention.

The ringing phone on the bedside table woke agent Ball. He rolled over, glancing at the illuminated face of the alarm clock. It was after one o'clock in the morning.

"Who in the world," he mumbled to himself, reaching for the receiver. His wife Beth stirred beside him, but appeared to remain asleep.

"Hello?" Ball said his voice deep and sleepy.

"You're meddling in things you shouldn't," a man with a slightly unusual accent replied.

"Who is this?" Ball was instantly awake.

"It doesn't matter who this is. What's important is that you mind your own business. And to make sure you understand we're serious, look out your front window."

"What?" Ball demanded, as the caller abruptly hung up.

Agent Ball swung his feet to the floor. Wearing nothing but his boxer shorts, he moved barefoot through the darkness. When he entered his living room, he noticed a glow dancing around the edges of the drapes that hung across his front window. Pulling back the curtains, he saw a cross burning in his yard.

Still in his underwear and without his service revolver or shoes he recklessly rushed outside, going to the side of his house where a garden hose was attached to a faucet. Turning on the water he began spraying the flaming cross. The funk of kerosene and smoke fouled the air.

By now his wife was out of bed. She saw the blaze and called the fire department. When the fire department and police arrived, the cross was still smoldering. The firemen hosed down the yard and finished extinguishing the cross.

While Agent Ball was giving his statement to the police, another cross was being burned in front of the Sanctified House of Prayer Apostolic Church. Peter's plan in the cross burnings, was to prompt the authorities to turn up the heat on the Klan. Which he hoped would result in the white supremacist retaliating against blacks for the increased scrutiny and badgering by law enforcement.

"What is this about?" Beth asked her husband after the fire department left.

"My best guess is my investigation is getting close to the person who murdered Hercules Jones."

"What are we going to do?"

"I think the best thing for you to do is to stay with your parents until I solve this case, which, based on what happened tonight, shouldn't take long."

*

The Balls tossed and turned in bed for the remainder of the night and by sunrise they were ready to walk out of the house. Agent Ball was going to follow his wife over to her parents then go to work but just as they were leaving, the telephone rang. Special Agent in Charge Sam Reid, Ball's supervisor, was on the other end of the line.

"I hope I didn't wake you, but I have some important news," Reid said.

"No problem, we've been up for hours," Ball said, not planning on giving any further details until he was in the office.

"The police just found what we believe to be the vehicle used in the murder of Hercules Jones."

"Where was it found?"

"Where interstate fifty five is being built close to south Parkway; the truck was discovered by some workmen behind some large mounds of dirt."

"I have to take my wife to her parents, and then I'll make my way over there."

"Wait, there's more," Reid said. "Last night, a cross was burned in front of the Sanctified House of Prayer Apostolic Church. Now some guy calling himself the Apostle is calling every law enforcement agency and city official insisting that something be done to protect him and his church. He's also demanding that we spare no expense to bring the culprit to justice. He woke up the mayor at five o'clock this morning insisting that something be done today."

"Last night a cross was burned in front of my house," Ball said, more than a little surprised by the news about the Sanctified House of Prayer Apostolic Church.

"This is starting to get out of control," Reid said. "And I guess we have to assume that we are not dealing with a lone assailant but an organized conspiracy."

"It could be, but maybe we can find some clues in the truck."

"While you go to South Parkway I'll have a tech team go to your house and investigate."

When Ball arrived on the scene of the discovered pick up, Gillespie was already there. Several Memphis policemen were dusting for fingerprints as Gillespie swept the area looking for additional clues. The wrapper to the C-4 used as the fire accelerant was found on the floor board of the pickup, confirming they had discovered the vehicle linked to the murder. Otherwise, the Datsun was empty. The truck's VIN number was removed, making it impossible to trace. The police were able to obtain several good fingerprints from the pickup. Ball took the prints back to the FBI field office where they matched the ones found in Mrs. Isabel Carter's garage apartment.

When Ball arrived home that evening he called his wife who was spending the night with her parents. He told her he was tired, and he would see her the next day. He stretched out on the couch to relax and watch television. Within minutes, he was sound asleep.

At one o'clock in the morning, Agent Ball was awakened by the telephone ringing.

Chapter 14

July 1961 continued

Maurice sat with his feet hanging off the weathered wooden porch, watching the two men load his furniture onto their truck. Each time the men came out of the house with some of his effects, Maurice became more infuriated. Mary held Trifecta close. They both managed to bridle their tears.

Maurice's cousin pulled up and parked his car behind the furniture truck. Maurice went to the car and leaned into the passenger's side window.

"What's happening, man?" Maurice's cousin asked.

"I need to split," Maurice responded.

"Are they repossessing your stuff?"

"No, man, I'm selling out."

"Where you need to go?"

"I need to dump the kid, and get to the bus station."

"That's cool. Where are you headed?"

"Chicago."

"Is she staying here?" Maurice's cousin asked, hopefully nodding towards Mary.

"No, I'm taking her with me."

"Are you ready?" The cousin asked disappointed Mary was leaving town with Maurice.

"Give me a sec."

Maurice returned to the porch, picked up the suitcase and ordered Mary and Trifecta to come with him. Mary and Trifecta picked up the remaining grocery sacks and piled into the car. Mary and Trifecta huddled in the back seat while the two men sat in the front. Driving away, Maurice and his cousin passed a half-pint of whiskey back and forth while they cursed employers, furniture stores, landlords and white people in general.

They drove to several of Maurice's relatives to borrow money that would never be repaid. Next they went to a liquor store where Maurice bought a pint of whiskey. After a few swigs, Maurice told his cousin to go the Lemoyne Gardens housing project. Caledonia had lived in the Gardens since she became eligible to receive Social Security disability.

Lemoyne Gardens was as dismal as the economy of the people residing there. The projects were built in the 1930s by WPA workers, and looked like any other institutional building constructed during that period. The buildings were made from reinforced concrete with a red-brick face. The complex was comprised of 842 apartments in 108 buildings, connected by a maze of sidewalks and retaining walls into clusters of buildings called courts and malls. The complex was large, over populated and intimidating. Even at his age, Trifecta recognized the evidence of addictions, street violence, domestic abuse, and mental illness in the Gardens.

Caledonia qualified for SSI (Social Security income) disability because she suffered from high blood pressure, diabetes, and arthritis, which prevented her from working. She also received AFDC (aid to families with dependent children) because she kept two of her grandsons who had been abandoned by Josephine. It had been so long since Caledonia had heard from Josephine, and she presumed her daughter was dead.

Both of Josephine's children were older and rode roughshod over Trifecta. They were one of several reasons Trifecta never enjoyed being at his grandmother's and was now agonizing about staying with her for an extended time.

When Mary and Trifecta entered the small apartment, containing an eclectic array of sagging and mismatched furniture, Mary kissed her mother on the cheek.

"Trifecta, speak to your Madea," Mary commanded.

"Hello Madea," Trifecta said shyly as he embraced her.

"What's all this?" Caledonia asked pointing at the sacks Mary and Trifecta were holding.

"Mama, we need your help," Mary said.

"How's that?" Caledonia responded, anticipating Mary's request and thinking: *I've raised my children; now I have to bring up theirs.*

Trifecta's cousins Tyrone and Willie strutted into the room. Not wanting to contend with their foolishness, Caledonia harshly ordered the boys out of the apartment.

"We need you to keep Trifecta for a while," Mary said, once Trifecta's cousins had left the room.

Hearing the words of his mother, an oppressive sadness weighed on Trifecta.

"Baby, you know I'd like to help, but I've got a house full with your sister's kids."

"Mama, I ain't got anybody else to turn to," Mary pleaded.

"Baby, I ain't got any money. My little checks don't go far enough as it is."

"I know, Mama, but you can have my check." The welfare department was unaware of Mary's living arrangement with Maurice, and she continued to receive an ADC check for Trifecta.

"I'll have to call the case worker," Caledonia said.

"I ain't got the time, Mama. Maurice is ready to leave now."

"Maurice ain't anything to me," Caledonia replied.

"I know, Mama, but he's all I got."

"You got a baby," Caledonia said, raising her voice.

"That's why I've got to go, Mama, so Maurice can get a good job and take care of me and Trifecta. And we'll start sending you money just as quick as Maurice gets work."

"I wouldn't depend on that worthless man going to work."

"You don't understand, he wants to do the right, he's just having a hard time."

"Why can't he get a job in Memphis?"

"He says the white peoples here are keeping the colored folk down."

"If he thinks it's going to be any different in Chicago, he's crazy."

"Quiet, Mama, he'll hear you."

Trifecta prayed silently that his grandmother would refuse to keep him. Unfortunately, his grandmother relented.

"Well, he'll have to sleep on the couch. There isn't any other place."

"Thank you, Mama," Mary said, standing up and embracing Caledonia.

With a hug, a kiss, and a few tears, Mary was out of the apartment and gone with Maurice. Watching his mother leave, Trifecta was in such emotional turmoil he felt like a boil was festering on his soul.

"Try to find you a place to put your things. We'll have to do the best we can," Caledonia said with a sigh as she walked out of the apartment to sit on the porch.

The apartment had a living room and kitchen on the main floor. Upstairs were two small bedrooms and a bath. Trifecta's cousins' shared one bedroom, while Caledonia slept in the other.

Trifecta found a closet under the staircase and was stowing his belongs there when his cousins returned from outside.

"What's this?" Tyrone asked, removing Trifecta's model airplane from one of the sacks.

"That's my plane," Trifecta said, moving toward his cousin who was at least a foot taller than him.

Tyrone threw the plane, but it wasn't built to fly. Instead, it tumbled through the air and slammed against the wall, then crashed onto the tile floor. A wing broke off and the tail assembly shattered.

"That plane sure doesn't fly very good," Tyrone said with a laugh as he pulled Trifecta's basketball from the paper sack.

"Leave my stuff alone," Trifecta screamed as he charged head-long at Tyrone.

Tyrone passed the ball to Willie just in time to catch Trifecta and shove him to the ground. Trifecta bounced up instantly and resumed his attack, but he was helpless against the larger boy, and quickly found himself on the floor with Tyrone on top of him.

"What's going on in here?" Caledonia hollered, standing in the doorway. "I told you boys to get out of here, and I mean stay out until it's time for supper."

"And you, "Caledonia said to Trifecta, "I told you to get your things put up."

"He broke my plane," Trifecta screamed, with tears running down his cheeks and blood trickling from his nose.

Willie started toward the door, still holding Trifecta's basketball. Trifecta tried to snatch the ball from his cousin. Willie was able to maintain his grip on the ball and spinning around sent Trifecta to back down to the floor.

"I said stop it!" Caledonia screamed, slapping Willie across the back.

"Give me that ball," she demanded.

Willie handed it to her, maintaining a look of defiance.

"Now both of you get out of here," Caledonia commanded. "Before I get a belt and stripe your legs."

When the two boys left the apartment, Caledonia turned to Trifecta, showing no compassion, and said, "Wash your face and get your things put up."

Caledonia walked out on the back porch and resumed a conversation she was having with a neighbor.

Trifecta picked up the pieces of his broken plane, wishing he hadn't been forsaken by his mother.

He put his basketball and clothes in the closet and realizing that his cousins had no respect for his belongings, he carefully hid his transistor radio underneath some storage on the floor of the closet.

***

When Mary failed to report to work, Mrs. Churchill grew concerned. Mr. Churchill told her not to worry because that was just the way those shiftless people lived.

Chapter 15

Spring 1960, one year earlier

In the spring of 1960, Yolanda went to Crenshaw's Country Store where she regularly traded. Mr. and Mrs. Crenshaw were always cordial to the share croppers and had customarily been willing to extend credit until the harvest.

"Hi Miss Crenshaw," Yolanda said, entering the store

Mrs. Crenshaw said nothing, which was unusual, but went into the back room of the store.

As Yolanda made her way through the store picking up some staples, Mr. Crenshaw entered from the rear of the room and stood at the cash register with a stern scowl etched on his face.

Placing her items on the checkout counter, Yolanda smiled and said, "It sure is a beautiful spring day, isn't it Mr. Crenshaw?"

Crenshaw, who was normally a pleasant man, stated flatly, "Ain't no credit today."

Still smiling, Yolanda said, "Beg your pardon, Mr. Crenshaw?"

"I said there ain't no credit today."

"Is something wrong, Mr. Crenshaw?" Yolanda asked, her smile turning to a look of concern.

"Nothing is wrong; there just ain't no credit."

"You know we always pay you, Mr. Crenshaw."

"It hasn't got anything to do with how you pay."

"I believe we're going to have a good crop this year."

"It hasn't got anything to do with the crops."

"I don't understand."

"You're on the list."

"What list?"

"The list the counsel says we aren't supposed to sell to."

"What counsel are you talking about, Mr. Crenshaw?"

"The counsel put out a list of all the coloreds who registered to vote, and they told us not to sell anything to you."

"Well, tell me how much these things are, and I'll go get the money from G.W," Yolanda said, confused.

"I told you I can't sell anything to you."

"Not even if I pay cash?"

"No."

"What am I supposed to do? Where am I supposed to buy what I need to feed my children?"

"I guess you'll have to go to Collierville, Germantown, or Memphis because there ain't anybody around here going to sell anything to coloreds who want to vote."

"After all these years, we've been trading here and been friends, you're going to let some counsel tell you who you can do business with?"

"I didn't tell you to vote, and I'm not selling to Negroes who are going to vote against me."

"I'm not against you, Mr. Crenshaw," Yolanda said with tears welling up in her eyes.

Yolanda went home and told G.W. what had happened.

"That doesn't sound like Mr. Crenshaw. My daddy and I have been trading there my whole life. I'll go talk to him myself," G.W. told Yolanda.

G.W. experienced a less friendly reception than Yolanda. Mr. Crenshaw ended up ordering G.W. out of his store and off his property. G.W. went to several other stores, but no one would sell to him.

Not being able to buy locally was inconvenient but it didn't cause enough hardship to make the blacks relinquish their right to vote. Throughout the summer G.W. and the other registered black voters traveled twenty or thirty miles to surrounding counties to buy supplies.

The summer of 1960 was a good year for Boll Weevils, but a tough year for cotton farmers. Despite all his effort, G.W. was unable to produce the anticipated amount of cotton even though the acres he worked did as well as any and better than most in the county. Once the cotton crop was in and sold, G.W. waited patiently for Bubba Simmons to pay him for his share of the crop.

One late September day while the children were in school, Bubba came to G.W.'s shack. G.W. was out in the fields and Yolanda rang the dinner bell to call him to the house. Yolanda was uneasy because Bubba was joined by the deputy sheriff and a couple of other white men who had less than favorable reputations with the black citizens.

When G.W. arrived, he removed his hat and wiped his brow before extending his hand to Bubba.

"How are you all today?" G.W. asked pleasantly, looking from one man to the other.

"Let me come straight to the point," Bubba said, not shaking G.W.'s hand. "The crop was bad this year, and I think you've been spending too much time stirring up the other coloreds around here and not enough time in the field. So I need you to get off my land."

"Come again?" G.W. asked in amazement.

"I want you off my land."

"Where are we to go?" Yolanda interrupted.

"Ain't my problem," Bubba responded.

"Now wait a minute." G.W. said. "The crop wasn't good, but we made as good a crop as anyone else around here, colored or white."

"That's your trouble, G.W.," Bubba said. "You've been getting mighty uppity lately. It's time somebody put you in your place."

"I ain't done anything to be thrown off this land," G.W. said, becoming more belligerent.

"Deputy," Bubba said.

"Bubba has the right to evict you, G.W.," the deputy sheriff said. "And I would advise you to leave peacefully."

G.W. looked at the men bitterly. The two men accompanying the sheriff had smirks on their faces.

"When are you going to pay me my money?" G.W. asked.

"You didn't make a good enough crop to get any money," Bubba replied.

"You ain't going to steal from me, Bubba." G.W. took a step toward Bubba. Bubba moved back several paces, afraid G.W. was going to attack him. The deputy inserted himself between the two men.

"G.W., I don't want any trouble," the deputy said, his two henchmen flanking G.W.

"I don't want any trouble either, but what about my money?"

"If you feel you're entitled to money you can sue Bubba in General Session's court. But that doesn't have anything to do with why we are here today. I need you to evacuate these premises immediately."

"What about our children, Sheriff?" Yolanda asked, as tears wetted her cheeks.

"What about your children?" the deputy asked, defiantly.

"They're in school. When they get out they'll come here."

"You have until six o'clock tonight to vacate."

"What's this really about?" G. W. asked, turning to Bubba.

"I done told you boy—you don't know anything about voting, and this is the price of your ignorance."

"Be out by six o'clock tonight G.W." the deputy commanded as he walked toward the squad car.

Chapter 16

July 1965, 1:00 a.m.

He faintly heard the telephone ringing; out of reflex, he opened his eyes. His mouth was dry. His body stiff, he was anesthetized with sleep. Still wearing the clothes from the day before, he stumbled from the couch where he had unintentionally gone to sleep. The television was broadcasting static and snow because the station had signed off the air an hour earlier. He looked at his watch, wondering who could be calling and hoping nothing was wrong with his wife.

"Hello," agent Ball croaked; his throat dry.

"I thought I made myself clear last night when I told you to mind your own business," the unidentified voice said stiffly.

"Who is this?" Ball asked, instantly feeling the surge of adrenaline.

"I guess we need to continue our lesson tonight." Without another word, the line went dead.

Ball cursed and hung up the phone. He retrieved his service revolver and a twelve-gauge shotgun, positioning himself in a chair by a window where he waited for the cross burners. After an hour of waiting, he fell asleep still sitting in the chair.

When Ball woke-up it was past time for him to report to work. He called Reid and told him what had happened. Agent Reid told Ball he would have his home patrolled throughout the day and ordered him to report in as soon as he arrived at work.

When Ball arrived at work he went straight to Reid's office.

"I'm still in contact with Cointelpro. Their informants in these white supremacist groups don't know anything about anyone attempting or even wanting to burn the Sanctified House of Prayer Apostolic Church. Keep in touch with your man at the police department and continue to put pressure on the Klan. It's apparent you have grabbed someone's attention." Reid said.

"I'd like to be comfortable bringing my wife back home."

"No problem; I'll assign a stakeout on your home to make sure nothing happens again. In fact, the best thing to happen would be to have this person or group try something, and for us to catch them."

Being personally threatened prompted Agent Ball to bring more pressure on known Klansmen. He brought some of the Kluxers into the FBI offices for interrogation. With others, he went to their place of employment and questioned them and their employers. In his investigation, he obtained information that led to the arrest of men involved in two unsolved crimes against blacks. One was the beating of a black teenager, and the other was for harassing a black family that had moved into a segregated neighborhood. Still, Ball failed to obtain any information about the murder of Hercules Jones. He continued to sporadically receive anonymous telephone threats.

Chapter 17

Summer 1960, five years earlier

On Trifecta's first full day in Lemoyne Gardens Caledonia ordered Willie to take Trifecta to a neighborhood park where each weekday throughout the summer a free lunch was provided by the city for underprivileged children. Willie, not wanting to associate with his younger cousin, walked several steps ahead of Trifecta for the entire trek to the park. As soon as the two boys arrived at the playground Willie deserted Trifecta for his buddies. Not knowing anybody Trifecta wandered aimlessly from the swings, to the box hockey game, to the tether ball pole, feeling alone and unwanted.

While he meandered around the playground he was being carefully scrutinized by several other boys. Within a few minutes he was approached by one youngster anxious to mark his territory.

"Who are you?" Levi Jones asked. Levi was 10 years old and had grown up in Lemoyne Gardens, and playing at the park.

"Trifecta Johnson."

"Where're you from?" Levi snapped.

"Orange Mound," Trifecta answered, reciting the name of the last neighborhood where he lived.

"What are you doing in South Memphis?"

"I'm staying with my Madea."

"Well, your Madea ain't here," Levi said.

"So?"

"So why don't you go back to your Madea?" Levi said, getting in Trifecta's face.

"Why don't you make me?" Trifecta said in defiance.

Without warning, Levi grabbed Trifecta and both boys fell to the ground with a grunt. The tether ball game stopped and children circled around the two scuffling boys. Levi tried to maintain a headlock on Trifecta, but Trifecta pried him loose by placing his forearm on Levi's cheek and pushing him away. Both boys groaned as they continued to grapple. The scuffle only lasted moments before the screaming children caught the attention of a park counselor who broke up the fight and then ejected the boys from the park for the remainder of the day.

The combatants walked away from the park together, no longer rivals but equals in their hierarchy. Neither Trifecta nor Levi wanted to return home and explain why they weren't at the park, so they wandered the neighborhood together. When they got hungry they went to the Four Way Grill at the corner of Mississippi and Walker where Levi treated Trifecta to a hamburger and a Coke.

When the two boys left the Four Way, Trifecta noticed an ominous group of young men standing menacingly on the corner across the street.

"Quit looking at them and let's go," said Levi, ducking his head and walking toward the projects.

"What's up?" Trifecta asked.

"That's the Mayor over there. We ain't got any business with him. There's nothing good going to happen being around him. You are going to get beaten up, robbed, or put in jail, so let's get out of here."

After they were a safe distance from the Mayor the two boys agreed to meet the next day and go to the park. Levi lived in Lemoyne Gardens with his mother and his older brother.

When Trifecta arrived home, Willie had already told Caledonia about Trifecta being kicked out of the park. Understanding a fight was the rite of passage for any new kid in the neighborhood, Caledonia gave him a half-hearted reprimand.

Chapter 18

A history of Jamison Elam, the Mayor of the corner

He was the self-appointed lord of the neighborhood, thereby becoming known as the Mayor. He administered his ghetto fiefdom from the corner of Mississippi Boulevard and Walker Avenue.

His given name was Jamison Elam. He never met his father. His mother was sent to prison when he was in elementary school for killing a man in the parking lot of Club Paradise, a local upscale juke joint catering to a black clientele.

Jamison's father, Jerry Elam, had deserted Jamison and his mother, Mabel Elam, shortly after Jamison was born. Jamison and his mother lived in a two-room apartment on Orleans Street. Mabel survived by doing day work and collecting welfare. She and her occasional boyfriend Riley Landers had been at Club Paradise several hours when Mabel became distraught. She had drank too much alcohol and became upset because Riley neglected her most of the night as he danced and flirted with Wilma Peppers, a one-time lover of Riley's. When Mabel could no longer stomach being ignored, she confronted Riley on the dance floor. She created such a commotion the couple was asked to leave.

Once outside in the parking lot Mabel continued to berate Riley. The more she screamed and cursed the angrier she became until she could no longer restrain herself and physically attacked him. She slapped and clawed at his face. Pushed beyond tolerance by her abuse, Riley punched back, sending her sprawling across the hood of a car. It felt so good to hit the woman who had plowed furrows into the flesh of his cheeks with her fingernails. When she pulled herself off of the car, he slapped her across the face, sending her down to the asphalt. When she got back to her feet, she assailed Riley with fists flying. It didn't take Riley long to pin her against a car. However, she continued to squirm, kicking him until she got in a position where she could bite the arm he was using to restrain her. Trying to defend himself, Riley slapped her repeatedly until a man pulled him off of her. With one punch the man cold-cocked Riley.

With Riley unconscious, Mabel reached in her bra and pulled out a straight razor. With a battle cry of "Leave my man alone!" she slashed at her intended defender. Her first swipe of the razor debilitated the man by lacerating his left eye and sending him to his knees.

"Leave my man alone!" she continued to wail, as she repeatedly hacked and sliced her protector. By the time club security was able to subdue Mabel, the man who interceded in her behalf was lying in a pool of his own blood. Mabel was arrested, and the man died later that night at the hospital.

After his mother was incarcerated Jamison stayed with an elderly aunt, who was actually the sister of his maternal grandmother. When his great aunt passed, with no other available relatives, Jamison was either in foster care, juvenile detention, or fending for himself on the streets of South Memphis.

In foster care Jamison was repeatedly placed with a dysfunctional family whose sole purpose in keeping children was financial. Those families were at times neglectful and abusive. Therefore, he rarely stayed with a surrogate family longer than a month or two before he returned to the streets. He had run away so often that children's services gave up trying to place him in a home. The only time he would be assigned a foster family was when the juvenile court released him into the custody of proxy parents. His time spent locked-up in juvenile detention usually involved petty crimes that Jamison committed in order to survive on the streets. Even though the duration of his sentences were short, his time with other delinquents made him increasingly nefarious.

When he began junior high school he bullied his classmates, even boys who were older, bigger and stronger. His fights weren't premeditated. He just couldn't restrain himself. Any interaction with him could turn violent. He had at least one fight each week, until no one in the student body was willing to challenge him. Even when Jamison lost a fight, he brutalized his opponent enough to discourage a return bout. Eyes, throat, and groin were Jamison's favorite targets. And if he ever got his enemy on the ground he would kick with all he had, aiming for the head and ribs. In the ninth grade he sent two boys to John Gaston Hospital. He was punished with a three-day suspension for each incident.

When Jamison reached the tenth grade at Booker T. Washington High School, he dropped out of school.

On the streets, Jamison would sleep anywhere he could find a bed, often compelling other children to beg their parents to let him spend the night. Once he was in a home he would stay until an adult insisted he leave. However, when he moved on, he usually took any essentials he needed or wanted from his host. Prior to Trifecta living with Caledonia, Jamison coerced Tyrone into convincing Caledonia to let him spend the night at her apartment, and a week later when Caledonia finally demanded that Jamison leave, he took Caledonia's last twenty dollars from her purse along with

Tyrone's favorite shirt and basketball shoes. Tyrone was wise enough not to try to recover the stolen money and property or even mention that it was taken.

Jamison was always welcome to stay with Clyde Mitchell. Clyde lived with his mother, Bedette, in the Lemoyne Gardens projects. Even though Bedette was not in jail, Clyde's situation was similar to Jamison's. His mother was bedeviled with drugs, alcohol, and men. Because of these compulsions she was often absent from home for days at a time. Any time she was missing Jamison spent the night at Clyde's apartment. When she returned home he always left. Clyde's mother was mean, and many of the men she brought home were dangerous. When Bedette and one of her men were at home living conditions became so intolerable that Clyde commonly chose to live on the street with Jamison.

Jamison and Clyde were seventeen years old the first time they sold drugs. They stole some heroin from a man who was high and had crashed in bed with Bedette.

The next morning when Cleo Flynn, Clyde's mother's overnight guest, awoke and found his drugs missing he went into a rage.

"What did you do with my smack?" he screamed in a drug withdrawal tantrum as he pulled Clyde's mother out of bed and onto the floor by her hair.

"What are you talking about?" Bedette cried, lying naked on the cold tile as she cursed Cleo, using vulgar language.

"You took my dope while I was asleep."

"I don't know anything about your dope. It was on the table when we went to bed last night," Bedette said, lifting herself to a sitting position while still on the floor.

"Liar," hollered Cleo, as he slapped her across the face and sent her sprawling.

Bedette continued to scream, calling him every filthy name she knew.

"Where's my dope?" Cleo demanded, unaffected by her intensity.

"I don't know," she said continuing to curse loud enough for the neighbors to hear.

Cleo grabbed her by the hair and pulled her to her feet. Her lip was split. He raised his hand to hit her again. She tried to block the punch with her arm but to no avail; he was too powerful. This time, he hit her in the eye with his fist. She fell across the bed.

"I'll kill you if you don't give me back my dope."

"I ain't got it." She tried to escape by crawling off the opposite side of the bed. However, he grabbed her by her ankle and pulled. She went airborne and landed prostrate on her back, on the tiled concrete floor, knocking the breath out of her.

"Where's my dope?" he demanded.

Gasping for air she was unable to speak so she shook her head.

"If you ain't got it, who does?"

She held up her hand, asking for a moment to catch her breath. Finally, she wheezed, "The only person I know who could have come in here last night is my son."

"What's your boy's name?"

"Clyde Mitchell," she said, trying to suck in more oxygen.

Cleo grabbed her hair and raised her to her feet, then took her outside and threw her to the ground in the courtyard where three buildings formed a squared horseshoe.

"Clyde Mitchell, are you here? You better come out and take care of your mother," Cleo screamed half a dozen times. The neighbors came to their doors and windows to see about the commotion. Clyde's mother sat naked in the grass, her mouth bleeding, her eye beginning to swell, and holding her side in an attempt to nurse a bruised rib.

When Clyde didn't show, Cleo glared at Bedette and growled, "You tell that boy of yours, if I don't get my dope back, I'll kill him and come back and finish you." Cleo stormed off, leaving her alone and naked in the grass. With no modesty, she slowly got to her feet and limped back to her apartment. Her neighbors closed their doors and blinds and quickly forgot what they had just witnessed in case any official asked what had transpired.

Cleo searched the neighborhood for Clyde and his drugs. Making inquiries on the street, he soon tracked Clyde and Jamison to a small clap board grocery store with peeling paint, on Florida Street. As Jamison and Clyde left the store and started up the street, Cleo stepped from the shadows.

"Are you Clyde Mitchell?" Cleo asked, confronting Jamison.

"Who wants to know?" Jamison sneered.

"The cat who's going to kill you if I don't get my dope back," Cleo said as he grabbed Jamison by the shirt, assuming he was Clyde.

"Let go of me, fool," Jamison said, knocking Cleo's hand away from him.

"I'm Clyde Mitchell," Clyde said.

Cleo instantly grabbed Clyde's shoulder. "Where's my dope, boy?"

"I don't know what you're talking about," Clyde said as he struggled in vain to free himself from Cleo's grasp.

Cleo cocked his arm to punch Clyde, but before he could strike, Jamison hit him in the head with a brick. Cleo staggered. Jamison hit him again, and Cleo crumbled to the sidewalk. Cleo remained motionless as Jamison and Clyde strolled away.

When Cleo regained his consciousness he was in total darkness at John Gaston Hospital. The blows to his head had permanently blinded him. Without his sight he was no longer a threat to Bedette, Clyde, or Jamison.

After Jamison and Clyde sold the heroin they stole from Cleo, they found a marijuana supplier and parlayed the profits from the heroin into the beginning of a lucrative pot business.

Once the boys began dealing in marijuana they could be found any time of day or night hanging out at the corner of Mississippi and Walker, providing the neighborhood with weed. By the time the boys were nineteen they had become the major suppliers of the devil's lettuce for Lemoyne Gardens and the adjacent neighborhood. Before Jamison turned twenty he had murdered one man and had at least two children by different women. Even though he had rolls of cash in his pockets, owned a fine car, wore fashionable clothes, and stayed in well-furnished apartments in the heart of the ghetto, Jamison provided no support for the children he fathered.

Chapter 19

Fall and winter of 1960 to August 1961

G.W. and Yolanda packed most of their possessions in their 1952 Chevrolet. G.W carried his hunting rifle and pistol in the front seat between Yolanda and him. The only things that couldn't be transported in a single trip were a few pieces of homemade furniture and a hand sown mattress. They planned to return for those items as soon as they found a permanent place to stay. After their children arrived home from school, G.W. instructed them to walk a mile to their Uncle Abe's house where he had arranged for his family to spend the night.

Abe's shanty was about the same size as G.W.'s, which meant that it was too small for both families to sleep. Some of the children were assigned to sleep outside.

"I heard there's been some other croppers thrown off their land in the last day or two," Abe said to G.W. as they sat on the tailgate of Abe's pickup after a supper of collard greens and corn bread.

"I heard that too but I didn't pay it any mind until today when Bubba and the sheriff showed up at my place," G.W. said. "It seems white folks have gone crazy about us voting."

"Jimmy Ray came around here yesterday asking me if I was going to get mixed up in all this and I told him it ain't none of his business," Abe lied. Actually, Jimmy Ray Dunlap, Abe's land owner, ordered him not to get involved in the voting. Abe assured him, "No boss; I haven't got anything to do with all that. I know us coloreds don't have any business voting." Now Abe was afraid that Jimmy Ray would find out G.W. and his family had spent the night at his place, and there would be repercussions for him and his wife and children.

Unknown to G.W. and Abe, Jimmy Ray had been teasing Bubba unmercifully, about the way Bubba had allowed G.W to be involved in the black voter's registration. More than anything, it was Jimmy Ray's ribbing at Bubba's expense that caused G.W. to be evicted.

"I heard there's a farmer who is taking in folk that have been ousted from their homes," Abe said, hoping G.W. would take the hint and go to the farm the next day.

"Where are they going to put all those families?" G.W. asked.

"I heard someone gave them some tents."

"Sure enough?"

"If I were you, I would go there tomorrow to see if you can get a spot," Abe said, hoping G.W. would be gone before Jimmy Ray Dunlap came by.

"I guess I'll do that," answered G.W.

*

The next day G.W. went to the farm that was housing evicted voters. Like Abe said, there were several large tents set up in a field. The farmer agreed to let G.W and his family move into one of the tents. A white merchant had donated the tents, wood-burning stoves, and a few other essentials for the displaced blacks. Because the merchant was afraid of retaliation by other whites, he insisted on remaining anonymous.

After settling in on the farm, G.W. thought he would sneak back to his shanty and get his homemade furniture. In the dark of the night, G.W borrowed Abe's pick up and returned to his shack only to find it empty. There were ashes on the outside of the crude cabin where Jimmy Ray and Bubba had burned G.W.'s meager possessions.

Within days the farm accommodated twelve tents to house the black refugees. A total of twenty adults and fifty six children became the first residents of what became nationally known as "Tent City." Within weeks the grass on the field where the tents were erected was worn bare, and when winter rains came, "Freedom Village," as its residents came to call it, turned into a huge mud puddle.

Wood had to be chopped for the stoves and water transported by hand. Lanterns and candles were used for light. Clothes were washed in boiling pots that sat on open fires amid the tents. The laundered clothes were put on bushes to dry. Because the tents could hold little more than cots for the families to sleep on, the canvas city was littered with furniture that couldn't be accommodated by tents.

G.W. tried to find work but no one in any of the surrounding counties would hire him or any of the other black registered voters.

In November 1960, the 1200 black voters of the county turned out to cast their ballots for Richard Nixon rather than John F. Kennedy. Doctor Martin Luther King Jr. endorsed Kennedy for president because Kennedy had intervened when Doctor King was arrested in Georgia while leading a civil rights demonstration. However, the blacks of this county favored the party of Abraham Lincoln and opposed Southern Democrats who supported segregation. The Federal Government monitored the election closely, having learned that registered blacks were not allowed to vote in the Democratic primary.

With no work the winter of 1960/1961 went slowly for the displaced share croppers. Churches supplied food, clothing, and other essentials to residents of the tent community.

Violence was a constant threat. Rocks, bullets, and fire bombs, along with racial slurs and abusive language regularly came from passing vehicles. When one of the citizens of "Freedom Village" was hit by a random bullet shot from a passing vehicle, the families decided to arm themselves and men took turns standing guard. When a second tent community was established, its location was kept a secret in an attempt to prevent more violence. The sheriff's department did little in response to violence other than sending a report to the Tennessee Bureau of Investigation and the FBI.

In the late summer of 1961, Minerva Williams, Yolanda's cousin from Memphis, braved the oppressive heat of "Tent City" and went to visit Yolanda.

"I've been hired by the Board of Education to work in the kitchen at Melrose High School," Minerva told Yolanda.

"That's wonderful," Yolanda responded, curious why her cousin had come all that way just to tell her about a job.

"It's a colored high school right there in Orange Mound where I live. I won't even have to ride the bus."

"You are blessed," Yolanda said with a forced smile.

"The reason I came here is because my white lady, Miss Dupree, who I've been working for the past three years, asked me to find her someone to take my place. The first person I thought of was you."

"Where does the white lady live?"

"She's in Morningside Park."

Yolanda was unfamiliar with Memphis. She looked at her cousin with a confused expression.

"Minerva, I appreciate you thinking about me, but I live here, not in Memphis. It would take me two or three hours to get there.

"Don't worry about that, you can stay with me until you get on your feet."

"What about G.W. and my children? I know you ain't got that much room."

"Don't worry about room. You all are heroes in Orange Mound. G.W. can stay with us and some of the neighbors will keep your kids. Anyhow, Miss Dupree will give me fifteen dollars for fetching you if she likes you."

"You think she will like me?"

"As hard as you work, she's going to love you.

Chapter 20

1962

During the summer of 1962, Levi and Trifecta became fast friends, always hanging out together in the park or around the housing project. Towards the end of the summer Trifecta and Levi left the park early planning to shoot some baskets at the outdoor basketball court at Lemoyne Gardens. Trifecta went into the closet under the stairs to get his ball but it wasn't there. Knowing Tyrone and Willie were upstairs, Trifecta and Levi went to their bedroom.

"You got my ball?" Trifecta demanded, standing at the doorway of the small bedroom.

"What ball?" Tyrone asked.

"My basketball."

"Do you see a ball in here?" Willie smarted off.

"My ball was in the closet last night, now it's gone. Do you know where it is?"

"We might," Willie said.

"You better tell me where my ball is."

"Or what?" Tyrone threatened.

"I'll tell Madea," Trifecta answered, realizing he and Levi were no match for Tyrone and Willie.

"Why don't you ask me nice, and maybe I'll tell you where the ball is?" Tyrone said, trying to provoke Trifecta.

Trifecta darted his eyes at Levi. Levi nodded his head, urging him to comply with Tyrone's request.

"Please, where is my ball?"

"At the playground," Tyrone replied.

"What's it doing there?" Trifecta asked with anger in his voice.

"We were playing basketball earlier and left it there." Tyrone lied, not wanting to tell the younger boys the Mayor had taken the ball and ran them off the court.

"Keep your hands off my stuff," Trifecta growled, leaving the room, with Levi in his wake.

Arriving at the basketball court, Trifecta and Levi found the Mayor and Clyde Mitchell shooting baskets with Trifecta's ball. He knew it was his ball because he had written his initials in large letters on the ball using a permanent marker.

"You know who that is?" whispered Levi as he and Trifecta stood courtside.

"Yea, I think so," whispered Trifecta, recognizing the Mayor.

"Let's go. We can come back later, and maybe they'll leave your ball."

"I'm not leaving without my ball," Trifecta said a little louder than he intended.

The Mayor stopped playing and looked at the boys.

"What do you want?" The Mayor snarled.

Panic rose in Levi like the ocean approaching high tide. He had heard several frightening and violent stories about the Mayor.

"You got my ball," Trifecta answered back, his colon drawing up in a knot.

"This ain't your ball, man. You need to get out of here."

"It's got my initials on it," Trifecta said, so scared he was beginning to hyperventilate.

"What's your name, boy?" The Mayor asked, glancing at the initials on the ball and then glaring at Trifecta.

"Trifecta Johnson."

"What kind of stupid name is Trifecta?" The Mayor asked as he and Clyde both laughed.

"I want my ball." Trifecta said resisting the urge to run away.

"People in the projects want money but look around: they ain't got none and you're not getting this ball. Now leave before you get hurt."

Levi followed Trifecta as he moved to a shade tree approximately fifteen feet away from the basketball court. The two boys sat silently beneath the tree watching the Mayor and Clyde Mitchell play basketball. Ten minutes passed when the Mayor threw up an errant shot that completely missed the backboard. The ball bounced in the direction of the boys. Trifecta jumped to his feet, scooped up the ball, and darted towards Caledonia's apartment with Levi a step behind him.

The Mayor and Clyde were in quick pursuit, and being much faster afoot, soon caught up with the younger boys. Clyde tackled Trifecta and wrestled the ball from him. The Mayor caught Levi. Clyde pulled a large folding knife from his pocket, as he sat high on Trifecta's chest using his knees to pin Trifecta's arms to the ground. Seeing the knife, Trifecta's heart shot into his throat thinking he was about to be cut. Instead, Clyde stabbed the basketball with all the force he could muster. Rather than piercing the ball the razor sharp knife deflected off the round surface, and the blade closed hard on Clyde's hand, cutting his fingers. Clyde cursed, grabbing his bleeding hand. With Clyde's attention turned to his wounded fingers Trifecta was able to squirm loose.

Trifecta jumped to his feet, grabbed the ball and tried to run. Clyde grabbed him by the shirt with his good hand and pulled him back to the ground. The ball slipped from

Trifecta's grasp. The Mayor forsook Levi and retrieving the dropped knife, knelt with the ball between his knees. He slowly inserted the blade into the ball, and the air hissed out. Clyde once again straddled Trifecta holding him on the ground, the Mayor picked up the deflated ball and smashed it into Trifecta's face breaking his nose and knocking him senseless. After flinging the punctured ball as far as he could, the Mayor jerked the front of Trifecta's shirt so hard that the buttons tore loose. Then he maliciously ripped the knife across Trifecta's naked chest cutting a deep incision into his flesh. Blood gushed from the open wound.

The next thing Trifecta knew, Levi was kneeling beside him, and the Mayor and Clyde were walking away. Clyde was cursing loudly as his hand continued to bleed.

"You're cut man, and your and nose is bleeding. Are you alright?" Levi asked.

"I'm alright," slurred Trifecta through lips that were quickly swelling.

With Levi's help Trifecta got to his feet. He was dizzy and jelly legged. Warm, sticky blood plastered the front of his open shirt to his body. His chest was numb. The hot copper smell of his blood nauseated him. Trifecta tried to walk but could only stumble and stagger towards Caledonia's apartment. Levi wrapped his arms around Trifecta, trying to hold him steady, but Trifecta's head was spinning and the earth beneath his feet felt like it was tossing and swaying. As they walked, Trifecta's chest continued to bleed, and he began to shiver. When they approached the parking lot behind Caledonia's apartment, the spinning in Trifecta's head seemed to reverse direction and he felt he was being turned upside down. Then everything went dark. Trifecta crumpled onto the ground. Levi attempted to hold him up. However, when Trifecta went limp, his weight pulled Levi to the earth with him.

"Trifecta, are you alright?" Levi wailed, struggling to his feet.

When Trifecta didn't respond, Levi ran for Caledonia.

Due to Yolanda's job she and G.W. had moved to Memphis and lived in Lemoyne Gardens next door to Caledonia. G.W. had just arrived home from work when he saw Levi and Caledonia scurrying across the parking lot. Caledonia was gesturing wildly toward Trifecta's still body caterwauling as she ran, "He's dead! My baby boy is dead!

Chapter 21

The fall of the 1966-67 school year. The first year Henry and Marcie attend Central High School.

Completing Junior High, Henry debated whether he would attend Tech or Central High School. Tech's curriculum focused on vocational training while Central's was considered college preparatory. Henry didn't choose the high school he would attend based on the course of study. He decided to go to Central because that's where Alan and a few of his other smoking buddies were planning on enrolling.

What Henry liked best about high school was, with parent's permission, students were allowed to smoke on campus before school and during lunch. The designated smoking area was the boys' restroom, located in the basement of the school. Rarely, if ever, did the faculty check to see if students who smoked had the required authorization from their parents. Henry didn't think his parents knew he smoked, and he never asked their permission to smoke at school, however he went to the "smoke hole" at every opportunity.

High school was also the first time he drank beer, which further besmirched his reputation with some students and the school's faculty.

Warren Adams was the first of Henry's friends to get his driver's license. Warren lived four miles from Henry's house. The first Friday night Warren was allowed to take his family's car out he picked up Henry, Alan, and Tommy Lane.

They cruised all the local hot spots, the Pig and Whistle on Union Avenue, Shoney's at Avalon and Poplar, the Krystal on Poplar across from East High School, and Shoney's on Summer Avenue.

"Where are all the girls tonight?" Warren asked.

"Who knows?" Tommy answered.

"You know what would be cool?" Alan asked.

"What?" Was a semi-unified response from the other boys.

"If we had some beer," Alan said.

"You think we could get somebody to buy it for us?" Tommy asked.

"No, there're too many undercover cops out to ask a stranger to buy it for us. We'd probably end up in juvenile court," Alan said.

"I know where we can get some beer," Warren said.

"Where?" Alan asked.

"There's a convenience store by my house."

"That sells beer to kids?" Tommy asked.

"No, but we can steal it," Warren answered. "It's easy."

"Have you ever stolen beer from there?" Tommy asked.

"No, but I've been in the store a million times and I have a fool-proof plan"

Henry sat in the backseat listening to his friends talk without participating in the conversation. However, when they parked a short distance from the convenience store, he was elected to perpetrate the crime.

"Just go in and tell the guy at the cash register you have to use the restroom. The restroom is in the store room behind the coolers. The beer that's not in the cooler is stacked next to the back door. Open the door, put a six- pack outside, then leave," Warren instructed.

"What if I get caught?" Henry asked.

"You won't get caught. But if you do, run, and we'll pick you up in the car."

The plan went off without a hitch. When Henry asked to use the restroom, the clerk pointed him to the rear of the store. Being more than just a little antsy, Henry moved quickly, placing a six-pack of tepid brew outside the back door then flushed the toilet in case the cashier was listening. Ironically, as he broke the eighth commandment, Henry prayed, "God, if you let me get away with this, I'll never steal again."

The clerk hardly noticed him as he walked out the front door. Soon he was relieved to be in the car full of boys, only to learn his friends expected him to go behind the store and retrieve the stash. They reasoned he could recover the beer faster because he knew exactly where it was.

"It's right beside the back door," Henry protested. Despite his objection he was sent to recover the stolen goods.

Drinking warm Falstaff, the boys drove north towards Poplar Avenue. The experience of stealing the beer was a bummer for Henry, but drinking it was worse. Henry didn't like the bitter beverage but he knew it wouldn't be cool not to drink it. So he would take a small sip, then several drags from his cigarette to keep the beer choked down. He thought he might throw-up any minute.

By the time they arrived at the Krystal on Poplar, the night had livened up and kids were swarming the hangout. Henry had only downed a fourth of his twelve-ounce beer, when they pulled onto the restaurant's parking lot and into a line of cars cruising around the hamburger joint. The lot was packed with kids in parked cars eating and socializing.

With a cigarette in one hand and his beer in the other, Henry took a swig from the can. With the beer at his lips he spied Marcie and several of her friends parked in her yellow Corvair convertible, staring at him.

"Don't those guys go to Central?" one of the girls in Marcie's car asked.

"Yea, the guy guzzling the beer was a neighbor of Marcie's. Wasn't he, Marcie?"

"Yes, we grew up together."

"I'm in class with Alan. He's kind of cute, but he stays in trouble," another girl said.

"Yeah, he's cute, but you would ruin your reputation going out with any of those guys. They're all losers."

"Hey man, isn't that Marcie McDougal?" Tommy asked when the boys passed Marcie's yellow sports car.

"Sure is," Alan answered.

"Let's go back and see if we can get something going with them," Tommy said.

"Forget it," chimed in Henry. He had never told anyone how he felt about Marcie, and was embarrassed to admit his extreme infinity for her now. "The cops cruise this place all the time and we don't need to get caught with this beer in the car."

"Henry's right," Warren said, concerned because they were in his parent's car.

"Marcie and her friends aren't going to have anything to do with us," Henry added. "They're all a bunch of snobs."

"Marcie sure is hot." Tommy answered.

In a moment of jealousy, Henry wanted to tell Tommy to shut up about Marcie. Instead, he said, "Let's go to Shoney's."

Henry had no idea that anyone at school gave him much thought. However, by the time school was dismissed the following Monday afternoon, many in the student body as well as several members of the faculty were aware that

Henry was seen drinking beer in public the previous Friday night.

Despite his rebellious reputation and less-than-average grades, Henry was allowed to work on the school newspaper staff because of his ability as a writer. Unknown to any of the faculty most of Henry's skills were the result of Scoop's mentoring and editing. However, Scoop was getting bored polishing articles about high school sports so he insisted Henry write more socially challenging articles.

Chapter 22

The day Trifecta was cut, August 1960

G.W. ran to where Trifecta lay on the ground, bleeding.

"I need some towels or something to try to stop the bleeding," G.W. said to Caledonia, as he knelt beside Trifecta.

"They killed my baby!" Caledonia bawled hysterically.

"Miss Caledonia, I need some towels."

Caledonia continued her hysterics. She was so emotional she was barely able to stand.

"Go to my house and get some towels, boy," G.W. ordered, turning towards Levi.

A crowd including Willie and Tyrone started to gather around Trifecta.

"Stand back so he can get some air," G.W. commanded.

The circle of curious onlookers barely moved.

Levi returned quickly with two thin white towels. G.W. wiped the blood from Trifecta's face with one towel and applied the other towel to his chest trying to stem the persistent bleeding. Then he picked up the wounded boy and carried him to his car.

Trifecta was only slightly conscious but could feel the strength of the person carrying him; at the same time he was aware of the stench that filled his nostrils while his head rested on the man's chest.

"You ride in the backseat with Trifecta," G.W. said to Levi. "Miss Caledonia, you can ride in the front with me."

Caledonia was on the brink of swooning. She continued to sob when G.W. laid Trifecta across the backseat. The smell in the car was as bad as the stink of the man.

"I need you to hold the towel tight against his chest," G.W. told Levi.

"Yes, sir," Levi said, even though he was feeling faint at the sight of Trifecta's blood soaking through the make shift bandage. Levi had seen people in the neighborhood shot or stabbed, but he had never been so close to a victim.

G.W. parked at the emergency entrance and carried Trifecta into the hospital. Blood was dripping from Trifecta's semi-conscience body.

Seeing G.W. and Trifecta, the nurse at the front desk ordered a gurney, and alerted a trauma doctor.

Caledonia struggled to walk into the building leaning heavily on Levi. She collapsed onto a chair, her head leaning back, her mouth wide open. G.W. helped lay Trifecta on a gurney, and an orderly wheeled Trifecta into an examining room to prepare him for surgery. G.W. started out the door and the nurse called to him, "Sir, sir! You can't leave. I need some information and the police are on their way to speak with you."

"I need to move my car," G.W. answered.

"Come right back."

"Yes ma'am."

When G.W. returned he tried to help Caledonia give the admitting nurse the required information but Caledonia was too overwhelmed to be much help, which frustrated G.W. and the nurse.

After forty-five minutes with no word on the progress of Trifecta, two policemen arrived.

"He was on the ground when I drove up," G.W. said in answer to the uniformed police officer's questions.

"I didn't know anything about what was happening until Levi told me," Caledonia answered the other policeman.

"Were you with him when he was stabbed?" the patrolman asked Levi.

Levi nodded yes.

The two officers took Levi out to the squad car for further questioning.

"Do you know the name of the person who stabbed your friend?" the patrolman asked from the front seat, while Levi sat in the back of the squad car.

Levi shook his head no, scared to rat out the Mayor.

Could you identify the person who stabbed your friend?"

Levi shrugged his shoulders. "Maybe" he said softly, knowing he would never finger the Mayor.

"Tell us what happened."

Levi recounted the events beginning with Tyrone and Willie leaving the ball at the basketball court. He was careful not to mention the Mayor or Clyde Mitchell and gave such a vague description of the assailants that it could apply to the majority of the men in the neighborhood.

"Where do Trifecta's cousins live?" one of the officers asked.

"With Miss Caledonia," Levi answered.

After confirming Caledonia's address, the two policemen went to Lemoyne Gardens to question Tyrone and Willie. The officers separated the two boys, one patrolman questioned Tyrone in the kitchen of Caledonia's apartment, and the other policeman questioned Willie in the patrol car.

Several people milled around Caledonia's apartment and the squad car trying to eavesdrop as the police interrogated Tyrone and Willie. Willie was scared, which hampered his ability to lie, and it was apparent to the policeman that Willie knew more than he was telling.

"You had something to do with this," the patrolman accused Willie.

"I didn't. I wasn't even there when he got cut," Willie said from the backseat. His head hung low; he couldn't make eye contact with the officer.

"You're not telling me the truth, which makes you an accessory to the crime."

"I didn't do anything," pleaded Willie.

"Have you been in trouble before?"

"No," Willie said with tears in his eyes.

"You're in trouble now unless you tell me the truth. Do you want to go to jail?"

"I don't know who did it."

"Answer my question. Do you want to go to jail?"

"No."

"Do you want to tell me what happened?"

"I don't know what happened, I wasn't there."

"I'm going to give you a few minutes to think this over and then if you don't tell me what I need to know, you're going to jail."

The officer got out of the squad car leaving Willie with his face cradled in his folded arms resting against the back of the front seat. When the officer entered Caledonia's apartment Tyrone was slumped in a kitchen chair. The policeman's partner was leaning against the kitchen wall. No one was saying anything. The cop who questioned Willie stood silently in the doorway for a good five minutes. Both police officers stared unmercifully at Tyrone. Tyrone looked at the floor; tension permeated the room. Then without a word the policeman who had interrogated Willie went back to the squad car.

When the cop left Caledonia's apartment he ran off several bystanders who had gathered around the squad car. He knew witnesses would hinder Willie's confession.

"Alright, here's the deal," the officer said, returning to the front seat of the cruiser. "Your brother has talked, now we need to confirm what he said is true. If your story matches his, you'll be free to go. If not, you're both going to jail."

Willie didn't know what to do, other than to tell the truth. He spilled his guts, telling everything he knew about what happened. However, he never mentioned the Mayor or Clyde Mitchell.

"Who did it?"

"I don't know."

"Who took the ball from you and your brother?"

"I don't know his name."

"You're lying, and you're going to jail if you don't tell me the truth."

Willie's hands were visibly shaking.

"If I tell, he'll kill me."

"If you don't tell you and your brother are going to jail."

"I don't know his name."

"You're lying," screamed the officer.

"No I ain't!" screamed Willie.

Willie wouldn't look at the policeman. He kept his head down but he could feel the cop's burning stare. After what seemed like several minutes of silence, he said, "They call him the Mayor."

"Where does the Mayor live?" the officer asked, much softer.

"I don't know."

"You're lying," the policeman said with a forceful whisper.

Willie swallowed hard. "All I know is he hangs out at the corner of Mississippi and Walker."

"Willie, you've done the right thing," said the cop in a calm almost fatherly tone.

"Please don't tell anybody I squealed."

The officer escorted Willie back into the house.

"Let's go," Willie's interrogator said to his partner, and they left without further explanation.

When the officers left, Tyrone was still sitting on the kitchen chair. "What happened?" Tyrone asked, confused by the cop's sudden departure.

"Nothing, I just told them what you already told them."

"I ain't told them anything."

"He said you told them what happened."

"He lied. Don't you know you can't trust white people? Especially pigs."

"I didn't know."

"What did you tell them?"

"I told them the Mayor took the ball."

"You're stupid. Now we're in real trouble. If the Mayor stabbed Trifecta for taking his own ball, what's he going to do to you for squealing?"

The two boys looked at each other. Finally, Willie asked, "Are they going kill us?"

"Shut up and listen. We're going to tell everybody it was Trifecta who squealed. This is his fault anyway. He can take the heat."

Chapter 23

The sound of the screen door slamming shut startled Trifecta out of a half sleep. His chest and face still hurt as he rose from the couch where he was recuperating from his injuries.

"Hey," said Levi approaching Trifecta.

"What happened to you?" Trifecta asked, noticing that Levi's eyes were swollen and his lip was puffed up.

"Some boys beat me up last night."

"Why?"

"They said we ratted out the Mayor."

"Did you?"

"No man, but I'm afraid they might be after you next."

"Why do you think that?"

"They want to make sure you don't press charges and I don't testify against him."

"Did they arrest the Mayor?"

"Yeah."

"Was it because he cut me?"

"Yeah, two cops pulled up at the corner of Mississippi and Walker looking for him and the Mayor took off running through some backyards. One cop ran after him, the other drove around the block. The Mayor was out-running the cop, but when he tried to climb over a tall wooden fence it fell apart because it was rotten. The Mayor landed flat on his face. That's when the cop caught him."

"Why do they think one of us told on him?"

"I don't know. I told them I didn't say anything but they whipped me anyhow."

"You know who did it to you?"

"It was those dudes who hang out on the corner."

"What are you going to do?" Trifecta asked.

"Try to stay out of their way."

"I wonder who squealed."

"I don't know…. did you tell the cops anything?"

"I haven't talked to the cops," Trifecta said.

"They talked to me when I was with you at the hospital."

"What did you tell them?"

"I told them Tyrone and Willie took your ball but I didn't say who cut you."

"I can't go anywhere for at least a week. Maybe it will be all over by then. Let me ask you something."

"What?"

"You ever smell G.W.? He stinks and his car stinks."

"That's because he's a garbage man. All that stinking garbage gets all over them."

"Man, its nasty."

"It's part of the job."

The screen door opened and Tyrone and Willie came in. Willie's nose was bleeding and his shirt was torn.

"I hope you're happy," Tyrone bellowed.

"About what?" Trifecta responded.

"Look what they did to my brother," Tyrone said, pointing to Willie.

"Who did what and why do I care?"

"Clyde Mitchell and those other cats on the corner jumped him. They accused us of squealing on the Mayor and said if you press charges or testify against him they're going to kill all of us," Tyrone said.

"So what're you going to do?" Tyrone asked when Trifecta didn't respond.

"What am I going to do about what?" Trifecta answered.

"'About testifying."

"I ain't going to squeal."

Later that day the police came to the apartment asking Trifecta to press charges against the Mayor.

"I don't think he did it," Trifecta said.

"We have a witness who said he did; plus he had blood on him when we arrested him."

"Who told you it was him?"

"Your cousin told us the whole story."

"Which cousin told you?"

"Willie, the youngest one."

"He doesn't know what he is talking about."

"Are you afraid to press charges?"

"I don't want to press charges on the wrong person."

"Who stabbed you?"

"I don't know, but it wasn't the Mayor."

"What did the guy look like?"

"He didn't look like the Mayor."

"Next time he might kill you."

"I'll take my chances."

As the police were leaving the apartment one said to the other in frustration, "This is the reason we can't stop crime in the ghetto. No one has the guts to stand up for law and order."

The Mayor was released from jail that evening. The next day Tyrone walked to Mississippi and Walker, where the Mayor and a quartet of his lackey's were hanging out and selling dope.

"What's going on?" Tyrone asked, sauntering up to the Mayor.

The Mayor stared at him without responding.

"I took care of that business for you," Tyrone said. "There ain't anyone going to press no charges. I guarantee it."

"Cool," the Mayor said without a smile. "As long as you're sure there ain't anybody going to tell the pigs anything."

"If Trifecta was going to testify they wouldn't have let you out of jail."

"I guess not but if this ain't over I'm holding you responsible. You dig?"

"I dig."

"Cool. You got a smoke?" The Mayor asked.

"No."

"Why don't you go get me some smokes?"

"Sure."

Tyrone and the Mayor stood looking at each other.

"What are you waiting for?" The Mayor asked.

"Money," Tyrone said tentatively.

"I'll take care of you later."

Tyrone only had fifty cents, and he spent thirty-five cents on a pack of Kools for the Mayor. In exchange for the cigarettes, Tyrone was allowed to spend the rest of the afternoon on the corner.

Tyrone was never repaid his thirty-five cents or any of the other money he regularly spent on the Mayor, for the privilege of running errands and standing on the corner of Mississippi and Walker. Tyrone's primary job was to ferry marijuana from the corner to cars waiting at the curb, collect money, and deliver the money to the Mayor. Occasionally he was assigned other duties including shoplifting and burglarizing homes and neighborhood businesses.

Chapter 24

Within a few days the swelling in Trifecta's face disappeared, the pain from the stab wound began to subside and he regained most of his strength.

"I need a way to keep my cousins from stealing my property," Trifecta told Caledonia as she came downstairs that morning.

Caledonia went into the kitchen in search of something to eat for breakfast, apparently ignoring Trifecta's statement. Moments later she returned to the living room with a plate containing two slices of buttered toast garnished with white sugar.

"We'll go to town today and see what we can find," Caledonia said.

They rode the bus to town, where Caledonia renewed her loan at a finance company. With money in hand, they walked to Beale Street and perused several pawn shops. Caledonia received thirty dollars by renewing her loan, and adding another six monthly payments of eighteen dollars each to her account.

They found an army foot locker for five dollars at Nathan's Pawn Shop. Then they crossed the street and bought a combination lock for fifty cents at Schwab's Department

Store. Before leaving Schwab's, Caledonia spent seven dollars on good-luck potions, hoping the concoctions would help her pay back her loan.

Returning home, Trifecta retrieved his transistor radio from its hiding place in the closet and locked his last remembrance of the Churchills in the foot locker. Caledonia put the foot locker in front of the couch where it doubled as a coffee table.

By the time school started in the fall of 1960 neither Trifecta nor Caledonia had any communication with Mary. They didn't know where she lived or how to contact her.

*

When Mary and Maurice arrived in Chicago, they moved into a small apartment with Maurice's brother, his wife, and two children. Due to the limited space in an already crowded two-bedroom apartment, Maurice and Mary slept on the living room floor. Notwithstanding his hopes for a better life in the north, the only job Maurice found was working as a dish washer in a small black-owned restaurant. Mary worked in the same restaurant as a waitress. In Maurice's opinion, being a dishwasher in a black restaurant was less prestigious than being a yard boy working for rich white people in Memphis. So in frustration and self-pity, Maurice began drinking more than ever and his abuse of Mary became increasingly frequent, not only cursing her but often punching her. Maurice's sister-in-law hated the way Maurice treated Mary and made sure Maurice understood the way she felt, causing even greater stress in the congested apartment.

To compensate for the abuse Mary sought comfort from a patron of the restaurant. His name was Rufus and he worked at a nearby meat packing company. Every day he came to the restaurant for lunch and due to a combination of Mary's looks and the attention she gave him, he always sat at one of her tables and left generous tips. The friendlier Mary was the more substantial her tips. What began as an innocent flirtation between a waitress and her customer soon advanced beyond propriety. They began intentionally touching and brushing against each other when ordering and serving a meal. With each passing day their discreet touches became more and more intimate and titillating. They laughed, smiled, and talked; often making suggestive comments to one another. When her special customer was in the restaurant Mary was always close by unless Maurice came out of the kitchen busing tables.

At his wife's insistence, Maurice's brother finally told Maurice if he was going to continue drinking he had to do it somewhere other than in their home and in front of the children. So Maurice began staying out late every night, sharing bottles of cheap wine in alleys and on corners with newfound friends. He began coming home drunk every night, long after Mary had fallen asleep alone on the floor.

One day when Rufus was leaving the restaurant and no one was looking he slipped a three-dollar tip down the front of Mary's blouse for a two-dollar meal, and then he suggested she let him drive her home from work.

After work Mary had always waited for Maurice to finish cleaning the kitchen and they would walk home together. When he began staying out until all hours of the night drinking, she started walking home alone. That night as she headed home, a large Buick parked alongside of her. At first she was frightened because she was by herself on the dark desolate street. Then she realized it was Rufus, who was reaching across the front seat and opening the passenger-side door for her.

"Need a ride?" he asked with a toothy grin.

"I can walk. It ain't much farther too where I stay," Mary said with a seductive smile.

"Who said anything about taking you to where you stay?"

"What do you have in mind?"

"The same thing you do and we're just wasting time talking."

.   Mary got into the car and scooted across the seat until she was side by side with Rufus. She asked, "Where are we going?"

"Paradise," Rufus said.

Mary smiled and put her head on his shoulder.

They parked on a side street, kissing and groping for about an hour before Mary said she had to go home. Later that week they met again, and the next week Rufus took Mary to his house. In the fourth week of Mary and Rufus' rendezvous, Mary arrived home after Maurice. However Maurice was drunk and asleep and never acknowledged she was absent.

Several days later Mary walked into the living room of the apartment and found the contents of her purse scattered across a small coffee table. Maurice was sitting on the couch counting a wad of money.

"What's this?" Maurice asked, holding out the cash.

"That's mine," Mary said, trying to snatch the bills from his hand. Most of the money was from tips that Rufus had given her.

"You've been holding out on me." Maurice said as he stood up.

"It's mine!" Mary screamed, reaching for the money.

"Shut up," Maurice said, pushing her away and holding the cash over his head out of Mary's grasp.

Mary slapped at the arm Maurice used to push her, still attempting to retrieve her money.

Maurice back handed her across her face. Mary fell to the floor, blood forming on her lip.

"What's going on in here?" Maurice's sister-in-law screamed, entering the room and seeing Mary on the floor.

"He's got my money," Mary growled.

"You ain't got anything. Everything is mine," Maurice said, stepping towards Mary.

Maurice's sister-in-law stepped between the brawling couple. She put both her hands on Maurice's chest in an attempt to keep him away from Mary.

Maurice started to knock her hands off his chest when she said, "Don't you dare. You do anything to hurt me or Mary, and you'll be sorry."

Maurice backed off. "We'll settle this later," he snarled at Mary, and then stomped out the front door, cursing Mary, still clenching her money in his hand.

Before Maurice returned his sister-in-law insisted that her husband tell Maurice that he and Mary had to leave.

That night Mary slept in the kitchen, sitting on a chair with her head cradled in her arms on the dinette table. Maurice was passed out on the living room floor. The next morning they packed their clothes and left. Maurice was worried about where they would stay that night but said nothing to Mary. Even though Mary was tired and her mouth sore where Maurice had hit her, she left for work with a smile of confidence on her face.

At lunchtime when Mary saw Rufus' car pull into the parking lot, she retrieved her suitcase and met him before he reached the entrance of the restaurant.

"What happened to you?" he asked, seeing her swollen lip and blood shot eyes.

"I'll tell you in the car. Let's go."

Eight months later Marquis was born. Neither Mary nor Rufus ever returned to the restaurant, nor did they see Maurice after that day. Soon after Mary moved in with Rufus, it was evident that she was pregnant. She insisted that Rufus give her a gold wedding ring, but she never mentioned wanting to have a wedding ceremony and Rufus never brought it up.

Chapter 25

In the spring and summer of 1961 freedom riders were taking commercial buses through the south to test the Supreme Court decision that ended segregation for people engaged in interstate travel. The freedom riders' purpose was to desegregate buses and bus terminals, including restrooms, lunch counters and water fountains. The freedom riders met with immediate and oftentimes violent resistance from white citizens.

As Caledonia and the three boys watched the evening news, they saw black people being abused because they staged sit-ins at lunch counters and rode buses through the south. Tyrone and Willie would chatter, "Won't any white people do that to me. If I was there I'd show them. Someday I'm going to freedom ride and eat at any restaurant I want."

Listening to his cousin's rail against white people as they watched the news, Trifecta was surprised to see the number of whites involved in the freedom rides and other civil rights protest.

In September of 1961 four white Memphis elementary schools had their first grades integrated by thirteen black children. This concerned Trifecta because he reasoned he might have to go to a white school.

Furthermore, during September 1961, Caledonia and Trifecta received a letter from Mary along with a ten-dollar bill for Caledonia and five dollars for Trifecta. Trifecta immediately sent a postcard to his mother who still lived in Chicago. Mary began sending Caledonia between ten and twenty dollars each month, and she always included a few dollars for Trifecta. Trifecta stashed most of the money he received from his mother in his foot locker.

Almost a year later, in August 1962, Trifecta and Levi were coming home from the park when he noticed a late model Buick parked behind Caledonia's building. Looking closer, the boys noticed the car had Illinois license plates.

Inside the apartment Trifecta was surprised to see his mother holding a baby. A man Trifecta didn't know was sitting next to her. When Trifecta entered the room Mary passed the infant to the man and approached Trifecta with open arms. She was wearing a nice dress with a necklace and shiny high-heel shoes. Trifecta thought she looked beautiful.

"Oh baby... I've missed you so very much. I'm so glad to see you," Mary whispered embracing Trifecta. "And here are some important people I want you to meet."

"This is your baby brother, Marquis." Mary motioned towards the child in the man's arms.

"And this is your new daddy, Rufus." Mary walked across the room and placed her hand on the man's shoulder

"It's a pleasure to meet you. Your mother has told me so much about you," Rufus said.

"Does the cat have your tongue?" Mary asked Trifecta.

"He doesn't know what to say," interjected Caledonia. "All of this is coming at us so fast."

"We're here for three days. Trifecta has plenty of time to get adjusted." Mary said with a smile.

Mary and Rufus were staying at the Clark Hotel on Beale Street, which advertised the "Best Service for Colored Only." Trifecta spent the nights at the hotel with his mother, Rufus, and baby Marquise. Mary told Caledonia and Trifecta that she and Rufus were married and she called herself Mrs. Sanders.

Chapter 26

Central High School 1966

Even though Lois was not as high in the pecking order as Marcie, they both belonged in the same social circle. The two girls ate lunch at nearby tables in the lunch room and conversations frequently spilled from one table to the other.

"He's kind of dorky but cute," Lois said, speaking with Marcie across the small divide between the lunch tables.

"What's his name?"

"Henry something or other," Lois replied.

"It wouldn't be Henry Murphy would it?"

"I think so. Do you know him?"

"Yeah, I grew up with him."

"You did? What's he like?"

"He was my best friend until the seventh grade. Now he's turned into a real jerk."

"Why do you think he's a jerk?"

"We were really close until I moved to Hein Park. He went to Fairview. I went to Snowden. I didn't see him again until this year, now he won't even speak to me. He's turned into a real snob."

Lois was intrigued by anyone who dared snub the popular Marcie McDougal.

"Well, he doesn't say much in art class either; maybe he's shy around girls."

"I've known him all my life. There is no reason for him to be shy with me. Anyway, we're in the tenth grade he should know girls don't have cooties."

Art was different from most classes. The students sat at tables rather than desks. Each table accommodated two students who sat across from one another. As long as they worked on their projects and the teacher wasn't addressing the class, students were allowed to talk softly.

"You're Henry Murphy, aren't you?" Lois asked as they began to sketch with charcoal.

"Yes."

"Do you know Marcie McDougal?"

"Sure."

"She says you're a jerk."

Henry looked at her with a blank expression. He was embarrassed by her comment and had no idea how to respond.

"Don't get your panties in a wad. She thinks a lot of guys are jerks," Lois continued, realizing she had rattled Henry.

"She does?" Henry asked a little shocked that a girl would talk about panties when speaking to him.

"She probably thinks Jimmy Morris is a bigger jerk than you."

"Why does she think Jimmy Morris is a jerk?" Henry asked, relieved he was no longer the subject of their conversation.

"He's kind of arrogant, don't you think?"

"I don't know him."

"You don't know Jimmy? I thought everybody knew Jimmy. He's got to be one of the most popular boys in the tenth grade."

"I think I know who he is, but I don't know him," Henry replied, embarrassed he couldn't claim Jimmy as a friend.

"Jimmy, Marcie, and I went to Snowden. Jimmy has liked Marcie as long as I can remember, but she's never had any interest in him."

"I imagine a lot of guys like Marcie."

"Yeah, why don't you?"

"Who said I didn't like her?"

"She did."

Mr. Green called the art class to order to give them additional instruction in the use of charcoal. Henry was amazed that Marcie thought he didn't like her.

During the first semester, Lois and Henry chatted every day during art class and developed what Henry thought was a friendly relationship. Because Marcie was what Henry and Lois had in common she was a regular topic of conversation, and it was soon apparent to Lois that Henry really had a thing for Marcie, but she never told Marcie because she was developing her own interest in Henry.

Lois wasn't as pretty as Marcie but Henry thought she was cute.

Henry's friend Alan thought of himself as a Romeo. Even though many of the girls he dated weren't very popular, Henry was envious of him because Alan always had a girlfriend, and Henry had never been on a date.

"Just ask someone," Alan prompted. "You don't have to marry the girl. We're just going to a movie."

Alan had gotten his driver's license during the Christmas break and was trying to persuade Henry to double date with him.

"I don't know who to ask," Henry answered afraid whomever he'd ask would turn him down.

Lois passed the boys on her way to art class.

"Hi Henry," she said with a bright smile.

"Who's that?" Alan asked, after Lois sashayed into classroom.

"She's just a girl in my class."

"Good, ask her and we'll go downtown to a movie."

"I don't know if she'll want to go with me."

"That's why you need to ask. Quit being stupid and ask the girl for a date."

The bell rang. As Alan started toward his classroom he looked back at Henry and said, "ask her."

Mr. Green was lecturing and showing slides on the techniques of water color. Not knowing how to ask Lois out, Henry decided he would write her a note.

He wrote as legibly as he could. Would you like to go to a movie tomorrow night? He folded the piece of notebook paper four times hoping Mr. Green didn't notice. Then he gave Lois a gentle kick under the table. She looked at him and he showed her the folded piece of paper and then passed the note to her under the table.

She discreetly opened it, making sure Mr. Green's attention was on the slide he was discussing. Henry was tense and flushed, his breathing became labored, and his stomach puckered as he anticipated that Lois might laugh at him for asking her out.

When Henry finally looked toward Lois, she was smiling and nodding excitedly. His shoulder dropped slightly and he began to relax until he noticed Mr. Green was behind Lois and had taken the note out of her hand.

"I'm sure the rest of the class would be interested in what Henry thought was so important that he couldn't wait to tell you until after class," Mr. Green said. Several of the other students in the class giggled as he read the note out loud

"Are you going to accept Henry's invitation?" Mr. Green asked Lois.

"Yes," Lois responded without a hint of embarrassment, while Henry's face turned crimson.

"Now, that we have that settled may I have your attention, Henry?" Mr. Green asked.

"Yes sir," Henry answered, being humiliated by the continued snickering in the class room.

When Mr. Green turned his attention back to the slides he was lecturing on, Lois gently pulled a piece of paper out of her notebook, wrote something, and passed it to Henry.

Amazed by Lois' spunk, Henry cautiously opened the note. It said, **Call me, 472-3742.**

Chapter 27

Trifecta 1962-January 1964

Mary and Rufus left for Chicago the Sunday before Labor Day, and on the Tuesday after Labor Day Trifecta started junior high school.

Junior high was a far cry from elementary school. The boys were bigger and much meaner. It seemed that there were fights almost daily, usually taking place during lunch break or after school. The girls wore makeup and perfume and many of them had breasts large enough to make the front of their blouses protrude.

A lot of the teachers in Trifecta's school spoke of the freedom rides that had taken place over the summer. His Tennessee History and Civics teacher, Mrs. Hightower, was particularly vocal about the widespread civil rights activity that had occurred during the previous months. When she spoke about civil rights and the plight of blacks, Trifecta was fascinated. She became particularly emotional when explaining the abuse to which the civil rights workers and protestors were subjected. She explained how black people had been beaten, deluged with fire hoses, arrested, sent to prisons, and attacked by police dogs. Even though

Trifecta had seen the reports of injustice on television, Mrs. Hightower's rendition had a profound effect on him.

On September 20, 1962, James Meredith, a black man, was barred from enrolling in The University of Mississippi, which was an hour and a half drive from Memphis. Mrs. Hightower was from Attala County, Mississippi, the same county as James Meredith. Mrs. Hightower's class followed the drama at the University in Oxford until October 1, 1962, when James Meredith was finally admitted to the University. His admittance was preceded by a campus riot which required U.S Marshals and federal troops to squelch the violence. By the time James Meredith attended his first class at Ole Miss two white people were killed and over seventy marshals and federal troops were injured.

Mrs. Hightower was always careful to temper her civil rights talks advocating non-violence, but Levi's older brother didn't agree with Mrs. Hightower or the non-violent philosophy of Dr. Martin Luther King.

Levi's brother, Jefferson Davis Jones, was ironically named after the confederate general. Jeff was a part-time student at Lemoyne College, which was a black college located across the street from Lemoyne Gardens. He worked full-time for minimum wage at Lee's grocery, a neighborhood store owned by a Korean. When Jeff had nothing better to do he talked to Levi and Trifecta about black history, frequently discussing the slave riots in the United States and the Caribbean. Unfortunately, his view of history was not nearly as accurate as Mrs. Hightower's, but for Trifecta and Levi, it was just as believable. He said the only way black people would ever be free was through violence. He used the United States Civil War as an example.

"There has never been a war where so many white Americans were killed, but you see what happened: when enough of them died, they abolished slavery."

The event that caught the attention of Jefferson Davis Jones and therefore the attention of Trifecta and Levi was the murder of Medger Evers in Jackson, Mississippi.

Medger Evers was the field secretary and leader of the NAACP in Mississippi. As such, he organized voter registration, demonstrations, and economic boycotts in the name of civil rights. Medger's home was fire bombed in May 1963, and he was shot and killed in his driveway on June 13, 1963. Even though it widely known who the murderer was, there was never a conviction.

*

In January 1964, Caledonia had a telephone installed in her apartment and Trifecta spoke with his mother every week. She would ask how he was doing in school—he always told her that he was doing fine, but in reality, with the exception of Mrs. Hightower's class, he had lost all interest in school.

Chapter 28

1966

Henry, Alan, and Alan's date arrived at Lois's house at exactly 6:15, the time Henry told Lois he would pick her up. Henry felt awkward as he approached the house. When Lois's mother came to the door, Henry introduced himself.

"Hi," Henry said with a smile. "I'm Henry Murphy, is Lois here?"

"Henry, I'm Lois's mother, Mrs. Lovett, please come in." Mrs. Lovett stepped aside so Henry could enter. "You certainly look nice tonight," she said.

"Thank you," Henry said. He was wearing an India Madras sport coat, dress slacks, a yellow shirt, a tie, and too much English Leather cologne.

Entering the front door, Henry saw Mr. Lovett leaning back in a recliner, watching the evening news.

"Henry, this is Mr. Lovett, Lois's father."

"Nice to meet you," Henry said with a smile.

"How are you, son?" Mr. Lovett asked, not bothering to get up.

"Have a seat on the couch, Henry; I'll see if Lois is ready," Mrs. Lovett said, disappearing into the back of the house.

Henry wondered if he should try to start a conversation with Lois' father. Mr. Lovett continued to watch the television ignoring Henry. The news was about a civil rights protest in another city. During a commercial break, Mr. Lovett turned towards Henry and said, "The coloreds are never satisfied. They're always marching, complaining, and stirring up trouble."

Henry didn't know how to respond so he just said, "Yes, sir."

"You know they're all communists."

"Yes, sir."

"Nikita Khrushchev, Fidel Castrol, they're the ones behind all this civil rights stuff."

"Yes, sir."

"If Martin Luther King and that bunch want to be communists, why don't they go to Russia or Cuba?"

When the commercial break ended, Mr. Lovett turned his attention back to the television until the next advertisement, and then he returned to his lecture.

"And I'll tell you something else. All these boys who are copying those British musicians and growing their hair long, they're falling right into the hands of the communists! All this hair on boys is a plot to feminize our young men, so the communists can defeat us without a fight. It's hard to tell if some of these guys are boys or girls."

To Henry's relief, Mrs. Lovett and Lois entered the room, and Mr. Lovett turned silent. Henry was pleasantly surprised at how attractive Lois looked when she was dressed up.

Driving downtown, Alan and his date sat as close Siamese twins, while Henry and Lois sat in opposing corners of the backseat. Henry was thankful that Alan included Lois and him in his conversation because he couldn't think of anything to talk about, which was strange because he and Lois talked non-stop in art class. For some unknown reasons, the dynamics of their relationship changed on a date.

In downtown Memphis there were several grand movie theaters with lush carpeted lobbies, lighted by elaborate chandeliers and uniformed ushers carrying small flashlights. "Clambake," starring Elvis Presley and Shelly Fabres was playing at the Lowes Palace Theater on Main Street. As the boys purchased tickets, the girls stood off to the side of the box office under the flashing lights of the marquee, talking and giggling. Once inside the theater, the boys each bought two Cokes and a large box of popcorn. Alan suggested they go to the balcony.

Knowing why Alan wanted to sit in the balcony, Henry hesitated and looked at Lois. She smiled at him, her signal that it was alright to be in the balcony, so they followed Alan and his date.

The balcony was empty. Alan went to the next-to-the-last row.

"Is this okay?" Alan asked in a low voice.

Lois shrugged her shoulders, indicating her approval, so Henry and Lois sat down on the comfortably padded seats. During the previews and commercials for the theater's concessions, Alan and his date whispered and giggled, which stressed Henry because he wanted to talk to Lois but he struggled with what to say. So instead, he unfolded the top of the popcorn and offered some to Lois, which she took with a smile. The two sat silently, looking at the big-screen while eating popcorn and drinking their Cokes.

The movie was similar to other Presley movies. There were continuous scenes of girls in bikinis, jiggling and shaking while Elvis sang.

Alan and his date began making out as soon the movie began, which made Henry feel awkward. This was Henry's first date and he was uncertain of the kissing etiquette.

Henry was also concerned that Alan and his date might be making Lois uncomfortable with their amorous activity and he was unsure what he should do. On the other hand Henry thought Lois might feel neglected because he wasn't making advances towards her, but he was unsure how to test the waters.

Lois was wishing that Henry would follow Alan's lead and get busy. Trying to entice Henry to be more affectionate, Lois moved as close to him as the armrest between them would allow. Henry assumed she was attempting to give Alan and his date as much privacy as possible. During one scene where Elvis was competing in a boat race and almost had a wreck, Lois gripped Henry's forearm as if terrified by the action on the screen. Henry wondered if her touching him was a signal that she wanted a little more intimacy. Henry looked at her and smiled. He thought about kissing her but decided against it, thinking she might not want him to. He turned his attention back to the screen. She removed her hand from his arm, disappointed.

Now more exasperated, Henry decided to try to put his arm around her. After several minutes of building up his courage, he put his right arm on the back of her seat and leaned into her. He smelled her perfume and felt the heat from her body, which made him so exhilarated that he became slightly dizzy. He whispered, "Are you enjoying the movie?" He could feel himself blush, and his heart was beating in his ears.

She turned; her face was inches from his as she nodded her head and whispered, "Yes." It seemed like an opportune time to kiss her but he didn't. Thinking things were going well, and with her facing him, he put his cheek next to hers and whispered, "Do you like Elvis?"

"Sure," she whispered.

"He's pretty cool," Henry said as he sat back in his chair coyly letting his arm drop across her shoulders. She didn't seem to mind, but he remained tense.

To his surprise, Lois reached across her body with her left hand and gently grasped his hand that was draped over her right shoulder, encouraging him to keep his arm around her. He turned towards her again trying to think of something else to whisper, but she leaned her head back and looked up into his face. He thought she had her lips puckered. He tried to control himself, thinking he was about to hyperventilate. Gathering all the daring he could and disregarding any thought of decorum, he closed his eyes and briefly brushed his lips on hers. A tantalizing electric shock coursed through him. He drew back slightly with his eyes open waiting for her reaction. To his surprise and delight, with her eyes still closed, she parted her lips. Instinctively he kissed her. His mind and body instantly went numb, delighted with his first kiss. Lois, on the other hand, had been making out as often as she could find somebody to kiss since the seventh grade when her mother allowed her to meet her friends at the Paris Theater on Summer Avenue. Henry and Lois remained locked in each other's embrace until the credits for the movie started rolling. When they separated, Henry sat back to catch his breath and settle down, emotionally drained. The foursome sat in the theater until the lights came up. The girls took their compacts from their purses, straightened their hair and refreshed their makeup.

As the foursome descended from the balcony Henry held Lois's hand, thinking he was in love; until he noticed Marcie standing in the lobby. Then thoughts of Lois vanished as quickly as a rabbit in a magician's hat.

"Look who's here," Lois said, spying Marcie. "We've got to go say hi to her."

"You go. I have to use the restroom," Henry said.

"You can go later. Come with me," Lois said, practically dragging Henry toward Marcie.

"Hi, Marcie," Lois said as she and Henry approached.

"Hi," Marcie said a little surprised seeing Lois and Henry together.

"Did you like the show?" Lois asked Marcie.

"It was alright for an Elvis movie, how about you?"

"Henry and I both thought it was great, didn't we Henry?"

"Sure," Henry said, not looking at Marcie and having no recollection of the movie after they started making out.

"It looks like you enjoyed the show," Marcie said as she reached up to Henry's face and wiped Lois's lipstick off of his cheek.

"Who are you here with?" Lois asked. She was proud Marcie noticed that she and Henry had been getting it on.

"Jimmy Morris."

"I thought you didn't like him," Henry blurted out, with somewhat of an accusing tone.

"Whatever gave you that idea?" Marcie asked, as Jimmy walked towards to them.

Henry looked at Lois.

"We've got to go... see you later," Marcie said, as she locked her arm in Jimmy's and walked away.

"I thought you said she thought Jimmy was a jerk?" Henry said to Lois.

"You know Marcie. She's fickle."

Chapter 29

In 1965 there were 18,815 marijuana arrests in the United States.

In September of 1963, Tyrone was arrested for shoplifting a wristwatch at Goldsmith's Department Store on Main Street. He spent one night in detention because Caledonia didn't have transportation to the juvenile hall. The following day she rode the bus downtown, and arranged bail. After Tyrone was given a court date, he was released into Caledonia's custody.

After his arrest Tyrone was put on probation and he dropped out of Booker T. Washington High School where he was a senior. Soon he was spending all his waking hours with the Mayor and other criminals on the corner of Mississippi Boulevard and Walker Avenue.

*

That year, Trifecta barely maintained adequate grades to get promoted to high school.

*

The summer of 1964 was called "The Summer of Freedom" by many, and the "Mississippi Summer Project," by others. The "Summer of Freedom" was a joint effort of the NAACP (National Association for the Advancement of Colored People), CORE (Congress of Racial Equality), SCLC (Southern Christian Leadership Conference), and SNNC (Student Non-violent Coordinating Committee), to register black voters in Mississippi. Many young white people from the north participated in the project organized by a coalition of the four minority groups. Registering blacks to vote was met with strong resistance in most of the affected communities. The interference of outside instigators (whites from the north) particularly enraged many of the good ole boys in Mississippi and the surrounding states. The result was local governments, police departments, the Ku Klux Klan, White Citizens Counsel, and other militia groups being involved in counteracting voter recruitment. During the summer, three civil rights workers were murdered; two of the three were white. Four others were critically wounded. Eighty summer volunteers were beaten. A thousand people were arrested. Thirty-seven black churches and thirty homes belonging to blacks were either bombed or burned.

While northern outsiders were trying to right wrongs in the south, racial unrest turned violent in the north.

In July 1964, riots erupted in Harlem, and Rochester, New York, and Jersey City, New Jersey. In August, rioting, looting, and burning occurred in North Philadelphia, Pennsylvania, Patterson, New Jersey, Elizabeth, New Jersey, and Chicago, Illinois, leaving the American public paranoid and divided over the future of the nation. Across the country, city police and state National Guard were being trained in riot control.

Racial tension was high in Memphis and Trifecta and Levi, under the influence of Jeff, were thrilled that black people across the country were violently battling white oppression. Throughout the summer and fall of 1964

Trifecta, Jeff, and Levi talked and fantasized about being involved in riots and voter-registration drives.

*

In the spring of 1965, Tyrone was arrested for the possession of marijuana with the intent to sell.

Two young white men, who appeared to be college students pulled their car to the curb at Mississippi and Walker and turned their attention towards the Mayor and his cohorts who were loitering in front of a store. The Mayor warned Tyrone to be careful. Tyrone slowly strolled towards the car.

"What's happening man?" Tyrone asked.

"We're looking to take a magic carpet ride," the man in the passenger's seat said.

"Don't know what you're talking about man," Tyrone said, trying to determine if he was talking to customers or cops.

"We are looking for a dime bag, and I got a twenty, if you have the good stuff," the man in the passenger's seat said holding up a bill bearing the image of Andrew Jackson.

After quickly looking up and down the street, Tyrone snatched the bill and stuffed it into his pocket. The Mayor and his flunkies watched the transaction without expression.

"Be back in a minute."

Tyrone disappeared behind the store and then quickly returned with a small plastic bag. As soon as he handed the bag to the passenger, the occupants of the vehicle were out of the car with pistols drawn. Three black-and-white police cars appeared instantly from every direction, making escape impossible.

While everyone else panicked, the Mayor calmly watched the drama unfold before him.

"Put your hands behind your head and lie face down on the ground," ordered the Narc that bought the dope.

Tyrone and the two boys standing beside the Mayor dropped to the ground. The Mayor remained standing with a cold smile.

"Get on the ground," a uniform patrolman screamed while aiming his revolver at the Mayor.

"Who, me?" the Mayor asked.

"Yes, you, you're under arrest."

"For what?"

"For possession of drugs with the intent to sell."

"I ain't got any drugs, and I'm not selling anything."

"You're an accomplice in a drug sale."

"I'm an accomplice to who?"

The uniform looked at the Narc.

"This is the only guy selling," the plain clothes cop said, pointing at Tyrone with his pistol.

"You're an accessory to a crime," the uniform accused the Mayor.

"What are you talking about?"

"You saw a crime and failed to report it."

"How was I to know a crime was going down, man? I didn't know what was in the bag."

Looking at his buddies lying face down on the ground, the Mayor said, "You cats get up, we ain't done anything wrong. We don't even know who the cat is that they say is selling dope."

When Tyrone was put in the backseat of one of the squad cars, he looked at the Mayor with pleading eyes, hoping the Mayor planned to bail him out of jail. To his surprise, the Mayor said to no one in particular, "Jail time is part of the job description."

Tyrone was taken to jail and bail was set at $5,000.00. Caledonia tried to borrow the 10%, for the bail bondsman, but that late in the month all the social security checks, welfare checks and ADC checks in the projects were spent. The most money she could scrounge up was $125.00.

When Sammy Mitchell asked the Mayor if he was going to bail Tyrone out of jail, the Mayor said, "We lost enough money when the pigs found our stash of grass behind the store. As far as I'm concerned, they can keep him in jail."

No longer considered a juvenile, Tyrone stayed in the city jail for three weeks while he waited for his trial. During that time he was beaten twice by other prisoners and constantly threatened.

At his sentencing, the judge gave Tyrone the option of going to prison for fifteen to twenty years or joining the army. After his experience in the Memphis city jail and the potential length of his sentence, he opted for the army.

*

Tyrone had to be at the army recruiting station by six-thirty in the morning to leave for basic training. Caledonia arranged for a neighbor who worked downtown to give him a ride. Caledonia was out of bed at five-thirty getting Tyrone ready to leave. While Caledonia was preparing a special breakfast of eggs and bacon, Tyrone quietly pried the hasp and lock off of Trifecta's Foot Locker. The locker contained fifteen dollars, the transistor radio, and two Baby Ruth candy bars. Tyrone took it all. The radio didn't have any batteries in it, and Tyrone threw it away at the recruiting station before he boarded a Grey Hound bus used to transport the recruits to Fort Campbell.

When Trifecta woke up he noticed his foot locker had been ransacked. Caledonia and Willie were eating cereal at the kitchen table. Trifecta went into the kitchen, cursing and calling Tyrone names.

"You better shut your mouth about my brother," Willie said.

"Your brother is a thief and belongs in jail. I hope he gets killed in the army," Trifecta shouted.

"Shut up!" Willie screamed.

Trifecta didn't say another word, but let his rage control his actions. He jumped on Willie. The two boys, a chair, and the table crashed onto the floor. After having a bowl of cereal dumped in her lap Caledonia struggled to her feet. Trifecta began pummeling Willie with his fists.

"Stop it!" Caledonia cried.

Trifecta continued punching Willie.

Caledonia wobbled to the back door as fast as her sore feet would take her.

"Help me; they're going to kill each other!" she pleaded.

G.W. heard Caledonia's screams and came out on his porch to investigate the ruckus. Caledonia was hysterical. She pointed to her apartment. G.W. went in and found the two boys locked in battle on the floor. Trifecta had worn himself out punching and was holding onto Willie trying to prevent him from fighting back.

G.W. pried the two boys apart. G.W.'s strength continued to surprise Trifecta.

"Break it up," G.W. said, pulling Trifecta to his feet.

Trifecta acted like he wanted to continue the fight, but it was all a bluff. He was happy G.W. came in when he did. He was past being ready to quit.

Willie got to his feet.

"What's this about?" G.W. asked.

"He's been talking bad about my brother," Willie whined.

"Your brother is a liar and a thief," Trifecta said, faking a threatening move toward Willie.

"Now, now," G.W. said, putting his hand on Trifecta's chest to keep him separated from Willie.

"You're coming with me," G.W. said to Trifecta. "And you're going to help Miss Caledonia clean up this mess," he instructed Willie.

"This mess ain't my fault," Willie said. Then pointing to Trifecta, he asked, "Why doesn't he have to help?"

"I'm going to take care of him. You mind me and help your grandmother clean up."

By that time, Caledonia was standing at the kitchen door.

"Excuse me, Miss Caledonia," G.W. said as he pulled Trifecta by the arm. "I'm going to take this one with me. The other one is going to help you. If you have any more problems, you call me."

"I will. Thank you for your help, and say hi to Miss Yolanda for me," Caledonia replied, having regained some of her composure.

All of G.W.'s children, along with several neighbors, were gathered around Caledonia's porch to see about the commotion. When G.W. walked onto the porch still gripping Trifecta's arm, he ordered his children to get ready for school. And the small crowd dispersed.

As soon as G.W. was out of the apartment, Willie went to his room without helping Caledonia clean the kitchen.

G.W. sat Trifecta down at his kitchen table. Wetting a wash rag he wiped a trickle of blood from Trifecta's face.

"What was that about?" G.W. asked.

"His stupid brother stole all my stuff when he left for the army."

"What did he steal?"

"He took fifteen dollars, a radio, and some candy."

"Were those things worth getting your grandmother upset?"

"He took everything I own except my clothes."

Feeling empathy for the young man, G.W. took his wallet from his hip pocket.

"Here, take this," G.W. said, handing Trifecta six one-dollar bills, which was all the money he had until he got paid in four days. "It ain't fifteen dollars, but it will get you by."

"I don't want your money."

"I want you to take it and promise me you ain't going to fight with Willie anymore or cause Miss Caledonia any further trouble. Is that a deal?"

Trifecta took the money.

*

After Tyrone finished his basic training at Fort Campbell, Kentucky, he completed his Advanced Infantry at Fort Polk, Louisiana.

The war was escalating in Viet Nam, while racially motivated rioting continued in the United States.

Chapter 30

Henry's second date with Lois was another double date with Alan and his girlfriend. They went to the Plaza Theater in Poplar Plaza Shopping Center to see "A Patch of Blue," which followed the story of an abused, blind white girl who fell in love with a black man. The black man was determined to help the young white girl escape her life of poverty and violence.

Leaving the movie, Lois made a general announcement to the others. "Don't say anything to my dad about seeing this movie; he really doesn't approve of whites and Negroes mixing."

"I don't either," Alan replied. "But I still thought it was a pretty cool movie."

"Yeah, it kind of makes you rethink the whole interracial thing," Alan's date added.

'I wouldn't go that far," Alan said. "You got to remember it was just a movie. That's not the way things really are."

"Yeah, my dad would say movies like that are made by communist to stir up problems between the races," Lois said as they were getting into the car. "Of course he thinks everything is a communistic plot. He actually believes there are Russians in this country instigating all the problems with the colored people. And don't get him started on the hippies and the Beatles; they're all communists according to him."

From the theater, Alan cruised to several of the high school haunts, but they saw very few people they knew.

"What do you want to do?" Alan asked the group.

"I know," Lois said, "let's roll someone's yard."

"That would be fun," Alan's date replied. "Whose house do you want to roll?"

"How about Marcie McDougal's? I know where she lives," Lois said.

Henry's stomach twisted into a knot at the suggestion, however, Alan and his date thought it was a great idea. They stopped at several gas stations and swiped the toilet paper from the restrooms. By the time they started toward Marcie's house they had eight rolls. The plan was for the girls to crisscross the yard with strips of the paper while the boys threw streamers of the tissue into the two large trees.

When they parked in front of Marcie's house, Henry had mixed emotions of dread and excitement. He just hoped they didn't get caught. It had been years since he had seen Mr. McDougal. However, he still had more than a healthy respect for the man. He had a healthy fear of him.

As the girls rolled the toilet paper across the lawn, the boys heaved it into the trees. Alan threw a roll high into a tree leaving behind a stream of paper in the branches, but the roll broke loose from the trail of paper and fell on Lois's head. She wasn't hurt, but the unexpected blow caused her to scream in surprise. The two girls giggled.

"Shhhhh, be quiet," Henry whispered, but the girls continued to snicker. Henry stood motionless, staring at the house, expecting Mr. McDougal to come out of the front door at any moment.

Seconds passed and the girls curbed their laughter and returned to crisscrossing the yard with the toilet paper. Henry's nerves settled and he softly threw a roll of toilet paper into the tree, wishing the other three would finish, so they could leave. Abruptly, the flood lights on the eves of the house came on exposing the four teenagers. They all dashed toward the car. When Henry was almost there, he was brought to a halt by a beam of light in his eyes coming from a flashlight held by Mr. McDougal, who was leaning against Alan's car.

"Henry?"

"Yes, sir."

"You kids having fun?"

"Sir," Henry said, not knowing what to say.

"Don't let me stop you from what you're doing. But Henry, I expect you and your friends to be here first thing in the morning to clean up this mess. Do you understand?"

"Yes, sir."

"I'm sure your parents wouldn't approve of what you have done here tonight."

"No, sir."

"Then this will stay our secret as long as you get this cleaned up."

"Yes, sir, thank you."

Mr. McDougal turned off his flashlight, walked across the yard and into the house.

The four got in the car and drove away. Henry wanted to say what a stupid idea that was, but it was Lois's idea, so he didn't say anything. Marcie lived close to Southwestern College. Alan found a secluded spot near the athletic fields on the college campus where they parked and made out for an hour before they went home. Kissing Lois made Henry temporarily forget about being caught by Mr. McDougal.

The next day, Henry was the only one to return to Marcie's house. He carried a rake and a couple of large paper grocery sacks. When he arrived he started raking the toilet paper that was on the lawn. The tissue raked up easily but pulling the paper out of the trees was another story. Mr. McDougal let him use a ladder, and told him that when he pulled out all the toilet paper he could from the branches, he had to use the hose and spray the tree until the remaining paper disintegrated.

By the time Marcie came out of her house, Henry was soaking wet from using a water hose. She was wearing shorts and a green Central High sweatshirt with a gold profile of an Indian chief embossed on the front. Her hair was combed and neat but was different from the way she wore it at school. She didn't appear to have on any makeup, and Henry thought she looked more sensual than he had ever seen her.

"Dad said you can quit now. It looks good enough."

There were still flakes of toilet paper on many branches of each tree.

"I'm sorry," Henry said.

"Don't be, I take it as a compliment. Usually when people roll your yard it means they like you. So did Lois help you?"

"Yeah, Lois, Alan, and his date."

"Well, I'm glad you like me enough to roll my yard because I still like you."

Henry blushed but was unsure what Marcie meant. Maybe she liked him as a friend, or it could mean she liked him romantically.

"So are you and Lois going steady?" Marcie asked.

"No, we've just dated twice."

"Are you going to ask her to go steady with you?"

Henry didn't know what to say. If Marcie meant she liked him romantically he didn't want to jeopardize his chances with her, so he said, "I don't know."

"Well, she's a sweetie pie."

"Yeah, I guess she is."

"I'll see you at school on Monday."

"Okay, I'll see you Monday," Henry said as Marcie went back inside her house.

Henry rolled up the hose, put the two sacks of unrolled toilet paper in the garbage can, and walked home. However, as he walked, his heart surged within him as he thought about Marcie and what she meant when she said she liked him.

When he went to school on Monday he discovered his relationship with Marcie didn't change much. They spoke as they passed in the hall but Marcie was still constantly surrounded by the school's elite social circle, which Henry couldn't penetrate. So Henry continued to date Lois and make out with her at every opportunity.

Chapter 31

Vietnam 1966

During 1966 the number of Americans killed in Vietnam more than doubled and the number of wounded quadrupled. It was also the year Tyrone was sent to Southeast Asia. Despite the ever-present threat of death, Tyrone was cool with being in Vietnam because even in the boonies, marijuana was easy to obtain, and if its use was not blatant it was broadly overlooked. Vietnamese grass was superior to anything sold or produced in the United States and could be purchased inexpensively. Its packaging was identical in appearance to American cigarettes. The joints came ready-rolled with filters, being exact replicas of state-side manufactured cigarette brands. The ways to distinguish a joint from a tobacco cigarette included the taste, smell, and the effects of smoking on the mind and body. The only appearance that distinguished a reefer from a cigarette was the unfiltered end of a joint was crimped so the marijuana wouldn't shake out of the cigarette paper.

Few soldiers questioned how Vietnamese living under primitive conditions could so skillfully disguise marijuana. However, the masqueraded reefers were manufactured in the

Soviet Union and exported to Vietnam in order to weaken the American troops while using the money obtained by selling drugs to U.S. soldiers to finance their war effort in Southeast Asia.

After being in country for two weeks and receiving additional training, Tyrone was flown by helicopter onto L.Z. (landing zone) "Sitting Bull." The fire base was being temporarily secured by Company B of the First and Seventh, First Air Cavalry. The company clerk met Tyrone when he disembarked the helicopter, and escorted him to his assigned infantry squad. His squad leader was sitting in the afternoon sun behind a sandbag bunker at a large cable spool turned on side so it could be used as a table. He and two other soldiers were talking while enjoying a warm beer. Tyrone's squad occupied two bunkers located in the perimeter berm of the landing zone.

Tyrone was invited to join them and have a beer. Tyrone had never liked beer, particularly warm beer, but he drank it in an attempt to fit in. While the squad leader briefed Tyrone on their mission a white guy strolled up with glazed eyes and a goofy grin. The soldier wasn't wearing a shirt and he had a visible tattoo of the Zig Zag man on his right bicep (The Zig Zag Man was the logo for Zig Zag cigarette papers. Zig Zag was the preferred choice of cigarette papers for rolling marijuana).

"Tyrone, this is Mad Dog," said the squad leader, introducing him to the shirtless white boy.

"What's happening man?" the white guy said, rapping knuckles, interlocking fingers, tapping the back of Tyrone's hand in the elaborate handshake of black soldiers.

"Tyrone is joining our squad," the squad leader said.

"Far out," Mad Dog said. "I got a care package from home; some summer sausage, cookies, stuff like that. Some of us are getting together tonight to chow down on my goodies. Come on by and scope us out if you want; we're just going to munch and rap."

"Cool," Tyrone responded realizing Mad Dog wasted, "I'll be there."

That night Tyrone met up with Mad Dog and his cronies and spent the evening in a bunker rapping, getting high, and munching on Mad Dog's care package. All the while, they tried to stab field mice with their bayonets as the rodents scurried over the dirt floor.

There were only two other blacks in Tyrone's platoon, but that didn't make any difference. Tyrone found his soul brothers among Mad Dog and the other pot heads in his unit.

By the time Tyrone had been in the country for three months he had been involved in several skirmishes with the Viet Cong. He saw two Americans die in combat and three others wounded during fire fights.

One of Tyrone's favorite things about being in the air cavalry was riding in helicopters, especially when he was stoned. He always liked to sit in the door with his feet dangling outside the bird because it gave him the sensation of flying. He particularly enjoyed the takeoff when the chopper dropped its nose and lifted its tail for a fast takeoff.

In the field Tyrone's unit was resupplied every three days. To receive their rations Tyrone's company had to either find an open field to land helicopters, or they had to cut a landing zone out of the jungle.

Tyrone and his company received food rations, changes of clothes, two soft drinks and two cans of beer each time they were resupplied. They also received mail. While Tyrone rarely received a letter or package from Caledonia, every three days he and the other heads received a shipment of grass from a supplier in their base camp.

Tyrone always traded his two beers for one soft drink. Tyrone enjoyed drinking Coke when he smoked weed but he hated humping soft drinks through the boonies. So after he ate, changed clothes, and got his supplies, he regularly volunteered to guard the perimeter, which meant he would go several meters outside the landing zone and stand watch. At his guard post, Tyrone usually sat against a tree, drinking the sodas and smoking two or three joints, putting his platoon in jeopardy because of his inattention.

Tyrone was on watch and stoned when he was given the unexpected order to saddle up. Military intelligence had reported suspected enemy movement approximately twenty kilometers away and Tyrone's platoon was being sent to investigate the alleged Viet Cong activity.

The landing zone used to resupply Tyrone's platoon was only large enough to accommodate one helicopter. This meant each squads in the platoon would be airlifted separately and several minutes apart. Tyrone's squad was assigned to the first helicopter. He took his regular spot in the door of the bird with his feet dangling inches above the skid. The chopper rose straight up, swaying slightly side to side. Once they cleared the tree tops the helicopter rotated 180 degrees, dropped its nose, raised its tail, and sped away. Within minutes they were circling an open field in the jungle, Tyrone could see other helicopters approaching in the distance. Tyrone felt mellow from smoking pot and was tripping on the sound of the helicopter's blades beating the air. As they circled the field the sixty caliber machine gun next to Tyrone began firing, ejecting hot brass shell casing onto him. When the ejected shell casings hit him it felt like he was being attacked by a swarm of stinging bees. Tyrone cursed and screamed at the door gunner, trying in vain to be heard above the rapid firing of the machine gun and the sound of the rotor blades.

"What are you doing man?" he shouted.

The door gunner was oblivious to Tyrone as he fired tracers and bullets into the tree line with the brass constantly spewing onto Tyrone.

When the chopper was a few feet from the ground Tyrone jumped out without his rifle or backpack to escape the deluge of shell casings.

High and unaware of the incoming hostile fire, Tyrone turned toward the helicopter and continued his rant at the door gunner. When the bird touched down the door gunner continued firing into the tree line. Tyrone reached into the helicopter and grabbed his rifle and backpack as brass bounced off of him. Turning carelessly toward the tree line, two enemy bullets crashed into Tyrone's chest, the impact of the bullets driving him against the helicopter as he fell to the ground. When Mad Dog saw Tyrone on the ground, he moved quickly to his side.

"They shot me man." Tyrone breathed, barely audible above the sound of the bird's blades thrashing the air and the fury of gunfire.

"It don't mean nothing," Mad Dog answered as he retrieved Tyrone's pack which he knew contained marijuana.

"I'm scared that I'm going to die," Tyrone said, with terror in his voice.

Tyrone thought he heard Mad Dog say, "You're just trippin', man," as he ducked away with Tyrone's backpack in hand.

While other members of Tyrone's squad quickly loaded him and his rifle onto the floor of the helicopter, Mad Dog snuck into some tall grass where he searched Tyrone's belongings and confiscated all of Tyrone's pot. Leaving the remainder of Tyrone's possessions in the weeds, Mad Dog rejoined his squad and watched as a gun ship appeared in the sky and launched rockets at the enemy position.

Before the helicopter arrived back at Sitting Bull, Tyrone was dead.

Chapter 32

Tyrone's Funeral

Tyrone had a ten thousand dollar G.I. life insurance policy. Caledonia was listed as the beneficiary. The funds were not going to be distributed for several days after the funeral. In the meantime G.W. assisted Caledonia in arranging for a free burial in the National Cemetery in Memphis.

The day before the funeral Mary and Marquis arrived at Caledonia's apartment unannounced.

"Mama!" Mary called, opening the screen door and sticking her head into the apartment.

Trifecta was lounging on the couch watching television. "Mama!" he cried, jumping to his feet and flying into Mary's arms.

"Mama, Mama," he said, continuing to embrace her and burying his face against her neck. He was as tall as his mother.

"My goodness, what are you doing here?" Caledonia asked, hobbling down the stairs.

"Hi, Mama," Mary said, disengaging from Trifecta. "I've come to be with you during Tyrone's funeral."

"Ain't that something," Caledonia said. "And who is this?" Caledonia asked as she reached out to hug Marquis. "Ain't he getting big?"

"Say hello to your Madea, Marquis," Mary said.

Trifecta looked on, somewhat annoyed that Mary had turned her attention away from him.

"Where's Rufus?" Caledonia asked.

"He ain't here."

"Where's he at?"

"Don't know," Mary responded.

"What do you mean you don't know?"

"I mean we haven't been together for a while, Mama."

"You mean you ain't married anymore?"

"That's right, Mama; we ain't married."

Trifecta's heart leaped, hearing that Rufus was out of Mary's life. Now there was no reason for her to stay in Chicago.

"Where have you been staying?" Caledonia asked.

"With a friend."

"How did you get here?"

"Bus."

"Well, baby, what happened between you and Rufus?"

"Another woman."

"How long has it been?"

"It's been awhile."

"Why didn't you tell me?"

"I didn't want you worrying, Mama."

"What are you going to do now?"

"I don't know. I just thought I needed to be with you for the funeral seeing nobody knows where Josephine is."

Caledonia moved Willie from of his bedroom to the living room couch, allowing Mary, Marquis, and Trifecta to sleep in the second bedroom. Mary slept in one of the twin beds, Trifecta and Marquis shared the other, sleeping head to foot. Willie grumbled and complained at losing his room but to no avail.

Tyrone's funeral was on Thursday at three o'clock at the Jerusalem AME Church on Kerr Avenue where G.W. and his family worshipped.

The sanctuary of the little church was packed. Some of the attendees had to sit in the small choir loft, which consisted of ten folding chairs behind a railing located behind the pulpit. Most people waved paper fans, attempting to move the stagnant air in the overcrowded wood-framed building. Even the Mayor and some of his lackeys who hung out with Tyrone on the corner were in attendance. The Mayor's crew all wore tailored, two-pocket bell-bottom pants that were the rage among the Memphis' young black community, with Rayon shirts, sun shades with various colored lenses, narrow brimmed hats, and highly shined leather shoes. Trifecta admired their wardrobes and thought if he ever got enough money that's the way he would dress. However, the tailored pants with no hip pockets anchoring the ensemble cost a minimum of thirty-five dollars at any tailor shop in Memphis.

Caledonia was wearing a wig that looked more like a hairy hat than a human coiffure. She was sweating and fanning herself as the minister stood to begin the service. With a gasp from several of the attendees, Josephine Johnson, Tyrone's long lost mother, unexpectedly took her seat next to Willie on the front row.

Caledonia did a double take to make sure her eyes weren't deceiving her, but when she recognized her daughter, she prayed out loud, "Thank you, Jesus." Mary glared at Josephine and Josephine scowled at Mary.

The preacher spoke for twenty minutes then G.W. gave the eulogy. Many in attendance, including Caledonia and Josephine, wailed and cried. At one point it appeared that Caledonia had lost consciousness in her grief. When G.W. concluded, the minister asked if anyone else had anything to say. Several guests rose and gave short accounts of their experiences and affection for Tyrone. As Trifecta listened, he thought he had never heard so much inaccurate information in his life. It was almost more than he could tolerate until Jeff stood, and with great emotion railed against the plight of the black man in Vietnam, forced to fight a white man's war.

When the service ended, Josephine rushed to her mother and embraced Caledonia.

"Mama, what happened to my baby?" Josephine asked as she continued to sob.

"It's alright, child. Like the preacher said he died doing the right thing, he died for his country. He is a hero," Caledonia said, attempting to comfort her daughter.

Guests gathered around Caledonia and Josephine to offer their condolences. Even though many mourners had never seen or heard of Josephine, they spoke to her as if she had been a devoted mother.

Mary, Marquis, and Trifecta had originally planned to ride to the cemetery in the limousine with Caledonia, but when Josephine showed up, Mary decided she and her boys would crowd into G.W.'s car.

At the cemetery Caledonia almost fainted again when soldiers removed the American flag from the casket, and after folding it handed the flag to her. With Old Glory folded and resting in her lap, Caledonia had to be supported by Mary and Josephine to prevent her from sliding out of her chair.

Recovering from her fit of grief, Caledonia walked away from the grave site with her two daughters. By this time, Caledonia's wig was slightly lopsided on her head.

A neighbor of Caledonia's approached them, addressing Josephine. "I'm so sorry about Tyrone."

"Thank you," Josephine said.

"I've been worried about Tyrone ever since he told the police about the Mayor stabbing Trifecta," the neighbor said.

"What are you talking about?" Josephine asked.

"I figured that the Mayor would have killed Tyrone himself after Tyrone told on him."

"It wasn't Tyrone that ratted on the Mayor," Caledonia interjected.

"Who was it?" the neighbor asked.

"Tyrone told me it was Willie, but he said he took care of it with the Mayor," Caledonia said.

Sammy Mitchell was walking within ear-shot of the conversation. Up to that minute the Mayor never knew who told the police he was the one who stabbed Trifecta.

Chapter 33

The day after Tyrone's funeral, Trifecta got out of bed and went downstairs to find a white man wearing a suit and tie, in the kitchen with Caledonia, Mary, and Josephine. Apparently the three women hadn't been up long because they were all in their night clothes. The white man and Caledonia were sitting at the table; Mary and Josephine were standing over them.

Trifecta watched from the living room as Caledonia signed a piece of paper. The white man stood up, shook Caledonia's hand and left. As Caledonia walked him to the door, she saw Trifecta but didn't speak.

When Caledonia reentered the kitchen, Josephine said, "Mama, I'd like to talk to you about that money."

"We'll talk about it after we feed Trifecta breakfast," Caledonia responded.

"Mama, you know the money is rightfully mine," Josephine said.

"I said, we'll talk about the money after we feed Trifecta breakfast," Caledonia answered.

"I don't see why the money belongs to you. Mama raised your children," Mary said.

"It ain't any of your business," Josephine lashed out.

"She's my mama, and it's my business," Mary retorted.

"I guess you think you're getting some of the money," Josephine snapped.

"I said we'll talk about the money after we feed Trifecta," Caledonia said, raising her voice.

"It's Mama's money; she can do whatever she wants with it," Mary sassed.

"Well, you ain't getting any, so just get that idea out of your head," Josephine replied.

"You're making my head hurt, now you both get out of the kitchen so I can feed Trifecta," Caledonia ordered.

Mary went upstairs to the bedroom. Josephine sat on the couch where she had slept the previous night. Willie was demoted to a pallet on the floor.

By the time Trifecta had eaten the leftovers from the night before and gone upstairs, Mary was dressed and back in the kitchen.

Once dressed, Trifecta returned to the living room positioning his self out of sight but within ear shot of the kitchen. Despite the commotion, Willie remained asleep on the floor.

"I know I'm going to give five hundred dollars to Trifecta because Tyrone stole his money and his radio," Caledonia said.

"He didn't steal five hundred dollars from the boy," Josephine said.

"I know he didn't steal five hundred dollars but Tyrone was mean to Trifecta, and Trifecta deserves it.

"It ain't right," Josephine said.

"It's as right as me giving Willie five hundred dollars," Caledonia said.

"Why are you going to give Willie five hundred dollars?" Josephine asked.

"Because he's Tyrone's brother and he needs to have fond memories of Tyrone."

"That leaves nine thousand dollars plus the two hundred and fifty dollars you get from Social Security," Josephine said.

"I'm going to buy some new furniture," Caledonia said.

"What about me, Mama?" Josephine asked.

"What about you? Mama is the one that raised your babies, all you did was birth them," Mary said.

"I told you this ain't any of your business," Josephine barked at Mary.

"I told you she is my mama and you don't deserve anything. She raised Tyrone," Mary said, not backing down.

"She's my mama, and you need to shut up," Josephine said.

"All you came here for is the money. You don't care anything about Tyrone," Mary said.

"What are you here for? You didn't come just for a funeral, and you sure didn't come for Trifecta." Josephine shot back.

"Stop it, both of you!" Caledonia snapped. "I'll tell you what I'm going to do. I'm going to give five hundred dollars to Trifecta, and I'm going to give five hundred dollars to Willie. Then I'm going to buy a thousand dollars, worth of new furniture. That leaves eight thousand dollars plus two hundred and fifty dollars from Social Security. I'm giving Mary the two hundred and fifty for bus fare because she came from Chicago. Then Josephine if you'll take Willie home with you I'll give you half of the remaining eight thousand."

Trifecta felt a surge of joy at the thought of Willie leaving. Now he and his mama could live with Caledonia until they could find their own place.

"Wait Mama, how comes I only get two hundred and fifty?" Mary asked.

"Why should you get that much?" Josephine responded. "What does a round-trip ticket between here and Chicago cost, fifty or sixty dollars?"

"You haven't done anything to get four thousand. While I only get two hundred and fifty," Mary said.

"I've been telling you Mama, the reason she came here is to get money from you. She doesn't care about a funeral," Josephine said.

"Look who's talking. Where have you been the last fifteen years while Mama raised your children?" Mary asked.

"If you want to take Trifecta, I'll give you more money. If you aren't going to take him, I deserve the money," Caledonia said, speaking to Mary.

Trifecta's jubilation turned to confusion. His grandmother was willing to pay his mother to take him away. He was crestfallen when Caledonia asked Mary what she wanted to do and Mary told her she had to think about it.

Caledonia turned to Josephine. "What are you going to do? "Are you going to take the money and Willie?"

"What if I don't take Willie?" Josephine inquired.

"I'll give you two thousand dollars. Tyrone was your son."

"I need to think about it," Josephine said humbly.

"By the way, I'd like you to answer Mary's question. Where have you been for the last fifteen years and how did you know Tyrone was dead?"

"I've been in Tipton County, and I heard it on the Memphis TV station when they tell about the soldiers who've been killed," Josephine said.

"You mean you've been an hour or two from here, and you haven't come to see your children or send money to support them?" Caledonia asked.

"I'll let you know what I decide," was Josephine's only response as she started walking out of the kitchen and away from the uncomfortable conversation.

Mary smiled as Josephine left the room, her sins having been exposed.

Trifecta snuck back upstairs, went into the bathroom, shut the door, and cried. His mother's words cut him as severely as broken glass.

Chapter 34

1965-1966

Scoop was tired of having his articles edited by a high school teacher, and he was bored helping Henry write about high school athletes. It came to a head in early November, 1965, when the facility advisor for the school newspaper insisted that the basketball players be referred to as "cagers," at least once in the sports section during basketball season.

"That's the most asinine thing I've ever heard," Scoop protested as he read the edited article he helped Henry write.

"She says originally basketball was played inside a fenced court, and the players were called cagers because...."

"I know what cagers are, and I know they use to shot the ball into peach baskets instead of a net. But what does that have to do with good journalism? In fact, when you write about something other than sports, I'll give you a hand. Until then let little miss know-it-all help you. I'm done being critiqued by a high school editor and not a very good editor at that. And I'm just as weary writing about high school athletes who are mediocre at best."

That was the last Henry heard from Scoop until the early spring of 1966.

*

"Henry, telephone," Henry's mother called to him late one afternoon in April of 1966.

"Who is it?" Henry asked, leaving his bedroom and going to the kitchen phone.

"Some man"

"Hello?" Henry said.

"Hey kid, it's Scoop."

"Hi Scoop," Henry said, thinking Scoop might have read one of his articles in the "Warrior" paper and called to congratulate him. He wasn't writing as well as when Scoop was helping him, but in his own opinion he was doing satisfactory. At least he was still having articles published in the school paper.

"I just found out that Central is going to be integrated next year and thought you could use some help with a story."

"Negroes are going to be at Central?"

"Yeah, that's what I heard from a very reliable source and this is the kind of thing I think you should be writing about. So what do you say?"

"Yeah, I guess...... are you sure your information is correct?"

"Are you questioning my nose for news?"

"No, it's just hard to believe that I'll be going to school with colored kids next year." Henry's mother glanced at Henry with a startled look on her face.

"Well believe it, and I need you to decide if you want to be the first to report on it?"

"Yeah, sure I do. How many Negroes will be at my school?"

"I don't know."

"Will white kids be assigned to colored schools?"

"Not next year, but soon."

"I hope I'm not one of the kids assigned to a Negro school."

"It would make a good story if you were. I'll pick you up tomorrow after school and we'll start to work on the story; is that alright?"

"Sure."

When Henry hung up, his mother immediately asked, "Who was that?"

"Scoop."

"What was he talking about?"

"He said Negroes will be attending Central next year."

"I don't want you getting involved in anything that has to do with integration, do you hear?"

"Yes, ma'am," Henry said.

Defying his mother's instructions, Henry met Scoop the next day after school.

"Where are we going?" Henry asked, getting into Scoop's car.

"We're going to Booker T. Washington High School."

"What are we going to do there?"

"You're going to interview some colored kids, about how they feel about being assigned to a white school."

Henry had never been to Booker T. Washington High School and was surprised how much the school resembled Central. A male student was crossing the school yard when Scoop said, "There's a black kid by himself. Interview him."

"Interview him?"

"If you're going to get the story right, you've got to interview people."

"Aren't you going with me?" Henry asked, suddenly frightened at the prospect of approaching a black stranger. The only black person Henry had ever talked to was the maid who worked at Marcie's house and that was years ago.

"It's your story, not mine. Go interview him."

"What do I say?"

"Ask him what he thinks about the possibility of going to a white school."

"What if he doesn't talk to me?"

"If you're going to be a reporter you have to be able to get people to talk even when they don't want to. If you don't hurry the kid is going to be gone."

By the time Henry got out of the car the black kid had reached the sidewalk and was half a block ahead of Henry.

Henry looked into the car at Scoop.

"Go on, hurry up," Scoop ordered.

"Hey, wait a minute," Henry hollered as he started to jog towards the black teenager.

The black kid looked back and saw Henry but continued to walk, wondering what a white boy was doing at Washington High School.

"Wait a minute."

The kid looked back again, realizing that Henry was hollering at him. He stopped, assumed a defensive position and waited for Henry. When the black student stopped Henry slowed to a walk and smiled, trying to appear friendly.

"Hi, my name is Henry. I go to Central High School."

The kid didn't respond.

"I write for the school newspaper and I'm working on an article about integration."

The kid still didn't say anything.

"I hear that our school is going to be integrated next year and I was wondering what you thought about that?"

"I don't think anything about it."

"What if you're one of the students assigned to Central, how would you feel?"

"I don't want to go to school with you, if that's what you're asking me."

"So in my article can I write that you don't want to go to a white school?"

"I don't want to go to a school with white kids. I just want as good of a school as white kids," he said, parroting what he had heard black adults say about the quality black education.

"What's wrong with your school?" Henry asked.

"The food isn't good." The boy said, having a very little or no knowledge in the difference between black and white schools.

"Okay," Henry said, writing some notes on a pad. "We had bologna cups today. What did you have?"

"We had bologna, but yours is better."

"How do you know it was better?"

"Everybody knows it is."

"We have Negro women cook our lunch. Who cooks your lunch?"

"Don't call us Negroes, we're black."

"Sorry, I didn't mean anything by it. But you don't like bologna cups?

"It's alright."

"What else don't you like about the school?"'

"You got better teachers."

"Then you want to have white teachers?"

"I didn't say that."

"Then you just want better Negro teachers?"

"We're black not Negroes."

"Sorry, I'm a little nervous," Henry admitted.

"There's no air conditioning," Trifecta said dropping the subject of teachers.

"Okay," Henry said, "but you're not going to have any air conditioning at Central either. Is there anything else?"

"Our books are second-hand from white schools. They got stuff written all over them."

"How do you know the books came from white schools?"

"They got Tech High School, East High, White Station and Central High School stamped in them."

"So you don't want to go to white schools, you just want better books, is that right?"

"Yeah."

"Where do you want to go to school?"

"I want to stay right here, at Washington."

"Can I quote you?"

"Yes."

"What's your name?"

"Why do you want to know my name?"

"So I can quote you."

"I'm Trifecta Johnson, but don't put my name in your paper."

Chapter 35

Henry Submits His Article

The sixth period was when the newspaper staff worked.

When Henry entered the newspaper room he saw his name written on the black board with the assignment to go out and sell ads for the paper. He went to Mrs. Turner's desk to receive a list of the businesses he was to call on. Mrs. Turner was the faculty advisor for the paper.

"I wrote a story," Henry said, handing her the two and a half handwritten pages of notebook paper.

"That's fine. I'll read it while you're out," Mrs. Turner said.

Knowing Henry didn't have a car Mrs. Turner gave him a list of retail stores on Union Avenue just east of Central High School.

Henry went by a couple of businesses but didn't have any luck selling ads so he hitchhiked home.

The next morning he stopped by the Huddle House Restaurant, which was a block from the school, to have a last cigarette and drink a Coke. Alan would frequently meet him there but he didn't show up that day. Finishing his Coke and cigarette, he arrived at school a few minutes before the first bell so he went looking for Lois.

"What have you done?" Lois asked.

"What?"

"What have you done?"

"I haven't done anything, why?"

"I heard you're in trouble because of something you wrote for the school paper."

"I submitted an article yesterday, but I don't think there was anything wrong with it. Scoop helped me write it. It's probably the best thing I've ever submitted."

The bell rang.

"I hope you're right. I love you regardless of what happens," Lois said as she walked away.

Henry went to home room, worried by what Lois said. When the class had finished the morning ritual of roll call, pledge of allegiance, daily Bible reading, and reciting the Lord's Prayer, a student came into the classroom and gave a note to Henry's homeroom teacher. After reading the note the teacher said, "Henry Murphy, you're wanted in the principal's office."

Henry's nerves were on edge as he walked to the office, unsure of his offense.

"Who told you Central High School was going to be integrated next year?" the principal asked Henry.

"I can't reveal my sources," Henry said, afraid he might get Scoop in trouble if he told.

"Who wrote this article?"

"I did."

"Don't lie to me young man."

"I'm not."

"Henry, you don't write this well, no student in this school writes this well. I don't write this well, so who wrote this article?"

"I had help, but I wrote it."

"Who helped you?"

"I can't say," Henry said.

"Did the person who wrote this article tell you Central High School was going to be integrated next year?"

"Is it?" Henry asked, following Scoop's advice on taking control of a conversation.

"Is it what?"

"Is Central going to be integrated next year?"

"I can't say."

"If it is going to be integrated then I shouldn't be in trouble for writing the truth, and if you refuse to tell me if Central is going to be integrated, then I can refuse to reveal my source."

"You're in trouble, son."

"For what?"

"Rabble rousing; now tell me your source."

"I can't reveal my source."

"You say in your article that you interviewed a Negro student. Who was the student and where did you conduct the interview?"

"I interviewed him at Booker T. Washington High School. I don't know his name," Henry lied, remembering how odd the name Trifecta sounded.

"Did your parents help you write the article?"

"No, sir."

"Where are your parents from?"

"Memphis."

"They were born in Memphis?"

"No sir."

"Where were they born?"

"My dad is from Florida; my mom was born in Canada."

"Canada?"

"Yes, sir."

"That even makes matters worst."

"Sir," Henry asked baffled how his mother being from Canada could be worse.

"Are you going to Canada when you graduate?"

"I guess I might go to Canada to visit my relatives."

"Are you going to Canada to dodge the draft?" The principal asked with disdain in his voice.

"No, sir."

"Are you willing to perform your patriotic duty, if you are drafted?"

"Yes, sir."

"Don't lie to me son, are your parents encouraging you to go to Canada to avoid being drafted?"

"No sir."

"Are your parents communists?"

"Sir?" Henry asked, dumbfounded by the disarray of questions.

"I asked, if your parents are communists?"

"No sir, why do you ask?"

"Because the article is the kind of thing a communist might write to disrupt this school and our society."

"I was doing some investigative reporting."

"Do you consider yourself an instigator?"

"No, sir."

"Then why did you write such a controversial article?"

"Because it's news that is socially significant."

"It sounds like propaganda to incite our students, and their parents."

"I'm just reporting what I was told."

"Do your parents vote?"

"My dad does. My mom's not a citizen."

"She's not?"

"No sir."

"Why not?"

"I don't know."

The principal continued his interrogation for almost an hour, insisting that Henry's article was written to sow discord in the school and community. Finally, he said, "If you don't tell me who told you Central is going to be integrated next year, and who helped you write your article, I'm afraid I am going to have to suspend you."

"Yes sir."

"You won't be able to make up the work you miss."

"Yes sir."

"Are you going to tell me?"

"No, sir," Henry said, remaining calm on the outside while anxiety was churning on the inside. He knew that if was suspended his parents would kill him.

When Henry left the principal's office, the principal immediately called the FBI, concerned that Henry's family had some communist connection. His call was taken by Agent Ball. Ball didn't have much interest in what the principal was reporting until he found out that Henry lived on Eastlawn Cove. He was a neighbor of the Davenports whose license plates were involved in the murder of Hercules Jones and the cross being burned in his yard. Henry Murphy immediately became a person of interest for Agent Ball in the unsolved homicide investigation that had grown cold.

When Henry told his mother he had been suspended for three days, she grounded him from talking on the phone for the three days he would miss school, and from leaving the house except to attend school and church for a month. His punishment was not as extensive as he had imagined

The next night, Agent Ball and two other agents visited the Murphy's home. At times, the family was interviewed together; other times they were questioned separately. They were asked about the theft of the Davenport's license plates, the murder of Hercules Jones, and the burning of the Apostolic House of Prayer. They were queried about their affiliation with white supremacy groups, civil rights organizations, and the Communist Party. They were asked where they were at precise times, on specific dates. At the end of the interrogations, the two agents accompanying Ball were convinced the Murphy's had not committed any crimes nor were they a threat to United States interests. Still, something didn't add up for Agent Ball. He was determined to keep an eye on Henry.

Chapter 36

The day Caledonia received the life insurance check

When G.W. arrived home from work Trifecta was sitting on Caledonia's back porch waiting for him.

"Madea wants to see you," Trifecta said as G.W. approached his apartment.

G.W. could tell something was bothering Trifecta. "What's wrong, son?" G.W. asked.

"The insurance money came today."

"That doesn't explain why you're so glum."

"They've been fighting ever since the white man brought the money."

"It'll be alright," G.W. said, patting Trifecta on the back. As he passed, Trifecta could smell the stench of garbage emanating from him.

G.W. hollered through the screen door, "Miss Caledonia," and Caledonia told him to come in.

"I've been blessed today," Caledonia said, apparently oblivious to G.W.'s rancid odor. "I received the insurance money for Tyrone."

174

"I certainly am happy for you, Miss Caledonia. Now what can I do for you?" G.W. asked, standing just inside the threshold.

"I was wondering if you'd mind taking me to the Tri State Bank so I can get my check cashed."

"I'd be glad to. Let me put on some clean clothes and I'll be right back."

After about thirty minutes, G.W. returned to Caledonia's apartment. Trifecta accompanied Caledonia and G.W. to the bank. It was the only black-owned bank in the city.

While Caledonia attempted to cash her check, G.W. and Trifecta stayed in the car in the bank's parking lot. Trying to get Trifecta's mind off his family problems, G.W. started talking about civil rights.

"Have you ever heard of James Meredith?" G.W. asked.

"Yes, I learned about him in school," Trifecta replied.

"What do you know about him?"

"I know he was the first black man to enroll in a white college in Mississippi."

"Did you know he is going to walk from here to Jackson, Mississippi, next week to protest racism and to show he's not afraid of the white people in Mississippi?"

"No."

"He's going to encourage colored folk to register to vote at the same time."

"So?"

"You know why he be going all the way to Jackson?"

"No."

"You know who Medger Evers is?"

"I know he was an NAACP man that the white people killed and burned his house."

"That's right, and he lived in Jackson, Mississippi. I suspect that's the reason James Meredith is going to walk all the way to Jackson."

"Are you going with him?" Trifecta asked.

175

"Not in body, but my spirit will walk every step of the way with him."

"Why don't you go?"

"I've got to work. I ain't hardly got enough money to feed my family now. I sure can't take off work, but I am proud of what James Meredith is doing."

Caledonia spent an hour trying to cash her check. Finally she had to open an account, and then she was told she would have to wait a week for the insurance check to clear before she could get her money. For the time it took Caledonia to take care of her business, G.W. impressed Trifecta with stories of James Meredith, Medger Evers, Martin Luther King Jr., and other Civil Rights leaders. While he shared the stories with Trifecta, he tried to instill the importance of Negroes voting. He insisted freedom would be won through ballots and not through violence.

*

That evening, Trifecta built up enough courage to speak with his mother about what she had planned to do about him.

"Baby, you got to understand. I have a chance to go to Detroit and make some money. I know a man who owns a bar. He said I could make big money working for him. He said I will do real well with the men who work in the factories. They will tip a woman like me real good."

"You're not going back to Chicago?"

"No baby, there are too many bad memories for me in Chicago. I need to get a new start.

"But what about me, Mama, will you take me with you?" Trifecta pleaded.

"Baby I want to, but that's no life for a boy."

"What about Marquis?"

"I talked to Madea. Since Willie is going with Josephine she said she will keep him. She said she's too old to care for a baby. I assured her you would help look after your little brother."

"Mama, Madea said she will give you $2000.00 if you take me with you."

"I don't know who told you that lie, but living in Detroit and working in a bar, isn't any place for a nice young man."

"Why do you have to go to Detroit? Why can't you work in Memphis?" Trifecta asked devastated because his mother lied to him about the money Caledonia had promised her.

"What would I do in Memphis?" she asked.

"Same as you do in Detroit. There's bars here, or you could go back to work for Ms. Churchill."

"Baby there isn't any money in this town for colored folks. We've got to go north if we're going to make a living."

"If you got a job in Memphis, would you stay?"

"If I could get a good job I'd stay," Mary lied.

The next day while everyone else was outside, Trifecta looked up the Churchill's number in the telephone directory. It took all the will power he could muster to dial the phone. He was prepared to beg for his mother's job.

"Hello?"

"Hello, Ms. Churchill?" Trifecta said.

"Who is this?" she asked.

"Trifecta Johnson."

"Who?"

"Trifecta Johnson, my Mama and I used to work for you."

"Oh yes," Mrs. Churchill said, trying to remember who he was. "What can I do for you?"

"My mama needs her job back."

"Who did you say you were, and who is your mother?"

"I'm Trifecta Johnson. My mama is Mary Johnson, don't you remember us?"

"I'm sorry son. I'm not sure. I've had so many Negroes work for me. I can't remember everyone."

"Can she have her job?"

"I don't need servants right now. I wish I could remember your mother."

"You fired her boyfriend. He cut your yard, and you caught him drinking on the job, and he and my mama moved to Chicago the next day."

"Oh yes, I remember who you are now. Trifecta, you are a fine young man and I wish you the best. However, if I needed a new servant, I don't think I would rehire your mother. That was a very unpleasant experience for me."

Trifecta didn't know what to say, so he slammed the phone into its cradle and stormed out of the apartment, almost hitting Caledonia with the door as she sat in a chair on the back porch.

"What's wrong with you now?" Caledonia asked.

"I hate white people," Trifecta whined.

"What white peoples do you hate?" Caledonia said unaware of any contact Trifecta had with white people other than an occasional clerk in the bargain basement of Shainberg's Department Store or some other business.

"I hate Ms. Churchill," Trifecta cried.

Mary, who was standing within ear shot, asked, "What do you mean you hate Ms. Churchill? You mean the Ms. Churchill that I used to worked for?"

"Yes, and I hate her."

"Why are you talking about Ms. Churchill?" Mary asked.

"I called her and asked her for your job back. She hardly remembers us. Then she said we were a most unpleasant experience for her."

"You did what?"

"I thought if you had a job, you would stay in Memphis with me."

"First off, I ain't about to do day work. I told you there's a man who wants me to come to Detroit. Don't you understand your mama needs to be with a man?"

Trifecta jumped to his feet, ran into the apartment, and slammed the door behind him.

Chapter 37

Spring 1966

Charity Ramble sat next to Henry in algebra class. She was considered to be weird by most of the student body. She was a self-professed, counter culture hippy chick in an ultra-conservative high school. At first glance she didn't appear to be pretty, but on occasions when Henry really looked at her and studied her features, she was cute. She never wore makeup, and the rumor on campus was she didn't wear a bra or shave her armpits. It was mandatory for a girl to wear a bra at school.

Contrary to the popular scuttlebutt, Charity shaved her underarms regularly. However, she didn't wear a bra for the first week of the school year. Based on Charity's slight bust line, the principal concluded the only place anyone would notice she wasn't wearing a bra was when she changed clothes for gym class. So he asked the girls' coach to discuss the school's dress code and personal hygiene with her.

Henry had just sat down in algebra class the day after completing his suspension when Charity looked at him, smiled, and said, "Hi."

"Hi," Henry replied, surprised because she rarely spoke to him.

"I hear you were suspended."

"Yeah,"

"I understand most of the teachers are pretty upset about what you wrote."

"Yeah, I'm not looking forward to the rest of the year, and I'm not sure how I'm going to catch up with the work I missed. I got a zero for the three days I missed in each of my classes"

"None of the teachers are going to help you with the work you missed?"

"No, I'm pretty much on my own."

The second bell rang, announcing the beginning of class.

"I'll try to help you, if you want."

"Ok," said Henry, not knowing what else to say.

"I think I can help you with English. I have Miss Carter and you do to, don't you?"

"Yes,"

"And we both have Mrs. Rosenberg for World History?"

"Yeah, but it's no big deal. I don't think there is any way I'm going to pass World History." Henry answered, not sure how she knew the teacher he had for his various subjects.

"Maybe you'll pass with my help. And of course, I can help you with algebra."

"Charity and Henry, do you mind if we begin class?" Mr. Sides said, standing in front of the class with his algebra book in hand.

Charity and Henry both turned towards the front of the classroom.

"Henry, I'm glad to see you back in class." Mr. Sides said sarcastically, thinking Henry was not only a poor student, but also a trouble maker. "I hope you know you have a lot of catching up to do."

"Yes, sir," Henry said.

"I think you probably need to give me your attention rather than listening to Miss Ramble." Even though Charity was an exceptional student, because of her counterculture appearance Mr. Side held her in distain.

"Yes, sir," Henry answered to a few more giggles in the classroom.

"Sally," Mr. Sides said to a girl in the front row, "will you take this note to the office for me?" Mr. Sides handed Sally a fold piece of paper. "The rest of you turn to page 153 and work the odd number problems. Fold your papers and put the answers on the outside, but show your work on the inside."

On her way to the principal's office, Sally opened the note and read as she walked.

Please send a lady to my classroom to measure the length of Charity Ramble's skirt; she and Henry Murphy seem to have developed a friendship.

When the class began solving algebra problems, Charity passed Henry a note: *Call me, so we can get together and catch up your school work. My number is 243-5303.*

Henry read the note and then stuffed it into his shirt pocket hoping Mr. Sides didn't see the exchange.

Henry was flattered that Charity was interested enough in him to help him catch up on his lessons. Nevertheless, he didn't have any intention of calling her. Hanging out with Charity, even doing homework with her, would push him lower on the social ladder than he already was. Plus, he was sure Lois would get mad at him. Anyway, he was sure Lois could help him with his algebra because she also had Mr. Sides for math.

Shortly after Sally returned to class, Miss Printup, the school's guidance counselor, entered Mr. Side's classroom, carrying a yard stick. Henry looked up to see Mr. Sides point to Charity. Miss Printup walked down the row of desks to Charity's seat; she was sitting in the fourth desk from the front.

"Charity, please stand up," Miss Printup said sternly.

Charity looked at her quizzically and slowly rose from her seat.

"Please get on your knees," Miss Printup said.

"Ma'am?"

"You heard me; kneel down as if you were praying. You do know how to pray, don't you?" Miss Printup asked sarcastically, assuming the hippie girl was an atheist, or practiced some bizarre eastern religion.

Embarrassed, Charity knelt, and Miss Printup used the yard stick to measure from the floor to the hem of Charity's skirt.

Stooping in order to see the measurement, Miss Printup announced, "Just as I suspected: your skirt is too short."

"Ma'am?"

"The Order of the Red Man, clearly states that your skirt can be no shorter than two inches above your knee, and your skirt is almost three inches above your knee. Do you have an explanation?" The actual measurement was an eighth of an inch shy of two and a half inches from knee to hem.

"I guess I grew an inch because when school started it was two inches," Charity said, so embarrassed by being reprimanded publicly that silent tears shimmered in her eyes.

Charity claimed she didn't care what other people thought of her, but when Miss Printup humiliated her in front of the class, she was crushed.

"Don't be disrespectful young lady," ordered Miss Printup, "Come with me to the office so I can send a note to your parents. Then you will have to go home until you can dress properly for school."

As she was leaving the room, some unidentified male voice from the back of the classroom said, "Free love" to a classroom full of snickers and giggles. Tears began to creep down Charities cheeks.

Charity's parents were professors at Memphis State University. There were rumors that they weren't married and Charity was their "love child." Somehow the faculty and some of the students learned that Charity's parents had radical political ideas, and were suspected to be communists, and advocates of the new morality. Even though Charity's actions had never given anyone reason to question her virtue, she was judged guilty by innuendo.

When they reached Miss Printup's office, Charity sat silently across the desk from the guidance counselor as she typed a note to Charity's parents.

"I doubt you'll be able to return to school before the end of the day," Miss Printup said, "But I expect you to be dressed appropriately for the remainder of the year. I understand your home life may not be as favorable as some of the other children in school. However, we do expect you to dress according to the school's standards."

Charity was about to ask what was wrong in her home life but Miss Printup kept talking. "As for Henry Murphy, I would think you need to choose your friends more carefully. He's a smoker; we understand he drinks alcohol, and he is friendly with Negroes."

"What's wrong with being friends with African Americans?" Charity challenged.

"Nothing, as long as they stay in their place, but Mr. Murphy seems to be insistent on changing our social order. And that, combined with his smoking and drinking, doesn't make him a suitable companion for a young lady. Nor is he a good citizen of Central High School."

Before Charity could offer a rebuttal, Miss Printup handed her the note and sent her home.

Henry struggled through about three-quarters of each math problem before he was completely lost; he received a zero for that day's work, giving him a zero for the fourth consecutive day.

By lunch, the main topic of discussion among teachers and students was Charity being sent home because she was a friend of Henry's.

"It's time you break up with him," a lunch table friend told Lois.

"She was sent home because her skirt was too short," Lois protested.

"Sally read the note Mr. Sides sent to the office. She said the real reason Charity was sent home is because she was talking to Henry. Others in the class said they were flirting so much that Mr. Sides had to tell them to be quiet."

"Who said they were flirting?" Lois asked the group.

"What would you call it? There's only one reason he would talk to that hippie, and we all know what that is," Lois's friend said, rolling her eyes toward the ceiling.

"You're liable to get expelled for being his girlfriend," interjected another girl.

"What do you think he's doing talking to that hippie girl anyway?" the first girl asked again.

"Free love," another girl answered.

"You're committing social suicide if you don't break up with him," a fourth girl said.

Chapter 38

The week following Tyrone's funeral

Trifecta remained moody for several days, saying very little to anyone, particularly to his mother.

Sensing despair in Trifecta, G.W. tried to spend some time with him each day. G.W. took him to cut a yard for some white people and split the five dollars he earned mowing grass with Trifecta. Another time he took him for a hamburger. While they were together, Trifecta's mood lightened as they talked constantly about the heroes of the civil rights movement. G.W. continued to impress and excite Trifecta with his knowledge of civil rights leaders past and present.

Caledonia's apartment was crowded and tension was high while waiting for the seven days to pass until the insurance check cleared the bank. On June 5th, the same-day James Meredith started his solitary march through Mississippi; G.W. took Caledonia, Trifecta, and Willie to the Tri State Bank. Caledonia's check had cleared and she opened a five-hundred dollar savings account for both Trifecta and Willie and gave each of them a twenty-dollar bill for spending money.

The next day, June 6, Trifecta went to a tailor shop on Vance Avenue and put a fifteen-dollar deposit on a pair of two-pocket bellbottom pants. He chose an iridescent material that faded from a green gold to a gold green, depending upon the angle a person looked at the cloth. It would be several days before the tailor could have the trousers made.

When he returned home Jeff and Levi were sitting on Caledonia's back porch talking with G.W.

"They killed him," Jeff said as Trifecta joined the group.

"Who killed who?" Trifecta asked.

"White folks killed James Meredith," Jeff answered.

"When did that happen?" Trifecta inquired.

"Earlier today; they shot him in the back," Jeff said.

"He was about twenty miles from here when it happened," G.W. added.

Later that evening, as Trifecta watched television, he learned that James Meredith had been shot several times with bird shot but he wasn't dead. He had been taken to William F. Bowld Hospital and was in satisfactory condition. There was film footage on the news of Meredith lying on the side of the road where he had been shot. The white man who shot him was arrested.

On June 7, several civil rights organizations, announced they were going to take up Meredith's march from the point where he was wounded. That same day, Josephine took Caledonia's four thousand dollars and went back to Tipton County with a promise that she would return in a few days to get Willie. She told Caledonia she had to make some living arrangements for him.

Caledonia gave Mary two hundred and fifty dollars. Mary was planning on taking a bus to Detroit the next day without Trifecta.

"Are you still mad at me?" Mary asked Trifecta.

Trifecta didn't answer.

"You need to try to understand. This is the only chance I have."

"It's the only chance you have to do what?" Trifecta mumbled.

"To be happy."

"Why can't you be happy in Memphis, with me?"

"You're too young to understand."

"I'm too young to understand what?" Trifecta demanded.

"What a woman like me needs."

They were both silent. Mary finally said, "Do you think you could find it in your heart to let your mama hold some of the money Madea gave you?"

"Why do you need the money?"

"I wasn't expecting Josephine to be here and I thought Madea would share the insurance money with me. Dante is going to be disappointed if I don't have more than two hundred dollars when I go back home."

"Who's Dante?"

"He's my man in Detroit."

"How long have you lived in Detroit?"

"For a while."

"How are we going to get to the bank?" Trifecta asked in a defeated tone.

"I'll find a way for us to get there tomorrow. But please don't tell Madea you're loaning me the money."

"Okay," he responded in disgust, knowing Mary would never repay him.

That afternoon Trifecta went downtown with G.W. to make a payment at the finance company. Trifecta was glad to get away from the projects and his mother. However, he was shocked when he and G.W. entered the finance company. Once inside the loan office, G.W.'s demeanor changed immediately. He went from being a man Trifecta admired to a buffoon. It was like a minstrel show, but instead of a black-faced white man, G.W. transformed into the stereotypical Negro.

As they entered the finance office two young ladies were sitting behind a counter. Behind the ladies were three white men sitting at a row of desks that lined the left wall. Closing booths, where contracts were signed and money was loaned, lined the right wall.

"Hi, G.W.," said one of the young ladies, immediately recognizing him.

G.W. let out a horselaugh. "How are y'all?"

One of the men stood up. "We've been waiting on you, G.W."

"Yes sir, yes sir. I know old G.W. is late."

A young man sitting at the front desk rifled through a stack of ledger cards he was using to make collection calls.

"Here's his account," he said to one of the girls. "I was about to call your wife," he said to G.W.

"No sir. You ain't got to do that, I told you I would be here, and here I am." G.W. was laughing again, as he spoke to a young man.

"There's going to be a late charge," the young man spoke up again.

"I know. Old G.W. doesn't mind paying what he owes."

"You're a good boy," the young man said.

Trifecta cringed when the pubescent guy who was probably twenty years G.W.'s junior called G.W. a boy. However, G.W. wasn't fazed by the insult as he kept a ridiculous grin on his face.

"You have another payment due in two weeks," the young man said.

"I know," G.W. replied. "But you ain't got to call my wife. I'll be here. I may be a little late, but you don't have to worry about old G.W.," he said, continuing to laugh.

The five white people smiled at G.W. as he continued his Uncle Tom persona.

When they left the finance company G. W. immediately reverted to his customary demeanor but he noticed Trifecta was uncommonly quiet.

"Is something wrong?" G.W. asked.

"Nothing is wrong," Trifecta mumbled.

The next stop was a furniture store where G.W. had to pay a bill. When they entered the store a white salesman hollered across the store, "Hey, G.W."

G.W. reacted with the same goofy house boy grin he had at the finance company.

"How are y' all?" G.W. said with a wide silly smile.

They walked to the rear of the store to make the payment. The cashier was a young attractive black woman. G.W.'s manner changed again as he politely paid his bill.

"Mr. Smith, there is a late charge due with this payment."

"Yes, ma'am, I have the money," G.W. replied in a very businesslike manner, handing the lady some cash.

Back in the car, Trifecta and G.W. drove several minutes in silence before G.W. asked, "What's the matter?"

"Nothing."

"There must be something wrong. You haven't said a word since we've been in the car."

"Why do you act like that?" Trifecta snapped.

"Why do I act like what?"

"Why, do you act like a fool?"

"What do you mean?"

"When you're around white people, you act crazy."

"That's the way they expect me to act. If I don't act like that, they think I'm uppity."

"So, let them think it."

"You don't understand. When colored folks get uppity they get hurt. See, your problem is you haven't been around enough white folks. But I know how to handle them and I been doing just fine."

"I'm not going to act like a fool just because I'm around white people."

"I hope you never have to, but I wouldn't count on it," G.W. said, his feelings hurt by Trifecta's reaction.

189

When G.W. and Trifecta got back to the Gardens, Trifecta got out of G.W.'s car without a word and slammed the car door, displaying his disrespect for what had happened. He went straight to Levi's house. He found Jeff and Levi in the bedroom they shared.

"What are you uptight about?" Jeff asked as Trifecta entered the room with a pout on his lips and hate in his eye.

"I'm mad at Mama, at G.W., and at white people," Trifecta said as he recounted the experience he had with G.W.

"I hear you," Jeff responded. "Tell you what I'm going to do."

"What?"

"I'm going to march."

"You're going to march where?"

"I'm going to be in the March Against Fear. I just need a way to get to Hernando, Mississippi, by tomorrow. You want to go?"

"I don't know."

"Look man, if you're as angry as you say. It's time you did something," Jeff challenged.

"Are you going?" Trifecta asked Levi.

"No, Mama won't let me," Levi answered.

"Mama's not letting him go because she's afraid there's going to be trouble, but she's not stopping me. This is the opportunity I've been waiting for. Are you coming or not?" Jeff persisted.

"I don't know," Trifecta answered.

"You don't know? Man, we've been talking about this for years. This is our chance to get involved in the movement and all of a sudden you don't know?"

"How are we going to get to Hernando?" Trifecta asked, hoping Jeff didn't have an answer, and the idea would be dropped.

"How about your friend, G.W.? He's got a car."

"I told you, we're mad at each other."

"You need to cool it. We got to prove to white people we're not going to take what they're dishing out. So you go convince G.W. to take us to Hernando."

"I don't know."

"You're just like the rest of these people in the projects. You do a lot of big talking but you don't want to do anything. If you don't want white people pushing you around the rest of your life you need to go tell G.W. he's takin' us to Hernando."

Chapter 39

The day Henry returned from suspension continued

Lois hated being without a boyfriend. However, the girls at lunch had applied enough pressure that she had no choice. She prepared a note for Henry before she went into art class. When he took his seat across from her it was obvious that Lois was disconcerted. When she continued to be sullen while working on her project he asked her if something was wrong. With a phony smile, she responded, "Everything is fine."

When the bell rang, Lois gathered her books, handed Henry a folded note, and almost ran from the classroom. Henry anticipated that the note contained some bad news so he went to the restroom to read it.

Stepping into a stall, he lit a cigarette. Few people had spoken to Henry all day and he had heard a few racial slurs directed at him. Many within the student body unfairly judged him without reading his article. Scoop had warned him the public frequently blamed the reporter for the news.

When the second bell rang and the restroom emptied Henry stayed behind, leisurely finishing his cigarette. He opened the note.

Henry,
I hope we can still be friends, but the pressures of the past few days have made me realize it might be better if we broke up for a while. I hope you accomplish whatever it is you're trying to do, and maybe we can get back together when you have achieved your goal.
Love,
Lois

Henry finished his cigarette and then took out his pencil and wrote at the bottom of the note.

I thought you said you loved me regardless of what happened. What happened?
Henry

Henry went to Lois's locker and pushed the note partially into the vent in the door of the locker, leaving a corner of the paper exposed so Lois would see it. Then he left school, skipping his remaining classes, and walked home.

It took him two hours to walk home. The first hour he muttered a salvo of angry words and insults under his breath about Lois. The second hour his thoughts volleyed between Marcie and Charity. The more he thought about Charity the more excited he became.

By the time he arrived home he was no longer upset that Lois broke up with him, and he was anticipating a romance with Charity. Even though he was aroused by daydreaming about Charity, he was concerned what Marcie would think about him dating a hippie.

"Remember you're grounded Henry, so go ahead and do your homework and maybe you can watch a little television later tonight before you go to bed," Henry's mother said when he arrived home.

"That's the problem, Mom. I only missed three days, but it has really put me behind. A girl in my algebra class has offered to help me catch up," Henry said, joining his mother in the kitchen.

"Who is this girl?"

"Her name is Charity Ramble."

"It's awfully nice of a girl to help you with your homework when you already have a girlfriend."

"That's the kind of person she is."

"What does Lois think about her helping you?"

"She's okay with it." Henry said, not wanting to make a big deal out of Lois breaking up with him.

"Is this girl going to help you at school or where?"

"I'm not sure. I think she wants me to go to her house or maybe she'll come here. I planned on checking with you and dad before I made plans."

"Ask her if she minds coming over here; we'll let you use the car to pick her up and take her home."

Preparing to call Charity, Henry's anxiety rose. Even though she told him to call he was afraid she might have changed her mind, because he felt it was his fault she was sent home. Taking a deep breath, he dialed the phone.

Charity answered the phone on the third ring.

"Hi, this is Henry."

"Hi Henry,"

"I'm sorry about what happened to you today," Henry said, referring to Charity's embarrassment with her skirt.

"It wasn't your fault."

"That's not what everyone is saying. The word around school is they sent you home because you were talking to me before class and they are punishing you because they think you're my friend."

"That's silly, but I would like to be."

"You would like to be what?"

"I would like to be your friend."

"That's cool. I would like to be friends with you too." Henry said trying to flirt.

"Far- out," Charity said happily.

"I was wondering if you were serious when you said you would help me catch up on my algebra."

"Sure, I think it's stupid that they suspended you for writing a story about African Americans."

"I had no idea it was such a big deal. But the thing is I'm grounded because I got suspended and I was wondering if you could come over here."

"Alright, but I don't know where you live."

"I live on Eastlawn Cove, but I can come get you."

"That's fine. Is tomorrow night alright?"

"Yea, I'll probably get another zero in class tomorrow, but I bet you got a zero today too."

"Probably, but it's no big deal, I've got a 98 average in algebra and I'm doing real well in the other classes I missed. So I'm not worried about my grades."

"That's great; by the way, did you get in trouble with your folks for being sent home?"

"No, as a matter of fact my parents got pretty mad at the school and my dad is going to meet with the principal tomorrow."

"It blows my mind that your dad would take your side over the principal's."

"He believes in free expression and he thinks they were being unfair to single me out."

"You don't think that will make things harder for you at school?"

"If it does my dad will go to the Board of Education. He loves to fight the system."

Chapter 40

The evening before the start of March Against Fear

A wave of emotions swept over Trifecta, leaving him feeling weak as he walked through the projects to humble himself before G.W. and ask him for a ride to Hernando.

"I'd love to help you, Trifecta, but I've got work tomorrow. You heard the man at the finance company. I've got another payment due in two weeks."

G.W. was more forgiving than Trifecta expected. He didn't mention the words that passed between them earlier in the day.

"I'll give you fifty dollars. That's more than you'll make picking up garbage tomorrow, isn't it?" Fifty dollars was more than G.W. brought home in a week of collecting trash.

"Does Miss Caledonia know what you're planning?"

"It will be alright with my mama," Trifecta said. "Madea doesn't have any say when my mama is here. So do you want to earn the money or not?"

"I don't want to take your money."

"I can either pay you or someone else, but I'm going to Hernando."

"If your mama says you can go, I'll take you."

That night both Mary and Caledonia forbade Trifecta to participate in the March Against Fear because of the anticipated violence.

When Trifecta was alone with Mary, he persuaded her to let him join the march by threatening to withhold the money he promised to give her. When Mary agreed to let him participate in the march, Trifecta assured his mother that he would loan her the three hundred and fifty dollars.

The next morning G.W. chauffeured Mary, Trifecta, and Jeff to the Tri State Bank. Trifecta closed his account, withdrawing the entire five hundred dollars. Even though he had no idea where Jackson, Mississippi was, or how long it would take to get there, he did have the foresight to keep a hundred dollars to cover expenses during the march. He paid G.W. fifty dollars and gave his mother three hundred and fifty dollars.

Jeff only had fifteen dollars in his pocket when he got into G.W.'s car to go to Hernando.

G.W. took Mary to the bus station, then headed south on Highway 51. Arriving in Hernando, there was no sign of the march. For the first time since leaving Lemoyne Gardens, Trifecta's excitement turned to anxiety as they slowly circled the town square looking for evidence of the march. White people glared at them and Trifecta slumped in the backseat. Continuing south on Highway 51, G.W. stopped at an unpainted wood-framed country store with two black men sitting on the front porch. Apparently Jeff was as intimidated by the ride through Hernando as Trifecta, because neither said a word until G.W. returned to the car.

"They say several hundred marchers are probably a few miles down the road by now. He warned me that some white folks round here ain't happy about what is going on. Fact is they say that the colored folk already arranged for the deacons to participate in the march."

Sensing some apprehension, G.W. asked, "You boys sure you want to do this? It's not too late to turn back?"

Trifecta had the urge to return home, but Jeff spoke first. "We're going through with it."

"Who are the deacons?" Trifecta asked.

"They call themselves the Deacons of Defense and Justice. They are a group of ex-soldiers. They carry guns for self-defense and to protect other colored folks from the Ku Klux Klan and similar white people," G.W. responded. "So I expect they are preparing for trouble."

It took five minutes to catch up with a small group of people who were straggling behind the main body of protestors.

"You boys stay together and try to stay with a big group. Don't get caught out alone by some white people," G.W. said, cutting his head around towards Trifecta.

"I hear you," Trifecta responded quietly.

"I'm serious, Trifecta, don't get caught by yourself."

"I won't."

As they came to the main body of the march, G.W. saw a dirt road off the main highway.

"I'm going to let y'all out up here. Are you sure this is what you want to do?"

Even in the ninety plus degrees of a June day in Mississippi, Trifecta felt a chill as his stomach fluttered and his arms and face tingled. "We're sure," Trifecta said meekly.

G.W. turned off the road and then turned around in the seat towards Trifecta. He handed him a piece of paper. "Here's my phone number, if you need me, you call me and I'll come and get you." Trifecta took the piece of paper, feeling sorry for the way he had spoken to G.W. the previous day. With the fear he now felt, he began to empathize with the older man. With weak knees, he got out of the car, carrying a brown gym bag Caledonia insisted he take. Stuffed in the small bag was one clean pair of underwear, a pair of socks, a toothbrush, toothpaste, a bar of soap, a can of baby powder (in case he chaffed), a roll of toilet paper, a sandwich, and a quart mayonnaise jar full of water.

"If you ain't got clean drawers, you're not marching anywhere," Caledonia lectured. "You'll be sitting on the side of the road rubbing your sore butt. That's why I gave you the baby powder in case you get heat on your privates." Caledonia took a breath. "And another thing, I've been in the Mississippi cotton fields enough to know you better have some water if you're going to be in the sun all day."

As Trifecta and Jeff crossed the road and joined the march, Trifecta looked over his shoulder to watch G.W. drive back onto Highway 51 and motor north toward Memphis. He suddenly felt alone even though he was walking in a crowd of people.

Highway 51 was like a furnace. Still, as Trifecta walked he began to relax. The people around him were talking, laughing, singing and sweating. He was surprised to see a smattering of white people in the march. While whites were an extreme minority, their presence was evident in the crowd.

Trifecta and Jeff began their trek with exuberance but after hiking for two hours the romance of participating in the march was gone and the reality of a two-hundred-mile journey set in. The road seemed endless. Its long rolling inclines stretched into the horizon. The pavement radiated heat. The sun was harsh and glaring. Shade from the shadows of trees was sparse. Both boys were soon bedraggled with sweat.

Even as Trifecta's energy was waning he was determined to keep going, thinking how cool the other kids at school would think he was for having actively participated in a civil rights protest. Being a child from the city and especially the projects, Trifecta witnessed things he had never seen before; farm animals, crops growing in the field, groups of black field hands cultivating the land with hoes, small squalid tenant shacks with young black children wearing scraps of patched and torn clothing, playing in yards with no grass. He was quickly developing a new appreciation for where

Caledonia and G.W came from, and the hardships of being a sharecropper. While Lemoyne Gardens wasn't the best place to call home, he now realized that there were far less desirable places live.

Everyone who participated in the march didn't walk the entire way; some would join the march as it passed through their town and others would march for an hour or two, others for a whole day, some multiple days. On weekends the number of marchers always swelled. People carried various sizes of American flags, others carried signs with "freedom now" printed on them. Others carried signs with "UAW" stamped on it, or other Unions that supported the March Against Fear. The Black Panther sign read, "Move over, or we'll move you over." The Mississippi Freedom Democratic party signs said, "MFDP supports the march for freedom." Some signs simply read, "James Meredith March through Mississippi, March Against Fear." Some placards were professionally printed while others were homemade. Jeff proudly carried a Black Panther sign.

When they passed through a town, both blacks and whites lined the highway. Some were well- wishers others were detractors. The well-wishers waved American flags and shouted encouragement. Others were simply smiling and waving. Often, there seemed to be a greater number of opponents than supporters. The adversaries of the march often waved Confederate flags and heckled the marchers. White supremacist constantly concerned Trifecta. In every town there was always a large number of police, highway patrol and National Guard. While Trifecta walked he hoped and prayed that there wouldn't be any trouble with white people.

In one unincorporated community, Trifecta was walking on the side of the road when he noticed a small white child wearing a Confederate cap, waving a plastic whiffle ball bat in the air. As Trifecta walked past the boy, he heard the boy's father say, "Get you one." The boy immediately cocked the bat and hit Trifecta with all of his might. The blow stung but didn't hurt. The boy cocked the bat again and began to swing but Trifecta snatched the bat out of the boy's hand and threw the bat to the ground. Instantly, the boy's father was in Trifecta's face, hollering and screaming threats, obscenities, and racial slurs.

Immediately, a young white man wedged himself between Trifecta and the furious father. The young man sucker punched the father with an upper cut. Another white man who Trifecta guessed was a friend of the boy's father approached as the father lay on the ground. He was met with a punch squarely on the nose by the left fist of the young guy. The blow landed him on his butt. By the time the father was back on his feet a large highway patrolman was standing between him and his assailant. The highway patrolman had his truncheon in his right hand, and it pressed against the angry father's chest. His left hand was restraining the young man.

"Bernie, there isn't going to be any trouble here today. I want you to go home," the patrolman said to the father.

"This punk slugged me," the father replied. Then he spat a stream of blood out of his mouth.

"I saw the whole thing, Bernie. You can either go home, or you can go to jail. It's your choice."

"Are you going to take that outside agitator to jail?" Bernie asked pointing at the younger man.

"That's none of your business, but there isn't going to be any trouble here today. Get your boy and Hal and go home," the patrolman said, pointing his Truncheon at the man sitting on the ground with blood leaking from his nose.

"You ain't heard the last of this, Rick," Bernie said to the patrolman. "You're not supposed to be taking a Yankee's side against me." Bernie took his son's hand, and they walked away while Hal got to his feet and trailed behind them.

The patrolman continued holding the young man's shirt in his fist. He pointed his nightstick at the crowd of marchers who had gathered to see what was going on. "There isn't anything happening for you folks to see. If you're here to march, then get marching. If you can't demonstrate peacefully, then go home." The crowd moved away.

"You go ahead and march," the patrolman said, releasing the man's shirt with a substantial shove. "But don't ever let me see you around these parts again. You understand?"

The man didn't say anything; he just looked the patrolman squarely in the eye as he backed down the road.

When Trifecta and Jeff started walking again, the young fellow came beside them. He asked, "Are you okay?"

"I'm fine, thanks for helping out," Trifecta said.

"My name is Peter. Peter Smith," Peter Golovach said flashing a smile.

Trifecta shook the man's hand, wondering where he was from. He had a slight accent, definitely not from around Mississippi.

Probably a northerner, Trifecta thought.

Chapter 41

The second day Henry returned to school

The next day at school Charity wore a tiered peasant dress that extended below her knees. It had a low neckline that should have attracted more attention than the previous day's hemline except Charity's breasts were so flat the neckline caused little controversy. Before Algebra class began Charity told Henry her parents did meet with the principal and he assured her parents that Charity would be treated fairly. In light of all the rumors and wrangling that had emerged the previous day, Henry hoped there would be no further repercussions caused by their conversation. Charity didn't seem concerned. However, when the second bell rang she stopped talking and gave Mr. Sides her attention.

That evening Henry's mom allowed Henry to use the family car to pick up Charity with the understanding that Henry was to bring her right back to the Murphy house to study.

Meeting Charity's parents was an unusual experience for Henry; they were definitely bohemians. Charity's mother had fairly long hair, but Mr. Ramble's hair was longer than his wife's, and his face was accessorized with a beard and mustache. Both parents wore blue jeans, love beads and sandals. Incense was burning in the living room, making the air smell sweet and feel sticky. Henry thought the Rambles were cool because unlike other adults they made him feel like an equal.

Leaving the Rambles, Henry held the passenger door open for Charity to get into the car. She was wearing bell-bottomed blue jeans with tattered cuffs, a tunic top, love beads, American Indian moccasins, and a leather headband with three strands of beaded tassels dangling along the right side of her head. She dressed more like a rock and roll singer than a Central High School student. Henry was sure his mother wouldn't approve.

After a few minutes of small talk about school charity asked, "What's the real story?"

"The real story about what?"

"You being suspended."

"I don't know what the big deal is. I interviewed a colored kid…"

"Black," interrupted Charity.

"What?"

"They want to be called black, or African Americans."

"When did that happen?"

"That's what they want to be called."

"Okay, I interviewed a black kid on how he felt about integrating Central."

"Is Central going to be integrated?"

"Yes."

"Far-out; what did the black kid say?"

"He didn't seem very enthusiastic about coming to Central."

"That's a shame. I've been thinking I might go to an African American school. I might go to Booker T. Washington, Melrose, or Hamilton."

"Are you crazy, a white girl going to an all-black school?"

"Why do you say that?"

"How do you think they're going to treat a white girl at a Negro school?"

"Black."

"Okay, how do you think a white girl will be treated in a black school?"

"I imagine you think all blacks are sex crazed and I would be raped every day," Charity said with a sweet but sarcastic tone to her voice.

"Well, yeah; that's what I've heard about colored…I mean black people, but either way I don't think you would be treated very well."

"Why, because white people don't treat blacks fairly, you don't think they would treat me fairly?"

"I don't know why they would mistreat you; but I think they would."

"I don't think I would be treated any worse than I'm treated at Central."

"What do you mean?"

"Kids at Central don't like anyone who's different from them. If you don't rat your hair, wear wraparound skirts, blouses with Peter Pan collars, a circle pin and a charm bracelet, no one will have anything to do with you. You just found that out as soon as you started supporting integration. The real reason they suspend you is because you don't think exactly the way they want you to think."

"Wait a minute," interrupted Henry. "I didn't say I supported integration, I was just writing an article about Central being integrated and the perspective of a black kid." Henry was suddenly conscious he was wearing a button-down collared shirt, khaki pants and brown penny loafers, just like ninety-five percent of the other boys at Central.

"When is Central going to be integrated? Charity asked.

"Next year, I think."

"It's about time; Memphis State has been integrated for years and so have some elementary schools; but how do you know Central is going to be integrated next year?"

"A good reporter never reveals his sources," Henry answered with a smirk.

"If you don't support integration, why did you write the article?"

"Its news and Scoop told me I needed to write about real news rather than stories about mediocre high school athletic teams."

"I'm down with that, but who's Scoop?"

"It's a long story and my mom blames him for me being suspended so I'll have to tell you later," Henry said as he pulled into the driveway of his house.

Henry was correct; at first glance he could tell his mother didn't approve of Charity or the way she dressed. However, like magic, everything changed. Charity related to adults the same way her parents had related to him, and using her charm and manners, Charity quickly won over his mother's heart.

Henry's mother was in the kitchen washing dishes and cleaning while Charity and Henry sat at the kitchen table working algebra equations. Mrs. Murphy was impressed at how sweet and patient Charity was as she tried to help Henry understand the work he had missed.

Charity and Henry worked on algebra for about forty-five minutes and when they finished Mrs. Murphy offered to fix Cokes and popcorn for them. Automatically, Charity was up from the table helping Mrs. Murphy prepare the snacks. Mrs. Murphy sat down at the kitchen table, drank a Coke and ate popcorn with Henry and Charity. Henry started to feel out of place as the two women continued to talk to each other, almost ignoring him. Henry was surprised because Charity and his mother laughed and talked like they were old friends.

When Henry was ready to take Charity home, Charity hugged his mother and Henry was dumbfounded when his conservative father let the little hippie chick hug him.

On the way to Charity's house, Henry gave her the lowdown on Scoop. When the kids arrived at Charity's house, Henry walked her to the door and she hugged him goodnight. Charity meant the hug as a sign of friendship, but Henry was delighted by the embrace and convinced himself it was a sign of affection.

Driving home alone, Henry listened to Randy and the Radiants on the radio and thought about Charity. She wasn't nearly as pretty as Marcie, and not even as cute as Lois. However, she was cool. Not cool in the same way as Marcie was cool, but she was cool. He wondered what Marcie thought about Charity, and then he thought about Marcie the rest of the way home.

Henry had no problem with the math equations he was assigned to work the next day. Mr. Sides was stymied when Henry made a hundred percent on his daily work.

For the second night in a row, Charity returned to Henry's house and helped him catch up on the lessons he missed in English class. She wore a tie-dyed tee-shirt, blue jeans and cowboy boots. Henry wasn't sure how he felt about the tie dye, but her attire didn't seem to bother his mother.

Chapter 42

The March Against Fear

Several days into the demonstration Trifecta and the other marchers arrived at the outskirts of a small delta town. They were fatigued and many were becoming irritable from the inescapable heat, sore feet, and aching backs caused by the drudgery of endless walking. The mood of many marchers was further despoiled by concerns of entering a racially bigoted burg where any and all civil rights activity had been quickly squelched and oftentimes thwarted violently.

"I've heard the old men talk about this place," Jeff said as he walked with Trifecta and Peter.

"It's typical of most towns around here," Peter answered. "The blacks live in shacks on dirt roads, without indoor plumbing while the whites live in brick or well-painted houses on paved streets lined with shade trees."

"I heard they still lynch black folk just like they did a hundred years ago," Jeff said.

"You and Trifecta don't have anything to worry about as long as you stay with me," Peter assured his two companions.

"Why, do you say that?" Trifecta asked.

"This is why," Peter said, displaying the nasty little derringer pistol he used to murder Hercules Jones.

"In fact, we don't need to wait for these rednecks to start trouble. I think we should go ahead and burn this racist town to the ground," Peter said, putting his weapon away.

Moving closer to the business district, Peter continued speaking louder, making threats against the town and its white residents in an attempt to instigate the crowd to violence. The more boisterous Peter became the more embarrassed Trifecta was walking next to him. Peter picked up a rock slightly smaller than a baseball as they were passing in front of a line of stores with plate glass windows.

"I wonder what would happen if a rock busted out a window or two? What would the bigots do then? They can't lynch us all."

Several marchers were looking distrustfully at Peter when a large black man wrapped a country strong hand around Peter's arm.

"We're here to demonstrate against fear, not to create fear, so don't do anything to make me ashamed of you," the black man with the vice grip on Peter's said. The man was a head taller and obviously much more powerful than Peter.

Flushed by embarrassment, Peter dropped the rock he had intended to throw and silently continued to walk.

To the bewilderment of the white city fathers, the number of blacks participating in the demonstration swelled as the crowd of protestors gathered in the town square. In an attempt to prevent their black citizens from participating or even being sympathetic to the protest, the white politicians of the town, made several promises they had no intention of keeping. The city leaders had vowed that all public facilities, including the library, restrooms, and water fountains would be available to blacks. They also hired four black registrants to promote black voter registration.

Despite the promised concessions, local blacks attended the protest and brought a new enthusiasm to the road-weary throng. As the crowd swelled, the speakers became bolder and more zealous, several calling for black power.

In the exuberance of the event an American flag was placed on the Confederate monument and more than thirteen hundred blacks were registered to vote. While this enraged many whites, the city's leaders maintained control and there were no obvious repercussions until the march proceeded peacefully towards Jackson. With the demonstrators gone, the American flag was removed from the Confederate monument. The four black registrants were fired. Seven hundred of the recently registered black voters were disqualified on a legal technicality, and the 1964 Civil Rights Act was again ignored.

These actions prompted a black boycott of white businesses referred to as a "blackout." The "blackout" gained national attention and created additional tension between the city's black and white populations.

In a town farther south, the plan was for the marchers to spend the night in the yard of a black elementary school. However, local police informed the marchers they had to have permission from the Board of Education to camp on the property. Several blacks argued the school ground was public property and they couldn't be denied the right to stay there overnight. The police disagreed, and one of the black leaders who was particularly vocal and had worked in the town's SNCC office for two years was jailed. The arrest angered many of the demonstrators, but Trifecta and some others were as scared as they were mad.

As soon as the police left, Peter started talking to a small group of young men about breaking the arrested man out of jail. Trifecta was becoming concerned that Peter was just trying to stir up trouble, but because Peter and Jeff were becoming increasingly friendly, Trifecta kept his thoughts to himself. He overheard other people saying they objected to whites participating in their march, and they particularly didn't appreciate people like Peter trying to usurp leadership.

Peter's plans for a jail break were generally ignored and the leader was released that same evening to rejoin the marchers who had moved to a nearby park.

Trifecta and Jeff missed the arrested man's speech after being released from custody, because they took the opportunity to go into a black neighborhood and buy some new clothes. They had worn the same clothes for eight days, and while they tried to rinse them out every night, they both needed something else to wear.

When Trifecta and Jeff joined the marchers at the park, they were met by a wild-eyed and excited Peter.

"Man, you guys missed it. It was really cool. He talked about being united and about being proud of who we are. He called for an end to white supremacy and for the beginning of black power. He said he's been arrested for the last time and he wasn't going to jail any more. He said we needed to burn down every courthouse in Mississippi. And when he had finished speaking another guy shouted, "What do you want?" and many in the crowd raised their fists and shouted back Black Power!" Peter raised his fist in the air as an illustration of what the others had done.

Trifecta thought it was strange that Peter was speaking like he was a black man; however, Jeff appeared to be enamored with everything the white boy said.

Not all of the marchers, including many of the organizers, were enthusiastic about the speech. Rather than uniting the marchers, the speech seemed to bring division between those advocating non-violence and those espousing Black Power.

One evening when Peter and Jeff had wandered off from the campground like they had done almost every night since they met, the large black man who had prevented Peter from throwing rocks and causing trouble warned Trifecta that he needed to be careful of Peter and Jeff. "Not everyone who appears to be for the movement really supports the movement," he cautioned. He also told Trifecta that he needed to stay away from drugs. When Trifecta said he didn't have any interest in drugs the man nodded in the direction of Jeff and Peter. Trifecta saw what appeared to be the glow of cigarettes, and for the first time he realized Jeff and Peter were burning a doobie. As Trifecta leaned back on his cot, a wave of disappointment and confusion enveloped him, his stomach began to hurt, and he wished he could go home.

Chapter 43

Henry and Charity at the Bitter Lemon

With Charity's help Henry's school work was quickly brought up to date and he was making better grades than ever. Because Mrs. Murphy liked Charity so much she agreed to give Henry a reprieve and let him go with her to the movies a week before his grounding sentence was over. When Henry was about to walk out the door his mother asked, "You've met Charity's parents, haven't you?"

"Yes, ma'am."

"What are they like?"

"A lot like you and dad," Henry lied.

"I just wish they had a better taste in the way they let Charity dress. I think she could be a really cute girl if she cut her hair and wore some decent clothes."

Henry arranged to meet Charity at the Memphian Theater at 6:45. The theater was about a fifteen-minute walk from Henry's house. Henry arrived at the movie at 6:35 and smoked a cigarette as he waited by the box office for her to arrive. At 6:40, Mr. Ramble pulled up to the curb in front of the theater. Charity got out of the car with a bright smile. Her dad remained parked in front of the theater.

Charity was wearing her tunic top, black leotards, and several strands of love beads.

"Hi," Henry said.

"Hi," said Charity. "What are we going to do?"

"I thought you wanted to see a movie."

"It's just two reruns, "Beach Party" and "Beach Party Bingo.""

"So you don't want to see the movies?"

"Not really. I'm not crazy about beach movies."

"I'm sorry. I thought you wanted to go to the movies."

"No, I just want to be with you."

Henry blushed with embarrassment as he imagined some sexual tension between them.

"What do you want to do?" Henry asked.

"Furry Lewis is playing at the Bitter Lemon."

"Who?" Henry asked.

"Furry Lewis, a Memphis Blues Man. I think it would be cool to go see him."

"Okay," said Henry, "but I have to be home by 10:30. I'm supposed to be grounded, you know."

"No problem. The Bitter Lemon isn't any further from your house it's just in a different direction and my dad will take us there."

The Bitter Lemon was a coffee shop located about a mile east of Henry's house.

There was a dollar-fifty cover charge for the night's performance.

Charity and Henry were early for the show which began at seven thirty, so they were able to get a table close to the small stage.

A waitress took their order for two coffees. The menu was limited to coffee, passion fruit, and pizza. Charity warned Henry that the passion fruit was nothing more overpriced orange juice garnished with a paper umbrella.

Furry Lewis was a small man with missing teeth. He wore a straw fedora, a thread bare suit, and tie. He sat on a stool and played a well-traveled acoustic guitar and a bottleneck slide on his pinky finger. He sang without further accompaniment. Between songs he told humorous stories, oftentimes making himself the butt of the joke. Henry had a hard time understanding what he was singing about or even saying, but Charity was enraptured by the old black man.

Furry finished his second set at 10:15, singing *Good Morning Judge*; a song in which he tells about being arrested for forgery even though he can't write his own name.

"I need to leave for home," Henry said. "Will you be alright by yourself?"

"Sure, but I'll call dad, and we'll take you home," Charity said.

"No, I don't want you to miss the rest of the show."

"Let me walk you out."

Once they were outside, Charity smiled up at Henry. "I had a wonderful time tonight," Charity said, standing on the sidewalk with Henry.

"Me too," Henry said.

Charity leaned into Henry. In anticipation Henry moved closer toward her, but to his disappointment she limited him to an impotent kiss.

"Be careful going home," Charity said with a smile, as she broke their brief embrace.

"Good night," Henry said, and Charity disappeared into the coffee house.

Henry was walking home, wishing Charity would be more affectionate, when he heard a man call his name. The voice came from a car parked in front of the Bar-B-Q restaurant that Henry was passing by.

Distracted by his thoughts, Henry hadn't noticed the person sitting in the dark interior of the vehicle. When the man stepped out of the car Henry recognized it was agent Ball.

"I'm late. I've got to get home," Henry said.

"Get in the car, I'll take you," Ball said.

"That's alright, I don't live far. I can walk."

"Get in the car, son, we need to talk," Ball ordered.

Reluctantly, Henry got in the front seat next to Ball.

For the short but slow ride home, Henry was interrogated about his association with civil rights activists, hippies, and communists. Ball also questioned him about the article he wrote regarding Central being integrated. Every question Henry answered Agent Ball twisted, making Henry seem un-American.

Chapter 44

The March Against Fear

One of the greatest disappointments Trifecta experienced during the march was when someone slipped into his brown gym bag and stole his last fifty five dollars. With his spirit crushed, he told Jeff and Peter what had happened. Peter handed him a twenty-dollar bill and told him not to sweat it, because he had him covered. However, Trifecta did worry. It seemed that everything and everyone he had trusted his entire life had let him down.

With the recent theft, Trifecta was careful not to let his brown gym bag out of his sight. While the gym bag without his money had no value, he cherished his meager belongings.

One evening when Trifecta was dejected and homesick he called G.W. from a payphone. The two talked until Trifecta didn't have any more change to feed the phone. After hearing about his troubles, G.W. offered to come and get him but he also tried to encourage Trifecta to finish what he had started.

"I'm sure even Dr. King gets discouraged," G.W. said.

"Why would he ever be discouraged?" Trifecta asked, thinking the famous black leader never experienced any problems.

"Well, they put him in jail, turned police dogs on him, knocked him down with water from fire hoses, and that's just what the white people did to him. There are plenty of colored folks that talk about him as bad as the white folks, even though he tries to help them have a better life."

When Trifecta returned to the camp, Doctor King was shaking hands and talking with many of the marchers. Doctor King had seen Trifecta many times during the march, and smiled at him as he approached. Trifecta was impressed that Doctor King took time to speak with him even though many older and more influential people were vying for his attention. When Trifecta asked him about the obstacles he experienced. Doctor King told him that he did become disheartened with the movement from time to time, and he had been disappointed with some black people as well as white people. But he said the key to success was keeping your eye on the prize.

"What prize am I keeping my eye on?" Trifecta asked.

"Freedom," Doctor King said. "After two hundred years of slavery and prejudice we can't allow discouragement to prevent us from achieving the freedom of equality."

As he dozed off to sleep that night, Trifecta felt better having talked to G.W. and Doctor King. He thought about how impressed G.W. would be when he told him that he had personally spoken with the civil rights leader.

Trifecta was surprised the next morning when he told Jeff and Peter about his previous night's experience and they treated his story with disdain. He was quickly learning that all blacks did not support Doctor King and his nonviolence philosophy.

The longer the march lasted, the more divisive its participants became, one group chanting "freedom now" and adhering to non-violence, the other screaming "black power" and seeking rebellion. This tension between the demonstrators confused Trifecta and caused him to wonder which philosophy he should adopt.

On June 21, a large contingent of marchers led by Doctor King attended a commemorative service for the three civil rights workers who were murdered in the vicinity. Jeff and Peter decided not to join the excursion because two of the three martyrs were white boys. However, Trifecta was determined not to be discouraged, so he joined the group of marchers going into town to commemorate their fallen brothers. Entering the city, Trifecta was overcome by a feeling of uneasiness as evil seemed to permeate the air. As the marchers joined other civil rights sympathizers in the town square for a prayer service, the local police controlled hostile white onlookers. Due to his apprehension, Trifecta stayed close to the main body of marchers rather than wander away as he often did during the rallies and speeches.

When the prayer service ended, the marchers intended to exit the town through a black neighborhood, hoping to encourage some of the local blacks to register to vote.

As they started out of town a barrage of rocks and other debris battered the marchers as an angry white mob attacked. Trifecta was hit in the face with a rock that lacerated his cheek. Chaos ensued as Doctor King tried to move the demonstrators away from trouble. Disregarding Doctor King's instructions, some marchers, including Trifecta stood their ground, throwing whatever they could find on the ground at the white mob. Police and sheriff's deputies stood idle when the whites attacked the demonstrators. As soon as the blacks retaliated law enforcement moved in, shoving and pushing the blacks away from the white throng. Trifecta was shoved to the ground, ripping his recently purchased pants, and scraping his knee. As he jumped to his feet, he left the brown gym bag on the ground and before he could retrieve it a white officer pushed him away. He struggled to break through the line of police who were herding the blacks with nightsticks and the butt ends of shotguns, but all his attempts were unsuccessful. After catching an elbow across his nose, sending additional blood streaming down his face, he forsook the bag and joined the other marchers as they retreated out of town. He had nothing left but the torn and blood-stained clothes he was wearing and the few dollars he had remaining from the twenty dollars Peter gave him.

When he returned to camp Peter and Jeff congratulated him for fighting back against white abuse, as others who participated in the confrontation bragged about their prowess. A nurse who was participating in the march tended to Trifecta and the other injured marchers. Another lady sewed Trifecta's torn trousers.

Even though Doctor King had not recovered from the stress of being attacked, he was taken to another town where he made a speech against violence. He pointed out that blacks made up ten percent of the population so they needed to focus on peaceful reform and not violence. According to reports Dr. King's speech was met with a mixed response. Some shouted "black power" with their fists raised above their heads while others answered with the mantra, "freedom now."

Two days after the confrontation at the commemorative service, the March Against Fear entered another town. Once again the plan was to pitch the tent and spend the night in the yard of a black elementary school. Marchers were also encouraging another "Blackout," telling local blacks to boycott downtown businesses. They called for blacks to participate in a one-day citywide strike.

Claiming they were trying to avoid a crisis, the authorities forbade the demonstrators to stop within the city limits. When the marchers proceeded to the elementary school, they were met by state troopers who used tear gas, nightsticks, and the butt ends of rifles and shotguns to disperse the crowd.

During the fracas Trifecta was subjected to large doses of tear gas. The fumes not only stole his breath but blinded him. When he tried to escape he couldn't see and he crashed head-first into a swing set, knocking him to the ground and putting a knot on his forehead. On the ground, he was under the noxious fog that hung over the playground. Crawling on his hands and knees he was overlooked by the state troopers who were beating marchers unmercifully. Inching his way on the ground, he was terrified that he was about to die due to the foul gas, or unrestrained violence.

The conflict was over in less than thirty minutes and a majority of the marchers found refuge in a nearby church. Inside the church, several nurses, a doctor, and others with medical experience, treated the injured and wounded. Trifecta and Jeff only experienced minor injuries but Peter, who was identified by the police and state troopers as an outside instigator, was beaten severely.

After Peter had been treated for his injuries he found Jeff and Trifecta. "I guess we're blood brothers now," he told Trifecta, pointing to his battered and bruised face.

On June 25th, James Meredith rejoined the march, giving the demonstrators a new vitality as the dangerous excursion was coming to a jubilant end.

On June 26th, the march arrived at Tougaloo College, a black institution on the north side of Jackson, Mississippi. A party began as blacks from Jackson and across Mississippi gathered for a rally before marching to the state capitol. Helicopters and small planes circled the campus and law enforcement continuously patrolled around the school as state and city officials monitored the rally. Trifecta celebrated by participating with a group of young men who placed "black power" bumper stickers on police cars. He was almost caught twice, but it was easy to disappear into the crowd.

When the march left Tougaloo College, there were approximately fifteen thousand protestors choking the street. The demonstration became increasingly festive as the procession got closer to the capitol. Many of the participants were dressed in patriotic red, white, and blue. People were playing horns and singing as they walked. Helicopters continued to beat the air above them. Law enforcement officers lined the route. Some were dressed in blue uniforms others wore brown uniforms and helmets. Several pairs of law enforcement officers walked along the shoulder of the road with the marchers. The highway into Jackson was clogged with black people as far as Trifecta could see.

As they passed through black neighborhoods they were cheered. When they walked through white neighborhoods they were jeered. Regardless of where they were the mood remained merry. Due to the number now participating, there was no fear.

When the demonstrators arrived at the state capitol Trifecta began to panic because he hadn't seen Jeff since early that morning. He wormed his way through the crowd looking for Jeff as Doctor King spoke to the crowd. His stomach knotted as he searched the perimeter while others addressed the crowd. Still he was unable to locate Jeff. As the crowd started to disperse it was all Trifecta could do to keep from crying; he was certain he had been deserted by his traveling companion, and he had no way to get home. He imagined Peter and Jeff had gone away together to smoke dope and had forgotten all about him. The speeches had been over for more than forty-five minutes when Trifecta sat down on the capitol steps and tried to plot his course of action. He had seen a few black police officers and he thought if he could find one of them he would explain his dilemma and maybe they would help him. He sat for ten minutes, before he spotted a black patrolman speaking with a white officer. Trifecta decided he would wait until the white cop left before he approached the black police officer. As Trifecta sat on the steps of the Mississippi State capitol, exhausted from weeks of marching and emotionally shaken from the fear of being lost and alone, he heard a white voice shout.

"Jeff! He's over here."

Trifecta turned to see Peter walking down the capitol steps towards him.

"Where have you been man?" Peter asked, approaching Trifecta.

"I've been looking for you two," Trifecta said with a sigh of relief.

By that time Jeff was coming up the sidewalk.

"I'm going to call some friends and we're going to spend the night with them, then I'll use their car to take you and Jeff back to Memphis," Peter explained.

They had to walk a block to a payphone. After Peter made the call they walked another five blocks to the corner where Peter's friend agreed to meet them. They waited for about twenty minutes before a clean- cut white man who appeared to be much older than Peter pulled up in a cream colored, four-door, 1962 Chevrolet Belair. Peter sat in the front. Trifecta and Jeff were in the back. After Peter introduced them to his friend, Andrei or Andy Berk, Trifecta sat back and tried not to fall asleep.

Chapter 45

The Summer of 1966

The last day of the 1966 school year consisted of attending homeroom and picking up report cards. Thanks to Charity Henry passed all his courses, even making a D+ in World History.

To celebrate the beginning of summer, Henry and Charity went with Alan and his most recent girlfriend to Maywood swimming pool. Maywood was nestled in a wooded area of Olive Branch, Mississippi, located just minutes from Memphis. Maywood was a small lake that had been transformed into a swimming pool, carpeted with hundreds of tons of white sand imported from Destin, Florida. The pool's shore line rivaled any on the pristine gulf coast. The complex also contained numerous picnic tables, a snack bar, men's and women's locker rooms, and a pavilion with a juke box.

When the foursome arrived at the pool, the unpaved parking lot was packed with cars. Henry's group changed into their swimming suits and met outside the locker rooms. Alan led the way down some flagstone steps to the beach and spread their towels on the sand in the vicinity of the diving boards.

Charity was massaging suntan lotion onto Henry's back when a group of ten or twelve kids from Central High School got out of the pool and walked to their towels that were laid out a short distance from where Henry, Alan, and the girls were sitting.

Marcie and Lois were both in the group. Marcie was wearing a two-piece swimming suit that enhanced her nubile figure, making her the focal point of the group. Conversely, Charity wore a one-piece swimming suit that did nothing to help her almost flat chest and shapeless butt.

The group of Centralities was friendly; many spoke to Henry's group. Marcie even waved to them, displaying her perpetual smile as she held hands with Larry Jones. Henry finished his cigarette, lathered Charity in suntan lotion, and pulled her to the edge of the pool. Henry went head first into the water, but Charity was hesitant to get in the cold water, not wanting to get her hair wet. After Charity eased into the pool, she and Henry swam to the shallow end. Charity had pulled her hair back in a ponytail but because it was so thick it was more like the tail of a Clydesdale than a pony.

When they were in three feet of water, Henry grabbed Charity around the waist and threw her into the air. With a scream, Charity's slight body splashed down, completely submerging her and soaking her hair. When Charity buoyed to the surface she was ready for a playful fight. To Henry's sensual enjoyment they started wrestling, dunking, splashing, grabbing, and climbing on each other's slick wet bodies. When Charity grew tired she wrapped her arms around Henry's neck and he held her in the water like a bride being carried over a threshold. Charity surprised Henry by giving him quick platonic kiss.

Even though Henry and Charity had been dating for several months, Charity had only allowed him chaste kisses at her door when he took her home after a date. When she kissed him it was more a sign of fondness rather than an act of intimacy, which often frustrated Henry, particularly after dating Lois the make-out queen.

"What does your mother think of me?" Charity asked as she floated in Henry's arms.

"She likes you; why do you ask?"

"I just think its important what a boy's mother thinks about his girlfriend," Charity said matter-of-factly, which surprised Henry because Charity always said she didn't care what anybody thought about her.

"Have your other boyfriends' mothers liked you?"

"I haven't had any other boyfriends. But I have always dreamed that your mother would like me."

"You've always thought about my mother?"

"I didn't always know whose mother it would be, but I knew someday a boy I liked would come along. Now that you have, I hope your mother and I can be friends."

"She likes you; because even when I was grounded, she let me go out with you."

"What would she like to change about me?"

"I don't know."

"There must be something."

"What would your parents like to change about me?" Not wanting to tell Charity his mother would love to cut her hair, and revise her wardrobe.

"They wish you weren't so uptight and that you would talk to them a little more."

"I talk to them," Henry replied defensively.

"You asked and I'm telling you," Charity said sweetly." Now I'm asking you what your mother would like to change about me."

"Well, she has said she would like to take some scissors to your hair, but she thinks you're cute, and I've tried to explain that you are just showing your individualism."

"It's cool. I asked, and I appreciate you telling me the truth," Charity answered calmly, not taking any offense at what Henry had said.

When they got out of the pool and back to where Alan and his date lay in the sun, Henry was hungry, so he and Charity went to the snack bar. As they passed the other Central High students, Henry scanned the group but saw neither Marcie nor Lois.

Climbing the flag stone steps from the beach, a dance pavilion was on the left, the snack bar was on the right, and the locker room was in front of them.

While Henry went to the snack bar Charity sat in the pavilion on one of the benches that circled the dance floor.

The jukebox was playing "Soul Finger" by the Bar-Kays as a few couples wiggled and jerked to the music.

When Henry got in line at the snack bar Marcie exited the girl's locker room with money in her hand and a towel wrapped around her waist. She walked to the snack bar where Henry was waiting to order.

"Hi," said Marcie, getting in line behind Henry.

Henry turned around. "Hi," he replied, feeling as awkward as usual when he was near Marcie.

"How were your grades?"

"Mine were fine, how did you do?" Henry stammered.

"I finished with a B in Latin and an A in everything else. I guess you got caught up on your work after being suspended?"

"Yeah, Charity helped me," Henry said, then turned to the guy in the snack bar and placed his order.

"What did your mother say about you being suspended?"

"She took it better than I thought she would."

"What does she think of your new girlfriend?"

"Also better than I thought; what do you think of her?"

"She seems alright; of course she dresses in a unique way, and I understand she has some strange political views."

"She's an individual," Henry said as he paid for his order.

"Is she going to make you an individualist?"

"What do you mean?"

"Are you going to turn into a flower child?"

"I don't know," shrugged Henry, taking his food. "See you later," he said over his shoulder as he walked away, wishing he didn't feel like a dork every time he was near Marcie.

While Henry and Marcie were at the snack bar, Lois entered the dance pavilion and walked up to Charity.

"Hi," Lois said.

"Hi," Charity replied.

"How are things going with Henry?"

"Good, thanks."

"He's hard to love," Lois said, looking at the floor.

"What?" Charity asked, not sure what Lois was getting at.

"Henry's hard to love," Lois repeated.

"What do you mean?"

"Well, I wasn't his first love, and I doubt you're his only love."

"What?"

"Turn around and you'll see what I mean." When Charity looked over her shoulder, Henry was speaking with Marcie.

"He's been in love with her his whole life. I just thought you needed to know."

Charity continued to watch Henry talk to Marcie as Lois walked away.

When Henry returned with their food, "Cute" by Tommy Burke and the Counts was on the jukebox.

Charity asked, "What were you talking to Marcie about?"

"Just school."

"I didn't know she was your friend."

"We lived close to each other when we were in elementary school."

"Do you like her?"

"Yeah, she's alright," Henry said with a slight blush.

"I mean do you like her romantically?

"No," Henry said. "I like you." This was the truth. He just wasn't sure he liked or loved her as much as he loved Marcie.

Chapter 46

Ten days after Tyrone's funeral

Caledonia sent Willie to buy a pack of cigarettes. After he purchased the cigarettes and left the store he was met by the Mayor, Sammy Mitchell, and another thug.

"Where are you going boy?" the Mayor asked with contempt.

"I'm taking these cigarettes to Madea."

"What kind of cigarettes do you have?" Sammy asked.

"Kools."

"This punk not only squealed on you for cutting his cousin, now he's stealing your cigarettes," Sammy said to the Mayor.

"Is that right boy, did you steal my cigarettes?"

"I ain't stole anything. Madea gave me the money to buy these cigarettes and I didn't squeal on you for cutting anybody."

"Are you calling Sammy a liar?" the Mayor asked.

"You can ask the man in the store. I just bought these cigarettes."

"I don't believe that Korean any more than I believe you," the Mayor said moving into Willie's personal space.

"Are you telling me you aren't the one that put the pigs on me for cutting your cousin?"

"What do you want?" Willie mumbled, looking at the ground.

"Maybe I want to cut you, like I cut your cousin," the Mayor said through clenched teeth so close to Willie's face he could smell the cheap wine and tobacco on the Mayor's breathe. Willie's stomach knotted and he was visibly shaking.

Without warning the Mayor sucker punched Willie in the stomach. The blow caused Willie to double over and Sammy pushed him to the sidewalk. The Mayor reached down and took Caledonia's cigarettes from Willie's hand.

"What are you going to do now? Are you going to tell the law I took back my own cigarettes?" the Mayor asked looking down at Willie.

"I ain't ever told the cops anything. I'm not going to tell the law anything now," Willie said, remaining on the sidewalk in a semi-fetal position.

The three thugs walked away but not before Sammy kicked Willie in the ribs.

*

"Where are my cigarettes?" Caledonia asked.

"I lost them," Willie said, holding his arm against the ribs where he had been kicked.

"What you mean, you lost them?"

"I don't know what happened to them, I just lost them."

"Well, you better go find them."

"I don't know where they're at."

"Cigarettes don't grow on trees. You go find them."

Willie was down to his last dime but he went back to the store and bought five loose cigarettes for two cents each. As he walked out of the store he came face to face with Sammy Mitchel. Not anticipating the chance meeting, they stood motionless for a moment staring at each other. Suddenly

Willie made a break across Mississippi Boulevard and into Lemoyne Gardens. Not expecting Willie to run, Sammy was a few steps slow in his pursuit. Still, he managed to stay close behind Willie, racing through the projects.

Running through the pain and gasping for breath, Willie made it to Caledonia's apartment just as G.W. was entering his apartment. Willie rushed inside the apartment and hooked the screen door. When Sammy leaped onto the porch he rammed his fist through the screen to unhook the door.

"Hold on!" G.W. hollered, stepping off his porch and moving toward Sammy.

"What's happening here?" G.W. demanded.

"Mind your own business garbage man," Sammy said, with his hand still though the screen.

"You can't come around here breaking down doors and entering people's apartments."

"You know who runs this neighborhood, you old fool?" Sammy asked, removing his hand from the screen door.

"I know you're not breaking into that apartment," G.W. said, mounting the porch and grabbing Sammy's arm.

"Let go of me garbage man," Sammy said, jerking away from G.W. and jumping off Caledonia's porch.

"This isn't over," Sammy said, pointing at Willie. "You screwed up boy."

Sammy turned and walked away, talking loudly about how Willie was going to get hurt.

"What have you done?" G.W. asked Willie.

"I ain't done anything," Willie said through the torn screen. Caledonia came out of the kitchen at the sound of the commotion. Willie walked towards the stairs and when he passed Caledonia, he handed her the five slightly crushed cigarettes.

"Miss Caledonia, are you alright?"

"I'm fine."

"What is going on with those boys?" he asked.

I don't know," Caledonia said. "But it doesn't look too good."

"It sure doesn't."

The next day Willie went to the recruiting office and joined the army. He figured he had better odds in Vietnam than he did in Lemoyne Gardens with the Mayor for an enemy.

Chapter 47

After the March Against Fear

It was a fifteen minutes to drive to the Berk's home. They lived in a modest white asbestos-sided house with a green roof. The home had two bedrooms, a living room, small dining room, kitchen and one bath. Trifecta was the first to take a shower. Mrs. Berk found some clothes for Trifecta that were slightly too large. Trifecta made them fit by cinching his belt and rolling up the cuffs on the pants. He felt great being clean and wearing fresh clothes.

The sleeping arrangements were for Trifecta to take the single bed in the guest bedroom, Jeff was to sleep on the couch, and Peter had a pallet on the floor. While Jeff and Peter took their showers, Trifecta laid on the bed. Hearing the hum of the window air conditioner in the living room, he shut his eyes for a moment. The next thing he knew Jeff was waking him up to eat supper.

At the supper table, Peter excitedly told the Berks about the march. Every time Peter stopped talking long enough to take a breath, Mr. Berk quizzed Jeff and Trifecta about their opinion of the march. He was particularly interested in what they thought about black power and the use of violence to achieve civil rights. Both Jeff and Trifecta were guarded in their responses to Mr. Berk's questions. They were after all, talking to a white man. Now that Trifecta was rested and thinking clearly he began to feel uncomfortable being a guest in a white family's house, eating supper at a white family's table, and talking about civil rights. Eventually, Mr. Berk began explaining how violence was the only means to bring about change especially when it was an under-class trying to acquire rights from an upper-class, as was the case with the civil rights movement in America. Trifecta thought it strange that Mr. Berk spoke about the United States as if it were some place other than where they lived. After supper Peter, Jeff, and Trifecta adjourned to the living room to watch television while Mr. Berk went into his bedroom. When the ten o'clock news came on, he joined the boys in the living room.

The lead story on the news concerned the March Against Fear and the rally at the capitol. When the newscaster began talking about the war in Vietnam Trifecta lost interest but Mr. Berk listened more intently. As soon as the weather was reported Mr. Berk turned off the television. He again questioned the boys about what had been said in the speech by Doctor King and others. Then he talked about the injustice of the Vietnam War which according to him was illegal because we were sending combat troops into an undeclared war.

"What is your opinion of the war?" Mr. Berk asked Trifecta.

"My cousin was killed in Vietnam," Trifecta answered.

"What a shame that a young black man lost his life fighting an immoral war. Were you close to your cousin?"

"We both lived with my Madea," Trifecta said, not wanting to reveal how he really felt about Tyrone.

"Your Madea?"

"My grandmother."

Mr. Berk lectured the boys for another fifteen minutes about the Vietnam War and how it was fought by the country's lower classes of blacks and poor whites while the capitalist machine profited from the war's miseries. However, he was careful never to mention how the communist benefited from the war.

It took Trifecta quite a while to go to sleep that night. His trouble may have stemmed from his earlier nap, or possibly it may have been because he was sleeping in a house that belonged to white people. Despite his problem falling asleep, when he finally dozed off he rested soundly and had to be awakened the next morning by Jeff. When he went to the kitchen, Mrs. Berk had a breakfast prepared with bacon, toast, eggs, and coffee. She had also washed Trifecta's shirt, underwear, and socks, but had thrown away his pants because they were unsalvageable. She packed all his belongings in a paper bag, encouraging him and Jeff to keep the clothes they were given the previous day and were currently wearing.

After breakfast Peter and Mr. Berk went into the Berks' bedroom while Trifecta and Jeff watched television. Jeff fell asleep. Trifecta could hear Mr. Berk lecturing Peter but couldn't make out what he was saying. When Peter came out of the room he asked if they were ready to go and the three boys loaded themselves into the Chevrolet and headed for Memphis. Jeff wanted to get some more sleep so he told Trifecta to ride in the front seat.

"What's the deal with Mr. and Mrs. Berk?" Trifecta asked.

"What do you mean?"

"Why are they your friends? And why did they let you take their car to a Memphis?"

"We have a lot of things in common, especially how we think the world should work. We have a common goal and have to work together to accomplish our mission."

"Why are they concerned about black people, particularly Jeff and me?"

"They are concerned about all people who are oppressed by imperialists."

"What's an imperialist?"

"An imperialist is a person or government that unfairly rules other people or countries when they have no right to do so. Like what the United States is doing in Vietnam, or what white people are doing to blacks."

"And you're against imperialism?" Trifecta asked, trying to understand how Peter and other white people fit into the civil rights movement.

"Among other things."

"What things are you talking about?"

"I think people should work according to their ability and be provided for according to their need."

"What?"

"I think people should pursue careers in areas of work where they have interest and ability, and that society should provide for their food, housing, clothing, health care and so on."

"Who would pick up the garbage, clean the hotel rooms, and pick the cotton?"

"Those jobs would be done by people who have the ability and the desire to preform that type of work."

"There ain't no such."

"There ain't no such what?" Peter asked.

"People who want to pick up garbage."

"Perhaps that is all their ability allows them to do. The point is they would still have their needs met equally with people who perform other jobs."

"Who decides what a person's ability is?"

"The leaders in the community would determine each person's ability."

"How do they know what I can do?"

"Throughout a person's education they would be tested to see what they are best suited for."

"I don't believe anyone is suited to carry heavy tubs of stinking garbage on their head. So who would collect the garbage?"

"Like I said, that would have to be determined by a number of factors. Let me ask you, what do you want to do when you get out of school?" because he didn't have an answer to the question about collecting garbage

"I don't know, but I don't want to pick up garbage, clean hotel rooms, or pick cotton."

"How do you know?" Peter asked in his best philosophical tone.

"Because Madea and G.W. told me what it's like. In fact, I don't want to be a share cropper either."

"What do you want?"

Trifecta thought for a moment and remembering his earliest ambition said, "I want to be like the Churchills."

"Who?"

"The white folks whose house my mama use to clean."

"What do you mean you want to be like them?"

"I mean I want to have a family and a house. I want to know who my daddy is. I want a mama that wants to be with me. I want a brother who cares about me. I don't want to be scared. I don't want to be alone. I don't want to be hungry or cold." Trifecta had unburdened his heart before he knew it.

"With the right political, social, and economic system, all of those things will be available to you."

"How?"

The government will provide for you the same as they provide for the Churchills."

"Right now, all the government provides is the housing projects."

"There won't be any projects."

"Where will the poor people live?"

"There won't be any poor people."

"Where will the poor people get money?"

"The nation's wealth will have to be redistributed."

"You think the rich white folks are going to give some of their money to black people?" Trifecta asked with a sarcastic chuckle.

"After the revolution they won't have a choice."

"Are you saying the government is going to steal the white people's money and give it to the people in the projects?"

"Not steal it, just redistribute the wealth and the money to make everybody equal."

"If they don't have a choice, it sounds like stealing to me."

"It's for the greater good. But first we must get people's attention. That's where people like Jeff and maybe you come in. If you help people like the Berks and I get the government's attention, we can help people like you and Jeff break the cycle of poverty."

"How are we going to do that?"

"You already have by participating in things like the March Against Fear."

As their conversation continued Peter talked about the evils of industrial capitalism and almost persuaded Trifecta of his ideology until he mentioned that there was no God. The April 8, 1966 edition of Time magazine startled the nation and began a heated controversy with a cover story "Is God Dead?" G.W., along with the Christian community, both black and white, was outraged at the notion that God could possibly be dead. Even though G.W. hadn't read the article, he had expressed his concern to Trifecta about anyone who was so perverted that they could believe God no longer exist. When Peter mentioned that he didn't believe there was a God, he instantly lost credibility with Trifecta. Peter realized their relationship was seriously injured when Trifecta grew sullen.

When they stopped for gas, Jeff woke up. Peter treated Trifecta and Jeff to a Coke and a candy bar, but his generosity did little to reestablish his relationship with Trifecta. For the second leg of their trip, Jeff took the front seat which was fine with Trifecta. He was content to stare out the open window at the landscape, remembering several landmarks from the march. Because of the wind roaring into the four open windows in the car, Trifecta couldn't hear the conversation between Jeff and Peter.

After traveling several miles, Jeff leaned over the seat and in a raised voice asked, "What are you going to do about your pants?"

"What pants?" Trifecta responded in a semi shout so he could be heard over the rushing wind.

"The pants at the tailor shop."

"Nothing, I guess. I don't have any money."

Jeff turned and spoke to Peter but due to the wind whistling in his ears, Trifecta had no idea what they were saying or why Jeff had an interest in his pants. Trifecta's stomach tightened as he thought about all the money he had a few weeks earlier and now he was dead broke.

Once they arrived in Memphis Peter drove to the tailor shop on Vance Avenue.

"Wait here," Peter said to Jeff, then turned to Trifecta. "Are you coming?"

Trifecta didn't say anything but got out of the car, wondering what Peter was up to. The tailor shop was in a converted white framed house. The shop was furnished with several long rectangle tables, two clothing racks and four industrial sewing machines. One black woman and two black men were working at the sewing machines while another black man was sitting on one of the tables, hand stitching a hem in a pair of trousers. The man on the table hopped to the floor when Trifecta and Peter entered the shop. It appeared the man recognized Trifecta but couldn't recall his name.

"May I help you?" the man asked with a Dominican accent.

Trifecta looked at Peter, unsure of what to say.

"We've come to pick up a pair of pants for my friend," Peter said.

"What's the name?" the man asked.

"Trifecta," Peter hesitated, realizing he didn't know Trifecta's last name.

"Johnson," Trifecta interjected.

The man walked to one of the racks of clothes that held several dozen pair of brightly colored trousers. After examining several scraps of paper pinned to each pair, the man located the Trifecta's.

"Do you want to try them on?" the man asked.

"Sure," Trifecta said.

The man directed Trifecta to a bathroom at the end of the hall that doubled as a changing room.

While Trifecta tried on the pants Peter paid the tailor. Then Peter looked through several pads of material samples randomly scattered on one of the long tables.

When Trifecta returned to the room the tailor asked, "How did they fit?"

"Good," Trifecta responded feeling really cool about his new threads.

"Why don't you pick out some more material?" Peter said.

"You know I don't have any money," Trifecta answered.

"I'll buy you two more pair," Peter offered.

Trifecta looked through several pads of samples before deciding on the pieces of material.

"I'll need a fifteen-dollar deposit for each pair of trousers," the tailor told Peter.

"I probably won't be here when he picks them up. I need to pay in full."

Peter paid the tailor an additional seventy dollars.

Leaving the tailor shop they stood on the porch of the old house.

"Why did you do that?" Trifecta asked.

"I just want to be your friend."

"Why?"

"We all need friends," Peter said. "And I never know when I might need you as a friend."

"By the way," Peter continued, "you'll probably need some new shirts to go along with your pants." He took thirty dollars out of his pocket and handed it to Trifecta.

"I don't want your money," Trifecta said.

"I know you don't want the money, but you do need the shirts. Now be my friend and take it." Peter thrust the money towards Trifecta. Trifecta reluctantly took the cash.

Chapter 48

Two days after the trip to Maywood swimming beach, Henry was sitting on the living room floor watching a *Laurel and Hardy* rerun on TV when the doorbell rang.

"I've got it, Mom," Henry hollered.

When he opened the door he was shocked to see Charity. She was wearing a blue blouse with white polka dots. The top two buttons on the blouse were undone and the shirt tail was knotted above her naval, exposing her midriff. Henry was sure his mother would disapprove, particularly as her white shorts didn't come to the mid-point of her thigh. However, the thing that shocked him the most was her neatly combed pixy hairstyle.

"Is your mom here?" Charity asked, barely acknowledging Henry.

"Sure," Henry said, so surprised he didn't know what else to say.

"Who is it, dear?" Henry's mom asked, walking out of the kitchen and into the small dining room which was visible to the front door.

"It's Charity and she wants to see you."

When Mrs. Murphy saw Charity's hair, she squealed with delight.

"I wanted to show you my hair," Charity said, obviously excited by Mrs. Murphy's reaction.

"Henry, invite Charity to come in and shut the door, you're letting all the cool air out," Mrs. Murphy said.

"I love your top," said Mrs. Murphy, referring to Charity's blouse, "and your hair is wonderful."

"Thanks," said Charity.

"Come in and have a seat. When did you decide to have it cut?"

"I've been thinking about it for a while. It's so much cooler when it's short. It doesn't take a long time to fix and it dries quickly, even without a hair dryer."

Listening to the two women talk about hair and blouses; Henry felt ignored.

Finally, he interrupted, "I think I'm going to go ahead and start trimming the bushes." cutting the bushes was the top priority on Henry's list of chores.

"That's fine dear," his mother answered. "Charity can join you in a few minutes."

Henry had finished trimming and was sitting on the back steps taking a break when Charity came out of the house with two Nehi Grape Sodas.

"What have you and my mom been doing?" Henry asked.

"I helped her make up your bed. She said she has a terrible time getting you to do it."

"Thanks," Henry said.

Henry's brother was away at college and was taking a full load of summer classes so Henry had the bedroom to himself.

"I liked doing it. I enjoy helping you," Charity said, handing Henry a grape drink and sitting down beside him. The fragrance of her perfume aroused his senses.

"Why did you cut your hair?" Henry asked.

"Don't you like it?"

"Yeah, but I thought you liked your hair long."

"You told me the other day your mom thought it would look better short."

"So?"

"I want your mom to like me."

"What does your mom think?" Henry asked.

"She's okay with it. She lets me dress and wear my hair the way I want. She has since I was in the eighth grade. She wants me to be an individual and not go along with the crowd, unless I want to."

"But you did it because you thought my mother wanted you to?"

"I told you it is important that your mother likes me."

"Why?"

"I don't have many friends, and I haven't since about the seventh grade when it seems everyone got concerned about being popular, looking like everyone else, and hanging out with the in-crowd. I guess my parents indoctrinated me to march to the beat of a different drum. In fact, you're the only boy I've dated since I've been at Central. And I like you a lot. I've been hit on by older guys at the Lemon, or by some of my parent's students, but I'm not stupid. I know what they want, and I don't do that."

"Do what?"

"You know, sex and stuff."

"I thought you were a hippie, free love and the new morality," Henry said.

"Is that why you date me, because you think you're going to have free sex?" Charity asked very calmly.

"No, but…" Henry didn't finish his sentence.

"Some people think because I'm a hippie," Charity made quotation marks with her hands when she said hippie. "That I'm into drugs and free love, but I believe in what the Bible says about sex and self- control."

"I didn't think hippies or college professors believed the Bible," Henry said.

"Do you think I'm a hypocrite, because I embrace Christianity and flower power?"

"No," Henry said hesitantly, unsure of how to answer.

"If being an immoral agnostic is the criteria for being hip or educated then I'm neither a hippie nor an intellectual. However, I think there are a few similarities in the flower power and Christianity, such as peace and love. And I only accept the philosophies of counter culture that are consistent with Christianity. I think the only way a person can truly have peace and love is thorough the Lord Jesus Christ." Charity remained very calm and spoke in a soft conversational tone.

"Why do you dress the way you do."

"God created every person is unique, and I guess I'm trying to display my uniqueness by going against the norm."

"So you go to church?"

"Yes, I go to a small church."

"What kind of church?"

"An independent Christian church."

"Is that where your parents go?"

"No, they would probably claim to be agnostic if it wasn't for me."

"That's weird."

"I guess."

"Do black people go to your church?"

"A couple of black families attend regularly."

"I don't think my church believes that the races should be mixed."

"I know and I think that's kind of strange. Churches will send missionaries to Africa to share the gospel with black people but they don't let black people into their churches in America."

"My dad says all they do in black Churches is talk about politics and civil rights, and church is supposed to be about God. He says the only reason they want to attend a white church is to cause trouble."

"What are white churches doing when the pastor and the deacons stand on the front steps of their church and refuse to let black people attend services? What kind of message is that? It's not the message Jesus taught," Charity said, still maintaining a sweet tone.

"Black people don't do things the way we do in church," Henry rebutted.

"The Bible says you must worship in spirit and in truth. As long as you believe and are remembering that the Lord Jesus died and rose again for your sins, I think you are worshipping correctly whether that means you are sitting quietly in a pew, or dancing and singing in the aisle of the church."

"Do people dance in the aisle of the church that you belong to?"

"No."

"If someone wanted to dance in church could they?"

"It would be discouraged but there are churches they could go to if they had a conviction to dance."

"So the white people in your church don't mind worshipping with black people?"

"When the blacks first started coming to our church, it caused quite a debate. In fact, three families left the church. But looking at the scripture, it was apparent that God wanted the Jew and gentile believers to worship together, and they were even more segregated than the blacks and whites in our society."

"So only three families left?"

"There are probably other people in the church who don't like it but you don't have to like something or even agree with something to be obedient to what God wants you to do. We used to take the Lord's Supper from a common cup. However, when the black families began attending we went to individual cups."

Henry was silent for a long minute.

"Can I ask you something?" Henry asked, looking down at the ground, being careful not to make eye contact with Charity.

"About church?"

"Kinda."

"Sure."

Henry was silent for another long minute.

"What is it?" Charity asked softly.

"Is what you believe about God and being obedient the reason you don't kiss me?"

"I do kiss you."

"You kiss me the way my mother kisses me," Henry said, still not looking at Charity.

"Heavy petting can lead us to do the wrong thing."

"I know, but I would like a real kiss sometimes," Henry said, meaning he wanted Charity to kiss him the way Lois did.

"Let's clean up the bush trimmings. I'll rake, and you can carry them off." Charity said, seemingly avoiding the subject.

Charity raked and Henry dumped the twigs and leaves in a ditch behind their house. When they finished they went into the house so Charity could say goodbye to Mrs. Murphy and get her purse. Mrs. Murphy was still in the kitchen ironing.

"I really like your hair dear. You come back anytime you want," Mrs. Murphy said, giving Charity a hug.

"Thank you," Charity said and started for the back door.

Henry was confused. He thought Charity would go out the front door because her car was parked in front of his house. However, he didn't ask any questions and followed her out the back door. Outside, Charity walked around the right side of the house, the opposite side from her vehicle and where Mrs. Murphy was ironing and could see out of the window. Henry was still a step behind her. About half-way between the front and backyard Charity stopped, put her arms around Henry's neck and said, "Is this what you want?" She gave him a passionate kiss that made his heart pound. After Charity's conversation with Lois and seeing Henry with Marcie, she decided if she was going to keep him, she would have to start acting more like a girlfriend rather than just being his buddy.

After their lips parted she said, "I expect you to respect my wishes concerning sex". Then she gave him a quick peck on the lips and turned and walked away, leaving Henry numb and dazed.

Chapter 49

Trifecta Returns Home

On the short ride to Lemoyne Gardens, Trifecta sat silently, still trying to figure out what Peter was up to and why Peter had so much money. It occurred to him that all white people might have a lot of money and that's why so many black people were poor. He started considering what Peter said about redistributing the nation's wealth.

When they arrived at Lemoyne Gardens, Peter took Trifecta home first. As Trifecta walked up the slight incline to Caledonia's apartment he noticed two small air conditioners humming in the windows. One of the air-conditioners was downstairs and the other was upstairs.

As he entered the apartment carrying his new pants, he hollered, "Madea, I'm home."

The room was packed with new furniture. Between the couch, stuffed chair, coffee table, end tables, floor lamp, and console television, there was barely a small path to walk through the small room. Trifecta was shocked to see Willie sitting on the couch next to Marquis watching television. Caledonia came from the kitchen almost immediately.

"What's he doing here?" Trifecta demanded, pointing at Willie.

Marquis stared at Trifecta without saying a word.

"His mama hasn't come back for him yet," Caledonia said as she reached to embrace Trifecta. "How are you?"

"It's been almost three weeks," Trifecta announced. "Your mama ain't coming back, is she?"

"I won't be here long," Willie said.

"You fool. Your mama ain't coming for you." Trifecta spat.

"I didn't say she was."

"Then where are you going?"

"I joined the army."

"What did you say?" Caledonia asked.

"I said I joined the army."

"Are you crazy?" Caledonia asked. "They killed your brother, now you're going to let them kill you?"

"They said I'm not going to Vietnam because my brother got killed there."

"Who told you that foolishness?" Caledonia asked.

"The man at the recruiting office said I wouldn't have to go."

"Is he colored or white?" Caledonia asked.

"White."

"Don't you know white men lie to stupid colored boys like you?" Caledonia said.

"If I go to Vietnam, I got a better chance there than I got here."

"Why do you say that?"

"The Mayor said he's going to kill me if I stay here."

"What?"

"He got the idea that I'm the one who told on him for stabbing Trifecta. I figure he told him," Willie said, pointing to Trifecta.

"I haven't told anybody anything," Trifecta said. "But if you hadn't squealed on the Mayor you wouldn't be in this jam now. Why didn't you go to stay with your mama? Madea gave her money so she would take you to live with her."

Willie just shrugged, turning his attention back to the television.

"Auntie Josephine stole your money," Trifecta said, turning to Caledonia.

"Are you hungry?" Caledonia said, ignoring his accusation. "Let me fix you something to eat. Then you tell us all about the march. We watched the news every night hoping to see you but we never did."

Caledonia fixed Trifecta a sandwich and a Royal Crown Cola, after which she made Willie turn off the television so she could hear all about the march.

Trifecta talked about his adventures for two hours, embellishing his story to include police dogs, fire hoses and other brutalities. He was quick to show scars from his wounds that hadn't disappeared. Caledonia, Marquis, and Willie listened intently to everything Trifecta said. As Trifecta's story was winding down Willie asked, "Where'd you get them cool threads?" referring to Trifecta's tailor made trousers.

"You keep your dirty thieving hands off my pants." Trifecta suddenly broke into a rage. "If you touch them, I'll kick your black butt all over these projects."

"Trifecta," Caledonia said, "your cousin is just asking you a simple question. You shouldn't talk that way."

"He better not touch my stuff," Trifecta threatened as Willie frowned.

"You tell him where you got those clothes," Caledonia said.

"I bought them. Did you think I stole them?" Trifecta asked Willie.

Willie glared back at Trifecta but didn't respond.

"There's no reason for all this," Caledonia said. "You're going to sleep in the upstairs bedroom with Marquis, and

Willie is going to stay down here. You don't have to worry. Nobody is going to bother your pants."

Trifecta retold his story that evening to G.W. and his family where he embellished his conversation with Doctor King. He and Jeff became something of local celebrities in Lemoyne Gardens. Trifecta continued to wear his old clothes, saving his new clothes for school.

Chapter 50

Peter had sent newspaper clippings to his father from various Mississippi towns during the march. He insinuated in his reports that he was responsible for instigating the blackouts and the racial confrontations in towns along Highway 51. His father had received conflicting reports from communist operatives in the Memphis and North Mississippi area, so he didn't believe any of his son's overstated tales.

Returning to Memphis, Peter called his father in Brighton Beach.

"We have acquired a location on E.H. Crump Boulevard where you will pose as an automobile salesman. Are you familiar with E.H. Crump Boulevard?"

"Yes."

"Eight automobiles will be delivered to the location on Tuesday. The marijuana is being smuggled in the vehicles.

Money has been transferred into your account to hire a Negro to act as the proprietor of the car lot. I suggest you pay him one hundred dollars per week. You are paying him to keep our drug business and your identity confidential.

If you are going to impact the Negro community and raise the money we need, you will need to have many distributors because it is necessary to turn over the inventory quickly. We have discovered that young people serve our purposes very well. You will receive a shipment of cars containing the drugs each week and we expect all of the narcotics to be sold every seven days.

It is your responsibility to assist us in financing the war in Vietnam while causing the deterioration of the social structure in Memphis, particularly in the Negro community. Is that understood?"

"Yes," Peter responded, feeling the fervor of his father's mandate.

When Peter hung up the phone he immediately drove to Lemoyne Gardens looking for Jeff. Even though Peter took Trifecta and Jeff home a day earlier, he was now disoriented driving through the maze of buildings, parking lots, streets and common areas that all looked alike. With dusk covering the city, he gave up trying to figure out the sequence of addresses. He stopped at a cluster of young men to ask for directions.

"Does he owe you money?" asked one of the young men.

"No, I just need to speak with him," Peter answered.

"Do you have any money?"

"No, not really," Peter replied, realizing things might be turning bad.

"Does that mean you do or you don't have any money?" the man asked while leaning into the drivers-side window.

"I have a few dollars," Peter said, revving the engine slightly, hoping the man would move out of the window.

"What do you want to talk to him about?"

"I want to offer him a job."

"Some of us might need a job."

"Maybe we can work something out. If Jeff takes the job, he'll be looking for some help. Does he know you?"

"I suppose. It seems like everybody knows who I am."

"I'll tell him to look you up, what's your name?"

"They call me the Mayor."

"Okay, I'll tell him. Now will you tell me where Jeff lives?

"I might be able to tell you, but it'll cost you." The four other blacks surrounded the car.

"How much will it cost?" Peter asked, wishing he had his derringer.

"How much money do you have?"

"Three or four dollars, I guess." Peter always liked to carry a lot of money with him. He wondered what reason he could give the police for being in the projects if he made a getaway by running over the man standing in front of his car.

"Ain't that something, that's how much I get for giving directions," the Mayor smiled.

Peter discreetly opened his wallet. He had Eighty five dollars, four twenties and a five. He took out the five.

The Mayor reached through the window and took Peter's wallet out of his hand. Taking the eighty dollars, he threw the wallet into Peter's lap. Before Peter could react, he snatched the five out of Peter's hand.

"He lives over that way somewhere," the Mayor said, pointing in the general direction of an array of buildings.

"Thanks," Peter said sarcastically, knowing that it would not only be useless but dangerous to try and recover his money. The gang of blacks moved away from his car, allowing him to pass.

With the Mayor's vague directions Peter had to drive around another ten minutes before he found Jeff's address. Levi answered the door and told Peter that Jeff wasn't home and he didn't expect him back until later that night.

"Tell him to stay here until I return," Peter said. "Tell him it will be worth his time."

Peter returned to Lemoyne Gardens at nine o'clock that night. This time he was armed with his derringer. There was no sign of the Mayor. Jeff was home.

"Let's take a ride," Peter suggested.

Peter and Jeff went to the car lot on E.H. Crump Boulevard. The key was where his father told him it would be. The two men entered the twenty-by-twenty building. There was a metal desk on each side of the door, a metal swivel chair for each desk, and a couple of metal side chairs on each side of the desks.

"Have a seat," Peter said, pointing to one of the swivel chairs at a desk. Jeff sat down. Peter sat at the other desk. Both men positioned their chairs so they were facing one another.

"Here's the deal," Peter said. "I'm opening a car lot and I want you to run it for me. I'll pay you one hundred dollars per week, cash, plus you can drive any car you want on the lot. In fact, you can drive a different car every day if you want. The only thing is no one can know that I'm associated with the business. If anyone asks, you're the owner and you don't even know me."

One hundred dollars per week was considerably more than the minimum wages Jeff was accustomed to earning. So he readily agreed to Peter's proposition.

"Why can't anyone know you're associated with the car lot?"

"Can I trust you?" Peter asked, knowing that he could because they had gotten stoned together every day during the march.

"You know you can trust me."

"We're going to sell weed out of the garage in back. If you want in on that I can give you a piece of the action."

"That's cool."

"When I say sell, I mean distribute. I have several men ready to take to the streets in every part of the city."

"How many guys are in on this?"

"Four if I can count on you."

"Four dudes can sell a lot of dope."

"No, that's not the idea. We'll get teenagers and kids to sell to the users. That keeps you and me farther away from what's happening on the street. In fact, I ran into a guy here in the projects that we might recruit to help us in South Memphis."

"Who's that?"

"He called himself the Mayor."

"There ain't no way man. The Mayor's not looking for a job. Any dope sold in Lemoyne Gardens, the Mayor is going to get his cut."

"What?"

"Yeah man; he controls this neighborhood."

"The Mayor may have a surprise coming."

Chapter 51

Two weeks after Trifecta returned from Mississippi, Caledonia received a letter from the Board of Education. The letter was informing her that Trifecta was assigned to Central High School. Until then Central had been a white high school.

"I don't want to go to a white school," Trifecta protested.

"You don't have a choice," Caledonia responded.

"Why do they have to choose me?" Trifecta asked.

"I don't know."

"This was going to be my best year. I was going to be one of the coolest cats at school. I got the threads. I marched in the movement. Everybody at school was going to have to respect me."

"You'll still be respected but at a different school."

"White kids don't respect anybody who marches for civil rights. Matter of fact they will probably hate me."

"I thought the reason you marched was because you wanted to go to school with white folks."

"I don't want to go to school with white kids. I don't even like white kids."

"You don't know any white kids."

"Do so. Jeff and I met this white dude on the march. I don't like him, and I don't trust him. It's just like you said, white people lie."

"Well, honey, I'm sure they're not going to lie to you at school."

"What about my friends?"

"What about them? They might be going with you."

Trifecta picked up the phone and called Levi but his telephone was disconnected. Trifecta walked through the projects to Levi's apartment.

"You get a letter today?" Trifecta asked Levi.

"No."

"I got a letter, and it said I am supposed to go to a white school next year."

"What?"

"I've been transferred to Central High School," Trifecta said, holding out the letter for Levi to see.

"What's Central?"

"It's a white high school."

Levi took the letter and glanced over it. "You sure have, what are you going to do?"

"I don't know. I was hoping you'd get one too."

"Are they making you go because you marched?"

"I don't know." Trifecta shrugged, "Madea's acting like she's going to make me go, but I don't want to if you're not going."

"Maybe I'll get a letter tomorrow," Levi said, trying to be encouraging, but hoping he wouldn't be reassigned to a white school.

"What's wrong with your phone?" Trifecta asked.

"Jeff's gone to pay the bill. He said he won't let it happen again."

"Let what happen?"

"He told Mama he wouldn't let the phone get cut off again because she didn't have the money to pay the bill."

"How is he going to stop it from getting cut off?"

"He's got a new job, making lots of money. He's working at a car lot with that white guy who was in the march and brought you all home."

Chapter 52

The Remainder of the summer of 1966
Caledonia, Peter, Trifecta, and Henry

After Willie left for Fort Campbell to do his basic training, Caledonia wrote Josephine and told her Willie was in the military. Three days later Caledonia received a collect call from Josephine. Neither Willie nor Caledonia had heard from her since Tyrone's funeral.

"What has Willie done?" Josephine wanted to know.

"He joined the army," Caledonia responded.

"Why would he do that?"

"He was having trouble around here, and you never came to get him. So he joined the army."

"What kind of trouble?"

"He was in trouble with some of the other boys."

"Didn't he learn anything from Tyrone? He's going to get killed."

"They told him that he isn't going to Vietnam because his brother was killed."

"Who is his insurance made out to?"

"I don't know."

"Haven't you heard from him?"

"He called me from a pay phone when he got to Fort Campbell."

"Why didn't you ask him about his insurance?"

"If you want to know, why don't you write him and ask?"

"I don't have his address," Josephine answered.

"I'll give it to you."

"I don't have a pencil."

"Give me your number, and I'll call you back with the address."

"This is a neighbor's phone. They don't like anybody using it. They let me use it today because I told them this was an emergency."

"I'll mail you his address."

"Okay."

"Why haven't you contacted the boy since Tyrone's funeral?"

"I've got to go. The people need their phone. Goodbye, Mama."

Josephine never wrote to Willie.

*

Henry and Charity had fun all summer. Charity showed him a side of Memphis he didn't know existed. They went to the Bitter Lemon, the Tonga club, Gateway, and the Roaring Sixties, which were teen clubs in Memphis. They swam a lot at Maywood, Rainbow, and Clearpool swimming pools. Clearpool had a dance for teenagers every weekend. They occasionally went to CYO (Catholic Youth Organization) dances at Little Flower Catholic Church on Jackson Avenue. The dance started immediately after Saturday night Mass. They went to the Fairgrounds a couple of nights during the summer, along with Battle of the Bands at Lakeland Amusement Park, and the Mid-South Coliseum. Henry attended some evening services with Charity at her church. Henry's mother was always glad to have Charity in their home and Henry was welcome at the Rambles home. During the summer Charity relaxed her kissing policy.

Henry earned money cutting yards in his neighborhood. Charity earned a little money babysitting, plus her parents were generous. So the kids always had enough cash to do what they wanted. It was almost a perfect summer for Henry except he couldn't get Marcie off his mind.

*

Once Peter recruited Jeff to work at the car lot, Moneypenny, Sims, and Ross began recruiting young people to push pot in Memphis' black communities. Peter divvyed up the city into two sectors, North and South Memphis, with Union Avenue being the dividing line. Confident that Sims was capable of working independently, Peter assigned him to be responsible for North Memphis. Moneypenny was made responsible for South Memphis so he could stay close to the car lot and the watchful eyes of Jeff and Ross. Peter's east boundary was Cleveland Street because he thought selling drugs in the white neighborhoods of Midtown and East Memphis would draw the attention of the police.

Ross was to work at the car lot posing as a mechanic and supervise and manage the drug business. When automobiles were brought in they would be taken to the Quonset hut located in the back of the car lot that served as a repair garage. Ross would remove the pot from the vehicles and repackage the drugs in nickel and dime bags. Then he stored the inventory of marijuana behind a false wall until it was needed.

Moneypenny and Sims had no trouble hiring poor black kids from the ghettos of Memphis to sell the drugs to the end consumers.

The marijuana business was competitive in all of the black neighborhoods, but no place was as competitive as the area surrounding the cross roads of Mississippi Boulevard and Walker Avenue, which was controlled by the Mayor. Despite the competition the drug sales were brisk.

Peter continued to hold a grudge against the Mayor for taking his money and was biding his time to exact revenge.

Chapter 53

August 1966

By the time Mr. Leroy Masters arrived at Caledonia's apartment, G.W. had been speaking with Trifecta for forty minutes about attending a white school.

Mr. Masters was an austere man who was active in the national and local chapters of the NAACP. He worked diligently with other civil rights leaders to initiate integration in the Memphis public high schools. By the way he dressed and carried himself, it was apparent Mr. Masters was a very dignified gentleman. When Masters entered Caledonia's apartment, G.W. rose to leave but Trifecta asked him to stay.

After introducing himself and taking a seat, Masters said, "My daughter Avery and eleven other Negro children will be joining you at Central High School. Most of these children have been chosen based upon the location of their residence, their academics, and extracurricular activities. You, on the other hand, have been chosen based upon the location of your residence and your involvement in the civil rights movement. There are several schools where we are interested in making a favorable impression. Because of a long tradition of excellence, Central High School is one of those schools. Precautions have been taken to insure your safety. While there won't be a lot of visible police protection in the unlikely event of trouble, there will be enough officers on the premises to protect you and the other children. We do not anticipate trouble from the white children or their parents. Conversely, we don't anticipate we will have problems with any of our students. It is very important to the movement that our students conduct themselves as ladies and gentlemen, and they apply themselves to their studies. This brings me to one of my concerns and the purpose of my visit. Our investigation shows that you have adequate I.Q. scores, but your grades reflect that you are not performing up to your potential."

"Mr. Masters, you are aware that Trifecta participated in the March Against Fear in Mississippi this summer," G.W. politely interrupted.

"I am," Masters replied.

"Well, sir, during the march Trifecta had the opportunity to speak with Doctor King and he now has a new appreciation for the movement and education. I'm sure he will do his best to do what you ask him."

"Is this true?" Masters asked, turning back to Trifecta.

"I don't want to go to school with white kids, but if that's what the movement needs, I guess I will." Trifecta replied, starting to enjoy the importance of the situation.

"The movement not only needs you to attend classes with white students, but we need you to excel. Are you willing to put forth your best effort?"

"I will."

"I'll see to it that he does," G.W. interjected excitedly.

"Very well, we will arrange transportation for you along with the other black students for registration and the first week or so of classes. This will give you, as well as the white students, an opportunity to get accustomed to your presence. Our goal is that you blend in and become a natural part of school life so other black children will not only be accepted, but welcomed by the students and faculty. Central has a strict dress code which we will inform you of, along with other instructions prior to registration. If finances hinder you from conforming to the dress code, we understand and are more than willing to help. Do any of you have any questions?"

Trifecta, G.W. and Caledonia said, "No sir," in unison.

"My daughter is planning a get together for all of the black students who will be attending Central. We would consider it a pleasure for you to attend. I also believe knowing the other children prior to attending school will benefit you. If transportation is an obstacle, I will be glad to arrange for someone to pick you up."

"That won't be necessary," interjected G.W. "I'll be happy to take him to your house."

After Mr. Masters left G.W. was beside himself with excitement. "This is too good to be true. First you're in the march, and then you talk to Doctor King. Now you're one of the students who will integrate a Memphis high school. I'm so proud of you."

Caledonia, who barely said anything during Mr. Masters' visit, smiled wide at Trifecta. She too was about to burst with delight.

A few days later Trifecta had another meeting concerning Central High School. This time it was with Peter, Jeff, and Levi at Levi's apartment.

"I understand you'll be going to Central High School this year," Peter said.

"Yea," Trifecta answered, wondering what interest Peter had in where he went to school.

"I think you can help the movement by being there," Peter continued.

"That's what they say," Trifecta said.

"Who are they?" Peter cross examined.

"What?"

267

"You said, that's what they say. Who else said you would be helping the movement by going to Central?"

"Mr. Masters; he's a big shot in the NAACP. His daughter is also going to Central."

"When did you talk to him?"

"He came to the house the other night," Trifecta answered, thinking this was none of Peter's business. But for Jeff's sake, he continued to answer Peter's questions.

"What did this Masters guy say to you?"

"He said it was important that I excel and make a good impression so other black children will be welcomed into white schools."

"Black people don't need to be welcomed into white schools. It's your right. If they don't welcome you, we'll either force them to let you in, or we'll burn the school down." Peter said, thinking he could use this situation to convince his father and the communist party that he was exploiting the social problems in Memphis.

"Right on," Jeff said.

"Mr. Masters said we are to behave ourselves and abide by their rules and dress code."

"Dress code?" Peter raised his voice. "You need to dress like a brother and not like some white kid. They're trying to steal your culture. When you go to that school you act black; you don't have to change who you are to go to their school. They're the ones who have to change. If they don't like it, tough; they are going to have to learn to like it and we will do anything necessary to teach them to like it."

"Right on," Jeff said again.

Trifecta cut his eyes at Levi and he could tell that Levi was as shocked as he was by the anger in Peter's voice.

"You dress the way you want. To be sure you can, I'm going to give you a job working at our business. Jeff and I are partners in a car lot on Crump Boulevard, and we'll hire you and Levi to work there."

"What are we going to do at a car lot?"

"Clean up cars, maybe sell a car; just whatever needs to be done."

"How much money will we make?" Levi asked.

Peter hesitated, "a dollar an hour."

A dollar an hour sounded like all the money in the world to Levi and Trifecta. Levi was excited but Trifecta remained skeptical about Peter. The next day Jeff took Levi and Trifecta to Brothers Motor Company on E.H. Crump Boulevard.

Both Trifecta and Levi worked at the car lot a few hours every day washing cars, picking up trash, cleaning the small office, and calling customers who were past due on their weekly car payments. The boys hadn't worked there long before they figured out something other than selling cars was going on. One day while they were cleaning the lot they happened into the Quonset hut. They saw Ross filling small bags with a tobacco-like substance which they both assumed was marijuana. When Trifecta and Levi told Jeff what they saw, he told them to mind their own business.

Trifecta saw very little of Peter at the car lot. On the occasions Peter was there he always talked to him about attending Central High School.

"Don't put up with anything from anybody. If the teachers hassle you, tell them you got rights. If a kid gives you a bad time, don't hesitate to fight. If you get into a situation you can't handle let me know, and I'll take care of it because I have connections."

Trifecta always acknowledged Peter's advice but he never intended to follow his counsel.

Chapter 54

The Cookout at the Masters

A week before the 1966-1967 school year, Mr. Masters and his wife had a cook out at their home for the eleven black children who were attending Central High School. G.W. planned to take Trifecta to the Masters' home on South Parkway but Peter insisted that Jeff take him. Trifecta was instructed to call the car lot when the cookout was over and Jeff would pick him up.

The Masters lived in an impressive two-story brick home surrounded by a manicured lawn as well as immaculate landscaping.

When Trifecta arrived at the party, Mrs. Masters answered the door. At first glance, she literally took Trifecta's breath away. She was tall and elegant, her skin was smooth and light, like milk chocolate. Her hair was straight and pulled tight into a bun. She wore a sleeveless flowered sundress that complemented her full breasts and narrow waist. She was the most sophisticated and striking woman Trifecta had ever seen.

"Hi, I'm Mrs. Masters, Avery's mother," she said as she stepped back from the door, allowing Trifecta to enter her home. "Who are you?"

"I'm Trifecta Johnson," he said, feeling out of place and unsure how to behave in the presence of such a grand lady.

"I'm so happy to meet you, Trifecta," Mrs. Masters said, putting her hand on his shoulder. Her eyes were large. She had high cheek bones and her lips were full and red. Trifecta's legs began to feel rubbery, and he knew his hands were shaking.

"Mr. Masters and the other children are in the backyard. Let me show you the way."

Trifecta was impressed with the cleanliness of the Masters' home. The furnishings were as nice as any Trifecta had ever seen, including what he remembered about the Churchill's home. The only difference in the quality of Churchill's furnishings and the Master's was that the Master's had clear plastic slip covers on all the upholstered furniture in the living room.

They walked through the house and into the backyard. Mrs. Masters moved gracefully with long strides. Trifecta had to quicken his normal pace to keep up with her.

When Trifecta entered the backyard, Mr. Masters and another man stood by a grill. Both men wore white shirts and ties. Mr. Masters had his sleeves rolled up and was holding a spatula. Teenagers stood in small groups about the yard.

"May I have your attention," Mrs. Masters announced. "I would like to introduce you to Trifecta Johnson. We're so pleased to have him join us this evening."

After her announcement Mr. Masters and the other man walked over to Trifecta.

"It's good to see you again," Mr. Masters said, extending his hand to shake Trifecta's.

"I would like you to meet Mr. Erwin. Mr. Erwin is with the NAACP and will be helping you and the other students get acclimated to your new school. Mr. Erwin, this is Trifecta Johnson, one of the students who will be enrolling at Central High School next week."

Mr. Erwin shook Trifecta's hand.

"Mr. Masters has told me a lot about you, Mr. Johnson. I understand you had the privilege of meeting Doctor King this summer."

"Yes, sir."

"What did Doctor King discuss with you?"

"He told me to keep my eye on the prize."

"What prize was he referring to?"

"The freedom of equality for all people," Trifecta said proudly.

"Excellent, I hope you will take those words to heart in your current academic endeavor. You are going to be given the responsibility of making the prize available for many children."

"Yes, sir," was all Trifecta could think to say. He was happy some of the other kids began to gather around him and the two men.

"And this is my daughter, Avery." Mr. Masters said, putting his arm around one of the young ladies.

Avery was a small replica of her mother, except more beautiful. She had the same smooth milk chocolate skin, and Trifecta could swear she had a golden aura around her. She wore a rosy pink sundress with puffed sleeves. Her hair was straight and hung to her shoulders. She wore a pink ribbon in her hair that matched her dress.

Trifecta experienced a hot flash as he looked into her large brown eyes.

"Hi, Trifecta," Avery said with a huge sparkling smile.

"Hi," the smitten Trifecta replied.

Avery introduced Trifecta to the other students. There was only one boy he recognized from his junior high school, and he was one of the smart kids who thought it was fun doing math problems and diagramming sentences.

"Cool threads," another boy said to Trifecta as they rapped knuckles, and wrapped their fists around one another's executing the soul brother handshake. Trifecta smiled, he hoped Avery over heard the boys comment.

Trifecta wore a pair of gold two-pocket bell-bottom pants, a shiny lime green polo shirt, and sun shades with green lenses that matched his shirt. The other students were dressed much more conservatively. Trifecta wondered if Avery thought he was cool.

When the hamburgers were cooked the students took their seats around several card tables. Trifecta tried to sit with Avery but was unsuccessful because several girls were vying to be Avery's friend and sat at her table.

After they ate, Mr. Erwin spoke to the group about the importance of their school year. Their behavior and achievements would reflect on all black people either positively or negatively and could make future integration of Memphis schools easier or more difficult.

After Mr. Erwin's talk the kids listened to records by The Barkays, Otis Redding, B.B. King, Sam and Dave, Booker T and The MGs, Bobby Blue Bland and Isaac Hayes. Trifecta took the opportunity to dance with Avery. They did the Dog, the Boogleloo, and Watusi, but Trifecta was thrilled when a tune was played for a slow dance. Avery felt good in his arms. About 8:30, the cookout started breaking up. Trifecta called the car lot and told Jeff he was ready to come home. He was surprised when Jeff arrived and Peter was with him.

Peter was anxious to learn what Mr. Erwin had said. Because Trifecta was more interested in Avery than what Mr. Erwin had been saying, he didn't remember much; however, what little he remembered didn't sit well with Peter

Chapter 55

Beginning of the 1966-1967 School Year

"They're here," Tommy said as he barged into the smoke hole in the basement of Central High School.

Everyone knew that Tommy was talking about the black kids. Anticipating trouble, several of the boys flipped their cigarettes into the commodes and headed for the door. Henry stayed behind continuing to smoke and hoping Charity wouldn't get involved if there was a confrontation. The more he thought about Charity and the potential danger she could be in, the more his conscience bothered him. After a few minutes, he went to find her.

He discovered her sitting in a recessed window sill in the stairwell where they frequently met before homeroom.

"I heard they were here and came to make sure you were alright."

"Why wouldn't I be?"

"I just thought if there was trouble you'd be in the middle of it defending the black kids."

"There wasn't any trouble; two black men escorted twelve students to the office."

The bell rang and Henry and Charity went to their respective homerooms.

The school day went by without incident. Henry only saw one black student the entire day and he didn't have a black kid in any of his classes.

That evening as Henry was getting up from the supper table the phone rang. He was close to the wall phone in the kitchen, so he answered it.

"Hello?"

"Hey, kid," Henry immediately recognized Scoop's voice.

"Can you hold on while I switch phones?" Henry asked. He went to the phone in his parent's bedroom because he didn't want his mother to overhear his conversation.

When Henry was on the extension he hollered, "Okay, I got it." He waited to hear the kitchen receiver hang up before he said anything to Scoop.

"Hi, Scoop."

"Have you started your story?"

"What story?"

"Your follow-up article to the one you wrote last year about colored kids attending Central High?"

"They never published my story and now my job on the newspaper staff is selling ads, not writing articles."

"They can't stop you from writing. They don't have to publish your columns but they can't stop you from writing. Anyway, I might get your stuff published in the Press Scimitar."

"You could do that?"

"No promises, but if your story is good enough I might be able to get it published."

After Scoop hung up, Henry immediately called Charity and told her about the conversation he had with Scoop. Charity was excited about the idea of Henry writing an article about African-Americans attending their school.

Charity was assigned to the same history class as Avery. She intentionally sat next to the black girl on the first day of school. Over the first week of classes, Avery and Charity talked on a regular basis. Charity felt sorry for Avery because if she was enrolled in Melrose, Hamilton, Booker T. Washington, or any other black school, she would have been on the student council, homecoming queen and one of the most popular girls on campus. Instead she was despised by most of the white students and some of the faculty at Central.

"My boyfriend is on the newspaper staff," Charity said to Avery as they walked out of class together.

"That's cool," Avery replied.

"He would like to write an article about African-American students integrating Central; would you mind letting him interview you?"

"That might be alright but I need to ask my daddy," Avery answered. "We're in a sensitive situation and I just need to make sure I'm not going to jeopardize what we're trying to accomplish, but I'll ask tonight."

As Charity and Avery walked down the hall talking, they drew the attention of several students.

During their nightly telephone chats, Charity told Henry about the possibility of Avery giving him an interview.

The next day in history class, Avery told Charity she could give the interview with the understanding that her father had to read the article prior to it being published.

"I'm certain that won't be a problem," Charity told Avery. "Henry and I are on your side, and I'm sure the interview will be friendly."

After fourth period Henry and Charity usually walked together to their fifth period classes.

"Avery said she would give you an interview but her dad has to read the article before it's published."

"Her dad?"

"Yes, these are emotional times and I'm sure they want to take every precaution not to be misunderstood. Maybe I can help you with the questions you will ask her."

"Do you think I need your help with the interview?"

"No, I just thought it was something we can do together."

The next day when Henry went to school he and Charity had prepared ten questions to ask Avery. While he had never been introduced to Avery, he was well aware of who she was because she was the prettiest black girl he had ever seen.

Henry usually sat with Alan in the lunch room but that day he noticed there was a vacant seat at the black kids table directly across from Avery. Disregarding the uneasiness he felt sitting with the blacks students, Henry took a seat on the stool facing Avery. While he wouldn't admit it publicly, except for Marcie, Avery was probably the prettiest girl in the school.

"Hi Avery, I'm Henry Murphy—Charity's boyfriend," Henry said, trying to be inconspicuous.

"Hi, Henry, I'm glad to meet you," Avery said, looking up with a smile.

Not only were the black kids shocked when a white boy sat down at their table, but the white kids were wondering what Henry was up to.

"Do you have time for an interview now?" Henry asked.

"Sure, I guess."

"Great... so, where did you go to school last year?" Henry said opening his pad.

"I was at Hamilton."

As Henry continued his interview, Trifecta walked into the cafeteria. When he saw a white kid sitting at his place across from Avery, he was suddenly overcome with rage.

"Were you involved in any extracurricular activities there?" Henry asked Avery.

While Henry wrote the impressive list of school organizations and activities Avery had been involved in at Hamilton High school, he became aware of someone standing in his periphery. When he turned to see who it was, Trifecta was breathing heavily through his mouth, and his eyes blazed with anger.

Turning his attention back to Avery, Henry asked, "What extracurricular activities would you like to be involved in at Central?"

"What are you doing, man?" Trifecta snarled, interrupting the interview.

"I'm talking to Avery," Henry said calmly.

"Why don't you go sit with your own kind?"

"Trifecta, stop acting like that," Avery said.

Remembering the unusual name of the black boy he interviewed the previous year at Washington High School, Henry asked, "Are you Trifecta Johnson?"

"It doesn't matter who I am. You need to stay away from my girlfriend," Trifecta said as he shoved Henry with all the strength his anger could muster. Henry fell against a black girl sitting next to him, almost knocking her out of her seat as he tumbled to the floor.

"Stop it, Trifecta," Avery admonished as the other girls at the table screamed and scrambled out of the way. While lying on his back on the floor, Henry instinctively kicked the stool he had been sitting on into Trifecta's shins. Trifecta cursed as he half tripped and half jumped on top of Henry. Trifecta tried to punch, but Henry grabbed him and the boys wrestled on the floor for a few seconds before a male teacher intervened and took both boys to the principal's office.

The principal had been dreading the first time he had to discipline one of the black students. He was afraid things could quickly turn racial and the NAACP would become involved.

"How did the fight start?" the principal said.

"I was interviewing Avery and Trifecta came along and pushed me to the floor for no reason," Henry answered.

The two boys glared at one another.

"What do you mean you were interviewing Avery?"

"I was writing an article for the paper about how Negroes were adjusting to being at Central."

"Who assigned you to write such an article?"

"No one, it was my own idea."

"How do you explain the fight?" the principal asked Trifecta.

"He was talking to my girlfriend and I didn't like it."

"Mr. Johnson, at Central we don't settle things by fighting. Do you think Mr. Murphy was saying anything inappropriate to your girlfriend?

"I don't know."

"We don't forbid polite and appropriate conversation between students during lunch or between classes. We certainly don't feel such conversations constitute a reason for violence even if the exchange is taking place between a white and black student. I believe the purpose for black students being at Central is to gain friendship and cooperation between the races. If either of you think I'm going to allow any type of disturbance in this school, particularly racial disturbances, then you need to get that thought out of your head. Do I make myself clear?"

Both boys responded with a nod.

Turning back to Henry, the principal said, "I thought your assignment on the newspaper staff was to sell ads, not write articles."

"I thought I had a good idea for an article."

"Why did you think that?"

"Because I thought an article about how Negroes were adapting at Central was news."

"It's not going to be news in our paper. Henry, I'm going to suspend you from being on the newspaper staff for six weeks. If you stay out of trouble for six weeks you can go back to selling ads, but not writing articles. And I'm giving both of you boys a week of detention for fighting. Now I believe your lunchtime is over so you need to get to your next class."

As the two boys walked towards their respective classes, Trifecta said, "I think I remember you, you're the cat that came to Washington last spring asking me what I thought about integrating a white school."

"Yeah," Henry replied coolly.

"Did you write your article?"

"Yeah."

"How was it?"

"It never got published and I was suspended for writing it," Henry said, as he slipped into the boys' restroom for a cigarette before going to class.

The principal called Agent Ball and reported what had happened because he knew Agent Ball had an interest in Henry.

Trifecta called the car lot and told Jeff he couldn't work until Saturday because he had detention hall. Peter was thrilled when he heard about the problems at Central and paid Trifecta for the time he missed due to detention.

Chapter 56

The evening after Trifecta and Henry tussled in the lunch room, Mr. Masters asked Avery how things were going with the interview about black students integrating Central. She told him about the problem between Trifecta and Henry. Mr. Masters was upset that Trifecta had picked a fight, but he was equally concerned about the relationship between his daughter and the boy from the projects.

"Are you his girlfriend?" Mr. Masters asked Avery.

"No."

"Why did he say you were his girlfriend?"

"I don't know, Daddy," Avery answered, wishing she hadn't told him about the fight.

"Does he have any reason to think you are his girlfriend?"

Avery paused. "I don't think so."

"What do you mean you don't think so?"

"We eat lunch at the same table with the other black kids and we walk to a couple of classes together."

Avery was aware Trifecta had a serious crush on her, but knew better than to tell her father.

"Have you done more than talk with him?"

"What?"

"Has he kissed you or done anything else?"

"Daddy!"

"Has he?"

"No, absolutely not," Avery answered firmly.

"I don't want you involved with that boy."

"May I ask why?"

"He comes from the projects. He has an unstable family life. I'm afraid he is one of those people caught in a cycle of poverty. He displayed his ghetto mentality in the way he reacted when a white boy was speaking with you. He is not the type of boy you should be involved with."

"I thought you wanted equality for everyone?"

"I want equal opportunity for everyone, but all boys are not equally suited for my daughter."

"He seems like a nice boy."

"Is that why he starts fights in the lunch room?"

"What do you want me to do, Daddy?"

"I want you to be nice to Trifecta, but I don't want you to encourage him."

"You don't want me to encourage him to what?"

"I want you to make it clear you have no romantic interest in him."

Both father and daughter stared at one another for a moment.

"Do I make myself clear?" Mr. Masters asked, breaking the silence.

"Yes sir."

*

The next day in the "smoke hole", Henry was leaning against the restroom wall enjoying a cigarette. Several other boys were milling around, talking and smoking when two guys from the football team entered. Henry was surprised to see them because if the coach caught them in the smoke hole, they risked being kicked off the team. The two boys approached Henry.

"We don't like coloreds and whites mixing here at Central, particularly boys and girls." Wally Shoemaker said, referring to Henry sitting with Avery and the other black students.

Henry shrugged and said, "Okay."

Not satisfied with Henry's response, Shoemaker pressed, "Do you like that colored girl, or do you just like all colored people?"

Henry knew he was referring to Avery.

"I don't particularly like her, but I don't dislike her," Henry said, his colon cinching into knots.

"Do you think that colored girl is pretty? Do you want to make out with that girl? Do you want to kiss those black lips?" Mark Elder asked, loud enough for everyone in the tiled room to hear. Mark was the boy with Wally. The room went silent.

"Do you?" Even though he was scared Henry tried to be unflinching by looking Mark squarely in the eye.

"You make me sick," Mark growled as he moved closer to Henry, taunting him. Henry continued to lean against the wall, not wanting to rise to Mark's challenge. Wally put the back of his arm across Mark's chest to stop him from moving any closer to Henry.

"You don't need to be flirting with colored girls. You don't need to make friends with colored boys. And you need to tell your hippie girlfriend the same thing or there's going to be trouble. You got it?" Wally said between gritted teeth.

Henry nodded slowly. The two football players left. As Henry brought his cigarette to his lips, he noticed his hand was shaking uncontrollably.

Alan entered the smoking room in time to witness the confrontation. When things returned to normal, Alan came over to Henry. "Man it's getting harder and harder to hang out with you. If I'm not careful I'm going to be guilty by association. What is it with you and the Negroes?"

"Nothing, I'm just trying to write an article about something other than guys who think they're tough because they put on a jock strap every day.

*

When Henry and Trifecta's week of detention was over, they happened to walk out of the room together.

"I hope you're happy, man," Trifecta said.

"What now?" Henry said.

"Avery won't have anything to do with me."

"Sorry," Henry said sarcastically.

"She even moved where she sits at lunch."

"Tough break."

"I need you to talk to her for me."

"What?"

"I'm sure it's all because of that fight we had. I need you to tell her that you and I are cool."

"Sure," Henry answered, having no intention of talking to Avery and risk being beaten by Mark and Wally.

Chapter 57

November 1966

As the school year progressed Charity and Avery developed a close friendship. Both girls felt somewhat isolated; Charity because she was considered a flower child and Avery because she was black. While the other black girls were nice enough and were in awe of Avery's beauty and intelligence, Avery didn't feel close to any of them.

If Charity were black, Avery might not have been as enthusiastic about having her as a friend, but both girls thought it was cool, exciting, and even daring to have an interracial relationship, and spoke with each other regularly at school and on the phone at night.

*

WDIA was the first all-black formatted radio station in the country, broadcasting with 50,000 kilowatts from Memphis, Tennessee. WDIA had played an important part in the civil rights struggle in Memphis and the surrounding area since 1948.

Each year the radio station sponsored what they called a "Goodwill Review" where various black singers, musicians, and comedians performed to an almost exclusive black audience. For years the "Goodwill Review" took place at Ellis Auditorium in downtown Memphis. However, when the Mid-South Coliseum was built in 1963, the "Goodwill Review" relocated to that venue.

In 1967, the radio station had an all-star cast of performers scheduled. One night as Avery and Charity were talking on the phone they decided to get some dates and attend that year's performance.

Later that evening Henry called Charity.

"I was talking to Avery earlier," Charity said.

"Okay," Henry responded.

"We thought it would be cool to go to the "Goodwill Review.""

"The what?" Henry asked. Not having listened to the black radio station, he thought she was talking about something that had to do with disabled people.

"You know, the show put on every year by WDIA."

"Do you mean the Negro radio station?"

"I mean the black radio station."

"Are you and Avery going together?"

"I thought I might get a date."

"You mean me?"

"Man, you are dense. Of course I mean you, unless you want me to find some other cute guy to go with me?"

"Isn't that just for black people?"

"It's for everybody."

"But only black people go to it, right?"

"Not if you and I go. Come on! It will be fun, and they'll have some great music."

"You don't think it will be dangerous?"

"You'll be there to protect me."

"I don't know."

"Look, if it makes you feel better, Avery is going to bring some big strong football player."

"Great," Henry said sarcastically. He had never told Charity about his encounter with Mark Elder or Wally Shoemaker, but that's where his mind flashed back to at the mention of a football player.

"So, is that a yes?" Charity asked, even though she recognized the insincerity in his voice.

"I guess, but we don't need to let my parents find out where we're going."

Within the week both black and white students, along with some members of the faculty, were gossiping about Charity and Henry double dating with Avery and a black boy. The rumors created all sorts of speculation about the identity of Avery's date. Soon the gossip become muddled. Trifecta heard about the date during lunch period when one of the black students who had heard the story fifth hand, mistakenly asked him, "Have you heard Avery's going on a date with that white boy, Henry Murphy?"

Without answering or checking the facts, Trifecta went looking for Avery and Henry. Unfortunately, Trifecta found Henry first. Henry was standing by some lockers a short distance from the smoke hole having a conversation with another student. Luckily for Henry, a male teacher was standing close by and saw Trifecta run up and blindside Henry shoving him into the lockers. Henry ricocheted off the locker like a silver ball off of a pinball bumper and landed on the floor. Instantly, Trifecta was on top of him, punching wildly, but the male teacher interceded before Henry was seriously hurt.

The teacher, holding each boy's arm in his hands, escorted the boys to the principal's office where he sat them down in the outer office.

"What were you doing?" Henry asked quietly so as not to draw the attention of the office staff.

"I'm going to kick your butt," Trifecta whispered.

"Why?"

Before Trifecta could answer, the door to the principal's private office opened.

"Boys, he will see you now," the teacher said.

The two boys took a seat in wooden chairs in front of the principal's desk.

"Mr. Johnson, I understand you attacked Mr. Murphy without any apparent provocation. Would you like to explain yourself?"

"I had to get some things straight," Trifecta said.

"What sort of things?"

"Just things."

"I see, the principal paused and turned toward Henry. "Mr. Murphy, do you have any explanation for what happened?"

"No sir."

"Is it a racial problem?" the principal asked, turning towards Trifecta.

"Everything in this city and school is a racial problem," Trifecta said.

"What specific racial incident caused you to attack Mr. Murphy?"

"He just needs to stay with his own kind."

"I see," the principal said, having his suspicions confirmed. He had heard that Henry and Avery were dating and it seemed reasonable that the trouble between the two boys stemmed from the interracial romance.

"Mr. Johnson, this is the second time you have attacked Mr. Murphy. If this happens a third time you're going to be out, do you understand?"

"Yes," Trifecta answered.

"When I say out, I mean expelled, is that clear?"

"Yes."

"Also, I'm going to call Mr. Masters and your grandmother. I am not going to have racial problems on this campus, is that clear?"

"Yes."

"Mr. Johnson, you may go without any punishment, but this will never happen again, do you understand?"

"Yes," Trifecta stood and left the room.

With Trifecta gone the principal turned his attention to Henry.

"I understand you are dating Avery Masters."

"Sir?" Henry asked, startled by the comment.

"It's come to my attention that you are dating one of the colored girls."

"No sir," Henry said emphatically.

"You mean you are not dating Avery Masters?"

"No, sir."

The principal leaned back, studying Henry's face. When he was convinced Henry was telling the truth he asked, "Why did Mr. Johnson attack you?"

"I don't know."

"What did Mr. Johnson mean when he said you need to stay with your own kind?"

"My girlfriend…."

"You mean Charity Ramble?"

"Yes, sir."

"Go on."

"The only thing I can think of is that Charity and Avery have been talking about double dating."

"Mr. Murphy, I'm not going to interfere with your personal affairs unless it begins to affect what happens at this school, and it appears it has. So I'm going to recommend that you and Miss Ramble reconsider double dating with Negroes."

"Yes, sir," Henry said, knowing that if he told Charity about the principal's recommendation she would become more determined to double date with Avery and a black boy.

That afternoon the principal made three telephone calls. The first call was to Mr. Masters.

289

After listening to the principal's explanation of what occurred between Trifecta and Henry and his subsequent conversation with Henry, Mr. Masters said, "I hope you're not trying to dictate who my daughter sees socially?"

"No, but I think these children are going to make things more difficult at school than they already are and they are putting themselves in an uncomfortable situation."

"My daughter is already in an uncomfortable situation. We understand that we are going to be uncomfortable if we ever hope to achieve equality. And equality is the hope my family and I have."

The second call was to Caledonia.

"May I speak to Mrs. Caledonia Johnson?"

"She ain't here," Caledonia said, recognizing the caller was a white man and thinking it was probably a bill collector.

"This is the Principal of Central High School. Will you have her call me when she comes in?"

He left his number but Caledonia didn't write the number down and she never called back.

The third call was to Agent Ball.

Chapter 58

December 1967

Charity had her parents' car for the evening and her first stop was Henry's house. Mrs. Murphy wasn't sure she approved of a girl picking up a boy for a date, but accepted it as being a sign of the times. Henry told his parents they were going downtown to a movie and said nothing about the double date. Charity and Henry picked up Avery next and finally Avery's date. From the time Avery got in the car, she and Charity talked and laughed and generally enjoyed each-others company, while Henry and Avery's date said little. Henry could sense that Avery's date was as uncomfortable double dating with whites as he was doubling with blacks.

"Tell us about yourself, Hershel," Charity said to Avery's date.

"I play football, basketball, and baseball for Hamilton High School."

"And he's also on the student council," Avery interjected.

"That's cool," Charity said. "You and Henry have a little bit in common. Henry is a reporter for Central's newspaper and he covers a lot of sporting events."

"I used to be on the newspaper staff," Henry said.

"Why aren't you still?" Hershel asked.

"I wrote a few articles the school didn't approve of so they told me I couldn't write anymore." Henry was purposefully vague, thinking Hershel might be offended if he knew Henry's writing career had been cut short due to an article about black students.

"What kind of articles did you write?" Hershel said.

"One of his articles was about Avery," Charity said.

"Oh yeah, what did Avery do to have an article written about her?" Hershel asked.

"The article wasn't just about Avery as much as it was about Ne…….." Henry was saying when Charity interrupted not wanting Henry to say Negroes.

"……it was about Afro Americans attending Central," she said.

"What was wrong with that?" Hershel asked.

"The man" didn't like it, so he put a stop to it, just like he puts a stop to everything else that's cool," Charity said.

"What else did the man put a stop to?" Hershel asked, wondering if Charity always referred to people in positions of authority as "the man", or if she was just trying to pander to him.

"We don't get to have a prom because black kids going to Central."

"Yeah, I heard about that," Hershel said.

"Is Hamilton having a prom?" Charity asked.

"It is and he's taking me," Avery said.

Hershel made arrangements to take Avery to Hamilton's prom almost as soon as he and Avery began dating. He thought taking a beautiful girl from another school to the prom would not only make the other boys envious but the Hamilton co-eds jealous.

"That's pretty lame," Charity said.

"That he's taking me to the prom?" Avery asked.

"No, that an African American school can have a prom but we can't just because a few blacks might attend."

"Daddy says the white people are afraid that the black boys will go after all the white girls," Avery said.

"They might be right. Do you want to take me to your prom, Hershel?" Charity asked, teasing Hershel.

"No way," Avery said. "He might decide he likes kissing those skinny little lips of yours."

"My lips aren't that skinny."

"They're skinnier than a black girl's lips," Avery said as the two boys were becoming increasingly antsy with the way the light-hearted conversation was going.

"My lips aren't any skinnier than yours."

"I guess that's because some white man thought my great- great-grandmother was cute," Avery said, giggling.

"That's typical. It's alright for a white man to have a black woman but they're scared their precious white women will be involved with a black man," Charity said.

"Well why do they let a black school have a prom but they won't let us?" Avery asked.

"What do you think, Henry?" Charity asked, putting him on the spot.

Henry didn't like the idea of interracial dating and he wasn't sure he liked the idea of mixed double dating, so he diplomatically said, "It's a bummer we can't have a prom."

"What do you think, Hershel?" Avery said.

"I think you girls are crazy," Hershel answered, feeling the same as Henry.

"We need to do something about it," Charity said. "Avery and I are among the few black and white students who speak to each other and I think we're the only ones who are friends. If the black boys don't even talk to the white girls and vice versa, I don't know why everyone thinks they'll have babies together."

To Henry's relief they had arrived at the Coliseum and the topic of conversation stopped. Black people were converging on the round domed building from all directions. As Henry scoured the parking lot his fears were realized;

other than a couple of policemen directing traffic he didn't see another white person anywhere. When the foursome walked past a white police officer, the patrolman glared at Henry and Charity with contempt, adding to Henry's anxiety.

The four had purchased tickets in advance and were sitting in the middle of the upper deck. Because the building was round, Henry could see all of the ninety-five hundred people in attendance, and other than a couple of white policemen patrolling inside the building he didn't spot any white faces among the crowd. Being in such an obvious minority he felt a twinge of empathy for the handful of black kids attending Central.

However, Henry felt a little better when the show started and the master of ceremonies welcomed all of his black brothers and sisters and their white friends.

When the performance started, there was a steady stream of singers and musicians along with a smattering of comedians. Henry was surprised to see several white musicians on stage playing with Booker T and the MG's and the Memphis Horns. While Charity enjoyed the show, she couldn't help but think about what they could do about the prom situation.

When the show was over Charity suggested they get something to eat at the Pig, referring to the Pig and Whistle. However, Henry was afraid someone from school would see them and word would get back to Mark and Wally so he recommended they go to Leonard's Barbecue, located in Southside High School's district. Southside was a predominately white school that was quickly being surrounded by black residents. Henry reasoned to himself that they would be less conspicuous and probably unknown to any of the restaurant's patrons.

Like the Pig and Whistle, Leonard's had a drive-in as well as an eat-in restaurant. Despite the cold-weather, Hershel suggested they eat in the car. Even though by federal law a restaurant could not refuse service to anyone based on race, Leonard's was still considered a "white" restaurant and Hershel didn't want to go inside. They parked under the canopy and waited for a car hop. Soon a black man was at Charity's window ready to take their orders. Looking inside the car the car hop asked, "What are you children doing?" The foursome understood that the waiter wanted to know why they were double dating.

"We're ordering something to eat," Charity said confidentially, "and I would like a Coke and a piece of lemon pie." Next to pulled pork bar-b-que, the lemon pie was Leonard's specialty.

The other three ordered the same. Within minutes the waiter attached a tray to Charity's car window and she passed the drinks and slices of pie to the others.

"I couldn't help thinking about our dilemma all night," Charity said.

"What dilemma?" Avery asked.

"Not having a prom our senior year," Charity answered.

"There's nothing we can do about it," Henry said.

"There is so," Charity said.

"What?"

"You could write an article," Charity answered.

"Then I would be suspended again and it wouldn't get published anyway."

"I don't mean for the school newspaper, but you could write a letter to the editor for either the Commercial Appeal, (the morning paper) or the Press Scimitar (the afternoon paper). And maybe your friend Scoop can help get it printed.

If he was suspended for writing an article for the school newspaper, Henry wondered what the repercussions would be for writing a letter to the editor of a city paper.

Chapter 59

February 26, 1968

Peter's drug trade had flourished during the 1966-1967 school year. Lots of illegal money was being generated through the sale of marijuana. The high grade of ganja that was being imported into Memphis by the communists allowed him to charge premium prices for the narcotic. The excessive profits made it possible for him to skim money for personal use rather than sending all the proceeds to support the communist war effort in Vietnam. Soon Peter was living in a recently built luxury high-rise apartment located directly across the street from Central High School. Trifecta could see Peter coming and going every day as he stared out the window of his second-period class. Peter had always been secretive about where he lived. However, Trifecta could identify Peter easily because he had purchased a late model yellow Cadillac Coup Deville. Trifecta frequently would see Peter sitting in the back seat of his luxury ride while Ross chauffeured him about town.

Peter had been smoking weed since he moved to Memphis but in recent months he had begun injecting heroin and taking LSD. Life for Peter appeared to be good. He had plenty of money, a nice apartment, a cool car, drugs, and several girlfriends who were attracted to his lifestyle. However, he was having business problems in South Memphis, specifically in the Lemoyne Gardens area. The Mayor had robbed several of the young boys who sold marijuana for Moneypenny. The Mayor not only robbed the youngsters but he had beaten a few of them, hospitalizing one child for over a week. Peter wasn't concerned about the children but was afraid one of the young couriers would eventually say too much and an investigation would lead police to him.

When Jeff called Peter to tell him another one of Moneypenny's boys had been robbed of two hundred dollars in drugs and cash, Peter decided it was past time for him to retaliate. He ordered Jeff and Moneypenny to report to him at the car lot at midnight.

Moneypenny was the last to arrive. When he entered the office, the room was filled with sweet-smelling smoke. Peter, Jeff, and Ross were all toking on reefers.

"What's happening?" Moneypenny smiled nervously.

"Everything's cool," Peter answered with pharmaceutical eyes and a cannabis induced grin.

"Want a hit? Peter asked, holding out a joint to Moneypenny.

Moneypenny took the marijuana from Peter and puffed away, sucking the intoxicating smoke deep into his lungs while Peter, who was suffering from the munchies, began ravishing a bag of potato chips.

There had been several minutes of small talk when Moneypenny asked, "What are we here for?"

Peter leaned back in his chair, lit another joint and said, "We got a job for you."

"Oh yeah, what am I supposed to do?"

"You're making a lot of money, right?" Peter said with a giggle.

"I'm doing alright."

"I'm going to pay you more for this job."

"That's cool, what do I have to do?"

"You know the Mayor?" Peter asked, trying to look serious.

"Do you mean the mayor of Memphis, Bill Ingram?"

"No, I mean the cat that sells dope at Mississippi and Walker."

"Yeah, I know him," Moneypenny said hesitantly with suspicion in his voice.

"You know what he's been doing to you?" Peter said.

"He's been causing us trouble," Moneypenny replied quickly sobering up, afraid of where the conversation was going.

"He's been causing you trouble and causing me to lose money," Peter said more authoritatively and with a deep frown on his face.

"That's right," Moneypenny responded.

"Well it's time you put a stop to it."

"Okay," Moneypenny said, not sure what else to say.

"And I got a plan for how you can do that."

"You do?"

"I do," said Peter. "You're going to kill him."

"Now wait a minute. I ain't killing anybody."

"It's your responsibility. He is stealing in your territory, plus, if you take out the Mayor you eliminate your biggest competitor in South Memphis."

"You need to get somebody else."

"You're responsible for your territory," Peter said, leaning toward Moneypenny.

"I'm not getting electrocuted for killing anybody, even if they are stealing from me."

"Is that what you're worried about? You're scared you'll get executed if you kill the Mayor? You know nobody cares about a Negro getting killed. Negroes get killed every day and nobody gets arrested. I've even killed a Negro, and I never got arrested.

Jeff was taken aback by Peter confessing to killing a black man.

"What's your plan?" Moneypenny asked hesitantly.

"You're going to dress up like a Klansman, and then you're going to kill him. I remember you make a good Klansman, burning crosses in people's yards. And to avoid any problems, Ross and Jeff are going to be watching to make sure you get the job done."

"That sounds risky."

"The FBI didn't suspect you when you burned a cross in front of one of their agent's home. Posing as a Klansman is the perfect plan for wasting that colored boy."

Peter's arrogance and disrespect for soul brothers was beginning to concern and aggravate Jeff.

*

The car was stolen in Indianapolis and delivered to the car lot that day. The only flesh that was visible on Moneypenny was his black face; the rest of his body was covered with clothing and gloves. Peter and Ross made a makeshift hood out of a white pillow case. The hood fit awkwardly but Peter assured Moneypenny he would only have to wear it for a few minutes so the fit wasn't critical as long as no one could tell he was black.

At twilight Moneypenny drove by the corner of Mississippi and Walker and was relieved that no one was there. He turned onto Walker, thinking he would tell Peter he couldn't find the Mayor. Moneypenny was aware that Ross and Jeff were following a short distance behind him to ensure he carried out the murder.

At Walker and Lauderdale, Moneypenny saw three young men walking towards Mississippi Boulevard and recognized one of the men as the Mayor. Moneypenny's heart started pounding. His hands were shaking, and his bladder felt like it would explode. He turned right and drove around the block. When he arrived back on Walker the trio was nearly at the corner. He lost his nerve and instead of shooting he drove past the three of them. Turning right he saw Jeff and Ross in front of him. His colon drew up in a knot, knowing he had no option but to carry out the plan. Moneypenny sped through the residential neighborhood, making the block again and hoping the Mayor and his two friends were still on the street. Returning to Mississippi Boulevard, he struggled to slip the pillow case hood over his head as he drove.

When he turned onto Walker his vision was slightly impaired by the hood. He pulled to a stop beside the three pedestrians. They were on the passenger side of the car. Unfamiliar with power windows, Moneypenny fingered the electric window button and instead of the front window, the back window went down. He quickly changed buttons and the front window retracted into the door. The three young men had stopped and were looking curiously at Moneypenny, unaware of what he was doing. Moneypenny's hands were shaking violently as he pointed the semi-automatic .45 caliber pistol in the general direction of his target. He pulled the trigger, jerking off a shot. Inside the confines of the vehicle the sound was deafening. The bullet hit the interior roof of the car blowing a hole in the top of the vehicle. He shot two more times. Both rounds made it out of the car but missed the intended victim. Moneypenny's ears were ringing. The boys started to scurry like roaches exposed to light, all going in different directions. The Mayor broke into a run, going in the same direction as the car. Moneypenny floored the accelerator while shooting randomly out of the window. As the car fish tailed down the street, the Mayor fell. He was hit by two of the haphazard shots.

Moneypenny tried to rip the hood from his head but it became twisted over his face leaving him sightless. He hadn't gone twenty yards before the car smashed into a wooden telephone pole. Time seemed suspended for an anxious moment, and then the broken pole crashed onto the roof of the car, injuring Moneypenny and interrupting electricity and telephone service to the neighborhood.

When Ross and Jeff turned back onto Walker they witnessed the carnage as neighbors swarmed from their houses to investigate the pandemonium. The two men quickly sped away, not wanting to be seen in the vicinity of the shooting.

The Mayor was dead on arrival at John Gaston Hospital. Moneypenny was admitted to intensive care, also at John Gaston. Peter and Ross were both concerned that Moneypenny might identify them as conspirators to the murder. So through contacts Ross had within the hospital and in exchange for five hundred dollars, Moneypenny died in the hospital that night without regaining consciousness. There was no autopsy so the cause of death that was recorded on his death certificate was an automobile accident. The investigation into the murder of the Mayor was immediately closed.

It didn't seem to Jeff that anyone cared to make the effort to investigate the cause of Moneypenny's death and he concluded that Peter was right when he said, "Nobody cares if a black man gets killed."

*

With the Mayor dead, Willie was safe to return to Lemoyne Gardens, except he had five months left of his tour in Guam where he served as a cook in the army. Despite the size of the small island, Willie enjoyed being in the tropical paradise, especially when he had a pass to leave the military installation. The people of Guam treated G.I.s very well, particularly some of the unmarried ladies.

Willie wrote a letter to Caledonia about once a month and Caledonia would always write him back. Willie hadn't heard from or written a letter to his mother since he joined the army.

Chapter 60

Mary returns home

Trifecta was overcome with pride. He had four Cs and a B. For the first time since enrolling at Central there were no Ds or Fs on his report card. At lunch he proudly passed his report card around the lunch table where the black students ate.

When Trifecta arrived home he rushed into the house, eager to show Caledonia his grades.

"Madea," he shouted as he stepped inside the apartment door. He had to look twice, unsure of who he was seeing. She looked weary and worn. Her clothes hung loose from her slight body. Her watery eyes appeared to be half closed. She smiled weakly when she saw him.

"Mama?" Trifecta questioned, not sure it was her.

"How are you, baby?" Mary said. Her hoarse voice was slightly louder than a whisper.

Trifecta crossed the room and hugged his mother. She felt frail in his arms. He could feel her shoulder blades as they jutted out from her back, having almost no meat on them. Her arms were like broomsticks covered with skin. He had never seen his mother in such a poor condition.

"When did you get here?" Trifecta asked.

"I haven't been here long."

"Are you going to stay?"

"I have some bad news for you." Mary said, ignoring Trifecta's question.

"What's wrong, Mama?"

"Your brother is dead."

Trifecta's eyes widened. His breath caught in his throat. "What happened?"

Since Willie had gone into the army, Trifecta and Marquis had become much closer. Trifecta had even begun to consider Marquis his brother.

"He didn't have a chance," Mary said.

"What are you talking about?" Trifecta asked in a panic, concerned about Marquis.

"He wasn't healthy."

"Mama, are you alright?" Trifecta asked as Caledonia and Marquis came down the stairs.

"I'll be fine."

"My brother isn't dead—he's right here," Trifecta said, pointing at Marquis.

"It ain't Marquis that died; it was Ramon."

"Who?"

"It's your brother, Ramon."

"I don't have a brother named Ramon," Trifecta said, beginning to wonder if his mother was delusional.

"Sure you do. He was born eight months ago, and that's why I'm here."

"Did you and Dante have another baby?"

"No honey, I haven't been with Dante for a while."

"What happened to the baby you had with Dante?"

"He's with his Madea on his daddy's side."

"Who is Ramon's daddy?"

"Terrance; I had two healthy babies with Terrance. That's why I kept telling him it's not my fault."

"What happened to Ramon?"

"He was sick. We didn't have any money for the doctor and one night he died. After that, Terrance went crazy and started beating me. Some of the neighbors heard us and called the law. The police took him to jail but I never did press charges so he was out the next day. After that he began beating me regular. The last time he was beating me it got out of hand and the neighbors called the law again. When the police came Terrance started fighting with them. He snatched one of the cop's pistols from his holster and shot him in the leg. The other pig hit him on the head with a nightstick and Terrance went down hard. When Terrance was on the floor the pig kept hitting him; I thought he was going to kill Terrance. Then more police arrived and they took Terrance to jail. His head was covered in blood. I don't know why he fought with the police. I wasn't going to press charges. Now he's locked up and I ain't got the money to bail him out. And I didn't have money to pay the rent so I got evicted and came here. But Ramon dying isn't my fault; I have eight healthy babies."

"I have seven brothers?" Trifecta asked.

"You have four brothers and three sisters, and Ramon is dead."

"Why, didn't you tell me about my brothers and sisters when you came to Memphis, for Tyrone's funeral?"

"I didn't think it was important."

"You didn't think it was important that I know about my brothers and sisters?"

"No."

"Where do they stay?"

"With their grandmothers and aunties, or whoever will keep them."

"You left them with relatives just like you left me?"

"How was I going to take care of all those kids? There ain't a man willing to take care of all of us. If there was, I would have sent for you."

Trifecta didn't want to hear any more so he left the apartment to be alone and collect his thoughts.

Chapter 61

Letter to the Editor

For the entire week following the Goodwill Review Charity talked constantly about the letter she wanted Henry to write to the editor of one of the newspapers. By Tuesday night he agreed that he would go to her house the following Saturday and they would compose a letter together.

When he arrived at Charity's house on Saturday morning, Avery was there. He found out later that she had spent the night. Charity's parents had always been more than friendly to Henry, but with Avery in their home, they practically ignored him. Initially, he was concerned he had done something wrong. Soon it was as apparent that Charity's parents were trying to show Avery they were progressive liberals who supported the black movement.

"What do you think, Avery?"

"Sit here in the good chair, Avery."

"Look at this picture of us and some of our black friends, Avery."

"Do you want to hear about the civil rights marches we've participated in, Avery?"

"We're members of the NAACP, Avery."

"What can I get for you, Avery?"

"It's been like this all last night and this morning," Charity whispered to Henry. "It was funny at first, but I'm starting to get a little bummed out now. And I think it's beginning to embarrass Avery."

Charity's dad asked, "What do you kids have on the agenda for today?"

"We're going to write a letter to the editor of the Press Scimitar."

"Great, what are you writing about?"

"Not having a prom, because the school is integrated."

"What do you think about that, Avery?"

"She thinks it's stupid, just like we do. That's why she's here, dad," Charity interrupted, hoping her dad would take the hint and leave them alone.

"Could you guys use some help? I've written plenty of letters to the editor."

"Henry's going to write it. He's a writer," Charity said, dismissing her father.

"Okay, I'll leave you kids with it. Avery, if there is anything you want just make yourself at home."

"What about Henry, Dad?" Charity asked, thinking her parents were as racist as anyone because they treated black people differently than they treated white people. Even though in this case they seemed to be favoring black people.

"What do you mean?"

"Is he supposed to make himself at home?"

"Certainly, Henry knows that."

After her dad left, Charity apologized to Avery for her parents. "They aren't usually like this. They just want to make sure you understand they support civil rights."

"I understand."

The three set to work on their letter. The girls told Henry the thoughts they wanted to convey and Henry put what they told him into his words.

The problem as they saw it was: paranoid old white men were worried that black boys would try to be overly friendly with the white girls. And that seemed improbable because there was little or no communication between the races at school. Thinking that would change because they attended a prom together was unlikely. Avery doubted that many of the black students would attend the prom anyway.

The girls were impressed with how well Henry expressed their thoughts in the letter but Henry wanted Scoop to read it before they mailed it. The three drove to Scoop's apartment, which was located on the corner of Poplar and Stonewall.

Scoop rearranged a few sentences and changed a word or two.

"You know the paper won't publish this letter unless it's signed and your home address is on it."

"I know."

"There might be some unpleasant repercussions."

Henry looked apprehensively at Charity, who was sitting in a dusty worn chair. Charity nodded hesitantly. Neither of them was as convinced as they once were that this was a good idea.

"Okay," Henry said.

"I don't know if you're reporting the news or if you'll be making news," Scoop said.

"Do you think they'll publish it?" Henry asked.

"Yeah, if they believe it's an actual letter and not some prank."

"Do you think they'll believe it's a real letter?"

"Against my better judgment, I'll call the paper and let them know it's legitimate but you need to consider the consequences when it is published."

Considering the possible fallout, Henry refused to allow the girls to include their names and addresses to the letter. He took sole responsibility for its content.

While Henry was sealing the letter in the envelope Charity noticed Avery's milk chocolate face was masked with concern.

Once on the elevator Avery broke the silence. "We don't have to mail the letter."

"No, we don't," Charity said, embracing Henry's arm.

"It's a good letter. I'm going to mail it," Henry said, trying to convince the girls he wasn't scared even though he was terrified.

There was a mailbox on the corner of Poplar and Stonewall. Leaving the apartment building, Henry went straight to the mailbox and dropped the letter in.

Chapter 62

A few days after Henry's letter to the editor was published.

He was brought out of a deep sleep into semi-consciousness by the telephone ringing. Within moments his father entered the room, shaking him violently. "Henry, wake up and get into the bathroom with your mother."

"What?" Henry asked, still in a fog.

"Don't ask questions. Just go to the bathroom with your mother."

Disorientated, Henry stumbled out of bed.

"Stay down," his father ordered.

Henry was puzzled by the unusual command, and then he noticed his father was holding a pistol. Henry didn't know his father owned a gun. At the same time he saw a flickering light coming from the front yard and sirens in the distance.

"Both of you sit in the bathtub," Henry's father instructed.

Mr. Murphy wanted his family to be as safe as possible in the event shots were fired into the house. He hastily determined the tiled bathroom was the most fortified room in the house.

Hearing the sirens quickly approaching, Mr. Murphy went out on the front porch to meet the police in his robe and pajamas. Without thinking, he carried his pistol with him.

"Gently place your weapon on the ground and raise your arms above your head," one of the policemen said, approaching the house with his service revolver aimed at Mr. Murphy.

Firemen were running to attach their hose to the fire hydrant that was located at the top of the cul-de- sac.

Henry's father placed his pistol at his feet and raised his hands.

A blast of water from the fireman's hose knocked the burning cross to the ground, extinguishing the flame.

A second officer began frisking Mr. Murphy. "Who are you?"

"I'm Jim Murphy. I live here."

"You can put your hands down," said the cop, figuring the bare foot man dressed in his pajamas was telling the truth.

"What happened here tonight? The officer asked.

"I don't know for sure. I received a call from one of my neighbors saying my front yard was on fire. When I looked out I saw the burning cross. I told my family to get in the bathroom. By the time I came outside you were here."

The policeman picked up Mr. Murphy's revolver and opened the cylinder.

"Do you have any idea why this happened?" one of the policemen asked as another patrol car arrived.

"Yes, my son wrote a letter to the editor that has caused quite a stir. He's been given a hard time at school by the other kids and we've received some threatening phone calls for the past two days. When my neighbor called to tell me the yard was on fire, I thought it was a prank call."

"Do you think its kids from your son's school making the calls?"

"No, they sounded like adults."

"Any idea who that might be?"

"One guy said he was a concerned citizen."

The cop tilted Mr. Murphy's pistol up and the cartridges fell into his hand.

"There's probably not going to be much that we can do tonight; it's too dark to look for evidence and between the firemen walking across your yard and all that water, any evidence that was here is certainly destroyed. We'll have someone come by in the morning to look around and speak with your neighbors to find out if anyone saw anything. In the meantime, try to get some rest."

The policeman handed Mr. Murphy his pistol and the ejected bullets then returned to his car and started writing a report.

When Mr. Murphy went inside the house both Henry and Mrs. Murphy were at the living room window.

"Let's go to bed," Mr. Murphy said. "Tomorrow could be a long day."

"Dad, I'm sorry I caused all this trouble," Henry said, feeling repentant about the backlash from his letter to the editor.

"Go to bed and we'll talk about it tomorrow."

Mr. Murphy reloaded his pistol and the family went to bed. No one in the Murphy family got much sleep the remainder of the night.

The next day Henry was late for school, so he didn't see Charity before classes began. With so much on his mind he had trouble concentrating in class so he wrote a short article about the previous night's events. He gave the article to Charity in the hall between classes. As soon as school was over he had to give a complete recount of what happened to Charity even though his article had accurately chronicled the events.

That afternoon as Henry was walking to the corner of Union and Cleveland where he usually hitch-hiked home, a car pulled to the curb alongside him.

"Get in the car, Henry."

Henry stooped to look and see who was driving. He immediately recognized Agent Ball. Henry hesitated.

"Get in the car, son. I'm holding up traffic."

Henry got in the car.

"How have you been, Henry?" Ball asked as he pulled away from the curb.

"Good."

"I guess we're becoming friends, meeting as regularly as we do."

Henry didn't respond.

"I understand you had some excitement last night."

"Yes sir."

"I had a suspiciously similar incident happen to me a few years ago."

Henry continued to look straight ahead recalling the interrogation Ball and the other FBI agents subjected his family to concerning the murder of Hercules Jones, the cross burning in the agents yard, and the stolen license plates of Dr. and Mrs. Davenport.

"You don't know anything about that, do you?"

"I told you before I didn't." Henry was becoming less spooked each time he spoke with Ball.

"Why are you involved with so much civil rights activity?"

"I don't know," Henry said, trying to avoid giving a direct answer. It seemed every time he talked to Ball the agent twisted what he said into something questionable.

"Did you know a lot of communists are involved in civil rights?"

"I've heard that."

"Do your parents have the same opinion of civil rights as you?"

"My parents aren't particularly in favor of civil rights."

"But you are?"

"I don't know," replied Henry, realizing he had said too much.

"Then why did you write that letter to the editor?"

"It's stupid that the board of Education won't let us have a prom just because black kids go to our school. I bet the black kids wouldn't even come to the prom if we had one. And if they did, so what, we're in school with them all day long. Are you scared their color will rub off on white kids?"

"No, I'm concerned their thinking will rub off on white kids, and a lot of their thinking is red and not black. Do you know what I mean?"

"We're talking about a dance, not politics."

"When it comes to integration everything is politics."

Henry shook his head and looked out the window.

"Are your parents sympathetic to the civil rights movement?" Ball asked quickly trying to get Henry to contradict himself.

"I already told you, no."

"Are you absolutely sure?"

"Yes," Henry answered.

"Do you know any white people who are involved in the civil rights movement?"

Henry hesitated, "No." He lied, remembering that Charity's parents were members of the NAACP.

"What about your hippie girlfriend?"

"What about her?" Henry replied, trying to avoid the inevitable question.

"Is she involved in the civil rights movement?"

"No."

"Henry, it's against the law to lie to a federal agent. You can go to jail for withholding information from me. I want you to look in the backseat."

Henry turned around. There were two large cardboard boxes with lids securely attached. One of the boxes was labeled "Henry Murphy," and the other was labeled "Charity Ramble." Henry unwittingly assumed the boxes contained what teachers referred to as their permanent record, and the contents held Charity's and his life story. In reality the boxes were empty.

"Let me ask you again, is your girlfriend involved in the civil rights movement?'

"Not that I know of," Henry said, thinking the FBI was aware of Charity's convictions.

"She runs around with a colored girl, doesn't she?" The clip at which Ball asked questions continued to increase.

"She has one black friend. Is that against the law?"

"Are her parents active in the civil rights movement?"

"I don't know," Henry lied.

"Did you know they're members of the NAACP?"

"No."

"Why do you think they joined the NAACP?"

"I guess they're for equality."

"Are they communist?"

"I don't think so."

"Are they communist sympathizers?"

"I don't think so."

"Do they talk politics with you?"

"No."

"What do you talk about when you're at their house?" Ball asked at a slower pace, and in a conversational tone.

"What do I talk about with Mr. and Mrs. Ramble?"

"Yes."

"Not much."

"Do you know where they work?"

"They teach at Memphis State."

"Do your parents know the Rambles?"

"Not really, my mom has talked to her mom on the phone a time or two."

"What did they talk about?"

"I don't know. Parent stuff, I guess."

314

Ball turned onto a side street and parked against the curb. They were a few blocks from Henry's house.

"Tell me why a cross was burned in your yard?"

"Because some people didn't like the letter I wrote to the editor."

"Why did you write the letter?"

"Because we want to have a prom."

"What do you mean, we?" Ball snapped.

"Charity and me."

"Who else?" Ball quickly redirected.

"Just about everyone at school."

In a slow low register Ball said, "I'm watching you son and I don't know what you have to do with what's going on in this city, but you will slip up and when you do, I'll be there."

The two sat silently looking at each other. Henry felt compelled to say something but forced himself to remain silent.

"You can go," Ball said and Henry got out of the car.

*

When Charity saw the brief article in the evening paper concerning the cross burning in the Murphy's year. She called Henry.

"The article is almost identical with the one you wrote. The only thing that's really different is they said they talked to your dad by phone and he had no comment. You know what that means?"

"What?"

"It means you're as good of a reporter as the person who wrote the article for the paper."

For the remainder of the night Henry proudly replayed in his head what Charity said about him being a good reporter. He also thought about the boxes that Agent Ball had in his car.

Chapter 63

The Beginning of 1968

After Mary returned home, Trifecta was so distracted having learned about all of his mother's children, and her promiscuous lifestyle, that his school grades plummeted. After his mid-term exams which were a disaster. He considered dropping out of school but the guidance counselor convinced him to complete the year and try and graduate.

The first few days Mary was back in Memphis, She would be at the apartment when Trifecta came home from school.

However, within a week, she would leave before Trifecta was out of class and wouldn't return until after midnight. When asked where she was, she would say she was doing "this and that" trying to earn some cash. And almost as if by magic, she had unexplained money. Not a lot of money but enough to lead Trifecta to believe that his mother could soon have a place of her own. Knowing about all of his siblings she had abandoned he wondered if she would she take him with her if she moved out.

What Trifecta didn't know was that Mary was earning money by selling marijuana for Jeff.

The longer Mary was in Memphis, the more her health and appearance improved.

*

In the meantime Peter was preoccupied cooking his books. The marijuana business was good. However, the cash needed to support his decadent lifestyle, which included multiple women and a growing personal drug habit, was accelerating faster than the cannabis revenue.

When questioned about the lack of earnings, Peter told his father and the Soviets that he had to discount the weed he sold due to the competition from the Mayor. Now that he had eliminated his main rival he would be able to provide more money for the cause. He also promised them that he had plans instigate increased social unrest in the city.

The communists did not sit idly by while Peter and his father made excuses for past failures and promises for future successes. The Kremlin dispatched spies to find out the cause for low profits in Memphis and take any corrective action necessary.

*

Since Moneypenny was murdered for nothing more than the possibility that he might rat out Peter, Jeff became concerned if he was ever arrested he would be in danger of falling victim to Peter's paranoia. Jeff was convinced that Peter's psychosis was the result of his increasing drug use. He wanted to quit working for Peter but he was terrified how Peter would react.

*

Charity decided to go to Memphis State rather than prestigious Vanderbilt in Nashville where she had earned a full scholarship. She made her decision when Henry told her that he planned to apply to Memphis State. She decided she would stake her future with him rather than enjoy the prominence of graduating from a nationally recognized school for academics.

Henry was clueless concerning the significance of Charity's decision to give up a full scholarship to be with him.

*

After the cross was burned in their yard, Henry's parents forbade him to write anything about blacks or integration. Scoop told him it was un-American to censor the press.

*

The beginning of the New Year saw the City of Memphis' governmental structure change from a mayor with commissioners to a mayor with a city council. Henry Loeb, the new Mayor, was sworn in along with the new city council, which consisted of thirteen councilpersons. Three of those councilpersons were black. Mayor Loeb was a staunch political conservative and avid segregationist who had won ninety percent of the white vote while he only received minimal support in the black community. Due to the results of the mayoral elections, some black Memphians questioned the benefits of the democratic process for their community.

*

Doctor Martin Luther King had initiated the Poor Peoples Campaign and was planning the Poor Peoples March on Washington in April of that year.

Chapter 64

February 12, 1968 (Abraham Lincoln's birthday)

"What are you doing home so early?" Yolanda Smith asked, immediately sensing something was wrong as she entered her Lemoyne Gardens apartment. G.W. was sitting at the kitchen table, slumped in his chair with his hands folded and his face contorted by worry.

"We're on strike," he replied.

"Help us Jesus," Yolanda said, looking heavenward in prayer. "Is it because those men were killed the other day?"

*

February 1, 1968 was a cold rainy day in Memphis. Two relatively new sanitation workers were assigned to work together. Their job was to load garbage onto a truck that compressed the refuse. When they were finished for the day, rather than riding outside the truck in the bone-chilling weather using the steps and handrail designed to carry workers, the wet and shivering rookies opted to ride inside the compactor so they would be shielded from the wind. Somehow the compactor engaged, and because the stop button was outside the truck, the men were helpless. One of the men almost escaped. However, his raincoat got caught in the mechanism and he was pulled back into the crusher. The union blamed the deaths on faulty, outdated, and dangerous equipment.

*

"Partly because those men were killed," G.W. answered, "but it's more than that. Mayor Loeb only gave the men's families a month's pay plus five hundred dollars to bury them. So we're asking for the city to keep us safer. We're also striking because every time it rains the colored men working at the sewer and drain department get sent home with only two hours of wages, while the white bosses get paid for the whole day. Plus the union wants the city to take our dues out of our checks. And we're demanding more money."

"What do you have to do with the men in the sewer and drain department?"

"The union says we've got to stick together," G.W. said in a committed tone.

"Why have you, of all people, decided to strike?" Yolanda asked, perturbed because G.W. said he learned his lesson in 1966, and vowed he would never strike again.

*

Having migrated to Memphis in 1963, G.W. paid a white man his last twenty dollars to get him a job as a garbage man with the city. At the time there were positions available because thirty-two of Memphis' garbage men were led by a union organizer in a walkout. The result of the walkout was the firing of all thirty-two men. G.W. was one of the men hired to replace the striking workers.

When G.W. began working in the sanitation department, the garbage men carried refuse from backyards in wash tubs on their heads. They carried the trash to an orange truck equipped with a compactor. After a rain, the homeowner's garbage containers without lids were full of water, and because most of them objected to having the polluted water emptied onto their yards, the garbage men were required to remove both garbage and water. While transporting the tubs of waste, filth leaked onto the men as they went from the house to the truck. A tub could hold 30 or 40 pounds of foulness and rot.

It wasn't uncommon for G.W. and the other "tub totters" to be attacked by dogs. When they tried to protect themselves the residents hollered and cursed at the garbage men then complained to the city. While working, the men were only allotted fifteen minutes for lunch, and residents often fussed if the men ate their lunch and rested under trees in their yard. So the policy was the men had to eat their lunch sitting under the garbage truck. This was extremely unappetizing due to the smell of the garbage and the constant presence of flies. There was no provision for restroom breaks and if a worker got sick on the job he was left to find his own way home. The sanitation workers were responsible to provide personal clothing and gloves. The only thing the city furnished was a tub to carry the refuse.

When G.W. arrived home each night, Yolanda insisted he immediately strip down to his underwear just inside the threshold of their apartment. While G.W. showered, she would soak his vile clothes in a wash tub outside the door. Many of the garbage men claimed working for the sanitation department was worse than being in prison, which several of them had experienced firsthand.

In 1964, G.W. joined the union. Union dues were a dollar a week which G.W. paid when he could and didn't when he was able to avoid the union stewards. In August 1966 another strike was called. All public works departments were expected to participate. However, the strike was squelched by a chancery court injunction. Because G.W.

was an active participant in the 1966 strike, his job was in jeopardy. He promised God and Yolanda that if he didn't lose his job due to the strike he would never strike again. G.W did not lose his job. One result of the 1966 strike was that the city provided the sanitation workers with three-wheel carts to carry their tubs in instead of having to carry the tubs on their heads.

*

In answering Yolanda's question about why he walked out on strike, G.W. said, "It ain't right what happened to those men."

"How do you plan for us to eat? Is the union going to give us groceries? Can we get more food stamps? Can you draw unemployment? What are we going to do?"

The Smiths already qualified for food stamps because their two full-time incomes did not raise them above the poverty level, meaning their income was not sufficient to provide adequate food, shelter and clothing to preserve health. At the time G.W. was making $1.60 an hour, five cents more than minimum wage. Yolanda earned $5.00 a day doing day work. Her white lady also provided her with lunch and bus fare to and from work.

"I don't know, but you have to understand when I went to work, groups of men were standing around outside the fences drinking whiskey and talking. When I started to go through the gate a union boss told me, "No work today." I didn't know what to do so I asked what was going on and he just said, "No work today."

What G.W. didn't tell Yolanda was the temperature was in the low twenty's with gusting wind. So he wasn't disappointed when he was told not go out on a truck.

"Some of the men told me the union called for a work stoppage last night at the labor protest. They said it isn't a strike; it's just a work stoppage. Other people were calling it a strike. They claim it will be over soon because we're going to bring the white people to their knees. And it's going to be bad for anyone who goes to work while the work stoppage is on.

I waited around until six trucks started out the gate to pick up garbage. The men outside the fence went crazy. They started hollering and cussing, calling the men on the trucks all kinds of names and making threats against them and their families. It seems to me we're damned if I go to work because the men on strike mean business, and damned if I don't go to work because we might starve. I figure we have a better chance at not starving than we do with all those strikers mad at us and wanting to hurt us."

"It seems to me you've been trying to bring white people to their knees all your life," Yolanda said. "And all you get is more trouble. But you do what you think is the best. Just remember we have children to feed."

Chapter 65

The Strike

On Sunday, February 11, G.W. had opted to go to church and pray rather than attend the called strike meeting at the Firestone Union Hall. At church he prayed for the families of the men who died on the garbage truck. He prayed for the union. He prayed for Mayor Loeb and the city council, but most of all he prayed for his family.

Monday morning, only thirty-eight out of one hundred and eighty-eight garbage trucks went out on routes. Nine-hundred and thirty out of eleven-hundred sanitation workers refused to work for a city that produced twenty-five hundred tons of garbage per day.

Among the demands given by the union was a wage increase to $2.35 an hour for laborers, $3.00 an hour for drivers, and daily overtime for more than eight hours of work. In addition, the union wanted a safety program and a regulation that trucks could not travel over forty miles an hour, a newsletter and union dues check off.

Due to the number of men involved in the work stoppage, the strike organizers made arrangements with the Firestone Tire and Rubber Union to use their auditorium for daily meetings. Because G.W. owned a car, he always took several of the sanitation workers who lived in the Gardens to the union meetings.

*

Two days into the work stoppage, G.W. was watching the news on television, when Yolanda arrived home from work.

"What happened today?" she asked.

"The television said that no progress has been made between the city and the union. Some of the boys and I went to a meeting at Firestone. They were saying the city isn't ready to negotiate so we aren't going back to work. The union said it won't be long. The union man said he was ready to go to jail because he's breaking the law by telling us not to work. The man with the city said there isn't anybody going to go to jail. So the union man said if they ain't going to arrest him, it means the strike won't last long."

"I hope not. Did he say what we're to do about food?"

"Nobody said anything about food."

On the night of February 14th, an inch of snow closed down the city, but by February 16th skeleton crews of sanitation workers were at their trucks collecting garbage in white neighborhoods. The sanitation workers who were on their routes were escorted by police officers.

Three days after the work stoppage began the NAACP and several local ministers stepped in attempting to settle the strike. Mayor Loeb was relentless in his position that a strike by municipal employees was illegal, and there would be no negotiations until the men returned to work.

Many black churches along with several community activists began to provide food for the strikers.

G.W. began to do most of the house work, including getting the children off to school every morning. He made sure to be home every day when the children returned each afternoon. That's why Yolanda was concerned when G.W. didn't arrive home until almost six o'clock on the evening of February 22.

"Where have you been?" Yolanda wanted to know. She had already fed the children and cleaned up the kitchen. "'I've been worried sick. It's been dark almost an hour and we haven't heard a word from you."

"It was something," G.W. said.

"When I went to the Union Hall this morning they said the union men, along with some preachers, were attending a public works meeting at City Hall. They said Fred Davis, the colored council man, is in charge of the public works. We think that's a good thing because we can have Mr. Davis put pressure on Mayor Loeb to recognize the union. We're sitting around talking and having a good time, figuring things are about to go our way when all of a sudden some of the men who went to the public works meeting came busting in saying we all have to go to City Hall. Because Mr. Davis doesn't want to hear from union bosses; he'd rather hear from the garbage men. So we all load up in cars; I had five other men with me. When we got to the council room, it was about full and there were more men coming behind us. Some preachers who had been there that morning got up and gave us their seats.

"Mr. Davis was standing at the microphone calling for us to come to order. Some of the men started hollering back, "You wanted the men, the men are here!" And more men kept coming in. When there weren't any more chairs, they started lining the walls. Mr. Davis said the fire department was making us clear the aisles. There were so many peoples in the room we were told we had to move to Ellis Auditorium. This caused more confusion and people start hollering, 'What do you want?' Some of the men hollered back, 'We want a union!' They hollered again, 'What do you want?' More of us hollered, "We want a union!" Some of the garbage men told Mr. Davis, if you ain't with us you're against us. Mr.

Davis got madder than ever so we started shouting, If you ain't with us," G.W. cupped his hands around his mouth to act like a megaphone as he said, "You're against us!"

"Finally, one of the white council men said the meeting was going to take a break until two o'clock and we would resume this meeting in Ellis auditorium. But a colored man, who I think is a preacher, said "We're not going anywhere."

"We started singing," G.W. began to sway. "We shall not be moved. We're waiting for the council, and we shall not be moved. We're waiting for the Mayor, and we shall not be moved." Then they started singing other songs. Before I knew it, one of the preachers started preaching about slavery. About how Memphis was built by colored folks, and it's time we got justice in this city."

"By this time it was getting past dinner and some people were getting hungry. So they started to bring in bread and cheese and bologna. Some women started fixing sandwiches right there in the room on one of those big fancy tables.

After we ate there was more preaching and singing. The longer we were in there the more folks started talking. Eventually they began saying they were going to burn the building down. Others started saying they were going to burn the entire city and I started to get a little concerned. Finally, they told us that the public works people voted to recognize the union, but the entire council had to vote on it and it would be tomorrow before the council could get together. We left City Hall feeling good that we got our way with the white folks."

*

The next day G.W., along with several hundred sanitation workers, met at the Union Hall; the mood was jubilant with the smell of victory in the air. Some union leaders spoke, criticizing the two Memphis newspapers for their opposition to the work stoppage. The meeting concluded with a speech encouraging the men to march to Ellis Auditorium where the full city council was scheduled to vote on the resolution by the public works subcommittee.

The group was instructed that there was to be no disturbance or reason for police to make any arrests. If anyone had been drinking they were told not to go to the auditorium.

No one at the Union Hall was aware that the City Council had already met that morning, and the previous day's resolution was changed. The amended resolution called for the sanitation workers to have the right to join and be represented by a union. The city promised a better promotion procedure, insurance and pensions, and an unspecified raise in pay at an unnamed date. There was nothing in the new resolution about dues check off or a written contract between the city and the workers.

When G.W. arrived at the auditorium there was a larger crowd than was at City Hall the previous day or at the Union Hall that morning. The mood remained enthusiastic but there was some tension as rumors began circulating that the resolution had been changed. G.W. was also aware of a strong police presence inside and outside the auditorium.

Once the meeting was underway there was an uneasy quietness among the spectators that troubled G.W. When the resolution was read the spectators remained silent. However, when the roll call vote concluded, the strikers rose to their feet, jeering, cursing, and complaining that they had been lied to and cheated. G.W. stood but said nothing. He just looked at the angry faces around him and was scared of what might happen. The three black councilmen and one white councilman voted no to the revised resolution, and the eight remaining councilmen voted yes. So the revised resolution passed.

The police turned off the microphone and escorted the council from the stage. As soon as the city council was gone the lights in the auditorium were turned off and more chaos erupted. Several men began taking to the stage. Shouting above the confusion, they proposed bringing several notorious black power advocates to Memphis to help in the protest. They urged all the blacks in the city to bring their garbage to City Hall.

The meeting concluded when the attendees were directed to march to Clayborn Temple, a black church on Hernando Street, with a small congregation and a socially active white pastor.

Chapter 66

Yolanda had been home several hours when a couple tub toters helped G.W. into the apartment. When Yolanda first saw him, she covered her nose and mouth with her hands and prayed, "Sweet Jesus, please help us."

The skin on G.W.'s swollen face was peeling; his shirt was unbuttoned and bandages were wrapped around his ribs. He had to be supported by the other men as he hobbled gingerly to his chair.

"What happened to you?" Yolanda asked, as the children looked on silently in shock.

Aware of the commotion outside and next door, Caledonia, Trifecta, and Marquis went to the Smith's apartment.

"It was terrible, Miss Yolanda," said one of the men who had helped G.W. into the house. "When we came out of the meeting ready to march to Clayborn Temple, the police were lined up across the street with their arms locked together, keeping us from going anywhere. They said we didn't have a permit to march. So we just stood on the sidewalk, talking and cutting up, and most folks were having a good time.

Then they changed their minds and told us we could march to Clayborn Temple. When we were on Main Street the police tried to keep us on the west side of the street and the traffic on the east side, but there were too many of us and we began to slip into the east side of the street. G.W., me, and these boys," the man said, pointing to his cohorts who helped him bring G.W. home, "we were in the middle of the march and when we were about at Court Square police cars pulled onto Main Street. The police cars were bumper to bumper. Each car had four or five policemen in it and they had guns and clubs. They used their cars to try to push the crowd to the west side of the street but there wasn't enough room. Some people got their feet run over by the police cars. Some of the marchers started cussing and hitting the police cars. All that did was make the cops mad.

When we were getting close to Monroe Street, the police started getting out of their cars. They were all wearing gas masks. They started squirting us with something they called mace. The police were saying to each other, "Use the mace." The mace was awful stuff. It burns and it makes you fall to the ground. If it gets on your skin it will make your skin peel. We tried to cover our faces with our coats and run from the cops but two or three of them got G.W. pinned up against the wall of a jewelry store. His arms were above his head and they began spraying him with mace and hitting him with their nightsticks. A bunch of us shoved up against the police that were beating G.W., and they turned on us. When they let G.W. go, he fell to the ground like a rag doll. Some of us were able to lift G.W. up. We got him to his car and took him to John Gaston Hospital. The emergency room was full of people from the march. Some of them were bleeding. Other's heads were swollen. Some couldn't see because they had been blinded with that spray. There were grown men crying likes babies, and preachers were praying over folks. It was a long wait but a doctor finally patched G.W. up the best he could and here we are."

"That's right," the other men said, confirming everything that was said.

Trifecta like the others stood quietly in the crowded room listening in disbelief at what happened. After G.W.'s companions went home, Yolanda, her children, Trifecta, Caledonia, and Marquis stayed and talked. Other neighbors came in and out of the Smith's apartment to hear G.W.'s account of the day's events. Trifecta became angry and bitter at the way G.W. was abused. He was furious at the police department. He was mad at the city government, and he was incensed with the white community in general.

The next morning the Memphis paper condemned the protestors and commended the police. The paper continued to report that the strike was a labor issue and not a racial issue. The paper went on to say it was un-American influences that were insisting the strike was about race. Peter Golovach sent every article from the paper to his father, hoping his father would attribute the unruliness in Memphis to his efforts. Even though he had done nothing to initiate or support the work stoppage.

Despite what the paper reported, the consensus among the black community was that prejudice was the root cause of the strike. It was no longer the sanitation workers striking against the city, but it was the entire black community opposing bigotry.

The attack on the sanitation workers occurred on a Friday. On Saturday, G.W. remained inside his apartment, either in bed or on the couch recovering from the beating. Even though he was up and moving around Sunday, he continued to experience some pain so he stayed home from church.

Sunday afternoon there was a knock on Smith's door. Yolanda answered the door to find Reverend Wilks, the pastor of Morning Glory AME church.

"Come in, Reverend Wilks," Yolanda said.

"Thank you, I just came by to see how G.W. is getting along."

As Reverend Wilks entered the apartment, G.W. struggled to his feet.

"Please don't get up, Brother Smith," Reverend Wilks said. "I heard you had quite an experience and I just come by to see if there is anything I can do."

"No, thank you. I'm feeling better now. I will be at church tonight."

"You better stay at home and rest," responded the Reverend. "I understand they beat and maced you severely."

"I appreciate your understanding," G.W. said, seeking absolution for missing that day's church services.

"I thought you might be interested in hearing what has transpired since you've been laid up," continued the pastor. "There was a big meeting of the black preachers yesterday at Clayborn Temple. I suspect every black pastor in town was there. Whether they had a large church or a small church, regardless of their faith, we all came together. I guess God works in mysterious ways to unite so many people. It was decided that every preacher across this city would speak about the strike in today's sermons. In addition, we decided to boycott all of the downtown stores, as well as all the Loeb Laundries and Barbecue restaurants (the Mayor's family owned laundries and restaurants across the city) and Pryor Oldsmobile (Downing Pryor was on the city council). No colored people are to buy Easter clothes. Our motto is "Keep your money in your pocket." We aren't going to put our garbage on the curb like the mayor requested. We are going to write letters to the mayor's office demanding he recognize the union. We are to stop having the paper delivered to our houses. Whenever we talk to white people we are going to tell them the reasons we support the strike."

"That sounds like quite a plan," G.W. said.

"We took an offering to support the strike and we collected twenty-seven dollars which I have for you."

"Say what?" G.W. asked.

"We took up a collection to help you with your expenses throughout the strike. I pray there will be more money collected for you," Reverend Wilkes said, handing G.W. an envelope full of change and dollar bills.

"I don't know what to say," G.W. said.

"You don't have to say anything; we just want you to know your church and churches across this city are behind you."

"What do you think will happen next?" G.W. asked.

"There's going to be a march tomorrow at 11 am, starting at Clayborn Temple and going to City Hall, followed by two marches every day except Sunday. On Sunday we will spend the day in church praying about the strike."

After the pastor left Trifecta went to G.W.'s apartment to see how he was doing. G.W. told Trifecta everything the preacher said. G.W. wasn't sure if he would be able to march on Monday, but Trifecta told him that he would skip school and march with him.

"I can't be a part of you ditching school," G.W. said.

"I can't bear to be with those white kids and teachers at school tomorrow. They're all against the strike and they're supporting Loeb."

"Miss Caledonia won't be happy if you skip school." G.W. said.

"It doesn't make any difference," Trifecta said. "This isn't about the union. This is about the movement and I'm keeping my eye on the prize. So I'm going to march."

*

The next day as the garbage men and their supporters assembled to march, many of the demonstrators wore placards, declaring, "I Am A Man" which was the mantra of the strike.

The march traveled from Clayborn Temple on Hernando Street, to Beale Street, to Main Street, to City Hall. The police required the marchers to walk single file on the sidewalks on both sides of the street. A helicopter hovered above the marchers.

By Tuesday, Trifecta returned to classes and G.W. attended the morning union meetings at the Firestone Union Hall and participated in the marches to City Hall. He also began attending nightly mass meetings at Clayborn Temple.

All strike activities were closely monitored by city policemen and the FBI.

Chapter 67

G.W. and the Strike

During the spring of 1968, every black person in Memphis was asked to support the strike, by marching, attending mass meeting, and contributing money and food. However, as the strike dragged on the union began to run low on cash. Some of the sanitation workers, as well as a portion of the black population, were losing enthusiasm for the work stoppage. Easter was approaching and the black community was expected to ante up the money they normally spent on the holiday to finance the strike.

"We have to do something," Yolanda said, while sitting with G.W. at the kitchen table. "We soon won't have enough money to feed the kids or pay any of the bills. I'm scared we're going to lose all of our furniture if we can't make our payments."

"I know it's a struggle."

"It's a struggle we can't win. How are you going to beat the white people in this town when they have all the power and all the money?"

"There are some colored councilmen."

"There are three; how are they going to do anything when the rest of the council is white and supporting the Mayor?"

"What am I to do?"

"Go back to work. My white lady asks me every day, how long are we going to keep up this foolishness. Some of the women around here, whose husbands are on strike, are beginning to ask the same thing."

"You better watch what you say or you're liable to get us in trouble, because you never know who is listening."

"We're already in trouble. We don't have any money. We barely have enough food. If things don't change quickly we won't have enough money for me to ride the bus to work or to buy gas for you to take me to work. This is just like it was when we were share croppers except we're not getting nearly as much help."

"We're better off than we were in Tent City."

"At least in Tent City a colored man owned the land; now we're living in a place owned by white people. I'm afraid we might be evicted any day."

"These projects are owned by the government, not white people," G.W. responded.

"The government is white people."

"Well that's what we're trying to change."

"We're going to starve and it ain't ever going to change."

Yolanda's employer insisted G.W. should be working and earning money to care for his family. However, she gave Yolanda an extra ten dollars every week during the strike because she felt sorry for Smith's children. It crushed Yolanda's spirit to receive charity from her employer but her children were more important than her pride. Still, she continued to talk to the other women in the Gardens whose husbands were on strike imploring them to urge their husbands to return to work.

"If Jamal goes back to work, then G.W. will," Yolanda said to one of her neighbors.

"I know, except Jamal is scared. He said the other men might kill our entire family if he breaks the strike."

Several evenings later there was a knock on the Smiths' door. When G.W. opened it he recognized a couple of tub toters from another garage and two younger men G.W. had never seen.

"Would you men like to come in?"

"No, what we have to say, your neighbors should hear," one of the young men said.

"Okay," G.W. said as he stepped onto the porch. Yolanda stood at the screen door where she could see and hear everything.

"We understand you're thinking about going back to work."

"I'm going return to work as soon as the strike is settled."

"We heard your wife's been telling people that you're going back to work whether the strike is over or not."

"I don't know who told you that."

"It doesn't matter who told us. We want to make sure it's not true."

"It's not."

"It would be dangerous to go to work while your brothers are on strike."

"I ain't working."

"So we have an understanding."

"That's right."

"What's about my children?" Yolanda asked through the screen door.

"What about your children?"

"How are they going to eat if my husband doesn't work?"

"You better teach your woman some manners," the young man said to G.W.

G.W. didn't respond.

"Are you going to be at the Clayborn Temple tomorrow?" one of the young men asked.

"I've been there every day except for when I couldn't walk because the police beat me."

"Good. We'll look for you tomorrow. Make sure we see you."

"Who are you?"

"We're the men who are going to make sure everybody who is supposed to be on strike stays on strike."

G.W. and the young man tried to stare each other down until the other young man said to his confederates, "Let's go."

The group of men walked away.

As G.W. entered his apartment, Yolanda said, "This strike is getting on my last nerve. Everybody is against us, the colored people and the white people."

G. W. didn't answer; he just sat down in a chair and stared silently at a lifeless television screen.

The next day at Clayborn Temple, when the garbage men and their supporters were assembling to march, the two of the young men who visited G.W. the previous evening approached him.

"We're glad to see you, G.W.," said one of the men as they positioned themselves in front and behind G.W.

During the daily marches, shoppers and business people shared the sidewalks with the strikers. The marchers walked in a single file on the sidewalks on each side of the street.

As shoppers passed G.W., the two young men began taunting them. The closer to City Hall they were, the worse the haranguing of shoppers became. Finally, a couple of police officers arrested the two young men and G.W. for disturbing the peace. While G.W. hadn't said a word, the two men made sure he was guilty by association, and G.W went quietly to jail.

Despite the union moving quickly to arrange bail, it was after six that evening when G.W. arrived home. Yolanda had already heard about G.W. being arrested.

"Here you are a church man, and you spent time in jail."

"It's not my fault."

"They said you were harassing the shoppers."

"It wasn't me. It was those boys who come by here last night. I just got caught up in it all when the police arrested them."

"What are we going to do?" Yolanda asked, covering her face with her hand to hide her tears.

"It'll be alright. Some of the union men who bailed us out said that some preachers have sent for Martin Luther King."

Chapter 68

March 1, 1968

Peter's marijuana business was booming. Yet it continued to be impossible for him to increase the amount of money he was contributing to the war effort because he was unwilling to change his deviant lifestyle. In order to divert his father's and the Russian's attention from the lack of drug revenue, Peter decided he would put emphasis on the garbage strike. After all, his assignment was to disrupt the social order in Memphis.

Peter called a late night meeting at the car lot with Jeff, Ross, and Sims. Peter was already there when the others arrived. He was drinking whiskey straight from a bottle and the stench of marijuana permeated the small room.

"We need to exploit this garbage strike to our advantage," Peter said.

"How are we going to do that?" Ross asked. Baffled how the sanitation strike could benefit their drug business.

"We're going to take the strike to another level," Peter answered. He was obviously stoned. His eyes were glassy and his pupils dilated.

The others looked at Ross.

"What's the plan?" Ross asked, not sure he really wanted to know.

"You heard Mayor Loeb met with the black preachers again today?"

"So?"

"So nothing; nothing happened. The preachers are cowards. All the coloreds are cowards. They didn't even put up a fight."

"What about the boycott?" Ross asked, trying to understand Peter's reasoning.

"What about it? Nothing is changing. The white folks are still getting their garbage picked up. I'm still getting my garbage picked up. The only people who aren't getting their garbage picked up are the garbage men and their supporters. Garbage is being picked up every day; it just doesn't get picked up in the colored neighborhoods."

Jeff took it personally that Peter was calling the blacks cowards and it infuriated him that Peter continued to call African Americans, coloreds.

"That's because they're afraid to go into the black neighborhoods," Ross emphasized.

"Maybe they're just using that as an excuse not to pick up the colored's garbage," Peter said. "The white mayor and the city council don't care if your neighborhood stinks. Fact is they're probably laughing because the only people the strike is hurting is the coloreds. This strike is a way for the Mayor to punish the people who didn't vote for him.

"So what does that have to do with us?"

Ignoring Ross's question, Peter took a drink from his bottle and continued. "Claude Armour, one of the mayor's men said on TV that our coloreds won't riot."

Anger continued to boil in Jeff.

"So what is your point?" Ross asked gently, not wanting to offend Peter.

"My point is that we have to do something that will cause the coloreds in this city to fight."

"What would that be?"

"I think we ought to attack Henry Loeb himself."

Jeff stirred in his chair.

"What do you mean?" Ross said apprehensively.

"You guys need to give the mayor a scare."

"Alright," Jeff said, not understanding, but liking the idea of terrorizing the mayor.

"How?" Ross asked.

"Get some bricks and go to his house. Give him a sample of what it's like to be in a riot."

"What if we get caught?" Ross asked, remembering that Moneypenny was murdered because he was caught carrying out one of Peter's schemes.

"Why would you get caught?"

"I imagine Mayor Loeb has a lot of security, and a car load of black men driving through an east Memphis neighborhood is going to draw some attention."

"If you're scared, then I'll drive you. If anyone stops us, I'll tell them you are my boys," Peter slurred arrogantly, which made Jeff even madder.

They took a car from the sales lot and Peter drove surprisingly well considering his condition. When they turned onto Mayor Loeb's street, Peter turned off the car's headlights. They passed the house once and then turned around.

Jeff and Sims got out of the car in front of the mayor's next-door neighbor's house. Each man had two bricks. They scurried towards the Loeb's home, while Peter shifted the car into neutral and coasted in front of the mayor's house. Two panes of glass crashed and a split second later two more panes of glass were smashed, including a large picture window in the Loeb's living room. To facilitate a fast escape, both men dove head first through windows of the car. Sims flew through the back passenger's side window while Jeff jumped head first through the front window. Peter had the car in gear and was speeding away before Jeff could pull his legs completely inside the car.

Once the two brick throwers were inside the vehicle the three black men crouched out of sight on the floor board of the car. The vandals hadn't gone far before police cars seemed to come from every direction speeding toward Mayor Loeb's home.

Still crouching on the floor board, Jeff said, "They must have every pig in Memphis looking for us."

"That gives me an idea," Peter said after a moment of silence. "How many bricks do we have left?"

"There're two or three back here. I guess we should get rid of them in case we get pulled over by the cops," Ross said.

"No, just wait, we can still use them."

Peter turned onto a street that ran north and south through the city. They came to a small shopping area in a white neighborhood where a Loeb's laundry was located. Peter pulled into the parking lot and Jeff put a brick through the plate-glass window.

Going north they found a Loeb's Barbecue restaurant, and a brick went through another window.

Peter, having previously informed his father of his plan to attack the mayor's home, sent the newspaper article to him showing where the mayor accused the strikers of vandalism. The police made the attack on the mayor's property a priority. After extensive interrogation of black garbage men, they had no suspects.

Chapter 69

March 20, 1968

The affluence of Americans was envied by many Russian spies serving in the U.S. in the nineteen fifties and sixties. Covetousness, when combined with opportunity, led many Soviets into corruption. One advantage of having authority in a totalitarian government is that the leaders are entitled to all the wealth they can pilfer. However, when excessive embezzlement occurred at the lower levels of the bureaucratic food chain, it became imperative that the elite had to take steps to protect their interest.

Ivan Golovach was awakened by a pounding on his front door. It was two in the morning according to the luminous dial of the clock on his bedside table. Picking up his pistol next to the clock, He put on his robe and went to the door.

"What do you want?" Golovach demanded as he turned on the porch light and looked through a peep hole in the door.

"We need to talk." The reply came in perfect Russian.

"What do you want?" Ivan said again, this time in his native language.

"We were being followed earlier, let us in before we are seen."

Ivan cracked open the door as far as the safety chain would allow.

In Russian, Ivan asked, "What do you want?"

"I am Mikhail Smirnov and this is Andrey Pavlor. We have most urgent business with Ivan Golovach."

Ivan had heard of Mikhail and he anticipated the reason they had come unannounced in the night was not good.

"What is your business?" Ivan asked.

"Patriot business; let us in before we are seen."

With pistol in hand, Ivan hesitantly released the chain and opened the door.

"Who is it?" Ivan's wife asked from the hallway leading to the bedrooms.

"Go back to bed," Ivan ordered his wife without explanation.

When Ivan's wife returned to the bedroom, Mikhail said, "You don't need a pistol comrade. Please put it away."

"We can talk in here," Ivan said, motioning towards the den but not relinquishing his weapon.

Ivan sat in a recliner and placed the pistol in his lap. Mikhail sat on a couch facing Ivan, while Andrey sat in a chair off to the side of the recliner. Ivan was uncomfortable that the two men were not sitting together.

"You have a nice home," Mikhail said. "Very luxurious."

"By Russian standards perhaps, but for an American businessman not so much," Ivan replied.

"You do need to keep up appearances."

"Yes, for the cause, I keep up appearances."

"The cause is the reason we are here for a visit."

"Rather late in the evening," Ivan said.

"Secrets are kept better in the dark." Mikhail said.

"It has been a long night. Before we start, perhaps you could provide us with some refreshment," Andrey suggested.

"What would you like?"

"Vodka."

Ivan placed his pistol on a table next to the recliner and went to the liquor cabinet, poured three glasses of vodka and placed them on a tray. When he turned to serve the drinks he saw Andrey had taken his pistol.

"What's going on?" Ivan protested.

"We are much more at ease when our comrade is not pointing a weapon at us," Mikhail said.

"This is a dangerous business we are in. You never know who to trust," Ivan replied slowly.

"You are right. Our business is full of thieves..." Mikhail paused and stared hard at Ivan, then said, "...and murderers. What we need to talk about tonight are the thieves. The revenues from your area of responsibility are decreasing while your demand for marijuana is increasing. And there seems to be extreme discrepancies from Memphis. I believe your son is in charge of our Memphis operation. Small shortages can be overlooked from a man in your position. However, your son is not in a position that has allowance for such inconsistency. He is greedy and that cannot be tolerated."

Ivan blushed but said nothing as he serviced the drinks to his guest. Then, returning to the recliner, he said, "The goal in Memphis is political unrest, not profits. And from the reports I receive the city is in turmoil with a garbage strike."

"It is true, but it appears your son's activities have been very lucrative."

"What do you mean?"

"He is leading a very opulent lifestyle with women, automobiles, and drugs."

Ivan blushed again and fear coursed through him.

"I know nothing about what you are saying."

"It is your responsibility to know and it is your obligation to make sure such things do not occur. This behavior, particularly in a time of war, is treason."

"Who sent you here? I report only to Boris Nikitin with the GRU."

"Treason has its consequences that even Nikitin cannot prevent."

"Are you the KGB? What agency are you from?"

"Bratva," Mikhail said, as he gulped the shot of vodka.

Ivan made a spitting sound. "You are not patriots. You are what Americans call gangsters."

"How do the Americans say? You are the pot calling the kettle black."

Ivan saw movement in his periphery; however, by the time he turned toward Andrey a shot was fired at point-blank range and Ivan fell to the floor, instantly dead from a head wound. Within seconds, Ivan's wife appeared across the room. Andrey shot quickly at Mrs. Golovach and missed. The second shot struck her but was not fatal. The third shot from Ivan's pistol finished the job.

Mikhail and Andrey spent the remainder of the night searching the house. They found fifteen thousand dollars in U.S. currency, several pieces of expensive jewelry, and many documents that would be harmful if they were found by the American government. They burned the documents in the fire place, and they took the money and jewelry and left in Ivan's car.

*

Alexander Koloff was a petty criminal who was in jeopardy of being deported from the United States. He worked as a waiter in a restaurant in Brighton Beach that served Russian cuisine. While waiting tables, he overheard a conversation between Mikhail, Andrey, and Boris Dyuzhenkovon concerning Peter Golovach. Boris was a former leader of the GRU and current ringleader of the Bratva, or the "Brotherhood." In lieu of jail or deportation, Alexander told the FBI the little information he learned from eavesdropping about the problems that the Soviets were experiencing in Memphis.

The FBI immediately began surveillance of Mikhail and Andrey.

The night Ivan and his wife were murdered Mikhail and Andrey were able to elude the American agents tailing them.

The next day the Golovachs bodies were discovered by a housekeeper. Because of their Soviet citizenship, the FBI was notified. It was soon discovered that the vehicle in the driveway was the car the FBI had been following the previous night. They also discovered the Golovachs' Lincoln Continental was missing. A nation-wide all-points bulletin was put out on the missing car.

Golovach's car was located, abandoned within a block of another reported stolen vehicle. Concluding the suspects had changed cars, an all-points bulletin was put out on the second vehicle. By mid-morning the stolen automobile was located, parked illegally at LaGuardia Airport.

With several FBI agents working the phones, it was discovered that Delta Airlines had a flight going to Memphis by way of Atlanta. By the time the discovery was made the plane was in route from Atlanta to Memphis.

There were no passengers on the plane by the name of Smirnov or Pavlor, but it was natural for Soviet agents to use an alias when traveling. A call was made to the Memphis Field Office of the FBI. Agent Ball and Swartz were assigned to meet the plane. If they discovered the Russian suspects, they were to follow them to determine what their business was in Memphis.

Chapter 70

March 18, 1968

Mason Temple was the home of the Church of God in Christ, an exclusively African American denomination. The Temple was the largest black venue in the south and served as a prominent location for civil rights activities in the nineteen fifties and sixties.

Mason Temple could accommodate seventy-five hundred people. On March 18, 1968, the Monday night Martin Luther King Jr. was to speak, the building and parking lot were overflowing with an estimated twelve thousand people. Against the recommendation of his advisors, Doctor King rearranged his itinerary to speak at Mason Temple in support of the sanitation strike. At the time, King's priority was the "Poor Peoples March on Washington" scheduled for April 22nd. However, in the excitement of a four-hour pre-speech meeting with Memphis' black leaders, Doctor King committed to return to Memphis on March 22nd to lead the sanitation workers in a march on City Hall.

It was late when G.W. arrived home from the meeting. Yolanda was in bed.

"Are you awake?" G.W. whispered as he slipped into the dark bedroom.

"Mmmm," Yolanda moaned, as she stirred.

"Are you awake?"

"What time is it?" Yolanda said starting to awaken.

"It's a little after eleven."

"Where have you been?" she asked with a yawn.

"I've been at the strike meeting."

"Why are you so late?"

"That's what I want to tell you about. There was singing, Bible reading, preaching, and praying. The white man from the union talked, and then a couple of tub toters walked into the meeting arm-in-arm with Doctor King. He called on the city to unite with the garbage men and he said we ought to have a work stoppage on Friday."

"What you mean a work stoppage?"

"He said no black people should work or go to school on Friday. He said the maids don't need to go to the white people's houses. The cooks don't need to go the restaurants...."

"He said what about the maids?" Yolanda interrupted.

"He said you shouldn't go to work. If no black people go to work this whole city will be shut down and that will help us win the strike."

"Well, that's a fine thing for him to say; he ain't got to live here," Yolanda said, sitting up in bed wide awake.

"That's the best part. He said he's coming back to lead a march on City Hall on Friday."

"What if I get fired?" Yolanda asked, not really expecting an answer.

*

G.W. didn't fall asleep until early Tuesday morning because he was so excited from the evening's events. Yolanda didn't go to sleep because she was worried about her job.

Yolanda fretted while she rode the bus to work, wondering how she was going to tell her white lady she was going to miss a day of work, due to the strike. However, when she arrived at work her employer said, "I understand you won't be working this Friday."

"Ma'am?"

"The morning newspaper said that your Mr. King has called for a work stoppage on Friday."

"Yes, ma'am, that's what I hear."

"Well, you need to make sure all your work is done by Thursday."

"Yes ma'am, it will be," Yolanda said, relieved about her job but still tired from lack of sleep.

*

When Yolanda arrived for work on Thursday, March 21st, her white lady asked, "Have you heard the weather report?"

"No ma'am."

"They are predicting a heavy snowfall this afternoon and tonight. I guess that will prevent your march tomorrow."

"Yes, ma'am," Yolanda answered, reasonably sure that a little snow wouldn't hamper a march led by Doctor King.

Throughout Thursday afternoon and night, a record seventeen inches of snow fell on Memphis, closing the city and the airport, preventing Doctor King's arrival and postponing the march.

Both sides of the strike claimed the snow was an indication that God was on their side. The sanitation workers pointed out that God honored the work stoppage by closing down the city, while many of Mayor Loeb's supporters claimed that God had sent the snow to prevent the demonstration from occurring.

In spite of all the talk, support for the strike achieved its crescendo on March 21st, and the heavy snowfall cooled some of the enthusiasm of the strikes supporters.

Doctor's Kings march was rescheduled for Thursday, March 29th.

The next Tuesday, when the snow had melted enough for Yolanda to return to work, her white lady asked if she intended on taking Thursday off to participate in the march and the work stoppage. "No ma'am. I'll be here, I need to work."

*

Charity said she supported the strike for humanitarian reasons as opposed to racial reasons. She also made it clear that she supported equality for every person as provided for in the Constitution and taught in the Bible.

"If the garbage men…" Henry started to say.

"Sanitation workers," Charity interrupted.

"Okay; if the sanitation workers don't like their jobs they ought to get different jobs."

"It's easy for you to say. If white people don't like their jobs they can get another one. But jobs aren't as readily available to Afro-Americans."

*

After the snow the sanitation workers resumed their two-a-day march from Clayborn Temple to city hall, but as they marched some young men who were not sanitation workers began chanting, "It's time to stop marching and start fighting."

Tension continued to increase throughout the week, particularly among the black youth of the city.

Chapter 71

March 27, 1968, the afternoon before Martin Luther King leads the rescheduled March in Memphis

"Hey man, you better tell your mother to get out of town," Jeff said when Trifecta entered the office of the car lot.

"What's up?"

"Peter's going to kill her."

"What are you talking about?"

"He found out she's been stealing money from the drugs she's been selling. Now he's going to make an example of her."

"What do you mean she's been selling drugs?"

"She's been pushing dope ever since she came back to Memphis."

"Who started her dealing?"

"Ain't nobody started her. She came to us and she been doing real good until she started ripping Peter off. Now he's saying he's going to kill her.

"When's he going to do it?"

"I don't know but he said he was going to take care of it personally. So I'd get her out of town as quick as I could."

"You know the number for the police?"

"It's in the book I guess," Jeff said. "What are you going to do?"

"I'm going to turn him in."

"Who?"

"Peter."

"Whoa man, you call the pigs and they're going to come in here and bust all of us."

"I'm going to send them to his apartment."

"How do you know where he lives?"

"I see him all the time. He lives in that apartment building across from school."

Trifecta reached for the phone. Jeff put his hand on the receiver. "I can't let you call the pigs man. I'm not a big fan of Peter's. Fact is he scares me. I think that he's blown his mind on drugs. But you're going to get us all busted and maybe killed if you turn him in. All you got to do is get your mother out of town. She's ripped off a couple thousand bills from Peter but she'll be alright if she gets out of here."

"That's cool. If I can't use your phone I'll call from somewhere else," Trifecta said as he walked out the door.

"Man," Jeff sighed to an empty room as he dialed the phone.

Peter answered.

"Hey man, Trifecta getting ready to have you busted."

"What do you mean he's going to have me busted?"

"He's calling the pigs to have you arrested before you kill his mom."

"How does he know I'm planning on killing his mother?"

"I don't know."

"You're the only person I've told that I'm going to kill her."

"Look man, I'm just trying to give you a heads up."

"I'll return the favor by giving you a heads up. If you don't find Trifecta and keep him from calling the law then you and I have a serious problem. Let me know when you find him and keep him with you until I get there."

Jeff considered his options and it didn't take him long to conclude that it was a good time to take his own advice and leave town. He cleaned out the cash box and was putting several kilos of marijuana in the trunk of his car when Ross showed up.

"What are you doing, man?" Ross asked.

"I'm out of here. This whole thing is about to fall apart."

"What do you mean?"

Jeff gave Ross a quick summary of Peter's plan to murder Mary and he assumed Trifecta had already called the police.

"This don't make no sense man," continued Jeff. "Peter's got us breaking windows in the mayor's house and the Loeb family businesses. The other night he had me set fire to garbage that had been piled up in some alleys. He's got us messing with the strike. We're going to wind up in the penitentiary if he doesn't kill us first."

"I hear you, man. Tell you what; let me have some of that dope and we'll set this place on fire so there's no evidence and then we'll get out of here."

"Cool, man."

The small wood frame office burned like kindling. The interior of the metal Quonset hut burned slower. Before leaving, Jeff and Ross took all of the keys to the cars that were on the lot. On their way out of town they drove through the Mississippi/Walker neighborhood and gave sets of keys to every seedy looking character they could find, telling them where they could find the vehicles that were theirs for the taking. They figured that the stolen cars would be enough diversion to allow them to leave town, and elude Peter and the law.

*

When Trifecta talked to the police department to make sure he had their attention, he told them that Peter was not only dealing drugs, but he was responsible for breaking the windows in Mayor Loeb's house. And to make sure he had their attention he fabricated a story about Peter planning to disrupt the march the next day.

*

Even though Peter had rented the apartment using an alias, the resident manager knew who the police were looking for by a description of his car.

Peter wasn't home when the police arrived with a warrant for his arrest. When they searched his apartment they found marijuana, LSD, miscellaneous drug paraphernalia, and several weapons.

By the time Peter arrived at the car lot in his yellow caddy, the fire department had come and gone. The office was burned to the ground and the Quonset hut stood charred and scorched with the windows and doors broken out. It was apparent that several cars were missing. Peter noticed a black man was in one of the cars preparing to drive away. Peter parked behind the car to prevent him from stealing the vehicle. However, after making an obscene jester the man jumped the curb and sped away in a 1965 Cutlass Supreme.

With his pistol in hand and curses on his lips, Peter got out of his car to survey the devastation. He thought Trifecta was somehow responsible.

Chapter 72

March 28, 1968
The Morning of the March

Henry slipped his school books under his bed and then rushed to the front door hoping to escape the house without his mother noticing he was empty-handed.

"I'm late for school, Mom. I have to go," Henry hollered, stepping into the spring day.

His mother emerged from the kitchen just in time to see the front door shut. In a trot, Henry cut through some neighbors' yards in case his mother was looking out of the window after him. He slowed to a walk when he was a block away from his home. He cut through the parking lot and across the yard of a church to the corner of Union Avenue and East Parkway.

Henry took his normal position, standing on the curb at the traffic light with his thumb outstretched to try and catch a ride from three lanes of traffic that were waiting at the red light. A horn blew catching his attention. Looking in the direction of the sound he saw Marcie's yellow Corvair in the second lane several cars back. She was motioning him to ride with her. Weaving through the idling cars, he reached

358

her vehicle seconds before the traffic light turned green and the surrounding motorist began to accelerate towards downtown.

"Hi", she said, smiling as he settled in the passenger's seat. The radio was tuned to WHBQ. "My Babe," by the Jesters was playing as she pulled away from the intersection. When he turned to look at her, he was so overcome with mixed emotions of pleasure and anxiety he grew light-headed.

"Thanks for the ride," he said awkwardly, as the fragrance of her perfume filled his nostrils. Her long straight hair was tucked behind her right ear and came to rest below her shoulders. She was wearing a sleeveless white blouse with a Peter Pan collar, accessorized with a circle pin, a plaid wrap around skirt, brown penny loafers and a gold charm bracelet dangled from her wrist. Her choice of clothing was not intended to be provocative, but seeing her slender arm exposed to her shoulder was strangely titillating for Henry, especially as she moved her arm to steer, and he caught a glimpse of the white elastic of her bra in the arm hole of her blouse.

"Where are your books?" she asked, glancing at him.

"I left them at home," he said, as he quickly turned his head hoping she wasn't aware that he had been admiring her.

"Don't you think you'll need them today?"

"I'm not going to school."

"Where are you going?"

"I'm headed downtown."

"What are you going to do?" she asked, aware of the problems that were anticipated at the demonstration led by Doctor King.

"I'm going to the march," he said guardedly, unsure what she would think about his plan.

"Are you crazy?" she asked with a raised voice.

"No," he said meekly.

"Do you support the strike?" Marcie asked, quickly glancing at him while still trying to keep her eyes on the road.

"No, I don't support the strike."

"Then why would you go and march with all those colored people?"

"I'm writing a story."

"What kind of story are you writing?"

"It's about the garbage strike and the plight of the city."

"Do you mean a newspaper story?"

"Yeah, maybe."

"What teacher gave you that assignment?"

"None, I guess I'm just freelancing."

"Do you have permission to miss school?"

"No, I'm skipping."

They stopped at a traffic signal at Cooper and Union. "My Babe" had finished playing, and a commercial for Chuck Hutton Chevrolet began. Marcie pushed a button on her radio, and the station changed to WMPS. "Keep on Dancing" by Larry Raspberry and the Gentrys was playing.

"Do you know how dangerous this is?" Marcie asked in a lecturing tone.

"I'll be okay."

"You'll be alright because you get along so well with colored people?" Marcie said sarcastically, remembering the confrontations Henry had with Trifecta.

"No, but I can take care of myself."

There was an uncomfortable silence for a minute or two. Not knowing what else to say, Henry asked, "How are things going with you and Jimmy?"

"We broke up," Marcie said casually.

"Oh," Henry said, a little embarrassed that he might have said the wrong thing. "So who are you going with now?"

"No one."

"It's unusual for you not to have a boyfriend," he said entertaining the possibility she might have an interest in him.

"What do you mean?"

"Boys are always after you."

"I guess; how are you and Charity getting along?"

"Good, we're both going to Memphis State next year."

"I heard she won a scholarship to Vanderbilt."

"She did but she wants to stay here with me."

"Really?"

"Yeah."

"Have you been accepted to Memphis State?"

"No, not yet."

"That's a pretty big sacrifice for her to make."

'Yeah, I know." Henry said, not really realizing the significance of Charity's decision

They arrived at Union and Bellevue.

"I'll get out here," Henry said. "I can catch a ride the rest of the way into town."

"It will be just as easy for you to go up Peabody," Marcie said, as she turned left onto Bellevue towards Central High School. "I wish you would reconsider and come to school. You can borrow some of my books."

Her concern caused Henry's heart to melt. He felt a connection with her he had yearned for since the seventh grade.

"No, I'm going to town," he said even though he hoped she would continue to try to persuade him not to go.

She didn't.

She pulled into an unpaved lot at the corner of Bellevue and Peabody where several students parked their cars.

When she was parked, Henry started to open the door but Marcie grabbed his left arm and turned to face him. "I want you to know that I think you're being an idiot, but I want you to be careful and if things start to turn bad I want you to leave. Will you do that for me?" She reached her arms around his neck and embraced him. He was so shocked he didn't know how to react but he managed to weakly hug her in return. As they pulled slightly apart he looked into her face and without warning she kissed him passionately on the lips. Her breath was warm but as clean and fresh as mountain air. His hormones raged inside of him.

No kiss had ever sensually excited him more, not when he was making out with Lois, nor when he kissed Charity.

He was delirious. His body tingled from head to toe, his breathing became heavy.

As they broke the embrace, Marcie said in a sultry whisper, "Will you promise to leave if things turn violent?"

"Yes," Henry whimpered.

Marcie turned Henry loose. She briefly primped in the rearview mirror and hopped out of the car wearing her perpetual smile. With her books cradled in her arms she sashayed across the teacher's parking lot and into the school building, leaving Henry sitting in the passenger's seat, debilitated from the kiss.

Alone in the car, Henry considered chasing after her and telling her how much he loved her. However, when she disappeared through the door of the school he exited the car, weak kneed. Regaining some of his composure he began walking towards downtown.

As he walked his mind resonated with pleasurable thoughts of Marcie and the kiss. He was convinced Marcie loved him. Weighing the option of going steady with Marcie or Charity, he decided it would be worth breaking-up with Charity to be with Marcie.

Marcie had no explanation for why she kissed Henry. Maybe it was an insuppressible adolescent urge or an act of concern for someone in danger. The more she thought about the kiss the more embarrassed she became, and she hoped no one had witnessed her indiscretion. It would have been one thing to give him a friendly kiss on the cheek but she had kissed him with all the carnal fervor she had within her. She thought she must have been temporarily insane.

Chapter 73

Waiting for the March to Begin

Walking slowly up Peabody Street, Henry tried to map out the strategy he was going to use to break up with Charity. When he noticed the time, he realized he needed to catch a ride if he was going to be at Clayborn Temple for the beginning of the March.

Seeing a bus lumbering towards town, Henry raced to the nearest stop. When he boarded the bus, he dropped his fare into the coin box, and sat in the first seat behind the driver. There were three other passengers, a white woman close to the middle of the bus, and two black women near the rear door.

As the bus made a dogleg turn onto Vance Avenue Henry saw clusters of black teenagers walking towards downtown. At Vance and Lauderdale Street, a large group of loud and rowdy black adolescent boys boarded the bus. They all seemed to be talking at once, pushing and shoving as they crowded through the doorway and up the three steps unto the bus. Henry was shocked when he saw that Trifecta among the group.

When their eyes met Henry blushed and Trifecta frowned, but neither acknowledged the other. The black teenagers elbowed and nudged their way towards the middle of the bus, chattering loudly. Much of what was said was laced with profanity, racial slurs, and hatred towards the city's mayor and the police department. Henry noticed the middle aged white bus driver kept his eyes glued to the road, ignoring the commotion trying to avoid trouble. The white woman found herself surrounded by the loud vulgar crowd of black teenage boys. Henry felt sorry for her but he didn't know what he could do to help her.

The best Henry could discern from the intense jabbering was that there had already been a confrontation at Booker T. Washington High School between the police and some black students. However, other than the profanity, much of what was being said sounded like Swahili to him and the two other white people on the bus. As it turned out there were unconfirmed rumors that the police had arrested several students at Booker T. Washington High School and a female student who attended Hamilton High School was beaten to death by the police. The reports of the arrest and the beating were later found to be untrue. It was becoming increasingly apparent that this bus was not the place for a white guy. So when the white woman exited through the back door of the bus at Danny Thomas Boulevard, Henry disembarked through the front door.

"That was an experience," the woman said to Henry as they stood on the corner of Danny Thomas and Vance plotting their next move. Like Henry, the lady had intended to ride the bus all the way into downtown where she worked.

"Yes, ma'am," Henry said, still embarrassed by the language the boys on the bus used in her presence.

When the woman spotted a bus going east on Vance, she said, "if that is any indication of what is going to happen in town today, I think I'll go back home." She crossed the street and boarded the east bound bus.

In pursuit of a less crowded and unruly street, Henry started walking north on Danny Thomas, but found all of the streets were congested with cars and pedestrians going towards town. He turned north on East Pontotoc Avenue and made his way to Hernando Street. The closer to the church he traveled the more concerned he became at being the only white person in a sea of black faces that appeared considerably less friendly than the crowd at the Goodwill Review. Despite what he told Marcie, he was beginning to think he might not be able to take care of himself.

Once in the general vicinity of Clayborn Temple, Henry took refuge in a recessed doorway of a neighborhood grocery. He constantly looked at his watch, wondering what was delaying the march from getting underway. The more time that elapsed past the scheduled start time, the more unruly the crowd became and the more uncomfortable Henry grew. The older folks who were waiting for the march to begin seemed edgy, some of them drinking wine and whiskey. Henry was aware that alcohol in such an emotionally charged atmosphere could easily cause the situation to turn hostile. What concerned him even more than the drinking was the anger displayed by the teenaged boys.

The crowd swelled beyond expectations and tightened around Clayborn Temple. The police had the area covertly surrounded, with the only visible evidence of law enforcement being a helicopter circling overhead.

As Henry stood in the doorway, a group of boys about his age were walking single file, hugging the edge of the crowd. When they passed Henry one of the boys lurched at him. Henry jumped back, terrified. The black boy laughed and with a few racial slurs continued following his friends. Moments later Henry was conscious of someone beside him. He turned to see Trifecta.

"I don't know what you're doing here, but if I were you, I'd go stand by the group of white people that are over there." Trifecta pointed across the crowd. Henry looked but didn't see any white faces.

"Thanks," Henry said, and he started moving cautiously through the crowd. When he looked back Trifecta had disappeared.

Weaving through the crowd trying to be as inconspicuous as possible, he spotted a group of white Southwestern College students. He identified them as such because several were wearing the college's sweatshirts. Standing close to the group of students he asked one of the guys, "Why hasn't the march started?"

"I think they're waiting for Doctor King to arrive."

"What are you doing here?" another one of the Southwestern students asked, genuinely concerned about a lone white teenager in a racially tense crowd.

"I'm a reporter for my school paper," Henry answered.

"Groovy, there is a reporter from our paper with us. .....Marsha," the boy hollered at a girl standing close by.

As a girl approached, the student with Henry said, "Marsha, this kid is a reporter for his school paper."

"Cool," said Marsha. "What grade are you in?"

"The twelfth," Henry answered.

"Come with me, and we'll do some interviews."

Marsha and Henry started working their way through the crowd, confidentially speaking with various people. Many of the older people assured them it was going to be a non-violent demonstration. One man pointed out that Dr. King had never led a march that escalated into a riot even though some of his marches had been disrupted by police brutality. Some of the younger people were suspicious of Marsha and Henry, thinking they were undercover police. However, that didn't prevent several of the boys who they interviewed from making threats against the white establishment.

The farther towards the back of the crowd Henry and Marsha moved, the more hostility they experienced. Some of the aggression was fueled by alcohol; some by anger, and some by rabble rousing. Many people were carrying signs: "**MACE WON'T STOP TRUTH**", "**JOBS, JOBS, JOBS**," "**JUSTICE AND EQUALITY FOR ALL MEN**," and the most popular placard worn or carried by the sanitation workers was "**I AM A MAN**."

It was obvious to the young reporters that communication among the march's organizers was almost nonexistent. While the march's marshals, who were identified by yellow arm bands, tried to maintain order and control, the mass of demonstrators began to show signs of turning into a mob. As the marshals moved through the crowd they hollered, "If you can't follow instructions, then go home. Don't stay here." However, the crowd continued to grow impatient.

Some of the teenagers began writing vulgar and profane slogans on the back of the "**I AM A MAN**" placards expressing their contempt for Mayor Loeb. Many of the placards were tacked onto three foot long wooden handles. Some of the teenage boys ripped the placards from the handles and started waving the wooden weapons in the air.

As Henry and Marsha made their way to the back of the march where most of the teenagers had gathered, cries of "Black Power" could be heard regularly. Others hollered the name of their schools, "Hamilton!" "Lester!" "Manassas!" "Washington!" along with shouts of profanity aimed towards Mayor Loeb. Becoming uncomfortable, Marsha recommended that she and Henry rejoin the white students.

Almost as soon as Henry and Marsha reunited with the college students, the march began. As the crowd started to move the marshals tried to keep the marchers off the sidewalks and in the street. The organizers of the march wanted Dr. King and his entourage to lead the march, followed by the various ministers of the city and the C.O.M.E workers (Community On the Movement for Equality, whose members had been instrumental in the strike and march).

The Southwestern students, along with Henry and a smattering of other white people, gathered as close to the front of the procession as possible.

Chapter 74

The Riot

It was almost ten thirty when Avery and Mr. Masters saw Dr. King arrive at Clayborn Temple. They had been waiting at the church since 7:30 that morning. Dr. King was late because he was in New York longer than expected, promoting the "Poor Peoples March on Washington." In addition to Avery and her father, many of the estimated 15,000 protesters had been waiting two hours or more for the demonstration to begin, causing widespread annoyance and a chance for a number of the dissidents to get drunk. Mr. Masters and Avery were lined up with the C.O.M.E workers, four deep behind the front row of the procession and Doctor King. When Doctor King was finally in place, and had his arms interlocked with other Civil Rights leaders, the cavalcade began to move. Walking in front of Dr. King and his associates was Henry Lux, the Assistant Chief of Police and the highest ranking police officer on the scene. In front of Assistant Chief Lux was a flatbed truck carrying reporters and black march marshals. Clearing the street ahead of the march were a group motorcycle policemen riding ten abreast.

From Clayborn Temple the march moved north on Hernando towards Beale Street. When the peaceful demonstrators began to turn onto Beale Street, a gang of high school boys barged in front of Mr. Masters and Avery.

"Get out of my way old man," one of the boys said as he jostled Masters.

Mr. Masters pushed back concerned the street punks might harm Avery.

"If you can't behave, then go home," Mr. Masters commanded. "We will not tolerate any trouble today."

The punk stared hard at Masters. "You want to take me home, grandpa?"

"Come on, man," one of the punk's co-conspirators said, pulling his partner away from Masters.

"I'll catch you later," the punk said, looking at Mr. Masters as he shoved his way into the third row of marchers.

Mr. Masters took Avery's hand and joined in the singing of, "We Shall Overcome," unwilling to allow the minor disruption to ruin Avery's experience of marching with Doctor King, even though he sensed the day would not go as well as planned.

*

G.W. and the other sanitation workers marched together. They were located in the middle of the parade. The mood among the tub toters turned festive as soon as the procession began moving. Most of the marchers were carrying signs or wearing placards held in place with string tied around their necks. Some of the people were chanting "Down with Loeb" while others sang freedom songs. Still others carried on conversations with their neighbors.

When Doctor King and the front line of marchers turned onto Beale Street, those at the rear of the procession were just beginning to move. Trifecta and Levi were near the back of the procession, along with high school students and young men from all over the city. Like Trifecta, many of the boys were dressed in flashy reds, purples, greens and golds.

While waiting for the march to begin the teenagers and young men had worked themselves into a frenzy speculating about the rumored police brutality that allegedly occurred at several black high schools. The unsubstantiated rumors lead to talk of rioting and looting.

Trifecta overheard several of the boys talking:

"Man there is some cool threads in Pape's."

"Man I dig Lanskey's. Have you seen those shirts they have in the window?"

"I was in Paul's Tailoring the other day, and that place is full of cool material. My mama could sew me some pants that would be out-a-sight."

"Have you seen the horns they have in the window of Capitol Pawn Shop?"

"You can't play a horn."

"I could learn if I had one."

"What I want from a pawn shop is a gun. Things would change around here if I had a piece."

When the last of the marchers began to press forward, many of the young men who were bringing up the rear were armed with metal pipes, bricks, bottles, and wooden handles that once held picket signs. As the armed boys passed in front of Clayborn Temple, the marshals were able to confiscate some of the contraband, but much more slipped by the scrutiny of the untrained and over worked volunteers.

As soon as the last of the marchers turned the corner onto Beale Street pandemonium broke out. Groups of teenagers broke rank and ran up the sidewalk, shattering store-front windows as they went.

*

When the sanitation workers were approaching Second Avenue, a swarm of teenagers running across Beale Street crashed into the city employees. The teenagers were hollering and screaming. "Get out of my way!" "I'm coming through!" "Move!" One young man ran directly into G.W., causing G.W. to stumble, but the boy bounced off G.W. and fell onto the street. The boy who was wielding a wooden handle that once held a picket sign rose from the street cursing and screaming at G.W. When the boy cocked his arm to hit G.W. with the wooden handle some of the other garbage men restrained him. The boy squirmed loose and quickly disappeared among the crowd.

More young people began to run on the sidewalks throwing rocks and bottles at store windows.

"Stop, stop, stop!" some of the garbage men hollered at the troublemakers.

"They're ruining the march!" others shouted.

They're going to get us killed!" still others screamed.

*

As the people leading the march were approaching Main Street, sounds of breaking glass and uproar could be heard behind them. Orders were given to keep marching. Several of the marshals were dispatched to find out what or who was causing the disturbance and to bring it to an end.

Masters suspiciously eyed the street punks in front of him. They remained in the formation. However, they were forcing the pace of the march by physically pushing Doctor King and the front row of men who had their arms locked.

*

When the other boys began running Trifecta and Levi naively followed, darting innocently up the sidewalk. When windows started breaking and merchandise from window

ROBERT HUMPHREYS

displays was thrown into the street the two friends became separated.

*

As the front of the march turned right onto Main Street, the boys behind Doctor King abandoned the march and started running up the sidewalk, breaking store windows as they went. As soon as the windows were broken the looters came, assaulting the vulnerable stores like buzzards on a dead carcass.

"Burn it down. Smash the glass!" screamed the crazed young men as they ran, skirting the marchers and entering stores through broken windows, then exiting seconds later with arms full of merchandise.

The march hadn't traveled more than a few blocks on Main Street when the procession stalled as it was met by a line of police officers wearing gas masks and carrying truncheons. With bedlam increasing, a car was flagged down on McCall Avenue, which ran off of Main Street. Doctor King was placed in the vehicle and ushered away. The police provided a bull horn to a remaining leader of the march and he instructed the crowd to return to Clayborn Temple.

The marchers became a chaotic tangle. Some people were attempting to return to Clayborn Temple, others were pushing and shoving to get to City Hall; still others were looking for a way to escape the violence.

When Mr. Masters turned around and saw the chaos that was occurring on Beale Street, he and Avery abandoned the march, continuing south on Main Street where minor looting had begun, but they were able to get back to their car and sped away safely.

Mr. Masters felt a twinge of guilt deserting the demonstration but Avery's safety was paramount. Still, he silently cursed those who had started the riot and wished they would rot in jail.

*

On Beale Street anarchy and the destruction of property escalated. The police began converging from every direction wearing gas masks, with batons at the ready. At first the police didn't bother the sanitation workers but were attacking the looters, forcibly trying to stop the pillaging and plundering. The looters and hoodlums responded by randomly throwing bottles, bricks, and rocks into the crowds of marchers.

"Go Back, Go Back!" chanted demonstrators who had been in the front of the procession as they now turned towards Clayborn Temple.

"Walk, don't run!" shouted the parade marshals, scared the very young or elderly might be trampled if the panicked demonstrators stampeded.

Marchers continued to push and shove as they changed directions in the street. Looters continued to ransack the stores, escaping quickly in every direction with arms full of booty. As the rioting continued, in frustration, the police turned on some of the peaceful demonstrators. Occasionally an officer would identify the sanitation workers he had trouble with during the previous weeks of the strike and took the opportunity to inflict vigilante justice.

Tear gas rose like smoke over a forest fire. The violence and turmoil continued to intensify as the street thugs who had not originally been in the march found a cache of bricks from old buildings that had been torn down. It was one of those bricks that first hit G.W. in the back of his head, sending him to his knees.

*

When Trifecta realized what was happening he stopped running. He moved into the street, trying to distance himself from the looters on the sidewalk. Several of the older demonstrators accused him of being one of the rioters.

"What you did was exactly what the white folks wanted you to do," said a woman, wagging her finger at Trifecta.

"You sure ain't helping the sanitation men," a skinny, hunched back old man said.

"You and your friends have disgraced us in fronts of Doctor King," someone else said.

"I hope you're satisfied. There's going to be innocent people hurt because of this foolishness," another chimed.

As Trifecta tried to distance himself from the troublemakers and his accusers he saw G.W. sitting in the middle of the street. His hat was off and the back of his head was bleeding.

"Come on, get up and let's get you out of here," Trifecta said, reaching to help G.W. to his feet.

"Why did they do it?" G.W. asked, looking into Trifecta's face.

"I don't know, come on and get up," Trifecta said, trying to pull G.W. up by his arm.

"It was colored boys throwing rocks at us that hit me."

"I know."

"It don't make no sense. They supposed to be on our side."

"I know, come on now. We got to get you up before you get trampled."

When G.W. stood he was weak-kneed and stumbled back and forth trying to keep his balance.

"Can you walk?" Trifecta asked.

"I'm a little dizzy and nauseated, but I think I can walk if I hold onto you."

With his arm draped over Trifecta's shoulder the two neighbors started walking toward Clayborn Temple when out of the blue G.W. was clubbed across the back of the neck, sending him back to the street. As he fell he almost pulled Trifecta to the asphalt with him. Before Trifecta could react, a police officer's nightstick clipped Trifecta's chin and hit him solidly just below the throat, sending him tumbling backwards to the pavement.

The man wearing the police officer's uniform was not a cop, it was Peter.

"Get up you little snitch or I'll kill you where you lie," Peter snarled.

Trifecta hesitated. Peter raised his baton to hit Trifecta again. Trifecta shielded his face with his forearm. But the blow never came. Instead, he felt someone tug at his arm. It was Henry trying to pull him off the pavement.

"Get up and let's get out of here," Henry grunted.

Confused but relieved, Trifecta saw Peter getting up from the street where he had fallen. Apparently, Henry had somehow knocked Peter off of his feet. As soon as Trifecta was up, he and Henry bolted towards Main Street. The two boys weaved through the menagerie of people, with Peter trailing a short distance behind them, pushing and shoving his way through the crowd.

When the boys arrived on Main Street, they ran north with Peter close behind. Passing a large department store, the boys tried to open the front doors but the doors were locked. Peter was gaining on them. The boys cut down a side street and ducked into the store's parking garage.

On the main floor of the parking garage was an area where shoppers waited for attendants to bring their car from the multi-level parking lot. In the waiting area were four restrooms, one for white men, another for white women, another for colored men, and another for colored women. The two boys went into the colored men's restroom and locked the door. The lock was a small barrel door bolt, which Henry barely latched before Peter crashed into the door. The door visibly shook from the force of Peter ramming into it.

"Come out or I'm going to start shooting through the door," Peter screamed.

The restroom was tiny with barely enough room for a toilet and a sink. The two boys had their backs against opposing walls but there was only a foot or so separating them.

"What are we going to do?" Henry asked in horror.

"I guess I have to go out there," Trifecta responded, even more terrified than Henry because he knew that Peter was after him.

Trifecta unlatched the door and stepped into the garage. Peter had a thirty eight caliber, police special revolver pointed at him. Henry stayed behind, clinging to the restroom wall. Praying or more accurately begging God to somehow protect him.

"Don't shoot!" Trifecta screamed, with tears running down his cheeks.

"Why did you call the cops, and why did you burn the car lot?" Peter asked wanting Trifecta understand and confess to his treachery before he died.

"I had to stop you from killing my mama, but I didn't do anything to your car lot."

"Your mama isn't nothing but a doped up whore that ain't worth dying for, but now I've got to kill you."

Not understanding the conversation between Trifecta and the cop, Henry wondered why a policeman wanted to shoot Trifecta.

"Hold it comrade," the voice came from the entrance to the parking garage. Trifecta turned his head and saw a man with both hands gripping the handle of a pistol pointed at Peter. The man was Andrey Pavlor. Mikhail Smirnov sat in the driver's seat of an idling car just outside the garage.

"What do you want?" Peter asked, not taking his eyes or his pistol off of Trifecta.

"We have come for you."

"Why?"

"Because you've been stealing," Andrey answered, as he began to walk slowly toward Peter.

"No, I haven't."

"We've had you under surveillance. We've questioned people concerning your activity. We have searched your apartment. We have tapped your phone. You talk too much and we know what you have been doing."

Knowing it was useless to beg for mercy Peter turned and pointed his pistol towards the man with the gun. Peter shot first, but his shot was quick and wild. Instinctively, Trifecta fell to the ground as more gunshots reverberated like a string of firecrackers exploding in rapid succession. Stray bullets hit and ricocheted from the floor and walls of the parking lot. When the shooting stopped, Peter was dead.

With the smell of spent gunpowder clouding the air Trifecta remained prone and motionless. Andrey rummaged through Peter's pockets, making sure he didn't have anything that would lead the authorities back to the Russian government.

When Andrey finished searching Peter's body he pointed his pistol in the direction of Trifecta.

"What to do with you?" Andrey said to himself in Russian, referring to Trifecta.

He no sooner got the words out of his mouth than a black car squealed into the parking garage. The car stopped short of Andrey. Two men jumped out of the vehicle with pistols drawn. Henry instantly recognized one of those men as Agent Ball.

Andrey high-tailed it further into the garage. Ball followed the Russian on foot while Ball's partner pursued in the car. The sound of burning rubber came from outside the garage as Mikhail Smirnov drove away, leaving Andrey to fend for himself.

"Let's go," Henry said, as he burst out of the restroom. During the confusion the two boys scurried out of the garage, ran down an alley, crossed Front Street, and slid down the grassy bluff to Riverside Drive. The boys sat at the bottom of the bluff looking at the Mississippi River trying to recoup from their horrific experience. Both were physically shaking, and their ears continued to ring from the gunfire in the garage. The traffic on Riverside Drive was light and there appeared no urgency in the drivers even though just a block or two away the riot raged.

"Why was that cop after you?" Henry asked.

"He's not a cop, he's a drug dealer, and I told the law all about him."

The boys sat silently, reflecting for a few moments on what they just experienced. Henry was wondering how Trifecta knew a drug dealer, and why the drug dealer was in a police uniform. While Trifecta was thankful that he was still alive, and wondering who the man was that killed Peter.

"What now?" Trifecta asked, breaking the silence. A car that just passed them had pulled over to the side of the road and was backing up towards them.

"It's okay," Henry said, recognizing the vehicle.

Chapter 75

Clayborn Temple under siege

G.W. limped and staggered towards Clayborn Temple. He was dizzy, nauseous, and his head continued to bleed. As he made his way down Hernando Street, whiffs of tear gas floated lightly in the air. When he was closer to the Temple, the smell of gas nearly overwhelmed him. A crowd of young people and the police were engaged in combat. The blacks were throwing bricks, rocks, and bottles, while the police responded with tear gas, mace, and truncheons.

When G.W. labored up the steps to the church a cop with a night stick tried to prevent him from entering the building. However, a brick intended for the police officer missed its target and struck G.W. on the right shoulder knocking him to his knees. The errant brick caused the policeman to turn his attention away from G.W. and back to the rioters.

Tears ran down G.W.'s cheeks as he battled with his battered body to get to his feet. He didn't know if the tears were caused by the gas, the pain in his body, or a combination of both. Once erect, he attempted to pull the door to the church open, but as soon as the door began to open it was snatched shut from inside. A whiskey bottle shattered at G.W.'s feet as he continued to feebly tug at the door.

"Please let me in. Please, I'm hurt and need sanctuary." G.W. squalled as he continued to strain at the door. In answer to his pleas, the door was finally released and G.W. was allowed to enter. He was surprised anyone would try to keep him from entering the building because the chaos inside was bordering on the pandemonium outside.

G.W. painfully eased into a pew in the back of the church. Some young people who were taking refuge from the police were making as much commotion as a herd of braying jackasses, cursing and hollering against the police and Mayor Loeb. A minister went to the pulpit.

"Please, everyone sit down and be quiet. We are on the phone with the police, asking them to retreat so we can get these folks who are injured to the hospital."

The minister's request was met with increased cursing and protest.

"Please, this is a house of God. Show some respect."

The jeering continued.

"I have asked you nicely, now either settle down or leave."

"We'll burn this place before we leave," shouted a young man who was standing close to G.W.

"Show some respect," G.W. repeated.

"Shut up, old man," said the young troublemaker.

"Did you hear the man? He said if you can't act right you should leave," G.W. said, glaring at the young man.

"You're the one that's going to leave."

The troublemaker grabbed G.W. by the shirt collar and tried to pull him to his feet, but G.W. had all the abuse he intended to take. Standing up, with a surge of adrenalin stimulating him, G.W. swatted the young man's hands, forcing the boy to let go of his shirt. Even with his right shoulder injured, he hit the boy squarely on the jaw, sending him crashing to the ground. Immediately several of the boy's friends were on G.W., knocking him to the floor where they not only punched him but kicked him unmercifully. Several of the tub toters attempted to help G.W., but it was a losing battle. G.W. might have been beaten to death if the front door hadn't been pushed open and a canister of tear gas lobbed inside.

As gas filled the sanctuary of the church, the ruckus grew with people trying to escape the noxious fumes. One of the other tub toters named Jamal Reese, who also lived in Lemoyne Gardens, helped G.W. crawl out of a window. Half blinded by the tear gas the two men shuffled through some residential properties trying to distance themselves from the bedlam. When G.W. couldn't go any further he collapsed in a yard behind a small clapboard house.

"What are you men doing in my yard?" a thin, gray-haired black lady said through her screen door.

"This man has been beaten by the police and by some colored boys. I'm afraid he's hurt bad."

"You ain't robbers are you?"

"No ma'am; we're garbage men."

"Have you been marching?"

"Yes, ma'am, and a bunch of those young boys started a riot."

"I saw what they did on TV."

"My friend here didn't do anything but he still got beat by the police. When we went to Clayborn Temple he was attacked by some colored boys."

"I go to the Baptist Church."

"Ma'am?"

"I said I don't go to Clayborn Temple. I go to the Baptist Church."

"I wonder if a Christian woman like you could get my friend a glass of water and some damp rags, so we can wash the gas out of our eyes."

Within moments the woman was in the backyard with two glasses of water and wet wash cloths.

"Thank you ma'am," Jamel said.

G.W. sat slumped on the ground.

"Your friend looks bad," the lady said.

"Yes, ma'am, he took a beating." By this time G.W.'s face had begun to swell where the young boys punched him and his ribs hurt where he was kicked. The back of his head continued bleeding.

"Are you finished wiping your eyes?"

"Yes, ma'am."

"Let me have those rags."

The lady took a damp cloth and applied it to the back of G.W.'s head. G.W. flinched at first, but soon the wet cloth began to soothe the wound.

"Hold this rag here," the lady said to Jamal.

The lady went into the house and returned a minute later.

"Can you drive my car?" the lady asked Jamal.

"What do you mean?"

"I was a nurse's aide before I retired, and I believe this man needs medical attention."

"Yes, ma'am."

"Does that mean you can drive my car?" the lady asked, pointing to a 1958 Ford parked on a gravel driveway.

"Yes, ma'am."

"We won't be able to wait on him because you'll have to bring me back home, but we can get him to John Gaston and leave him there until a doctor can see him."

Normally it would have taken less than fifteen minutes to travel to the hospital, but having to detour around the riot areas, it took more than a half hour. When they arrived at the emergency room it was full of people suffering from trauma received in the riot. Looking around, G.W. thought hospitals in Vietnam couldn't be any busier.

G.W. gave Jamal the keys to his car and told him where the car was parked. By the time Jamal got the lady home the activity around Clayborn Temple had subsided. He soon found G.W.'s car and went back to the hospital.

It was hours before G.W. was released from the hospital. By that time a curfew was imposed from dark to dawn throughout the city. G.W. and Jamal were driving towards Lemoyne Gardens as sundown darkened the sky. They were stopped by the police three times and asked what they were doing on the street. Jamal pointed to G.W., who was bandaged, medicated, and holding a bottle of prescription drugs in his hand. "I'm bringing him home from the hospital."

The police let Jamal and G.W. go with a warning to get off the street as quickly as possible.

When they turned onto Mississippi Boulevard, it was apparent that the riot had spilled over into the Lemoyne Gardens neighborhood. Almost every store had broken windows. Even the stores owned by blacks were sacked.

"That don't make no sense," Jamal said.

"What's that?" G.W. asked.

"Why those boys would tear up Miss Leona's Hat Shop. Everybody knows Miss Leona is a colored woman and a strong supporter of the strike."

Miss Leona owned a millenary shop on Mississippi Boulevard a block away from Walker Avenue and was one of the neighborhood's most respected citizens.

"They don't care who they hurt. They just want to cause trouble, and it ain't got nothing to do with the strike." G.W. said, talking about the rioters.

Jamal helped G.W. limp into his apartment. G.W. could hardly walk, not only because of his wounds but also because of the pain medication.

When the two men entered G.W.'s apartment, Yolanda looked at her battered and swollen husband, then looking upward prayed. "Dear God, please, I can't take any more."

Chapter 76

Scoop gets the story

"He's with me," Henry told Scoop as Trifecta got in the back seat of the car.

Scoop pulled back onto Riverside Drive going north.

"I tried to get close to the demonstration but most of the streets are blocked. What did you see?"

Henry gave a quick account of his experience during the riot. Scoop turned to Trifecta. "How about you son, what happened to you?"

"Pretty much the same as Henry…"

"Tell him what you were talking about when you got on the bus this morning," Henry said.

Trifecta looked at Henry like he had said something wrong.

"It's okay," Henry said. "Scoop's a reporter, not a cop."

"You colored people have been complaining that the papers aren't giving you a fair shake, but if you'll tell me your side of the story, I'll do what I can to get it printed. I'll even give you and Henry the byline."

"The what?" Trifecta asked.

"I'll put your names on the article."

"I'll tell you what I know, but I don't want my name in the paper."

"Why not?" Henry asked.

"We came close to getting killed today and if our names are in the paper there's no telling who will be after us next."

"What do you mean you almost got killed?" Scoop asked.

Scoop turned east towards the newspaper office, as Trifecta told about Peter being murdered and the men in the parking garage.

"The FBI was there too," Henry said.

"Wait, I'm confused. Let's start from the beginning," Scoop said.

Henry gave Scoop an abbreviated account of his involvement with Agent Ball.

Trifecta quickly told Scoop about Peter.

Neither boy knew anything about the man who killed Peter.

"Tell him what you and the other kids were talking about when you got on the bus," Henry said to Trifecta.

"I decided to skip school and go to the march. I went to Booker T. Washington to see what was happening before I went to Clayborn Temple. When I got there some men were telling the kids to cut classes and join the protest with Doctor King. I caught up with some of the cats I knew who were skipping school and going to town. The cops started stopping kids who were walking off campus, telling us to go back to our classes. Some of the kids got to hassling with the cops. They were hollering and screaming, but me and the guys I was with ignored the cops and just kept walking.

We got on the bus that Henry was on. Next thing I know Henry was getting off of the bus. When I got to Clayborn Temple a bunch of cats said there was some white dude standing by himself. They were figuring on beating him up. When I saw it was Henry, I told him to go stand with some other white people."

"How many white people were participating in the march?" Scoop asked, turning into the parking lot of Scripts Howard Publishing Company where both the morning and afternoon papers were printed.

"Not many. Most white people are against the garbage men." Trifecta said as the three got out of the car.

Scoop and the two boys entered the building that was a whirlwind of clamor and activity. Telephones were ringing. Voices constantly rumbled and typewriters were clacking as people rushed up and down the aisles that separated the desks, trying to meet deadlines. Finding an empty desk with a typewriter, Scoop started interviewing Henry and Trifecta. He wrote as fast as he could to pound out a story. Scoop called the FBI field office to confirm the story about Peter being murdered. No one would verify that a murder had occurred. After questioning the boys further, and both boys insisting, he included the murder in the article. He noted that the reported murder was an unconfirmed account from a reliable but undisclosed source.

Just prior to the final deadline the article was completed with Henry's name on the byline. Henry considered the possible repercussions from having his name on the article, but he couldn't resist having the by line on a real newspaper article.

Scoop drove the two boys to Central High School. Due to the riot classes were dismissed so they walked a block to the Huddle House restaurant. Entering the diner they were given disapproving looks by short order cook. Despite the civil rights act, the well-established restaurant was generally considered for whites, causing Trifecta to feel uncomfortable. The boys went to a table in the back corner away from the counter where the cook was stationed.

"Why did you do it, Man?" Trifecta asked after the waitress had taken their order for two Coca Colas.

"Why did I do what?"

"Why did you stop Peter from beating me when you thought he was a cop?"

"I don't know. I saw him getting ready to hit you with his billy club and I just shoved him. It was instinct I guess."

"I owe you because he would have killed me."

"You don't owe me. You saved me from getting beat up when we were waiting for the march to begin."

"Okay, we'll call it even. I'm going to tell you about a decision I've made."

"What's that?"

"I'm quitting Central."

"You're dropping out of school?"

"No, it's too close to graduation. I'm going back to Washington to finish school with my friends."

"You don't have any friends at Central?"

"No, after today you're the closest thing to a friend I have at Central and all we've done is fight since we've known each other."

"Aren't the other black kids your friends?"

"They're all smart and I'm not. I tried to get something going with Avery but that didn't work out. I came to Central to help the movement, but going to school with white kids hasn't made any difference. All I've ever wanted to do is be with my mama. Since she's been back in Memphis, I found out she's been involved in some bad stuff. Now that Peter is dead she can get straightened out. I'm going graduate high school with my own people, and then I'm going to take care of my mama."

"I've made a decision too."

"What's that?"

"I'm going to break up with Charity and start going steady with Marcie."

*

Henry was home by five. However, it took two hours of fretting for him to work up the courage to call Charity.

"I read your article in the paper. It was great." Charity said.

"Thanks," Henry said. He was so preoccupied about breaking up with her, he had forgotten about the article Scoop wrote under his name.

"It sounds like you were right in the middle of the riot."

"Yea, I was."

"Were you scared?"

"Yea, I was scared some of the time. But the reason I called is we need to break up," Henry blurted out, unable to control the anxiety of ending the relationship.

There was silence on the other end of the line. Henry's stomach knotted tighter waiting for a response.

"Did you hear me?" Henry asked no longer able to tolerate the muteness.

"Yes," Charity said with a sob.

"Okay, I'll see you around" Henry said, relieved, thinking the worst was over.

"Wait, I need an explanation," Charity said with a whimper. "I gave up my scholarship to Vanderbilt for you and I want to know why you're breaking up with me."

Henry was speechless as he thought of all the reasons he had rehearsed for breaking up with Charity.

"I think I'm holding you back. The best thing for you is to go to Vanderbilt and forget about me," was Henry's impromptu reply.

"You're kidding, right?" Charity said sounding aggravated. "Does this have anything to do with Marcie McDougal?"

"No," Henry said, blushing. If Charity could have seen him she would have known he was lying. Even without seeing him she suspected he was lying.

"I've got to go my mom is calling me," Henry said, thankful he had a reason to end the conversation. He quickly hung up the phone before Charity could rebut.

While Henry was on the phone with Charity there was a knock on the Murphy's door. Being cautious due to the riot and the ensuing curfew, Mr. Murphy looked out the window before opening the door. When he saw a white man in a suit he opened the door.

"Mr. Murphy, I don't know if you remember me, I'm Agent Ball from the FBI."

"How could I forget you after you interrogated my family for hours? What can I do for you?"

"If you have a few minutes, I would like to ask Henry a few questions. I assure you it is very important."

"Sure, come in." Mr. Murphy said, afraid his family was about to be put through the wringer again, but feeling he had no other option.

Mrs. Murphy called Henry and after hanging up with Charity he joined his parents in the living room.

When everyone was assembled, Agent Ball turned towards Henry and said, "I'm here to talk to you about what happened today."

"Yes, sir," Henry answered, as his parents looked towards him, befuddled.

"I guess you saw your story has been edited quite a bit?"

"No sir, I haven't read the paper."

"What story?" Mr. Murphy asked.

"Have you seen today's paper?" Ball asked, turning towards Mr. Murphy.

"Sure, it's right here," Henry's father answered, picking up the newspaper from an end table next to the couch where he was sitting.

"Look at the bottom right hand corner of the front page."

Glancing at the paper and then looking at Henry in amazement, Mr. Murphy asked, "Did you write this?"

"Yeah, kind of," Henry said.

Mr. Murphy scanned the article as Mrs. Murphy looked on, confused. When Mr. Murphy looked up from the paper Mrs. Murphy asked, "What is it?"

"Henry wrote about the riot," Henry's father answered.

"What riot?" his wife asked.

"The garbage men who rioted on Beale Street today," Agent Ball commented.

"How could you write about the riot when you were in school?" Mr. Murphy asked.

"Did the school let you go downtown today?" Mrs. Murphy asked.

"No ma'am," Henry said, looking at the floor.

"Then how did you write about the riot?" his father asked.

"I skipped school."

"What caused you to skip school and go downtown? You could have been killed," Mr. Murphy said.

Henry didn't answer. Instead Agent Ball interjected, "That's why I'm here; we need to talk about what happened today."

Henry's parents turned their attention to Agent Ball, thinking Henry was in real trouble.

"Henry witnessed a murder today." Both Mr. and Mrs. Murphy gasped. Henry continued to stare at the floor.

"It had nothing to do with the strike," Ball continued. "It had to do with international espionage. That's why the information about the murder was taken out of your article. And that's why I need you folks not to mention this to anyone. The reality is if you do tell people what happened they aren't going to believe you anyway. Who would think a kid from Memphis would be involved with a Soviet spy?"

"What happened to you today?" Mrs. Murphy asked Henry.

Henry looked at Ball as confused as his parents.

"Go ahead and tell them son; I would like to hear your version of today's events."

Henry rehashed the day omitting the part about Marcie. He still didn't know what any of it had to do with a Russian spy.

"I knew Scoop or whatever his name is was trouble. Every time you're around that man you get into trouble. I don't want you seeing him anymore," Mrs. Murphy lectured.

"He's just trying to help me, Mom."

"Well, he's not doing a very good job of it."

Agent Ball briefly told them about Peter and then he said, "I'll leave you folks to work this out. I appreciate your time and hope what we have talked about will remain confidential."

"You can depend on that. We are a very patriotic family and we try to do everything our government asks," Mr. Murphy said as he shook hands with Agent Ball and led him to the front door.

After Ball was gone Mr. Murphy said, "I really don't know what to say. What you did was very foolish, and you are a lucky young man because you didn't get hurt or worse. Why don't you go to your room and get ready for bed? We'll talk about this tomorrow after I have had time to think."

As Henry left the room he noticed his mother carefully reading the article.

In the meantime Trifecta called Avery. At first, Mr. Masters wasn't going to let him speak to her, but when Trifecta told him it was about the march, he relented. After briefly discussing the riot, Trifecta told Avery that he was leaving Central and finishing the year at Booker T. Washington. He also told her about Henry and Marcie and Henry's plans to break up with Charity.

As soon as Trifecta hung up, Avery called Charity. Both girls were soon crying.

Chapter 77

Henry, the day after the riot

The following morning Henry had plotted his route between classes to avoid Charity. Now all he had to do was find Marcie and ask her to go steady. When he approached Marcie's homeroom he noticed she was wedged between the lockers and Dan Partee. Dan was quite a bit taller than Marcie and she was looking up at him with dreamy eyes.

The bell rang and Dan left to go to his classroom. Before Marcie entered her homeroom Henry stopped her.

"I need to talk to you," Henry said sounding desperate and confused.

"It's only a few minutes before homeroom."

"I know, but I wanted to let you know that I broke up with Charity."

"I'm sorry."

"You don't understand. I broke up with Charity so I could go steady with you."

"Why would you do that?"

"Yesterday, when you kissed me, I decided I loved you more than I love Charity."

"Kissing you was a mistake. I don't know why I did it, and I'm sorry you misunderstood."

"I misunderstood? What was I supposed to think after the way you kissed me? What am I to do now? I already broke up with Charity," Henry demanded.

"Dan asked me to go steady with him yesterday while you were downtown with the garbage men." Marcie held up her left hand to show Henry that she was wearing Dan's class ring. "I like you Henry, and I hope we can be friends. But these last three years have shown me that we aren't meant to be together romantically. You have no aspirations. I'm not sure you're even going to college. Plus you're immature, and your association with Negroes is not something I want to be involved with. Whereas, Dan is ambitious and he has a football scholarship to Ole Miss so we'll be together at the same college for the next four years."

The tardy bell rang.

"I'm ambitious enough to have an article published in last night's paper and I don't associate with Negroes, I was just writing articles that have social significance."

Marcie's homeroom teacher was about to close the door and she asked Marcie if she was going to join the rest of the class.

"Yes ma'am," Marcie said. Then, turning to Henry, she said, "Tell Charity you made a mistake, and you're sorry. Explain to her that you were experiencing a lot of stress yesterday." Marcie disappeared into the class room and the door closed behind her.

Taking Marcie's advice, Henry went to Charity's homeroom. The class had already started so he waited in the hallway until the period ended. As soon as she entered the hall Henry confronted her. Her eyes were blood shot and it was apparent she had been crying

"I made a mistake, I was under a lot of stress" Henry said. "I love you, and I want you back."

Without a word, Charity handed Henry his class ring. She turned and walked away. He followed her grasping her arm to stop her from walking further.

"I want you to have my ring. I don't want to break up with you."

"Why? Has Marcie already dumped you?" Charity said, having learned what Trifecta told Avery.

"No." Henry lied. "I've just decided I want to be with you."

"You're a liar!" Charity screamed, drawing the attention of students and teachers alike. Charity had never used profanity in her life. However, this was the first time she had been jilted. With her emotions erupting, both tears and profanity gushed from her.

A female teacher quickly intervened and escorted Charity to the principal's office. Charity was sure she would be suspended for her outburst. Instead an empathic guidance counselor not only calmed her down but also assured her that her scholarship to Vanderbilt could be reinstated provided she had nothing else to do with Henry Murphy. Charity assured the counselor that her relationship with Henry was over. She received three days of after school detention for her tantrum which she considered a slap on the wrist in light of the language she used.

Chapter 78

March 29, 1968

Doctor King was determined to conduct a peaceful demonstration to support the striking sanitation workers so he mobilized his staff to organize another march rather than depending on well-meaning but inexperienced local workers.

The garbage men and their families were becoming increasingly discouraged. Not only because of the riot, but because the strike fund was being depleted and there was little money being distributed for them to pay rent, buy food and pay utility bills. Many of the strikers, including G.W., were considering returning to work or finding other employment.

The AFL-CIO was worried that if Mayor Loeb prevented city employees from organizing in Memphis, other southern cities and states would stop their municipal employees from forming unions.

The City of Memphis agreed to allow the sanitation workers to resume demonstrating but restricted the marches to four hundred public works employees and their adult supporters. Young people were forbidden to participate.

The marches were to be closely monitored by the Memphis Police Department to insure compliance. However, G.W. was in no condition to march.

G.W. struggled to attend church on Sunday, three days after the riot. He and Yolanda joined with the other church members in praying for peace and reconciliation in Memphis. It amazed G.W. that a city that boasted more churches than gas stations could be so full of hate.

On Monday, April first, it was announced that Doctor King would lead another march on April eighth. During that week various unions and civil rights groups across the country pledged to participate in the demonstration. The National Guard also withdrew from Memphis, and the curfew was lifted.

On April third, the city obtained a temporary restraining order, which prevented non-residents of Memphis, including Doctor King, from participating in the march on April eighth. The American Civil Liberties Union and several local attorneys immediately started working on having the restraining order lifted.

The day Doctor King arrived in Memphis to plan and organize the April eighth march, numerous death threats were made against him. The threats not only came from whites but also from some blacks, and though he was under constant surveillance by local and federal authorities, he refused protection. The first night he was in town he spoke to three thousand people at Mason Temple. The people in attendance braved severe weather to hear Doctor King.

The lawyers representing Doctor King met with the judge concerning the restraining order the morning of April fourth. Lawyers for the city pointed out that reliable sources reported blacks across the city were purchasing guns and ammunition, and the Ku Klux Klan also planned a demonstration in Memphis on April eighth. Concluding the hearing the judge ruled the march would occur as scheduled with certain restrictions that he would present on April fifth.

That evening Doctor King and his entourage were preparing to go to dinner at the home of a local civil rights leader prior to his nightly speech at Mason Temple. Doctor King was standing on the second-floor walkway of the Lorraine Motel waiting on some stragglers who were to attend the dinner, when he was shot. He died on the operating table at Saint Joseph Hospital at seven o'clock that evening. A curfew was immediately imposed on the city and the National Guard was recalled.

The news of doctors King's death was not taken well within the black community. Throughout the night fires were ignited, windows were broken, and looting was rampant. Police cars were shot at, and gangs of teenagers roamed the streets in black neighborhoods. While white neighborhoods, were as quiet and peaceful as midnight on Christmas Eve.

Instead of prowling the streets Trifecta went next door to talk to G.W. about the day's events.

"Now that they have killed Dr. King, is the civil rights movement over?" Trifecta asked G.W.

"No. The movement is bigger than one man. There are plenty of people to keep the movement alive. Dr. King was a charismatic leader, but he wasn't doing it all by himself.

"I guess black power is our only hope."

"If by black power you mean political power, you're right. If by black power you mean violence, then you're wrong."

"White people used violence on Dr. King."

"That was one white man. It wasn't all white people. Most white people don't want to be around a murderer, like the man who killed Doctor King any more than I want to be around black people who are burning and looting tonight."

"Have you forgotten that it was white people who made us slaves?"

"Have you forgotten it was white people that freed the slaves?"

Trifecta was beginning to get frustrated with G.W. and his defense of white people. "Doesn't what happened today make you angry at white people?" He asked.

"I'm mad at the person who murdered Doctor King, but not at all white people."

"If it wasn't for white people refusing to give the garbage men what they want, then Doctor King wouldn't have been in town, and he wouldn't have gotten shot."

"If there hadn't been a riot the other day, Doctor King wouldn't have been in town, and he wouldn't have gotten shot."

"All the white people in this town are against you and the rest of the black garbage men."

"I hope not," said G.W. precariously.

Chapter 79

On April eighth, Trifecta and Yolanda marched with G.W. in the memorial celebration for Doctor King. Yolanda asked Trifecta to walk with G.W. because he continued to have dizzy spells from the beatings he received during the riot.

Many people in the march wore signs that read, "Honor Dr. King, End Racism."

Caledonia invited G.W. and Yolanda over for some pie and sweet tea when they returned from the memorial service.

"How was the march?" Caledonia asked, as Trifecta, Yolanda and G.W. entered her apartment.

"There were too many long speeches," Trifecta replied.

"We had to stand for several hours," Yolanda said.

"I had to sit on the curb for a while," G.W. said.

When they were all seated at the kitchen table, Caledonia said, "I got a letter from Willie today. He said he's going to get married."

"That's wonderful," Yolanda said.

"Sure is," G.W. agreed. "Who is the girl?"

"She's from Guam. He sent me a picture of her." Caledonia pulled an envelope from the pocket in her house coat and extracted a picture of Willie and his bride-to-be.

"He says he'll be able to move off base, and the government will give him more money for a housing allowance."

"She's a white girl," Trifecta exclaimed, looking at the picture.

"Ain't either, she's from Guam," Caledonia snapped.

"What kind of people lives in Guam?" Trifecta asked.

"Looks like she's Asian," Caledonia said.

"Asian or white doesn't make any difference," Trifecta said. "She isn't black. It don't make no sense. Why would she marry him anyway?" Trifecta ranted.

"Well hopefully they're in love," interjected G.W., "and she probably wants to improve her life."

"How is her life going to be any better when they come here and live in the projects?" Trifecta asked.

"The projects may be a lot better than where she lives now. I know the projects are better than the tenant house we lived in when we were share cropping," G.W. said.

"It's not right for him to marry a girl from Gaum," Trifecta said.

"Are you a racist?" G.W. asked.

"I'm not white. How can I be a racist?"

"You don't have to be white to be a racist. If you hate somebody because of the color of their skin or the shape of their eyes, then you're a racist."

"Well then, there are a lot of black people that are racist."

"I imagine there are. We marched today to honor Doctor King and what he did to end racism. And that includes being racist towards peoples in Guam."

"I haven't even heard of Guam."

"That's the shame of it. You don't even know this girl, but because she's not black you don't think she's good enough for your cousin. We can't expect white peoples to stop being racist if we're going to continue to discriminate," G.W. said.

*

On April sixteenth, the city agreed to recognize the union, and the city met some wage and benefit demands which required a donation from the local businessman and philanthropist, Abe Plough, until a new budget could be adopted.

"Mr. Plough is a white man," G.W. said to Trifecta one day after the strike was settled.

"So?"

"So if it weren't for Mr. Plough, I don't know if I would have ever gone back to work. Remember I told you not all white people are against us?"

"I remember."

"I guess this proves that it ain't so bad to have a white man on your side."

"Maybe not," Trifecta admitted. He was as happy as anyone that the sanitation strike had ended.

Chapter 80

1968-1975

Mary met Sims when she was selling marijuana for Moneypenny. Sims was immediately attracted to her and the two began spending a lot of time together, particularly at night. Sims wanted Mary to live with him but she refused. There was no real attraction to setting up housekeeping with him. In their current relationship, she enjoyed the benefits of his money and affection without the hassle of tending to him or running the risk of being abused by him. An added bonus to their affair was that he taught her how to deal profitably in food stamps and introduced her to the neighborhood's Korean grocer who would buy food stamps for fifty cents on the dollar. Sims bought food stamps from people for twenty-five cents on the dollar, which gave him a hundred percent profit. His customers benefited because they could buy things with the cash they couldn't purchase with food stamps, and the grocer could redeem the food stamps with the government for a hundred percent of face value.

Soon after Jeff and Ross left town Sims decided his best course of action was to follow suit and get away from Memphis. He invited Mary to join him but she declined.

When Sims was gone Mary went to the grocer to negotiate a deal to sell him food stamps. At first he refused, saying she didn't have enough money to buy a sufficient quantity of stamps to make it worth his time or to take the risk. Using her womanly favors, Mary changed his mind and she was instantly in the food stamp business.

Mary applied for Social Security Disability when she first returned to Memphis. Soon after Sims left, she was miraculously awarded one hundred and ten dollars per month for disability benefits. Based on her Social Security income, she was able to receive free housing in Lemoyne Gardens and an allotment of seventy-five dollars in monthly food stamps.

Trifecta moved in with his mother while Marquis lived with Caledonia, enabling her to continue drawing ADC benefits.

Within a month of having her apartment in Lemoyne Gardens, it was obvious that Mary was pregnant. She wasn't sure if the baby belonged to Sims, the Korean grocer or one of two men who stopped by to see her on occasion. However, when the child was born it was obvious he was the offspring of the Korean.

"Why does the baby have slanted eyes, light skin, and thin lips?" Trifecta asked Caledonia as they looked through the glass window of the nursery at John Gaston Hospital.

"Lots of black babies have light skin when they are first born," Caledonia answered.

"That doesn't explain his lips and eyes," Trifecta said.

"Light skinned Negroes get along better in this world."

"Blacks, not Negroes," Trifecta said.

"I thought by now you knew enough to be able to figure out the baby's daddy ain't no colored man," Caledonia said.

"Black man."

"What?"

"The baby's daddy isn't a black man," Trifecta corrected Caledonia.

"Maybe those white folks are right. You sure are getting uppity about what folks call you."

"Maybe, but they sure aren't going to call me a Korean. I don't know what it is with Asian people and your family, but I'm not going to have anything to do with any of them and that includes Willie's wife and Mama's babies," Trifecta said as he walked away from Caledonia in a huff.

The grocer refused to provide any support for his child, but he continued to buy food stamps from Mary. She was buying and selling approximately two thousand dollars in food stamps per month, netting her five hundred dollars every thirty days. Unfortunately, it came to an end in 1973 when the police busted the Korean for food stamp fraud. In return for a significant fine, a suspended sentence and probation, the Korean turned in Mary and five other people who were selling him more than twelve thousand dollars in food stamps per month. Mary was sentenced to one year at the women's prison in Nashville and five years' probation.

Mary had been in prison for two months when spots of blood in her bra forced her to go on sick call. This wasn't the first time she had experienced a discharge but now her breasts were swollen. The skin on her bosoms looked pitted like the peel from an orange and her nipples were turning inward and becoming intolerably painful.

It only took the prison doctor a few minutes to diagnose Mary with breast cancer. While the prison wasn't equipped to determine exactly how advanced the cancer was, the doctor's prognosis was that it had probably spread into other areas of her body.

There were oncologists in Nashville who were interested in using Mary in their research. After examining Mary, the specialists concurred with the prison doctor's prognosis and gave her between twelve and eighteen months to live. They offered to provide her with free medical care if she volunteered for some experimental treatments that could add a year or two to her life. Mary agreed to the treatments, which not only proved to be horribly painful, but a complete failure. By the time she completed her prison sentence she was bedridden. Freed from jail, she was taken to Caledonia's apartment where she suffered day and night until she found relief from her pain through death in July 1975.

*

After completing high school, in order to avoid the draft and the war in Vietnam, Trifecta had enrolled in Lemoyne-Owen College with money provided by the United Negro College Fund. Through some personal attention by several professors Trifecta was convinced that his future was not determined by his past or his color but by the way he prepared for the future. Because this message was consistent with Doctor King's philosophy Trifecta became serious about his studies and graduated college with a 3.15 grade point average. While attending Lemoyne-Owen he met Lawanda Grandberry. They fell in love and were married during their senior year of college. After graduation Trifecta took advantage of new opportunities that were being made available to blacks and was able to land a job as a manager trainee at Union Planters Bank. He immediately noticed he was the only black in his class of six manager trainees. It was obvious to him that the training director was a racist and was looking for a reason to fire him. This worked to Trifecta's advantage because he knew he had to work hard to keep his job and the harder he worked, the more recognition he received. Due to Trifecta's superior work ethic he was the first one of the manager trainees to be promoted to assistant manager. He was assigned to the branch bank in Poplar Plaza shopping center, a branch whose clientele were predominately white.

Chapter 81

1968-1975

Because of his low SAT scores Henry wasn't accepted into Memphis State. Instead, he worked a minimum-wage job, until he was drafted in March 1969.

While in the army Henry submitted several unsolicited articles to *Stars and Stripes*, the military newspaper, but he never had anything published. When his two years of military service were complete, a year of which was spent in Vietnam with his unit making an unauthorized missions into Cambodia and Laos, Henry enrolled at Memphis State under the G.I. bill. During his sophomore year he joined the University's newspaper staff, but after what he'd experienced in Southeast Asia, writing about the struggles of dorm life, the failing football team and the expanding cafeteria were subjects so dismally boring to Henry he had to find something else. At the start of his junior year he ran across a daily newspaper published in a small West Tennessee town north of Memphis that was looking for a reporter willing to work full-time for part-time wages. Henry jumped at the opportunity to make less money than he received in G.I. benefits for attending college full-time. He gave up an apartment he shared with two roommates and rented a small single wide trailer on the outskirts of the West Tennessee town. His job included reporting on local politics, high school athletics, farm news, lady's socials, obituaries, births, and arrests. In addition, he had various other duties, including selling advertising and taking out the trash. He was poor, but enthusiastic about his career. However, it continued to be hard to write about the mundane.

On the fourth of July 1975, the Rolling Stones were scheduled to have a show in Memphis. For an unexplained reason, a press pass for the concert was mailed to the newspaper where Henry worked. The owner of the paper gave the pass to Henry. As an opening act for the Stones, Furry Lewis was brought onto the stage. Exactly like the Bitter Lemon, Furry sang some songs with no accompaniment other than his acoustic guitar and told stories.

When the concert ended fifty- five thousand rowdy fans began exiting the Liberty Bowl Stadium. Henry was amid the pushing and shoving of the crowd when he felt a tug on his arm. Looking around he saw Charity, the ever faithful Furry Lewis fan. Charity followed Henry as he moved out of the crush of people.

"Hi," he said with a smile.

"Hi, she replied.

"It's good to see you. How have you been?"

"I'm doing well, and yourself."

"I'm good, so what are you doing now?"

"I'm a lawyer."

"That's great," Henry said, as he glimpsed someone standing at a short distance from them. Looking closer he recognized the person was Marcie McDougal.

Realizing that Henry had seen Marcie, Charity said, "Marcie and I came to the concert together."

"Really?" Henry asked.

"Yes, I'm an associate at her father's law firm, and she's the office manager. We're also very close friends."

ROBERT HUMPHREYS

"Really?" Henry repeated somewhat astounded.

"Yes, we are. The reason I stopped you was to see if you knew Trifecta's mother died yesterday?"

"No I didn't."

"I found out because another lawyer in my office represented her pro bono on a food stamp fraud charge. I thought you should know as you and Trifecta were so close."

"I wouldn't say we were that close."

"I assumed you were close when you told him you were going to break up with me before you told me." Charity said with a smattering of bitterness.

"Are you planning on going to the funeral?" Henry said, not knowing how she knew he had told Trifecta he was going to break up with her, and trying to change the subject.

"I was considering it."

"Is she going with you?" Henry asked nodding towards Marcie.

"I don't think so, she really didn't know Trifecta."

"Are you planning on going alone?" Henry asked looking at her left hand to see if she was wearing an engagement or wedding ring. She wasn't.

"If I go, I will be alone."

"Do you think that's a good idea, a white girl going into a black neighborhood unescorted?"

"I told you a long time ago I'm not afraid of black people any more than I am of white people. As a matter of fact I am less threatened by African American men than I am of drunken fraternity boys at Vanderbilt."

"What I mean is, I would like to go the funeral, but I would like to go with someone I know. I'm not real good at funerals." Henry didn't care about the funeral but Charity had never looked so pretty, and he wanted an opportunity to try to rekindle their relationship.

Are you asking me to go with you?"

"Yes."

"Are you asking me out on a date?"

408

"I don't consider going to a funeral a date," Henry lied. "As long as it's not a date I'll go with you."

Charity wrote her address on the back of a business card and they made arrangements to go to the funeral on July sixth.

*

The Korean grocer could understand and speak English as well as anyone living the Lemoyne Garden area. However, his customers thought he only had a shallow understanding of the language so they felt free to speak openly while they were shopping in his store. This gave the Korean constant knowledge of what was going on the neighborhood, so he was aware that Mary had died, and that Trifecta and his wife were considering adopting Mary's Korean son. On the day of Mary's funeral the grocer closed his store and went to the church where the funeral was to taking place. His business was in dire financial straits. Since he was no longer able to accept or redeem food stamps his sales consisted of small quantities of cigarettes, beer and a few other items that were ineligible for government assistance. The grocer had no specific reason for attending the funeral other than being mentally unstable and economically desperate.

*

Since seeing Charity at the concert Henry could think of little else other than her. When he picked her up to go to the funeral she was wearing a short but traditional black dress, which was a drastic change from the way she dressed in high school, and from what she was wearing at the concert. He was wearing checkered bell bottom pants, a blue double breasted blazer, a Union Jack tie and as usual a liberal amount of English Lather cologne.

The funeral was held at the Morning Glory AME church on Kerr Avenue where G.W. and his family were members. When Charity and Henry entered the church there were only a few people in attendance. The two white people took seats close to the rear of the sanctuary. A black man and woman walked up the aisle of the church towards them. The man had a huge Afro hairdo, facial hair, and was holding the hand of a light skinned boy with Asian features. Charity was the first to recognize him.

"Hi Trifecta," Charity said standing up and hugging him.

"Hey Trifecta," Henry said standing up and extending his hand.

"We're sorry to hear about your mother," Charity said.

"Thank you," the woman with Trifecta said.

"This is my wife Lawanda," Trifecta said.

"I've heard a lot about you." Lawanda said shaking Henry's hand.

"I'm glad to see you cats are back together," Trifecta said.

"Don't get the wrong idea," Charity said. "We came together because Henry's afraid to come into a black neighborhood by himself."

"That's not true. I just needed an excuse to be with her," Henry confessed.

"That's sweet," Lawanda said.

"Isn't it," Charity said with a snide smile directed toward Henry.

"And who is this little person?" Charity asked.

"He's my mother's son and now that she's dead, Lawanda wants to adopt him," Trifecta said.

"That's nice," Charity said.

Trifecta and Lawanda had been having some heated arguments concerning Jermaine. Trifecta said he didn't want the Asian child, because it was the baby's daddy who sent his mother to prison. He was convinced that if she hadn't been incarcerated she would not have died of cancer. He also pointed out that no sooner had his cousin brought his

Guamanian wife to the United States than she ran off with another man. "You can't trust any of those people." Trifecta said.

Lawanda attributed Trifecta's reluctance to care for his half- brother as pure racism.

As the two couples were chatting the Korean grocer entered the church. When Trifecta saw him he hollered, "What are you doing here?"

Lawanda immediately ordered Trifecta to be quiet and not to do anything foolish.

Her reprimand only further enraged Trifecta. Incensed, Trifecta stormed toward the Korean.

"What are you doing here you slant eyed…..," Trifecta yelled at the grocer.

"I've come for my son," The Korean shouted interrupting Trifecta's diatribe. The Korean had no desire to take Jermaine, however he thought the boy was his first line of defense and the only advantage he had over Trifecta.

"You ain't getting anything that belonged to my mama," Trifecta screamed in the Korean's face shoving him with both hands. The smaller man stumbled to the ground.

"Stop," cried Reverend Wilks. He and G.W. simultaneously moved towards Trifecta and the grocer intending to break up the altercation.

The ghetto was not a safe place to have a business, and even though the grocer was on probation he carried a pistol.

Trifecta moved toward the prostrate grocer. Rising up on one elbow, off balance and afraid of the three men moving toward him, the Korean drew his gun and without aiming squeezed off four rounds. One bullet went into the ceiling, another shattered a window, the third put a hole in the casket and the fourth splintered the arm rest on one of the pews. Caledonia fainted and Lawanda screamed. Everyone in the church had either ducked behind a pew or dropped to the floor.

The grocer was the first one to his feet. Pointing his pistol at Lawanda he bellowed, "I want my son."

Having risen to her knees, Lawanda cradled Jermaine close to her breast.

"We're not giving you anything," Trifecta said coming to his feet.

"If you won't give me the child, you must pay me ten thousand dollars," the Korean said pointing his pistol at Trifecta.

"What?" Trifecta exclaimed, stopped in his tracks by the gun aimed at him.

"If you want to keep the boy, you have to pay me ten thousand dollars," The Asian barked.

"You can't sell a child," Lawanda protested.

"If you're not going to pay then give me my son."

"Wait a minute," Charity intervened. "Ten thousand dollars is out of the question. You have to come up with a more realistic number."

"I ain't giving him any money," Trifecta railed.

"Shut-up," Charity said to Trifecta taking control of the situation. Then turning to the Korean asked, "How much?"

"Five thousand dollars," the Asian said.

"No way, one thousand," Charity countered.

"Two thousand is the final offer. If you don't pay me two thousand dollars I am taking the boy now." The Korean said, He hoped those attending the funeral could raise two thousand dollars, because he had no desire to take the child.

"Twelve hundred," Charity continued to bargain.

After hesitating long enough to consider her offer, the grocer said, "Okay, twelve hundred.

"You ain't taking Jermaine," Trifecta said.

"If I have to shoot you, I will. I'm taking my son or you'll give me twelve hundred dollars," The grocer said, continuing to point his gun at Trifecta.

"How do we know you'll relinquish your rights to the child if I bring you the money?" Charity continued negotiating.

"You'll have to trust me."

"I'm a lawyer, I don't trust anyone."

"What interest do you have in this?" The grocer asked.

"I'm Mary Johnson's lawyer," Charity said, hoping the Korean had never met Mary's attorney.

"So what?"

"So I continue to represent Mary even though she is no longer with us.

Now, we have two problems. First someone will have to leave to get the money. Second before we give you twelve hundred dollars we will need a contract transferring parental rights to Trifecta and Lawanda."

"Do you have the money?" The grocer asked.

"In the bank," Charity lied.

"How do I know you'll return?"

"You've got the boy and all these other people as hostages."

"How long will it take you to get the money?"

"I can have the money and be back in two hours."

"I'll only wait one hour. If you're not back in one hour, I'll take the boy and leave."

"I will need at least an hour and forty five minutes."

"An hour and fifteen minutes," the Korean countered.

"An hour and forty minutes," Charity said, thinking this would be fun, if the circumstances weren't so serious.

"An hour and thirty minutes, and you better leave now because your time has already started.

Charity took Henry's keys and drove until she saw a pay telephone. Because she only had three hundred and twenty-five dollars in her savings account, she called Marcie and asked to borrow the ransom. Next she called the police and explained the situation and outlined a plan for capturing the grocer with no risk of anyone being harmed. Then she drove to her office which was fifteen minutes away and typed the contract.

Within an hour she met Marcie and several policemen down the street from the church. She reviewed her plan with the police. She was surprised that the police even considered her plan let only agreed to give it a try.

She walked back into the church an hour and fifteen minutes, from the time she left. In her absence the Korean had gone berserk, and was standing behind the pulpit screaming, cursing and using racial slurs at the people who were now coward down in the pews.

"Do you have the money?" The grocer shrieked as Charity entered the building.

For the first time Charity was scared. The Korean's eyes were crazed, and his movements were frenzied and turbulent. She calmly held up twelve, one hundred dollar bills as she approached the pulpit.

"I have the cash, but I need you to sign this contract before I give it to you," she said.

The contract simply read, in lieu of twelve hundred dollars he agrees to sell Jermaine Johnson to Trifecta and Lawanda Johnson, and release the kidnapped hostages.

The Korean signed the document without reading it, took the money without counting it. Carelessly waving his hand gun erratically about the room he naively walked out of the church. The police had the church surrounded and immediately arrested him and confiscated the money and the pistol. The contract served as a written confession to kidnapping and human trafficking. The only flaw in the plan was the police confiscating the Marcie's twelve hundred dollars as evidence, which wouldn't be returned until after the trial.

Before leaving the church Henry commented that every time he was around Trifecta he always had a good story. Trifecta responded, "You're pretty cool for a white cat, but hanging out with you is too dangerous for me." That was the last time Henry spoke with Trifecta.

Henry wrote articles about the incident for both of the Memphis papers.

The next day Henry asked Charity to have dinner with him. He told her he wanted more insight on how she cultivated her plan to foil the Korean grocer kidnapping plot. He said he thought he might be able to develop a story about her. Honestly, he wanted an opportunity to resume a romantic relationship with her.

During dinner Henry reminisced about the good times they enjoyed in high school. Anticipating where the conversation was headed, Charity reminded him how he vacillated between Marcie and her, and while she hoped he had matured, she had no desire to renew their relationship.

"If the subject came up, Marcie wanted me to tell you she has no interest in you either," Charity said. One thing life had taught Henry was resilience. He changed the subject, finished dinner and took Charity home telling her good night for the last time.

Epilogue

Lawanda soon had her way and she and Trifecta adopted Jermaine. Lawanda loved Jermaine as her own, and as he grew so did Trifecta's love for him. In an unusual way, Trifecta's life's dream came true. Trifecta and Lawanda successfully created a functional life, from Trifecta's dysfunctional family.

*

Eventually Henry wrote a book about the Memphis garbage strike, which gave him enough money to move out of the trailer and back to the city where he was able to keep writing. It even gave him a short lived job as a writing teacher at Memphis State, which he hated more than selling advertisements for the small rag that kept him going after college. He always kept girl friends in the city. He juggled them like some drunken clown who burns himself on the flaming clubs he tries to keep in the air. Henry could never find anyone worth loving. No one was as pretty or desirable as Marcie, and none of them could inspire Henry like Charity. He learned to prefer it that way. He spent his time looking for stories and remembering the ones already played out. The story that troubled him most, but the one he could never bring himself to write was about Avery.

Avery was so tormented by the assassination of Doctor King that her pain compelled her to leave the city where he was murdered. She attended Fisk University in Nashville for one semester. However, her misery did not subside. She arbitrarily chose to move to Boston seeking refuge from her pain and white bigotry. She soon decided it was useless to try to escape her agony, or prejudice against blacks within the boundaries of the nation that took the life of her beloved leader. Ignoring her parent's wishes she traveled to Africa where she was shot and killed. Inadvertently she found herself in Angola amid a civil war. She witnessed unimaginable atrocities, and gratuitous cruelty by blacks on other blacks. She justified the barbarity thinking they were fighting for independence from the Portuguese Colonist. To her disappointment and frustration, she discovered that the war involved more than patriotic blacks struggling for independence, but there were some Soviet supported rebels who simply wanted to change the government from Portuguese rule to the communism. It was during a gun battle between black socialist freedom fighters and black communist that she was killed.

When Henry heard about Avery's death, he wept. He mourned for her just as he grieved for his buddies who died in Vietnam. He believed his Army buddies and Avery died for the same reason and that was to benefit politicians and politics.

*

When Scoop died of old age, Henry spoke at his funeral about not giving up until you got the story right. He still didn't know exactly what that meant, but with every passing experience he learned getting it right was an impossible struggle he could never turn away from.

*

G. W. continued to work for the city sanitation department until he retired. He and Yolanda left Lemoyne gardens and were the first black family to buy a house on a block of Netherwood Street in South Memphis. Within a week every house on that block was up for sale. Within eighteen months every house on the block was owned by blacks.

*

As for agent Ball, he eventually retired frustrated each time he remembered he was unable to solve the murder of Hercules Jones or arrest the people responsible for burning a cross in his yard.

*

Most of the Music and bands mentioned in this book are from Memphis. However, each of the characters did have their favorite Top Forty music here is a top ten list of the songs they enjoyed.

Charity's favorite Top Forty Songs

1.	Somebody to Love	Jefferson Airplane
2.	Like a Rolling Stone	Bob Dylan
3.	Blowin' in the wind	Peter, Paul and Mary
4.	I Got You Babe	Sonny and Cher
5.	Ain't to Proud to Beg	The Temptations
6.	All Along The Watchtower	Jimi Hendricks
7.	Sounds of Silence	Simon and Garfunkle
8.	I saw Her Standing There	The Beatles
9.	59th Street Bridge Song	Harper Bizarre
10.	White Room	Cream

Henry's Favorite Top Forty Songs

1.	Satisfaction	The Rolling Stones
2.	Louie Louie	The Kingsmen
3.	House of the Rising Sun	The Animals
4.	I'm a Man	The Yard Birds
5.	All Day and All Night	The Kinks
6.	Get Around	The Beach Boys
7.	Wipeout	The Safaris'
8.	Good Lovin'	Young Racals
9.	Wild Thing	The Troggs
10.	Money (That's what I want)	Barrett Strong (covered by The Beatles)

Trifecta's Favorite Top Forty songs

1.	I'm Black and I'm Proud	James Brown
2.	(Reach Out) I'll Be There	The Four Tops
3.	Heat Wave	Martha and the Vandellas
4.	Finger Tips Part 2	Little Stevie Wonder
5.	Dance to The Music	Sly and the Family Stones
6.	Soul Man	Sam and Dave
7.	People Get Ready	The Impressions
8.	Midnight Hour	Wilson Pickett
9.	Sand By Me	Ben E. King
10.	I Feel so Bad	Little Milton

Marcie's Favorite Top Forty Songs

1.	Cherish	The Association
2.	Here Comes the Sun	The Beatles
3.	God Only Knows	The Beachboys
4.	Hang on Sloopy	The McCoys
5.	Do You Want to Know a Secret	The Beatles
6.	Leaving on a Jet Plane	Peter, Paul, and Mary

7. California Dreaming — The Mamas and Papas
8. I've Got You Under My Skin — Frankie Valli and The Four Seasons
9. Try and Catch the Wind — Donovan
10. Will I See You in September — The Happenings

Avery' Favorite Top Forty Songs

1. My Girl — The Temptations
2. Up, Up and Away — The Fifth Dimension
3. Ain't No mountain High Enough — Diana Ross (Avery's favorite version)
4. Walk on By — Dionne Warwick
5. Lover Concerto — The Toys
6. Your Love Keeps Lifting Me (Higher and Higher) — Jackie Wilson
7. Tracks of My Tears — Smokey Robinson
8. I Heard it through the Grapevine — Marvin Gaye
9. Your All I Need to Get to Get By — Marvin Gaye and Tammi Terrell
10. When a Man Loves a Woman — Percy Sledge

The End

Printed in the United States
By Bookmasters